PRAISE FOR

JUST ONE LOOK

"[A] wild ride of a novel . . . [*Just One Look* is] a delicious and marvelously controlled portrayal of one woman's delusions, and how they undo her, but also create something new and whole."
—*The New York Times Book Review*

"Fresh, fun, and totally wicked . . . a sharp, modern thrill ride with a witty heroine."
—*Entertainment Weekly*

"I inhaled *Just One Look*. I was going to read one chapter, then one chapter became the whole thing because it felt like HBO's *Enlightened* meets Patricia Highsmith's *This Sweet Sickness*. YUM."
—CAROLINE KEPNES, *New York Times* bestselling author of the You series

"Bitingly modern and totally addictive, *Just One Look* is a juicy entry into the unhinged-women canon. I loved it—it's propulsive, surprising, and deeply creepy. With wry prose and deliciously wicked twists, Lindsay Cameron's suspense debut is the freshest take on stalker fiction since *You*."
—ANDREA BARTZ, *New York Times* bestselling author of *We Were Never Here*

"Lindsay Cameron has penned a relentlessly gripping and cunning tale of the new Pandora's box—the inbox. *Just One Look* had me promising: just one more chapter, just one more page, just one, until—oops—I was done."

—CHANDLER BAKER, *New York Times* bestselling author
of *The Husbands*

"Lindsay Cameron's thriller will appeal to fans of *You,* in that readers get a glimpse inside the head of someone willing to go to extreme lengths for what they want. . . . Nothing and no one are as they seem in this thriller about envy, obsession, class, stalking, and revenge."

—*Oprah Daily*

"Will leave you chilled to the bone."

—*PopSugar*

"[This] is a highly entertaining narrative that positively sparkles with wit and insight into the mind of a young woman with much promise, hobbled by self-doubt yet insanely pursuing an impossible dream. This is the author's suspense debut, and it succeeds wildly. Highly recommended for all collections."

—*Booklist* (starred review)

"You will be obsessed after the first paragraph. Lindsay Cameron has created an unforgettable character that beckons from the page until you've devoured every last word. A delicious and irresistible read!"

—LIV CONSTANTINE, internationally bestselling author
of *The Last Mrs. Parrish*

"Lindsay Cameron takes obsession to a whole new level and I am here for it! With each twist, *Just One Look* becomes more intriguing, more shocking, and more fascinating. Once you pick it up, settle in for the night because you won't be able to put it down."

—SAMANTHA DOWNING, *USA Today* bestselling author
of *My Lovely Wife* and *He Started It*

"Gripping, darkly funny, and razor-sharp, *Just One Look* is a brilliant suspense debut. With a multifaceted, sympathetic heroine to root for, no matter how devious she may seem, and a perfectly paced sinister plotline, this addictive novel begs to be read in one sitting. I could not tear my eyes away for a second."

—SAMANTHA M. BAILEY, internationally bestselling author
of *Woman on the Edge*

"*Just One Look* is addictive and compulsive, with a wicked sense of humor. Clear your diary, because once you start reading it, you won't want to put it down."

—EMMA ROUS, bestselling author of *The Au Pair*

"Fast paced and thrillingly tense, *Just One Look* is a wild-ride reminder of the dangers of the digital age. Cameron ramps up the suspense from the first page, instilling each chapter with an impending sense of doom and a protagonist as sympathetic as she is sneaky. A terrifying tale of obsessive love that will have you changing all your passwords."

—KIMBERLY BELLE, internationally bestselling author
of *Stranger in the Lake*

"[An] entertaining, seamless story about obsession, stalking, and revenge . . . Cameron skillfully makes the unlikable Cassie sympathetic, even as her propensity for anger and violent fantasies grows. The twist-filled plot contains myriad surprises. Psychological thriller fans will be more than satisfied."

—*Publishers Weekly*

ALSO BY LINDSAY CAMERON

Biglaw
Just One Look

NO ONE
NEEDS
TO KNOW

NO ONE NEEDS TO KNOW

A NOVEL

LINDSAY CAMERON

BANTAM BOOKS

NEW YORK

A Bantam Books Trade Paperback Original

Copyright © 2023 by Lindsay Cameron

Random House Book Club copyright © 2023 by
Penguin Random House LLC.

Published in the United States by Bantam Books,
an imprint of Random House, a division of
Penguin Random House LLC, New York.

BANTAM BOOKS is a registered trademark and the B
colophon is a trademark of Penguin Random House LLC.

ISBN 978-0-593-15910-1
Ebook ISBN 978-0-593-15909-5

Printed in the United States of America on acid-free paper

randomhousebooks.com

2 4 6 8 9 7 5 3 1

Book design by Alexis Capitini

For Ethan and Elise
always the favorite part of my day

NO ONE
NEEDS
TO KNOW

"If you want validation, use your social media. If you want discretion, then turn to UrbanMyth. Your secrets are safe with us."

—Press release, UrbanMyth app launch

It was lauded as an alternative to the performative, show-your-best-self platforms, an anonymous social media app organized by neighborhood. All you needed to create an account was an email. No profile. No username. No way to track your identity. The anonymity worked like truth serum. We disclosed things there we would never discuss with our best friends or even our spouses. Especially not our spouses.

We bared our secrets.

It was supposed to be confidential.

And it always was.

Right up to the moment when it wasn't.

Prologue

———————

Before it happened, I never noticed how many times a day an emergency vehicle drove past my apartment building. Their sirens blended in with the cacophony of New York City, an ambient noise that never roused my attention. Today, though, I knew with absolute certainty that the wail emanating from the street below was the second police siren I'd heard in the past six hours. Instinctively, my ears now detected the shrill sound, the way a deer detects the snap of a twig beneath a hunter's boot.

A signal of imminent danger.

My body stilled, attempting to clock the proximity of the vehicle. Louder. Closer. Louder. Closer. I wiped my clammy palms on my cotton pajama bottoms, my mind cycling through wild scenarios. *Fists pounding on the door. Weapons drawn. The stupefied expressions of my neighbors. "Did they say 'murder'?" they'd whisper.* I pulled at the soft fabric on my upper thigh, debating whether I should change. If I was going to be perp walked, I didn't want to be wearing the same pajamas I'd donned for the past three days. Pushing myself off of the couch, the sound of the siren finally began to recede. I released a ragged breath and dropped back down.

Another bullet dodged.

Leaning forward on the cushion, I slid my laptop closer to the edge of the coffee table. The screen had gone black. I tapped the trackpad to bring it back to life, and the home page of the *New*

York Post stared back at me. Anxiety thrummed my veins as I scanned the familiar headlines.

In the long list of issues I hadn't considered when I'd pressed two fingertips against the fleshy neck of the lifeless form, confirming what I already knew, the ensuing media attention had to be at the top. But the news cycle was the furthest thing from my mind when I was staring down at the slack, ghostly face, the milky white eyeball bathed in red. Among the many feelings jostling inside my body in that heart-stopping moment—the fear, the horror, the shock—there was one, quiet but persistent, that took me by surprise. It was relief.

Because maybe, just maybe, you got what you deserved.

Chapter One

FEBRUARY

HEATHER

As THE BLACK Escalade inched down Park Avenue, Heather had the feeling she was being slowly marched off a cliff. She imagined a loud, male voice behind her bellowing out the orders—*left, right, left, right*—until she plunged blindly over the edge. Was it her husband's voice she was hearing in her mind or some generic movie voice, like Morgan Freeman's? It had to be the latter. If her husband had his way, she wouldn't be sitting in this car right now. "Are you sure this is a good idea?" Oliver had repeated, as she'd pushed her feet into the ballet flats beside the door, his brow crinkled with concern.

Yes, she was sure.

So why wouldn't Morgan Freeman shut the hell up?

Heather leaned her head between the seats, peering out the windshield at the river of illuminated red taillights. A mocking reminder of how little control she had over the evening.

"Can you take Lexington instead? This doesn't look like it's moving." If she was going to be marched off a cliff, it should at least be efficient.

The driver tapped the dirty iPhone mounted on the dashboard. "Waze says Park is better, but whatever you say." The car swung left and she slid back on the seat. She could already see the traffic was lighter on Lex. The knot in her stomach uncoiled a bit.

A good omen—she could use one of those.

She put her hand on her daughter's arm and gave it a reassuring squeeze. "It'll be more fun than you think. I promise."

"You and I have very different definitions of fun," Violet muttered, not bothering to raise her eyes from her phone.

Heather's jaw clenched. There were kids right now who were *weeping* to their parents because they couldn't get a ticket to this event, yet here her daughter sat, acting like she was about to spend the evening being waterboarded.

The driver jammed his brakes at the light, and an expensively clad woman holding the hand of a curly haired toddler stepped off the curb, lifting up an open palm to the cars, as if she had the power to stop traffic. Heather followed them with her eyes, feeling a pinch of nostalgia for when Violet was that age. Always at arm's reach. How easy it was to guide her through life back then. Organic food, music classes to stimulate her brain, teaching her to go down a slide rather than walk up it—there was a playbook, a comprehensive step-by-step guide that made perfect sense to Heather. "It's easy to feel like a good parent when you have an easy child," the director of Violet's preschool had told a roomful of eager parents, but Heather wholeheartedly disagreed. It wasn't genetic luck. Heather had prepared for being a mother the same way she'd prepared for the SATs—meticulously. And it had paid off. Violet could read an entire chapter book before she'd finished kindergarten, had a shelf full of squash trophies, and was a regular winner of the service award at her competitive Upper East Side private school. This type of success didn't happen by accident. Heather was a good mother.

Violet was proof of concept.

She tucked a stray strand of Violet's cinnamon-colored hair behind her ear. "I know this isn't what you want to be doing tonight, but you need to keep your eye on the prize."

Violet groaned. "You don't even know if she'll *be* there, Mom. I mean, where did you even hear she was coming? You said yourself it wasn't public knowledge." Violet tore at a cuticle with her teeth, and Heather gently moved her hand away from her mouth.

Violet looked like she might protest, but she let her hand fall into her lap.

"Eye on the prize," Heather repeated, ignoring the question. Again.

"Whatever," Violet mumbled, plucking a peppermint candy from the pile in the cup holder, twisting open the wrapper, and popping it into her mouth before Heather could protest. Heather pressed her lips together. She hated when Violet ate anything offered in an Uber. Who knew where those dirty little candies had been? Some pervert might find it humorous to unwrap them, lick, and rewrap, waiting for some unsuspecting rider to partake. Why wasn't her daughter more suspicious of candy from strangers? A suburban, poison-in-Halloween-candy-style paranoia had been drilled into Heather as a child, but she'd somehow failed to pass on a healthy sense of caution to her daughter. She added that to her mental list of things to teach Violet. But not tonight.

Heather checked the time on her phone. 6:55 P.M. Dammit.

"We'll get out here," she said, tapping a fingernail against the window.

"We're still five blocks away," Violet whined as she unpeeled herself from the leather bucket seat. "And these shoes you made me wear are *really* uncomfortable." She gestured to her sensible but fashionable one-inch-heeled pumps, the ones Heather had purchased last week after reading a study claiming people attribute significantly greater intelligence to taller children. While it might not be a fair assessment, who was she to argue with psychology?

"You'll be fine." Heather waved her out of the car impatiently. "The walk will be good for both of us."

By the time they swept through the brass doors and into the elegant foyer, most of the children had already descended the scarlet carpeted staircase. They weren't children anymore, Heather supposed. They were teenagers now, all dressed up and ready for their first Teen Night at The Doubles Club, the private dining club that catered to the elite social set, which Heather had spent years strategizing her way into. "It's so overwhelming, isn't it?" Heather could remember a perky southern blonde lamenting as she shook a small maraca over her three-month-old in their Music Babies class at Diller-Quaile. "New York City parenting, I mean. Like, we have to do all these classes to get them into the right preschools and we have to know about all this stuff, like, years in advance or our child is shut out. And apparently it only gets worse." She'd leaned in conspiratorially. "Have you heard about these teen dances at Doubles? My neighbor told me her daughter became a social pariah because they weren't members, so she couldn't go." Heather had arranged her expression to be appropriately shocked, but she'd gone home and straight to Google to investigate. Unlike her southern friend, Heather didn't consider it overwhelming. There was a formula. Formulas she understood.

A gaggle of girls congregated at the bottom of the stairs now, teetering like newborn giraffes in heels that were much too high, visibly vibrating with excitement. Heather scanned the preening crowd, hoping for a familiar face she could point Violet toward—a social crutch—but came up empty.

Violet needed to make more friends. Although, truth be told, the apple didn't fall far from the tree in that category.

"Place your mobile phones in these locked pouches," a goateed man in a dark suit bellowed to the group making their way inside, tendering a brown pouch to each outstretched hand. "They'll be returned to you at the end of the night."

Heather's fingers curled tighter around the strap of her purse. The first time she'd encountered these "privacy pouches" was at the latest Lin-Manuel Miranda musical, when ushers had informed the patrons that they were required to stow their mobile devices until the final curtain. "It's for your own enjoyment," the usher had explained, as he'd passed her a Playbill and a numbered pouch. But everyone knew the pouches were less about altruism and more about preventing an opportunistic fan from filming the show and plastering it online for all to see. It made sense for private clubs across the city to employ the same approach to "protect the integrity and privacy of the members of the club," as the president of The Doubles Club put it in a letter to its members. After Occupy

Wall Street, these old-school, old-money clubs were vilified and all it would take was one unfortunate video posted online and the media would be all over it. Heather had purposely not mentioned this new rule to Violet, though, treating it as a "cross that bridge" problem.

"Wait." Violet stopped short at the top of the stairway, the sole of her new shoes scuffing across the floor. Her eyes widened in horror. "What did he say?" She hugged her phone to her chest, as if it were a favorite teddy bear about to be ripped from her grasp.

Heather let out a weary sigh. "Don't be so dramatic, Vi. It's only two hours. I'll pick you up at nine, you'll have your phone back, and you can tell me all about the fun you've had."

Violet gave her another eye roll and Heather noticed a fleck of mascara on her lid. Heather had broken her moratorium on eye makeup, hoping a few swipes of mascara would give Violet a booster shot of confidence, but looking at her lashes now she wondered if it was a bit much.

This isn't New Jersey.

It was a common refrain, a silent mantra that ran through Heather's mind, to remind her that anything resembling a popular trait from her home state needed to be exorcised from their lives, like a lingering demon.

Heather used the pads of her thumb and forefinger to dab off a visible clump. "Everything is going to be *fine,*" she said, trying to will it true with the conviction of her voice. Heather was a firm believer that children were malleable, like clay. Violet just had to be pressed into shape properly. And it was Heather's job to do the pressing.

A group of blazer-and-tie-clad, floppy-haired boys piled into the foyer, calling out indistinguishable insults to one another. Heather watched her daughter shrink into herself and step out of their way, leaving the boys a wide berth. She suppressed a disappointed sigh. So much for that Turning Girls into Leaders camp Heather had sent her to last summer.

Taking hold of Violet's hands, she gave them a reassuring squeeze, the way she used to when her daughter would cling to her leg at kindergarten drop-off. "Violet, honey, listen." She struggled to keep her voice therapeutic as she looked into her daughter's anxious eyes. "I know you don't want to be here, but it's important that you—"

"Bye, girls!" a fur-vested woman trilled mere inches from Heather's ear, waving her shiny-red-manicured fingers in the direction of three swinging ponytails bouncing down the stairs, interrupting Heather's pep talk. Violet's feet rooted themselves even more firmly in place. Heather stole a glance over her shoulder before taking her daughter by the elbow and steering her back outside and down the sidewalk, away from the curious eyes of loitering parents.

"You need to channel this nervous energy you're feeling," Heather murmured, giving Violet's back a gentle rub as they rounded the corner. "Remember you're—" The thump of a body against hers cut Heather off mid-sentence, knocking the wind out of her.

"Oh!" a woman yelped.

Heather stumbled backward, struggling to get her balance, as the woman's iPhone clattered against the pavement.

"Oh my gosh, I'm so sorry," Heather said, flustered, bending down to retrieve the phone. She did a quick screen check, relieved there weren't any cracks.

"You should really watch where you're going," the woman grumbled in a tone that sounded like she was demanding to see the manager. It was only when Heather stood up straight that she realized, with horror, whom the sour voice belonged to.

Shit.

"Poppy!" Heather's voice sounded unnaturally high-pitched. "I didn't realize that was you!" Her cheeks burned as she attempted to rearrange her expression into one resembling "pleasantly surprised" and ran a hand over her hair to smooth down any harried-looking flyaways. "I'm so sorry. I didn't see you there."

Poppy's cornflower-blue eyes scanned Heather's face, consulting her mental Rolodex and apparently coming up empty.

"Heather Quinn," Heather supplied, putting a palm to her

chest. "My daughter goes to Crofton with your son." *And they've been in the same class for the past three years and we've been introduced no less than five times.* She wrenched her lips into a smile, which probably looked more like a grimace.

After a beat, Poppy's pinched expression relaxed and her finishing-school manners took over. "Oh, Heather. Of course. I didn't recognize you," she said smoothly, a smile spreading across her face like frosting. She leaned in for a quick cheek-to-cheek, which required Heather to stand on her toes. Poppy had one of those long, willowy frames that wouldn't look out of place on a runway in Milan. A stark contrast to Heather's five-feet-five frame, which clung to those extra fifteen pounds like her body was preparing for a famine. And no matter how many yoga positions Heather contorted her body into, there was no eliminating the slight hunch in her shoulders, implanted after decades spent stooped over a computer.

"Well, thankfully no damage done," Heather said, clearing an unexpected tremble in her voice and gently pressing Poppy's phone into her slender hand. "Not a scratch on it." She kept her smile zippered in place, reminding herself not to stare too long. Effortlessly beautiful people were always mesmerizing to her, like rare butterflies. She couldn't imagine anything in life not requiring effort. Her gaze flicked to Violet. The red patches that had bloomed on her cheeks earlier had migrated over her entire face and neck. This encounter was not helping.

"Anyway, we should—" Heather started just as Poppy blurted, "What are you two up to?"

There was an awkward pause where they each waved the other one to continue, before Heather answered, "I'm dropping Violet off at Doubles." She rested a proud hand on Violet's shoulder.

Poppy cocked her head. "I didn't realize you were a member." Her words peeled up at the end, making it sound more like a question.

"Oh, we're fairly new. I think it's been about six months," Heather said, as if it had been a spur of the moment decision to join the club, rather than the result of years of calculated social climbing to attain the right reference letters, accumulate enough disposable income to pay the membership fees, and convince Oliver of the intrinsic value of admission.

"How wonderful!" Poppy flashed a smile that displayed all twenty-eight of her pearly white teeth. Heather noticed a smudge in Poppy's petal-pink lipstick on the bow of her upper lip and couldn't help taking pleasure in this tiny hole in an otherwise perfect façade.

"A newbie then," Poppy continued. "Well, I just dropped Henry off. He insisted on arriving with a bunch of his friends. You know how boys need to travel in packs these days." She rolled her eyes theatrically and kept babbling.

Heather shifted her weight, waiting for an opportunity to interject, but Poppy—who had never uttered more than a handful of words to her—wasn't even pausing to take a breath between sentences. Bemused, Heather interpreted this as indisputable proof of what she'd believed all along—being a member of Doubles really *did* increase a person's social stock. She tilted her head, intrigued by this unfamiliar version of the woman who had only ever greeted her with a cold shoulder. She noted a quiver at the corner of Poppy's cheek, picking up on it like sonar. Heather had a gift for reading people, an uncanny ability to tune in to the slightest change in mood, discerning potential shifts from a crack in a voice or a bead of sweat on a hairline. Growing up, that skill had been a survival mechanism.

Heather's senses sharpened.

Something was off.

She tuned back in as Poppy said, "But I told Henry, 'You'd better be on your best behavior tonight if you want any *hope* of getting into Andover.'" Poppy froze, a faint pink sweeping over her ivory features. She had the expression of someone who had inadvertently revealed the existence of a surprise party.

Heather blinked at her, considering how to respond. She could feel the weight of Violet's gaze on her.

Careful, Heather. Careful.

Poppy must have heard a question in Heather's silence because she quickly added, "I . . . I heard that the director of admissions from Andover was going to be there tonight, so . . ." She tucked a strand of her freshly blown-out hair behind her ear.

Heather willed her facial features to remain impassive. "Really? I hadn't heard that." She tightened her grip on Violet's shoulder.

"Apparently, she thought it would be a good chance to observe the kids and make sure the candidates 'play well with others,'" Poppy explained with accompanying air quotes. "After everything that happened last year, you know, I think they want to be really cautious." She paused to lift a perfectly arched eyebrow. "But I can't remember where I heard that . . ." she trailed off, scrunching her face up as if trying to locate a long-lost nugget in her memory.

Heather bit back a smile. Poppy was many things, but a good actress was not one of them.

"Anyway, I should run." Poppy adjusted her purse on her shoulder and regained her self-assured edge. "But we should grab a coffee sometime."

"That would be great." Heather nodded. A coffee date with Poppy was about as likely as beers with Barack Obama. Having a quick conversation on a sidewalk was one thing, an organized social interaction was quite another. Still, Heather played along.

Heather always played along.

Poppy's platinum Cartier watch glinted on her wrist as she fluttered her fingers in a half wave. Heather and Violet watched in silence as her narrow hips sashayed down the sidewalk and disappeared into a black Escalade, which seemed to appear out of nowhere.

Effortless.

"Mom, why did you lie to her?" Violet asked, rousing Heather out of her temporary paralysis.

She let out a shaky breath. "Let's get you inside, Vi." She gave a light tug on Violet's elbow to get her moving, ignoring the question. When they rounded the corner, the crowd on the sidewalk had dispersed, a sign that she and Violet were beyond fashionably late. Heather hustled Violet through the doors, into the foyer, and smoothed a palm over her daughter's hair one final time, kissing the top of her middle part. "Eyes on the prize."

Resigned, Violet descended the stairs, relinquished her phone, and disappeared inside without so much as a peek over her shoulder. Heather lingered at the top of the steps, arms folded over her chest.

This was the right thing, she told herself. This was for Violet's own good.

"Excuse me," a young girl beside her mumbled, breaking into Heather's thoughts.

"Oh, I'm sorry." Heather stepped aside. The girl bounded down the stairs, and Heather noticed the dramatic pink on the ends of her beachy-blond hair. Heather cocked her head, wondering how that would go over. Would the admissions director think multicolored hair indicated a brilliant, creative mind, or would it put an automatic *x* beside her name? If Heather was a betting woman, she'd put her money on the latter. These traditional institutions claimed they welcomed candidates who colored outside the lines—the next Bill Gates or Steve Jobs—but boarding schools have a type, and they stick to it.

And Heather prayed to God Violet fit into it.

The pink-haired girl darted a glance over her shoulder and Heather realized, catching a glimpse of her profile, that she looked familiar. Heather watched as she surreptitiously slid an iPhone ensconced in teal leather into a pocket of her black skater dress, bypassed the distracted doorman, and entered the dance. A satisfied smile crossed Heather's lips. A rule breaker. Definitely the recipient of an automatic *x*. She pivoted to leave, hoping Violet didn't notice there was someone in the midst who'd managed to smuggle in a phone.

Later, Heather would wonder if everything that happened afterward could've been avoided if she'd called out to get the attention of the preoccupied doorman. *You missed one!* Or if she'd marched down the stairs and tapped the little rebel on the shoulder, reminded her that everyone had to relinquish her phone before entering. Rules were rules.

If she hadn't left.

If she'd somehow intervened.

If. If. If.

Chapter Two

NORAH

NORAH KNEW HARRIS was going to explode even before she looked up from her laptop and saw the telltale vein pulsing on the side of his forehead. Everyone in the conference room—five executives from Global Corp., six of Norah's gray-suited colleagues—all held their collective breath, waiting for him to speak.

"That's not what we fucking agreed to!" Harris slammed down his palm, his pointlessly elaborate wristwatch clanking against the table. Norah let out a beleaguered sigh and allowed her gaze to drift to the floor-to-ceiling windows. Four hundred and forty-five hours. That was the amount of time she'd sunk into this acquisition, and it was about to fall apart thanks to inflated male egos. But as frustrating as it was, Norah knew Harris's tirade wasn't the source of the large pit in her stomach, the one gaining in heft with every tick of the oversized wall clock.

Tick. Tick. Tick.

The ruddy-faced man on the other side of the table was talking now—something about a material adverse change—but Harris waved him away with a dismissive hand. "Don't shit in a bowl and tell me it's ice cream," he growled. The mound of loose skin hanging over his ill-fitting collar wobbled as he tossed the stapled document across the table.

Norah studied him from her position two seats over. With a potbelly that rivaled a full-term pregnancy and a horseshoe of salt-

and-pepper hair shellacked around his otherwise bald head, Harris was the kind of guy who had probably looked middle-aged since he was in kindergarten. Norah could picture him as a middle manager working at a nondescript office near a strip mall, which is probably where he'd be if he hadn't had the good fortune of being born into the Ridley family, a family that had donated enough to Harvard Business School to have a wing named after them. As it was, he was the founder of Orca Asset Management—a private equity firm with over twenty billion dollars under management—and Norah's boss.

She wondered what Harris would say now if she stood up, explained in her most confident tone, *You'll need to excuse me a minute. My daughter isn't answering any of my texts and I'm starting to worry,* and left the room. Norah could imagine the answer being along the lines of *You have a daughter?* Despite the fact that his son, Henry, had attended the same school as Caroline for the past eight years, Harris never failed to be shocked by Caroline's existence. Given the lack of photos in his office, Harris was never in danger of being labeled a "family man."

Norah tapped the screen of her phone awake. Caroline's response time usually rivaled the speed of an out-of-office email, but there was still no answer to any one of Norah's six messages, including the last one, sent over an hour ago. *I'm sensing you're ignoring me, but can you send me proof of life? An emoji? A thumbs-up?*

She chewed on her lower lip. Recently, Caroline had been distant, not her usual cheerful self. She was thirteen, and Norah had been a parent long enough to know that moods were part of being a teenager, but it was beginning to feel like more than that. There had been her sudden interest in boarding school, for instance. Apparently, it wasn't enough to be leaving home in four years for college, now she wanted to fast-track the timeline. There'd also been her uncharacteristic irritation with this work trip. "I don't see why you need to fly all the way to L.A. when you could Zoom instead," she'd moaned, the corners of her mouth tugging down as she watched Norah stuff her laptop into her carry-on bag. "Is that another dig at my aversion to technology?" Norah had asked in response, keeping her tone light as she'd zipped her bag closed and thrown it over her shoulder. She'd expected to see a smile on Caroline's face, but when she'd looked up, Caroline's mouth was flat. "I'll be gone less than twenty-four hours and you can reach me anytime," Norah had assured her, holding out her arms. Caroline, to her credit, had stepped into them. But replaying the conversation in her mind now, Norah wondered if she'd been too dismissive. Because Caroline *hadn't* tried to reach her. Not even once.

She drummed her fingers on the polished wood conference table, her eyes fixed on the screen, willing the three pulsing dots to appear below her message. *This is what it will be like,* she realized, her insides tightening. *This is what it will be like if Caroline goes off to boarding school next year.* A waning line of communication.

Time with Caroline had always been a cherished commodity for Norah, perhaps because it had always been a limited one. Working at Orca was a sixty-hours-a-week obligation, making spare time a premium, and preserving it was a driving force behind Norah's choice to live in the city rather than depart for a spacious suburb. Living a twenty-minute walk from her office gave her the flexibility to do things like read a book to Caroline's kindergarten class or attend middle school career day, while still making it back to her desk for an 11:00 A.M. work call. It also meant she wasn't beholden to Metro-North schedules, allowing Norah to make it home most nights before Caroline was in bed. Those pajamaed, sleepy conversations with her daughter constituted the entirety of Norah's wellness routine.

Time. That was what living in the city gave Norah. And she'd assumed she'd have eighteen years of it. The thought of having it reduced by four years was like someone wrenching her away from a once-in-a-lifetime vacation well before her prearranged checkout.

Norah wasn't unreasonable. She'd allowed Caroline to *apply* to boarding schools, with the understanding that they would discuss it if she was accepted. She could practically hear her business school professor pontificate: *The delaying tactic is a powerful strategic device that can give one party in the negotiation the upper hand by postponing the decision.*

Her index finger tapped the screen again. Nothing.

What if . . . Norah's heart rate began picking up speed. *What if . . . Caroline isn't answering because she's been hit by a car walking home from school, and she's unconscious in a hospital bed, and I'm sitting here in a conference room three thousand miles away.* She pushed her chair back. "I have to make a quick call," she announced to no one in particular, trying to make it sound work-related, before lowering her head and darting out of the conference room.

The hallway buzzed with power ties and pencil skirts walking with purpose. Norah gripped her phone with slick hands.

"Do you need the ladies' room?" a woman with crooked teeth and a messy ponytail stationed in a cubicle asked, raising a thin brow.

"I'm looking for a quiet place to make a call," Norah said, trying to keep the rising anxiety from her voice. The woman swept her palm toward a breakout room at the end of the hall, and Norah scurried past the row of cubicles and closed the door behind her. The room was small—maybe nine by nine—with a circular mahogany wood table and six wheeled, black leather chairs pushed underneath. Mini bottles of water were meticulously arranged in a square in the center of the table. Norah leaned against one of the chairs, fished her earbuds out of her blazer pocket, popped one in each ear, and dialed Caroline's cellphone.

Straight to voicemail. Dammit. She jabbed the red circle, ending the call, and dialed Bennett's number. He picked up on the third ring.

"I've been trying to get ahold of Caroline," Norah said, not waiting for a hello. "But she's not responding. Do you know where she is?"

"Yes." He drew out the word, confusion evident in his tone. "She went to bed a half hour ago. Are you okay? You sound out of breath."

Norah's shoulders sagged with relief. "Bed?" She peered at her watch, feeling slightly foolish. "But, it's not even nine-thirty there."

"She was tired from the dance." She could hear him open the refrigerator, twist open what she assumed was a beer, take a long pull. "Your voice sounds really panicked, Nor. Is everything all right? You should've texted me earlier and I—"

"I did," Norah guillotined his sentence, her tone sharper than she intended. "Twice."

She could hear the jostle of the phone, a long sigh expelled. "Oh shit, I'm sorry. I see it now. I don't know how I missed those messages."

"Wait." Norah's mind was slowly catching up now that her pulse was returning to normal. "Did you say 'dance'?"

"Yeah, she ended up going to that dance tonight."

"What dance?"

"The one at The Doubles Club." He said this like it was obvious. As if Caroline had ever stepped foot inside The Doubles Club. Caroline spending the evening at The Doubles Club sounded about as likely as her spending the evening piloting a plane at JFK.

"Very funny." She snorted. "Really, why did she go to bed so early? Is she getting sick?" Norah stuck her thumbnail between her teeth and began pacing the small space. "You know, she did seem a little lethargic before I left, but I'd chalked that up to—"

"Norah," he cut her off, chuckling. "I'm not kidding. Your little socialist daughter came into the living room wearing a dress and announced she was attending the Doubles dance. I told her that was fine as long as she understood that I would accompany her in an Uber with door-to-door service."

Norah dropped into a leather swivel chair, stunned. Now that she thought about it, somewhere in the recesses of her mind she could recall a dance being mentioned in the WhatsApp group titled "Crofton Eighth Grade Mamas," the one she'd joined because she thought the group messages would be helpful reminders, tips, or necessary school information. Instead, it wound up being gossip about Crofton teachers and recommendation requests for the best pool maintenance company in the Hamptons. She'd muted the notifications and ignored the *For those attending, anyone interested in meeting for cocktails while the kiddos are at the Doubles dance on Friday?* message that came in earlier in the week because a) the word "kiddos" was like an electric drill up against her eardrum, and b) who the hell goes to antiquated private clubs anymore?

Apparently, her daughter.

"But . . . how did that even happen? We're not members."

"Well . . ." He paused, and she could hear him smiling on the other end of the line. "My mom got her a ticket."

Norah sighed and raised her eyes to the ceiling, resting her head on the top of the padded chair. She should've known her mother-in-law's fingerprints were all over this. Waverley Stillman was a formidable and prominent socialite from old money, and she would like nothing better than to indoctrinate Caroline into her exclusive club. No matter how many times Norah politely declined Waverley's offers to take Caroline to her stylist at Saks, Waverley couldn't understand that Norah didn't want her daughter raised the way Bennett had been raised, with ridiculous social etiquette classes for eight-year-olds and using the word "summer" as a verb. Norah wanted Caroline to be grounded, to work to carve out her own path and see the world beyond her moneyed zip code. "I've never met someone who hates money as much as you do and it's surprisingly intoxicating," Bennett had teased her early in their relationship, after she'd confessed her aversion to diamond jewelry. But it wasn't true. She didn't hate money. Quite the opposite, in fact. Unlike Bennett, Norah wasn't born with a silver spoon in her mouth. She'd grown up in a rent-controlled two-bedroom apartment with her three siblings on the Lower East Side before the Wall Street bros deemed it cool, back before developers bulldozed the warehouses and public housing. She and her three sisters had attended a nearby public school, with steel bars curved around the classroom windows and a twenty-by-twenty strip of asphalt that doubled as a playground, until Norah was singled out as gifted and her mother led the charge to get her into a private school on financial aid, convinced a private-school education was the golden ticket to the high-paying jobs held by the parents of the children she taught piano to Uptown. And her mom was right. There was no doubt that Norah's years at The Crofton School, with its stellar reputation and penchant for getting its graduates into the right high schools to catapult them into the Ivies, set Norah on her life path. Full scholarship to Yale, Wharton for business school, and now, a managing director at Orca complete with the seven-figure salary that went with it. What Norah hadn't realized back then, as her mother's shaky hand was filling out the paperwork for the financial aid, was that as her own world was beginning to expand, her mother's body was slowly degenerating. Parkinson's disease, the doctors had informed them solemnly when Norah and her sisters had forced their reluctant mother to see someone after she'd tried to pick up a cup of coffee and it ended up in her lap. Norah was in her first year at Yale at the time, and had offered to drop out, get a job, help out with the astronomical medical bills that were piling up, but her mother wouldn't hear of it. "Just make sure you do well enough to get a job making millions and we never, ever need to worry again." So that was what Norah did. She paid off all of her parents' outstanding debt in her first two years at Orca and now her parents lived in a house near the beach on the southern tip of Long Island, outfitted for a wheelchair and a twenty-four-hour nurse. No, Norah didn't hate money. Making the amount of money she did had saved her family. What she hated was the invisible fence some rich people erected around their world to keep everyone else out.

Exhibit A: The Doubles Club.

"You sound pissed," Bennett said.

Was she? Maybe a little bit. She wished he'd consulted her on this. At the very least sent a text. But a more accurate description of what was sitting in her gut right now was regret. She should've paid better attention to Caroline's reluctance about this trip. Maybe what she'd been trying to communicate was *Stay home. I need you.* Norah ran a clammy hand down her face. She loved her job, she really did. But sometimes she hated it too. That's what working motherhood did to you; it kept you in a constant state of purgatory between the two.

"I'm surprised, that's all," she said, reaching for one of the Poland Spring bottles, twisting off the cap, and taking a slug of room-temperature water in an effort to put out the fireball of guilt.

"Well, don't be too hard on yourself, Nor. I think it was a last-minute decision. My mom told me she had to pull strings to get a same-day ticket."

"Hm." Norah picked at the label on the bottle with a fingernail, suppressing a pinch of unease. When she'd attended Crofton, decades ago, the wealth was less conspicuous. Norah was always aware her classmates had more money than she did, but not absurdly so. The world Caroline was inhabiting now was one of multistory penthouses and private islands, and sometimes the fear that Caroline would get swept up in it kept Norah awake at night. But it never seemed to affect Caroline, so Norah tried not to let it affect her, either. "Well, did she tell you anything about it?" she asked, trying to sound breezy.

"Yes, because teenage girls tell their stepfathers *everything,*" he said wryly.

Bennett had embraced his role as stepfather to Caroline since he and Norah had married two years ago. Norah had been parenting solo for eleven years at that point and had a good rotation of childcare between her full-time nanny covering the days and her sister for the overnights when she had work travel. "I don't know how you do it," the stay-at-home moms at Caroline's preschool would say whenever she breezed into the classroom for parent visiting day dressed in her suit, parking her overstuffed roller bag by the door. "It takes a village, right?" Norah would say with forced cheerfulness. But the truth was, she wasn't aware there was an option *not* to do it. She wanted to keep her job, and the nature of her work simply didn't allow for any less than one hundred percent.

But, unlike most of her colleagues, she didn't have a partner to pick up the slack at home. Caroline's father—in the loosest sense of the word—was a man she'd met through work who, when she'd announced she was unexpectedly pregnant, informed her he "Really wasn't *there* yet." As if they were talking about a destination along a bus route rather than the baby growing inside her.

"I can hear that mind of yours spinning, Nor," Bennett said now, his voice gentle. "But it was only one dance, and I made sure to snap a stealth photo of her all dressed up, and you not being home one measly night doesn't mean you're not an amazing mom. And Caroline knows that."

Norah closed her eyes and let out a long exhale. Bennett's words felt like a weighted blanket placed over her body. In his youth, Bennett had served as diplomat between his feuding parents, and it had given him supernatural insight into soothing a person's frayed edges. He always managed to pull Norah back from the ledge. Even when she didn't realize that was where she'd been perched.

"Thank you," she whispered.

"Anytime. We're a team."

She glanced at her watch. "Shit," she hissed, leaping to her feet, knocking over the bottle of water on the table in the process. A gray-haired man passed by in the hall, casting a sideways look. "I've gotta go," she said, grabbing a wad of tissues from the box in the corner and dabbing at the puddle. "I snuck out of the meeting, but I need to get back."

"Wait. Before you hang up, I should warn you about something. Don't be mad."

Norah dropped the damp wad in the trash. "Please tell me your mother hasn't signed her up for a debutante ball."

"Nothing that bad." He inhaled deeply. "Caroline was in the bathroom for a long time when she got home from school, and I figured she was doing teenage stuff, but it turns out she was coloring the tips of her hair pink."

"Pink?" Norah echoed, feeling her muscles unclench. *This* she understood. Typical teenage rebellion.

"Yeah, apparently there's some weird TikTok challenge where you soak your hair in beet juice."

"As long as she's not ingesting Tide pods, I think we're good." She ended the call and pressed her fingertips against her temples. A dull headache was spreading. Like storm clouds gathering.

Call it paranoia, call it helicopter parenting, or call it mother's intuition, but as she hurried back to the conference room, she couldn't shake the feeling that she was missing something.

Chapter Three

HEATHER

I THINK MY limp-dicked husband is cheating on me.

Heather's fingers froze on the trackpad, her lips curling up at the edges as her eyes ran over the words on the screen. She'd spent the past twenty minutes scrolling through UrbanMyth. The most sordid posts—the confessions of secret pregnancies, the trysts with the tennis pro, the confidential polls comparing net worth—were highlighted in the "most popular" column on the right side of the screen, but Heather had been digging through the weeds—the less scandalous "I found a hair in my gnocchi at Sfoglia" nonsense—hoping to track down a nugget of information about what went on inside Doubles tonight. So far, she'd come up empty. But discovering a juicy post like *this* before it was siphoned off into the "most popular" column, and at least fifty other users had chimed in with their thoughts, was akin to discovering an off-the-radar restaurant before it wound up in the *Times*. She settled back in her chair and continued reading. *I found a blister pack of Viagra in his coat pocket with two pills missing, but we haven't had sex in months (on account of the whole limp dick thing . . .) Should I confront?*

"Jesus," Heather muttered, reading the replies.

I hate to be the bearer of bad news, but your husband is getting it up for someone else.

Time to clear out the bank accounts and call your lawyer!

Everyone on here is so cynical. There could be an innocent explanation for all this. Maybe he was testing for side effects?

Heather let out a snort. Long live Pollyanna. Sliding her finger down the trackpad, she could feel her shoulders begin to relax. UrbanMyth was digital Xanax. The opposite of Instagram. On Instagram, Heather's eyes were constantly assaulted by people broadcasting filtered versions of themselves. *Look at me! I'm standing gracefully on a paddleboard, surrounded by crystal clear water, wearing a barely-there bikini and feeling #gratitude. Later, I'll bake Martha Stewart—worthy cookies with my perfectly groomed offspring.* Ten minutes of Instagram scrolling was enough to make her want to drink a bottle of Drano to escape her own inadequacies. The people of UrbanMyth, on the other hand, they were her people. And not just because the algorithm required them to live within a three-block radius. Their lives were messy. They had problems. And reading about theirs helped Heather ignore her own.

Like gawking at someone else's accident to distract from your own wreckage.

She rested her fingers on the keys, readying herself to type a response.

"So, how'd it go?" Oliver's voice boomed from over her shoulder.

Heather clicked the red *x* in the corner of the screen with the quickness of a snake, as if she were a porn addict who'd been caught feeding her habit, and swiveled around to see her husband standing in the doorway, grinning. This was the main problem with her home office—the back of her chair was to the door, leaving the eighteen-inch screen on the desk in full view. But there wasn't any other practical way to reconfigure the eight-by-eight windowless space that had doubled as a walk-in closet for the previous owners. Reason number thirty-two that she wished their apartment were bigger.

Location, location, location as they say.

"Did Violet see any of her friends there?"

"A few, I think." Heather blew on her cup of tea, watching the steam billow, avoiding his eyes. He knew as well as she did that

Violet hadn't carved out a social group at Crofton. Admitting that now, though, would only give him more ammunition in the "Maybe we should move out of the city" argument, an ongoing debate that had recently evolved into something resembling trench warfare, with each of them firing shots at opportune times from the safety of their respective barracks. Under no circumstances did Heather intend to budge. She'd seen firsthand what existed beyond the Hudson River and it reeked of Bud Light and mediocrity. The suburbs weren't *peace*. They were *stasis*. The opposite of what she wanted for her daughter. Oliver, on the other hand, had developed the irritating opinion that what Violet really needed was a "normal childhood." By this he meant a childhood that mirrored his, with a gaggle of neighborhood friends who happily embarked on adventures together on their bicycles before returning to their attentive parents and manicured homes in time for a roasted-chicken-and-mashed-potatoes dinner. But Heather's childhood had consisted of none of those things, so what the hell did that make hers?

Heather firmly believed that Violet didn't *need* a yard or a collection of neighborhood friends. She was *independent*. Oliver couldn't understand. He loved being around other people, and as far as Heather could tell, the feeling was always mutual. It was probably his most distinct character trait—likability. The two of them would be at a party, and she would sit back and watch the way people were drawn to him like to a pied piper. Heather, on the other hand, had once been compared to beige paint by an ex-boyfriend of hers. "You, like . . . blend in," he'd explained, as if it was a compliment rather than a searing insult she'd hold on to and reexamine for the rest of her life. All these years later, she still refused to have a single wall painted beige. Although, if she was being honest with herself, the comparison was understandable. With her high cheekbones and wide smile, she was attractive, but unremarkably so. It was one of the reasons it annoyed her so much when Poppy forgot her name—because it had happened to her so damn often in the past.

"Well, I hope she had fun," Oliver said, taking a gulp of amber liquid from the tumbler Heather only now noticed he was holding. "She didn't seem too happy when you guys left."

Heather rolled the warm mug of tea between her palms. "Fun" was probably not the word Violet would use to describe her evening. "I did what you said, Mom—I went," Violet had grumbled after Heather tried to probe for details, only peeling her eyes from the screen of her phone long enough to fix Heather with a surly glare. Heather didn't even want to think about what would've happened if she'd pulled that crap with her own parents. Lucky for Violet, Heather was committed to never raising a hand to her child. One of the many, many differences there would be in their upbringings.

"It's better than her spending another Friday night in front of her computer, right?" Heather said, taking the opportunity to find common ground. Violet's computer had morphed into an appendage ever since she took that advanced coding camp two summers ago, and they were in agreement that it was getting out of hand. "And I *do* think her going tonight will help with admissions. Even Poppy Ridley seemed to think so."

"Well, if the queen decreed it so, then it must be true," he said drolly, raising his eyebrows.

She swiped a pen off her desk and playfully threw it at him.

"Ouch!" he said through a laugh, the ice cubes rattling in his near-empty glass.

Heather's mouth twitched when she remembered Poppy's horrified expression after she'd inadvertently confessed to frequenting UrbanMyth. *The stakes are going to be high at Doubles on Friday. I heard DOA from Andover is going to be in attendance ensuring the candidates are the kind that can "play well with others,"* the anonymous post had declared earlier this week. It had garnered over one hundred responses and zipped to the "most popular" column. But despite the fact that it was named one of the "Start-ups to Watch" by *The Wall Street Journal,* frequenting UrbanMyth was still considered taboo on the Upper East Side. Or at least *admitting* it was. It was like paying your nanny under the table or combining a tummy tuck with your C-section—everyone did it, but nobody copped to it. Poppy dropping a direct quote from UrbanMyth into casual conversation tonight was further proof she was off. Heather couldn't help but wonder why. She tucked the thought away to ponder later.

"You *know* . . ." Oliver dragged out the word, a smile playing at his lips. "Many of the amenities that you'll find at Andover can also be found at a suburban public school. And we wouldn't need to parade Violet in front of an admissions director for her to attend." He made an exaggerated Vanna White–like gesture with his hands to what was meant to be an imaginary Violet.

"Keep talking and I'll throw this mug at you," Heather deadpanned.

He mimed zipping his lips before holding up an index finger. "Okay, but one last point. Think of the extra money we'd have if we didn't need to pay tuition. Or New York City taxes for that matter."

Heather rolled her eyes, attempting to smother her annoyance. She hated when Oliver brought up the cost of Violet's education, how taut it stretched their finances, as if this was news to her. Oliver was a partner at a Big Four accounting firm, but that didn't even come close to the top of the food chain on the Upper East Side. There were parents of children in Violet's class who were making *donations* larger than his entire salary. Maybe twice as much. Heather tried not to think about the eight ball that put them behind in the boarding school admissions race. "Tried" being the operative word. In reality, she studied the list of donors in the Crofton annual report as if there'd be a pop quiz, obsessing over whether it would be wise to give an additional five thousand dollars to move from the "friend" category to the "builder." But the distinction was moot. Parents like her—not poor enough to be interesting, not wealthy enough to underwrite a new gymnasium— were forced to get creative. For example, ensuring your well-mannered daughter is in the same room as the admissions director of her top-choice school.

Among other things.

"On that note, I'm headed to bed," Oliver said, running his palm along the stubble on his neck. "Are you coming soon?"

"In a bit. I need to get a few things done first." She gestured to her computer.

His face perked up. "Work on book two?"

"Yup." Heather wiped her damp palms on her lap. "I had a jolt of inspiration, so I want to get it down."

"That's great. How many words did you get done today?"

"Um . . . about a thousand." She lowered her gaze to her keyboard and noticed the wrappers scattered beside it. Was her stomach roiling because she'd consumed four snack-sized Snickers bars or because of this conversation? It was impossible to tell.

"Pretty productive day." His expression was pleased, his eyes as trusting of her as a golden retriever's. "That puts you at about fifty thousand then, right?"

She nodded, willing him to stop asking questions so she could stop lying.

"Looks like I'll have another book release party to plan soon," he said. "Okay, I'd better leave you to it then." He tapped a palm against the doorframe.

Heather waited until she heard the bedroom door close before getting up and quietly shutting her own. She dropped back down on the ergonomic rolling chair and finished her tea in a single gulp that scalded her throat.

Back on UrbanMyth, the Viagra-popping spouse was highlighted in the "most popular" column now. Thirty-seven comments. Heather chewed the cuticle on the edge of her thumb before catching herself and tucking her left hand underneath her thigh. She inched the cursor toward the words "create new post" and clicked. She hesitated for a moment before typing her question into the rectangular box and hitting enter.

She loved her husband. She did. What she was doing now didn't change that.

Her eyes stayed fixed on the screen, waiting for replies.

UrbanMyth Message Board

Has anyone ever received a loan from a bank without their spouse's knowledge? I'm curious how this would work.

> Depends how much you need . . . How much trouble are you in?

> I've found online banks are most reliable for this. Brick and mortar banks may say your account will be paperless, but they still mail statements your spouse can find.

> Make it a personal loan and don't secure it with any marital assets. Easy peasy.

> If you're willing to do murder for hire, I have a spouse I'd like offed.

I've started a relationship with someone outside my marriage. I'm not going to actually leave my husband, but does anyone on here have some tips for successfully keeping a man on the side?

> DO NOT use Apple products. Those linked devices have been the downfall of countless marriages.

> Are you both on the same page? This only works if he knows the rules. I had a fling get a little . . . obsessive.

> My husband and I have an open marriage in order to avoid this kind of deception.

> If you have kids, don't do it. I cheated on my husband and now I spend half my holidays alone. Nothing says depressing like a giant Christmas tree in an empty apartment.

Chapter Four

POPPY

THE HIGH-PITCHED SPUTTERING sound coming from the brushed-chrome appliance was the first sign that today was not going to go the way Poppy had planned.

"Shit," Poppy hissed, stabbing at the buttons until the power light dimmed. She inspected the mug she'd optimistically placed under the spout of the built-in Bosch coffee maker. A pool of brown sludge covered the bottom of the cup. She shook her head. This thing had been nothing but trouble since that overzealous designer had convinced her it was a must-have in any Fifth Avenue kitchen. "Small appliances sitting on top of countertops are reserved for apartments East of Lex," the designer had proclaimed, swiping her hand at Poppy's Nespresso machine as if she could make the unruly eyesore disappear. Poppy had relented, of course, as she always did when being upsold, and had the $4,000 device that promised to make Persian-café-quality beverages installed as part of her latest revamp. Her kitchen appliances would not have been out of place in a small restaurant now, although she never cooked.

Form over function.

It might as well have been written in neon over the entrance to her apartment.

This morning, though, function would've been nice.

She dumped the thick, grainy liquid in the sink and swished out the mug. Twisting her wrist, she caught sight of newly visible veins popping up on the back of her hand. She narrowed her eyes and ran the pad of her index finger along the offending imperfection. Poppy's dedication to her beauty regime rivaled that of an Olympic athlete's dedication to her chosen sport. Every inch of her body had been buffed, moisturized, botoxed, colored, manicured, pedicured, stretched, sculpted, lasered, massaged, tightened, trimmed, whitened, or some combination of all of the above. Lately, though, it was beginning to feel like an exercise in futility. It reminded her of a game she used to play with her brother during summer nights on Martha's Vineyard. When the tide would start to come in, they'd select a sandbar to "rescue" from the ocean. They'd set to work, knees fully in the sand, methodically building elaborate walls and drainage systems to fortress the area, and, when all else failed, used buckets to scoop up the seeping water and toss it back to the sea. Inevitably, they'd be standing in knee-deep salt water, forced to admit defeat.

"Beauty is currency," her mother had told her, after gifting Poppy a nose job for her sixteenth birthday. "Whatever you do, *don't* lose it." She'd said this like Poppy's beauty was a handbag that might absentmindedly be left behind on a plane. Poppy had dismissed it at the time, but now she could see her beauty for what it really was: a diminishing asset. One she feared losing the way some people feared the depletion of their life savings.

Turning off the tap, she made a mental note to call her cosmetic surgeon today. Surely there was some kind of reconstructive surgery that could be done for thinning skin on the back of her hands. It seemed impossible that an enhancement she valued could not be bought or procured for her.

She cinched the belt of her Egyptian cotton robe and leaned against the counter. Closing her eyes, she expelled a long breath. If last night was any indication, her currency was still highly valued. She touched a fingertip to her bottom lip, thinking about his lip pressed against it, and a delicious warmth washed up her thighs and down her spine. She wanted to bask in the heat like a cat stretched out in a sunbeam. But, try as she might, she couldn't shake the reproachful voice clawing its way into her consciousness, the one telling her it was a close call last night.

Too close.

She tried to imagine the scene if Heather had rounded the corner two minutes earlier. A shiver ran through her body thinking about what the fallout could've been. As it was, the conversation had been predictably bland. But there was something in Heather's expression that Poppy had found unsettling. The intensity with which she'd studied Poppy's face, as if Poppy were an abstract painting in the Guggenheim. Was it possible Heather *had* seen what Poppy had been doing? That woman had always been a little odd, Poppy supposed. Where some people emanate serenity, Heather emanated manic stress. Like a hummingbird on speed, vibrating with nervous, palpable energy. You could practically see the desperate, jittery waves radiating off of her. At the school benefit last year, Poppy had been stuck next to Heather at the table for dinner. Poppy had spent the evening trying to have a conversation with the more interesting woman on her other side, while Heather continued to try to poke her way in, nakedly eager, with some out-of-left-field compliment—"I love your dress, those shoes are beautiful"—straining for approval. It was unbearable. Poppy didn't have time for people who struggled socially. She was a firm believer in survival of the fittest.

Natural selection should've weeded Heather out of her social sphere long ago.

She pulled a bottle of organic coconut water from the fridge, tilted it to her lips, and took five long swallows, hoping the electrolytes would sweep away any lingering worries about Heather. What she really needed was a Xanax. It had been over a week since she'd taken one because it had started to make her groggy, but better to be groggy than to have her paranoia wreak havoc on her appetite and make her skin break out.

She located her purse where she'd dropped it in the foyer, sifted through for the vial, and headed back to the kitchen. She washed two capsules down with what remained of the coconut water and slipped her phone from the pocket of her robe, checking the time.

Eight-thirty A.M. Harris must've been held up on the work trip. Where had he gone again? Toronto? Or was it Chicago? Poppy could never remember. Or be bothered to care. All she knew is she had the apartment to herself. And having her husband thousands of miles away was making her feel particularly emboldened. She rested her thumbs on the screen, considering. *Should I, shouldn't I.* Her thumbs set to work drafting a text, repeatedly deleting and retyping.

"Good morning!" a voice sliced through the kitchen, startling her.

"Oh!" Poppy yelped, bringing her phone to her clavicle. "You scared the hell out of me."

"I'm so sorry, Ms. Ridley," Maya stammered, the smile dropping from her face, her doe eyes widening. "I was going to get started in here, but I didn't mean to sneak up on you." She bent her head as if readying herself for the guillotine. "I . . . I can come back later."

Poppy wrestled her breathing under control. "No, no, don't be silly." She forced a shaky smile, dropping her iPhone back into the pocket of her robe and cinching the belt tighter. "I didn't hear you come in, that's all."

Poppy was still having a hard time getting used to the new housekeeper. Her last housekeeper had retired abruptly three months ago—some nonsense about a sick mother—and Poppy had engaged an agency to find her replacement. Maya was younger than she would've preferred, probably late twenties, but she'd impressed Poppy during her trial week with the amount of work she was able to get done during her ten-hour shift. The energy of youth. What Poppy hadn't considered was how accustomed she was to the "old guard" of household help, who followed certain unspoken rules, one of which was that household help remained . . . well, generally unspoken. Maya, on the other hand, greeted her with twentysomething exuberance every time she entered a room. And her voice was always a decibel louder than what Poppy considered normal, as if they were actors on a stage and Maya was projecting her voice to the back of the theater.

It was probably in Poppy's head, but sometimes she felt like Maya sought her out, like a lonely puppy. The apartment was five thousand square feet for god's sake. There were places to clean other than the room Poppy was currently occupying. Of course, Poppy's low-key annoyance could stem from something her mother had said. "Never have someone working in your home who is younger than you, Poppy. That's like hiring your own replacement." If there was one person fully committed to the old way of doing things, it was her mother. Not that she knew much about a successful marriage. But that didn't stop her.

Poppy could see that Maya was conventionally attractive with her chestnut-colored hair, impossibly thick lashes, and soft curves that rivaled a forties pinup girl, but was Poppy really supposed to *fire* her because she happened to be attractive? Truthfully, if the circumstances were different, Poppy might consider it, but she'd already gone through four housekeepers in the past two years and knew firsthand the validity of the "You can't get good help" adage. Besides, Harris practically lived at the office. He probably couldn't pick his own housekeeper out of a lineup.

"I need to wake Henry up for lacrosse practice, so the kitchen is all yours," Poppy said, dropping her empty coconut-water bottle in the sink. "Oh." She paused mid-stride. "I'm going to have a service tech come by to take a look at the espresso machine. Can you make sure he doesn't leave a mess in here?"

"Of course," Maya replied, a tad too loudly, pulling a cloth out of the drawer and setting to work wiping the gleaming quartz countertop.

Poppy could hear her turn the tap, hear the water running, as she headed down the hallway, past Harris's home office, to her son's bedroom. She knocked gently before pushing the door open. Henry's golden-blond curls poked out from the mess of covers and one scrawny arm was draped over the side of the bed. If the faint, funky smell permeating his room wasn't enough of a reminder that she was now parenting a teenager, the fact that he would gladly sleep like the dead until noon every weekend would seal it. Henry's current sleep habits were a complete one-eighty from his toddler years when, like clockwork, his pajamaed feet hit the floor at five-thirty every morning. Poppy never understood how mothers without hired help endured those endless early mornings. She'd relied on a live-in nanny with a bedroom beside Henry's from the day he was born until two years ago when Poppy had finally let her go. And she never felt an ounce of guilt about delegating the dirty work of parenting. Perhaps that was because it was how her own mother had done it. Some women were hardwired for midnight breastfeeding and sticky-fingered toddlers. Poppy and her mother were simply not among them.

She rested a hand on Henry's shoulder, then hesitated, her gaze catching on the underside of his arm. Curves of blue and black ink covered the soft pale skin on his wrist and forearm, as if he'd made a pit stop at a tattoo parlor on his way home. Gingerly, she lifted the sleeve of his pajama shirt to get a closer look, a smile twitching on her lips. She'd forgotten all about that silly tradition. There were probably twenty phone numbers written in loopy, swirly handwriting across his left arm. Lucky for Henry, he took after her rather than Harris in the looks department. It was like her mother always said, "Children should inherit their looks from their mother and their trust fund from their father." Poppy had done both, but the trust fund was long gone. College, grad school, years of keeping her lifestyle afloat while working unpaid internships in the art world: the trust fund couldn't sustain her forever. Dad had left the lion's share of his money to Mom. And Mom was not about to part with any of it.

She gave Henry's shoulder a shake, and he responded with a groan.

"Henry," she whispered, as an iPhone buzzed on the night-stand, the glow of the screen illuminating the darkened room. She picked it up and flopped down at the base of the king-sized bed. If anything was going to get this boy out of bed, it would be the ter-ror of his mother's hands on his precious phone.

When Henry got his first mobile phone, the rule was that she could review his texts at any time. "Don't think of it as invading their privacy," the rigid-looking woman from Digital Media Coalition had advised parents in the phone safety seminar. "Think of your child's mobile phone as a car that you are helping him learn to drive. Because a child who doesn't know how to navigate the online world can cause as much damage as a child doing ninety miles an hour on the wrong side of the highway." The dramatics of the comparison had been met with a hard eye roll from Poppy, but she did as the presenter suggested and periodically reviewed Henry's text chains for the first few weeks. The worst things she saw were a couple of swear words and a little harmless needling among friends. Certainly nothing akin to a reckless driver poised to mow down fellow motorists.

She flipped the phone over in her palm. The text that had popped up on his phone was illuminated on the home screen. Poppy made a mental note to change this feature on her own phone. How many marriages was Steve Jobs responsible for destroying?

She squinted at the message.

Four simple words: *Did you see this?*

Her curiosity was piqued. She tossed a glance at the lump of down duvet. No movement. This wasn't snooping, she told herself. She was simply ensuring Henry knew how to safely operate his car. She tapped on the message, inputting Henry's birthday when prompted for the password, relieved to see he hadn't changed it, and a full-sized photo of a girl spread across the screen. Poppy's brow furrowed as she examined it, using her thumb and index finger to enlarge the picture, zooming in on her face. This girl looked familiar, but Poppy couldn't figure out why. She wasn't one of Henry's friends. Poppy was up to speed on who was in Henry's crowd because they always seemed to wind up at her apartment. Still, she recognized this mousy brown hair and oval face from somewhere.

After a moment, the penny dropped.

"Henry." She jostled her son's leg, harder than she meant to. "Henry, *what* is this photo?"

UrbanMyth Message Board

OK, someone explain to me this Doubles tradition of phone numbers on the arm.

> The first rule of Fight Club . . . Shhhhhh

> It is by far the most antiquated thing about that ridiculous club. If a boy dances with a girl, she writes her number on his arm. Boys collect them like it's a game of trick or treat. Toxic masculinity starts early on the UES.

> Don't listen to Debbie Downer above—it's all in good fun. The kids get a kick out of it, and nobody needs to actually call each other or date or whatever. It's just a game.

If my husband was impotent and cheating on me, I'd kill myself.

> Here we go again, the user who suggests everyone with a problem should kill themselves.

> Go away troll.

> Is this a reference to the cheating Viagra spouse? Keep message threads together—don't start a brand-new post!

Chapter Five

HEATHER

HEATHER RETRIEVED THE skim vanilla latte from the counter and slipped a cardboard sleeve over the cup, spinning it until the edge was precisely lined up with the spout. She'd already had her caffeine fix for the day, but sitting down at a table without making a purchase was too conspicuous. Cradling the warm cup in her hands, she made her way to the back of the narrow café and lowered herself into the banquette seat in the far corner, the one with the clearest view of the door.

Bean Around the World Café was a hole-in-the-wall with a sandwich board on the sidewalk boasting an "out of this world Nutella latte," but if the lack of customers at ten o'clock on a Saturday morning was any indication, the neighbors didn't agree with the proclamation. It was an isolated oasis in a sea of crowded Starbucks, thirty blocks from her apartment, far enough away to make it the ideal place for them to meet. The two of them being spotted together wouldn't immediately ring any alarm bells, she supposed, but it could raise some questions. Questions Heather preferred not to answer. Lately, her lies were multiplying like rabbits. And she did not need to add more to the colony.

She smoothed her hair down and ran a fingertip under each eye, ensuring the mascara she'd applied an hour ago hadn't migrated. Then she slid her phone out of her coat pocket and thumbed out a text. *I'm here at Bean Around the World. Table in the back.* Within seconds the phone vibrated in her palm. She stiffened when she saw it was a message from Oliver. *Where are you?* Without replying, she rested the phone on the table, screen-side up. Excuses gathered in the back of her mind: she didn't see the message, dead battery, service dropped in the subway.

She'd come up with a reasonable explanation. She always did.

Toying with the lid of her coffee cup, she tried to imagine what would happen if Oliver knew what she was doing right now or, god forbid, if Violet did. Violet was like a china plate these days. A hairline fracture could shatter her. She took a sip of her latte, hoping the warmth sliding down her throat would calm her nerves. Lately, her insides felt as pressurized as a shaken soda can. Thank god the boarding school admission process would be over soon. The deadline for applications was the last day of February, which was next week. Heather had submitted Violet's over a month ago.

A "try hard." That's what Heather's classmates used to call her in high school. It took weeks for her to grasp that it was intended as an insult. Because she did, in fact, try hard. Very hard. At everything. And for the life of her, she still couldn't comprehend why this would be considered a detriment. Yet, there was always someone telling her to dial down, ease up. Even Oliver. Especially Oliver. *We should really ease up on Violet, Heath.* She nearly choked on her latte now thinking about it. Name one person who's ever won a race by easing up on the gas. Easing up is how you lose.

There were many reasons for Heather to feel guilty right now, but she refused to feel an ounce of guilt for being an involved parent. The parents who *should* have felt guilty were the ones who raised their children like feral cats, parents who skated by with the barest minimum: keeping their child fed, housed, vaccinated. People like Heather's mother and father. Her father had attended one parent-teacher conference, and only because he'd somehow heard beer would be served. Not surprisingly, it wasn't. Afterward, he'd come into her bedroom, a contemptuous expression on his face. "You sound like a teach-ah's pet," he said in his thick New Jersey accent. It wasn't a compliment. Still, she'd kept her nose in a textbook and ignored the angry sounds echoing through the paper-thin walls of their small bungalow, imagining herself on an ivy-coated campus instead. But despite graduating top of her class with a perfect SAT score, Heather was inexplicably shut out of her dream schools. It felt like a cruel injustice at the time, but the full injustice only became evident later, when she realized the people who took her spots had their paths lubricated with legacy connections and reference letters written by presidential candidates. Heather had forged ahead, accepting a full academic scholarship to Rutgers, and had even managed to land a spot at a top New York investment bank after graduation. But the old boys' club stays that way for a reason, and when Heather was up for managing director she lost out to a guy who wouldn't have been able to structure a deal if he'd had a gun to his head but had Princeton on his résumé, which apparently was enough for the three alums on the management committee. When she left her job, she told everyone it was to spend more time with her family, and she *did* want that, but the truth was that seeing him in the position that was rightfully hers was more than she could bear.

The disappointment had sealed in Heather a cold, hard truth: Proximity is half the battle in this world. Every small decision she made for her daughter was like collecting an Action card in The Game of Life—send her to Crofton, spin again; gain admission into Andover, advance five spaces; earn a degree from an Ivy League school, collect the career of your choice.

Heather knew firsthand there was only so much room at the table. And she would ensure Violet had a seat if it killed her.

Her phone vibrated, bringing her back to the present. Another message from Oliver. This one was simply a row of question marks. She stared at the message, anxiety humming under her skin like a cut nerve. What was *with* him today? Taking a shaky sip of her now cooled latte, she checked the time again: 10:20 A.M. The coffee shop suddenly felt warm, and she realized she was sweating. Her fingers flew across the screen. *Where are you??? I'm still waiting at Bean Around the World.* Then added, *Table in the back,* as if anyone entering this café could miss her.

Setting the phone back down on the table, she rolled the cup between her palms. The barista was humming, wiping down the milk frother with what appeared to be a dirty rag, when the sound of Heather's ringtone pierced the quiet space. A photo of Oliver and Violet at the beach flashed on the screen.

"Shit," she hissed, tapping the green circle and lifting the phone to her ear.

"Heather?" Oliver's voice blared from the speaker before she could say hello. "Where are you?"

Her eyes darted to the top corners of the café, as if he'd spotted her on a hidden camera. "I'm . . . I'm running some errands," she said, clearing the wobble in her voice. "Why?"

"Right. Uhhhh . . . how close are you to home?"

"I'm at Whole Foods, so kind of close." She squeezed her eyes shut, regretting the corner she'd painted herself into. Now she'd need a Whole Foods bag in hand before returning to the apartment. Mentally, she adjusted her timeline. "Do you need me to pick you up anything?"

"No, there's . . . I . . . need to talk to you. It's too hard to explain over the phone." There was a hint of anger in his tone. "Can you come home?"

"Well, I need to finish up here and then . . . um . . ." Her fingers tightened around the cardboard sleeve on the cup. "I have an appointment I need to head to. Can it wait until after?"

"What appointment do you have?"

"I'm having trouble hearing you," she said, increasing the volume of her voice, buying herself a few minutes. The barista dropped her rag and shot Heather a curious look, so Heather angled her body away. "Sorry, a loud pack of kids went by, and I couldn't hear you for a sec."

"I said, 'What's the appointment?'" he repeated, his voice uncharacteristically sharp.

She started to speak, but he cut her off.

"Never mind. Heath, you've gotta come home."

"Oliver, what's going on?" Panic rose in her voice. The barista was staring openly now, but Heather didn't care. "Tell me what's going on. What's happened?"

"It's too hard to explain over the phone. You need to get home as soon as you can."

And then he was gone.

BY THE TIME the taxi delivered her to the front of her building, her breaths were coming fast and swift—out, out, out—as if she were in labor again. She bypassed the notoriously slow elevator and opted to take the stairs, two at a time, up to her twelfth-floor apartment. There was a small part of Heather that was in a permanent state of waiting for the other shoe to drop, as if this life she'd built was perched precariously on the edge of a cliff and at any moment the ground would give way.

Crash.

Her heart rate had built to a rapid staccato when the front door slammed behind her.

"In here." Oliver's voice came from the living room.

"Oliver, you have me completely freaked out," she called, wiping her palms on the sides of her pants as she headed down the hallway. "What could be so important that I needed to—" She stopped short.

Violet was huddled on the gray-blue sofa, arms wrapped tightly at her waist, clutching a squashed tissue. Her eyes were rimmed crimson and her cheeks were a splotchy mess. Oliver was seated on an upholstered chair across from Violet, head resting on the tips of his fingers. He was raking his bottom lip with his teeth, a tic he only had when he was angry.

The shaky smile on Heather's face instantly evaporated.

"What's going on?" she barked, her breath still choppy from the stairs and adrenaline.

Oliver and Violet exchanged looks.

"Can someone tell me what the hell is going on?" She raised her voice, crossing her arms over her chest. She could feel her heart pounding against the back of her hand.

"It's easier for you to see it than for me to try to explain it to you." Oliver slid an iPhone across the coffee table. "Here. Take a look."

Heather swiped it off the table and tapped an impatient finger, illuminating the screen. There was a close-up shot of a bored-looking musician with a guitar.

"Okay, what am I looking at?"

Violet craned her neck, peering at the screen. "No, not that." She held out her hand. A few taps of her thumbs and she passed it back to Heather. "It's from last night," she mumbled.

Heather refocused her eyes, pulling the phone closer to her face. There, staring back at her, was Violet, wearing the navy dress Heather had purchased, perched on a red velvet couch, her wiry legs crossed. Heather recognized the couch as the one stationed in a lounge inside The Doubles Club, a small area the members had designated the "rest stop" due to its proximity to the bathrooms and the lack of speakers in the room. Heather had sat on the same couch, cocktail in hand, when the music had gotten too much for her at the Doubles Fall Fling. Violet was clutching an object in her right hand. It wasn't a cocktail. It was cobalt blue and looked like an elongated flash drive or a pen that had been flattened by a steam-roller. Heather couldn't place what it was and for a brief, laughable moment she almost asked why there was a plume of visible breath coming from Violet's mouth, if it was some kind of filter that the kids were using these days. Then it clicked.

"Is this a . . . What is this?" she sputtered. "Is this a *vape*?"

Oliver rubbed a palm over his stubble and blew out a long breath. "Apparently our daughter was vaping at the dance last night."

She stared at him as if he'd spoken in a foreign tongue. She wouldn't have been more shocked if he'd stood up and slapped her across the face. And for reasons she couldn't explain, everything inside of her wanted to reach out and slap him across his.

Violet still had Beanie Boos in her room.

Violet slept with a nightlight.

Violet was thirteen years old, for god's sake.

Violet didn't vape.

"Mom, I'm sorry," Violet said.

Her attention snapped to Violet. The expression on her face was the same one Heather remembered from years ago, when she'd walked into the kitchen and discovered four-year-old Violet sitting on the tiles, chocolate frosting circling her mouth and a wet cupcake in her hand, the plate of twenty-four birthday treats reduced by three. Heather had taken a picture of Violet's adorably guilty face and sent it to Oliver with the caption *Busted!* After that, Heather and Oliver referred to the expression as "cupcake face," an instant tell that Violet had misbehaved. A full-blown admission of guilt.

"Violet." Her daughter's name came out shaky. "Where was the admissions director when this was happening?"

"Mom, it was really crowded and . . . I, like, never even *saw* her there." She wiped a tear running down her wet cheek. "Like, the whole night."

This was new information to Heather. Yesterday, it would've been a crushing disappointment, but now it flooded her with relief. "Well, this is *still* unacceptable," she said. "We've talked about the dangers of this kind of thing." Hadn't they? Heather could recall countless conversations about the dangers of falling behind in school and the dangers of not drinking enough water, but, to her surprise, she couldn't recall a single conversation about vaping. Or smoking. Or any drugs at all for that matter. Heather thought about the parenting book she'd read last year, *Raising Girls to Be Leaders*. There'd been a chapter titled "Teen Vaping: What You Need to Know" (Christ, a whole chapter on the subject), which Heather had only skimmed. *If you catch your daughter vaping, lend an ear. It's important to create an environment of disclosure.* She remembered highlighting the words "environment of disclosure," but now she wanted to grab that ridiculous book from her shelf and beat the author over the head with it, because that advice was useless. What should've been in its place was *practical* advice on how to create an environment where your daughter doesn't vape in the first place.

"I only tried it because I was really nervous and thought it

might calm me down a little bit and help me avoid a panic attack."
Violet pulled her skinny legs up to her chest. "I had like one puff.
Maybe two. I had no idea it would end up on Instagram."

"Instagram?" Heather's voice rose. "Wait. This photo is on *Instagram*?"

Oliver and Violet nodded morosely, practically in sync. Violet
slumped farther into the couch, hugging a throw pillow. "We
don't know who posted it because it was posted on the PSCON
account." She pronounced it like "piss-con" and Heather turned
to her husband to translate. Oliver gestured with his hand for Violet to keep going.

"The Private School Confidential Insta account. People send
their photos anonymously, and nobody knows who posts them.
Sometimes there's stuff about crazy parents or creepy teachers.
This one got posted this morning, I guess." She wiped her nose
with her balled-up sleeve. "Grayson texted me a screenshot someone sent her. Apparently, it's been going around."

Heather stared into her daughter's watery eyes and swallowed a
feeling of nausea. "Grayson did this?"

"No, Mom." Violet gave an exasperated huff. "Someone sent
Grayson a screenshot and she sent it to me because we're teammates
and she wanted to give me a heads-up." She swept fresh tears from
her eyes, smudging black streaks of day-old mascara across her face.

"A heads-up," Heather echoed. She ran her hands through her
hair, gripped the roots. Her mind was firing so fast that she felt
faint. "Do you mean to tell me that this photo of you is out there
for the *world* to see? Forever? For anyone to—"

"Let's not go to the worst place, here, Heath," Oliver interjected, his voice verging on a plea.

"We're already in the worst place, Oliver," she snapped. She
hated when he met her anger with that tone of his. It was his hostage
negotiator voice, as if she were a lunatic clutching a ticking bomb.

Heather could feel the ship unmooring.

"Jesus Christ, Violet," she fumed. "Everything you've *worked*
toward, and this is what you—" She bit back the rest of the sentence. Violet had buried her tear-splattered face in her hands.

Heather could see two pinpricks of blood where she'd chewed the side of a fingernail raw. She was so vulnerable. Broken.

Something split open in Heather's chest and two words bubbled up from somewhere deep and primal and raw: *Fix this*.

"Where's my phone?" Her eyes flicked around the room wildly before she remembered it was tucked in the back pocket of her jeans. Wrenching the phone from the tight pocket, she stabbed at the screen. Triage. Stem the bleeding. With a few taps, she'd opened Instagram and navigated to the PSCON account. The photo of Violet flooded her screen, assaulting her retinas again. Except now she was focused on the words captioned below the photo. *Need a little pick me up? Let me introduce you to Crofton's resident dealer. #ExtracurricularActivities #DoublesClub #TeenNight.*

The floor tipped, and Heather gripped the back of the upholstered chair, anchoring herself.

"Crofton's resident *dealer*?" The words exploded from her mouth. "You're selling *drugs*?" She could feel nerve endings in her brain snapping, her lips going numb. Was she having a stroke? The possibility seemed preferable to her current reality.

"Mom, no," Violet wailed, a fresh round of tears on her cheeks. "That's a lie. I swear. I've never even *touched* drugs."

"What the hell was in the vape then, Violet?"

"It was just *weed*. That's not really a drug. It's *legal*."

But Heather had stopped listening. She was reading. Twenty-seven comments already and more were accumulating. The words swam in front of her.

I think I bought Molly from this girl last week.

Anyone know her name? Can she hook me up with some Oxy?

That's why Crofton wins all the athletic titles—they're juiced up.

Private school girls aren't as hot as they used to be.

Heather was going to be sick. "Who . . . who *are* these people?" she asked, incredulous, her thumb bending and straightening, message after message scrolling by as her eyes scanned each post.

"Nobody we know," Violet said. She brought the cuff of her hoodie to her mouth, started chewing on a thread. "The only people who ever comment on these posts are trolls. Or sometimes people who have already graduated and want to keep themselves connected to the private school 'scene,'" she said, carving out air quotes.

Hot anger rushed through Heather's veins. She took several deep breaths through gritted teeth, as the practical part of her brain fought to take over. The photo wouldn't appear in a Google search of Violet's name, thankfully, but if an admissions director was willing to come to a dance at a private club to assess potential candidates, she was certainly capable of keeping an eye on an underground Instagram account. Heather's finger hammered at the words "report photo," and she scanned the list of reasons before landing on "bullying or harassment." *Thanks for letting us know!* flashed on the screen in an obnoxiously optimistic font.

She gave the phone a violent shake as if that might somehow destroy the photo.

Violet crossed her arms over her chest. "You're the one who *made* me go to that stupid dance," she said with a self-righteous sniff. "And now my whole life is *ruined*."

Oliver rose from the chair and sat down beside Violet, wrapping an arm around her shoulder. She buried her face in his chest. "It was a bad decision, honey," he whispered in her ear, running a palm down the side of her head. "And we need you to learn from it, but one bad decision won't ruin your life."

"It's not fair, Dad." Violet's voice was muffled, her face buried in the crook of Oliver's arm. "I didn't know anyone was going to take a *picture*."

Watching Oliver stroke Violet's hair, Heather's mind trickled back to the sight of Violet's ponytail swinging as she descended the stairs into The Doubles Club. There'd been an uneasiness niggling at Heather, a reason she'd lingered. A mother's intuition. That tiny voice that compels a mother to check on a sleeping infant, only to find the swaddle blanket dangerously bunched around its neck. Heather's gut was trying to give her a warning last night, and she'd foolishly ignored it.

"I still don't understand how it happened," Heather heard Violet say. "We weren't even allowed to *have* our phones in there, so who could've taken that picture?"

Who could've taken that picture?

The words popped a bubble in Heather's consciousness.

"I know who took it," she blurted.

Oliver regarded her, a deep crease of worry forming between his eyebrows. "I don't think this should be about who *took* the photo, this is about . . ."

Heather thrust her palm in his direction, severing the sentence. "Vi, who is that girl in your class who played Mary Poppins in the play last year?"

She lifted her head, leaving a wet spot on Oliver's shirt. "Why?"

"Just." She waved her hand impatiently. "What's her name?"

"Caroline Ryan?"

"Does she have pink tips in her hair?"

She lifted one shoulder in a halfhearted shrug. "She did yesterday."

All at once, the puzzle pieces slammed into place. Caroline Ryan was a bright girl and Violet's biggest competition in the boarding school race. Both girls were top of the class and had similar résumés, loaded with college-friendly extracurriculars. Andover was going to take only so many applicants from Crofton, most of which would likely be legacies. It was a zero-sum game. Too many passengers, not enough lifeboats. And everyone knew Andover would be hypersensitive for any signs of disobedience after the unfortunate incident last year when three Andover students used spray paint to express their discontent, tagging a large portion of the campus with the phrases *Harvard acceptances for sale, inquire within* and *Future white-collar-criminal training center* and *Overprivileged, underqualified assholes live here.* The damage had been so widespread it had garnered a six-minute segment on CNN, with Anderson Cooper earnestly posing the question "Are these kids sounding the alarm bell? Is the American education system rigged?" It was well-established lore that the alumni were so irate that the admissions director had to assure them adjustments would be made, including increased diligence into each candidate's "sociability." So, what better way to eliminate a member of the competition for an Andover acceptance than to post a photo of her blatantly breaking rules and label her an underground drug dealer capable of corrupting an entire student body?

Oliver was eyeing Heather now, as if she were a dangerous animal that needed to be handled carefully. "Heath, I don't know where your head is at right now, but I don't think we should jump to any conclusions here."

But Heather had already hurdled several.

"Oliver," she said, her voice rising. "Someone did this to Violet *purposefully*."

"Well, let's think this through before we—"

"We need a plan," she cut him off. Oliver winced. Oliver once said that her plans should have a mandatory waiting period, like purchasing a firearm. But Oliver walked through the world with the firm belief that everyone was as well intentioned as he was, and as much as she loved him for his blind naïveté, sometimes he reminded her of a baby rabbit nibbling on clovers in a field, oblivious to the python about to swallow it whole. Heather, on the other hand, was raised by two people who saw the world for what it was: carnivorous. "Don't let anyone mess with you, Heather" had been her mother's advice minutes before she boarded the bus for her first day of kindergarten, as if there would be an entire classroom of five-year-olds waiting for their opportunity to pounce.

The truth was so blaringly obvious now that Heather didn't know why it hadn't occurred to her sooner. Caroline Ryan had planted this photo of Violet like a bomb set to detonate Violet's chances of getting into Andover. Heather's job was to defuse it. Her jaw worked up and down as she evaluated her options. Could a forty-two-year-old woman punch a thirteen-year-old, physically force her to post a retraction accepting all culpability? Probably not.

Heather's phone vibrated on the table, and they all jumped.

"Let it go to voicemail," she barked.

Oliver slid the phone off the coffee table and peered at the screen. An image reflected in his glasses, two lit squares and a name Heather couldn't make out.

"Heather?" he whispered gravely, his eyes widening as he held the phone out to her.

She stared at the name on the screen, trying to decipher why on earth someone from that number would be calling her now. On a Saturday morning.

Her stomach dropped.

She had thought this day couldn't get any worse. It turned out it could.

Chapter Six

HEATHER

THE BUILDING THAT housed The Crofton School was once home to a member of the Carnegie family, back when wealthy New Yorkers built houses that took up entire city blocks, and was the only private school in the city on the National Register of Historic Places. Heather could still remember how impressed she was when their tour guide mentioned this tidbit as she led them through the classrooms adorned with ornamental fireplaces and thick crown molding, and down to the theater with its neoclassical ceiling that rivaled the rooms of Buckingham Palace. "Our history is important here at The Crofton School," the earnest tour guide explained. "But we also have an eye to the future too, as you'll see when I bring you to our STEM lab." Oliver had squeezed Heather's hand in a way that communicated he was as bowled over by the tour as she was. It was a far cry from the public elementary school Heather had attended, with the dilapidated play structure and rusty drinking fountains ringed in yellow tape and a sign that said DO NOT DRINK. *Sold!* Heather wanted to call out before they descended the steps to the STEM lab. Thankfully, Violet managed to impress the director of admissions and stand out from the thirty other five-year-olds being evaluated in her interview group. Rather than draw an elephant or an egg when asked to draw something beginning with the letter *e,* she'd scrawled down an equation and promptly solved it. It was single-digit addition, but still. All the hours that Heather had spent drilling through those educational flash cards had paid off, and Crofton, a school with a kindergarten admission rate that rivaled Harvard's, offered Violet a spot. It wasn't until weeks later, after they'd signed away fifty thousand dollars in annual tuition, that Heather realized the point of that tour wasn't to *sell* parents on the school, but rather to show parents that no other school could possibly live up to it.

"Mr. and Mrs. Quinn?" the petite woman with the punishing ponytail and icy expression called out from behind the lacquered wood desk.

Heather and Oliver rose to their feet.

"Dr. Krause is ready to see you now. Follow me." She turned on her heel and Heather and Oliver fell into step behind her.

It had only been a few hours since Heather had picked up the call from the school and a somber voice on the other end of the line introduced herself as the headmaster's assistant. "Sorry to bother you," she'd said, sounding not the least bit sorry. But the headmaster was requesting—or was it demanding?—a meeting with Heather and Oliver. Today, if possible. On a Saturday.

It did not bode well.

Heather watched the woman's sleek ponytail swish like a pendulum as she led them down the carpeted corridor, past framed inspirational quotes, displays filled with impressive student artwork, and a tapestry adorned with the school crest, the Latin words *Suos cultores scientia coronat* emblazoned in the middle. *Knowledge crowns those who seek her.*

Heather wondered what knowledge the headmaster was seeking right now. There was a part of her holding out hope that this meeting wasn't about the PSCON photo, but about something else entirely. *Surely,* she told herself, *one little vape wouldn't generate all this fuss on a weekend. Not even a school as straight-edged as Crofton would be that puritanical. Surely.*

"Heather and Oliver." Dr. Krause rose from behind his mahogany desk and greeted them with an outstretched hand. Heather assembled her most pleasant smile, despite the hurricane whirling beneath her ribcage. His grip was moist, or maybe Heather's skin was on fire, and she resisted the urge to pull her hand back. "Great to see you both again," he said, flashing a practiced smile and directing them to a walnut leather loveseat in the sitting area of his large office. He lowered himself into the damask chair opposite them.

Aaron Krause was young to be the headmaster of a prestigious New York private school, with his tortoiseshell, professor-chic glasses and fondness for phrases like "the whole child" and "the five selves," but he managed to balance it all out with a traditional edge. The school still had a uniform that included a blazer and tie for the boys, kilts for the girls, and the students greeted their homeroom teacher with a formal handshake every morning, maintaining an old-school aesthetic that Heather appreciated.

Heather shifted the throw pillow on the loveseat and perched herself on the edge. The office was orderly yet comfortable, with framed awards peppering the walls and the Crofton crest adorning most of the items on Dr. Krause's massive desk, from the stainless-steel travel mug to the brightly colored stress ball positioned beside the computer screen.

The chair squeaked as Dr. Krause leaned back and steepled his fingers. "I'm sorry we're not seeing each other under happier circumstances," he started, the residue of a smile disappearing from his face, taking Heather's last shred of hope along with it. His tone was disappointed, and Heather could feel her cheeks getting warm. "I thought it would be best if we discussed this together as soon as possible. This is a little, um . . . delicate, but I think we should get right to it." His expression resembled that of a doctor about to deliver the news that they had three weeks to live.

Heather lowered her gaze to her hands, firmly gripping her knee. The cuticle on her index finger was ragged. Violet wasn't the only one who'd developed the horrible habit of picking her cuticles lately. Heather hadn't done that since her college days, but in the past couple of weeks she'd noticed red, raw patches blooming around her nail beds, thanks to boarding school application stress.

She wanted to lift up her hands and shove them in Dr. Krause's face. *See? I'm literally bleeding for this!*

He took a deep breath in through his nose, blew it out. "It's come to our attention that there was an incident at a dance last night." He trailed off and raised his eyebrows in a way that seemed to ask if they were all on the same page.

Heather adjusted herself on the loveseat and cleared her throat. "Yes, Violet made an unfortunate decision at the dance, one that she says she deeply regrets." She emphasized the word "deeply" in hopes of conveying her sincerity. "I'm sure you can imagine how much of a shock it was for us, given Violet's track record, and we appreciate that you wanted to check in." She stole a glance at Oliver, who gave her an encouraging nod. They'd rehearsed the response on the walk over, and she was delivering it with the right mix of authority and remorse. "We can assure you we will be handling this family matter appropriately."

Dr. Krause shifted uncomfortably in his seat. "Unfortunately, from our point of view, this has moved *beyond* being a family matter."

Heather felt her eyebrows raising toward her hairline, eased them back down. This conversation was not going in the direction she'd expected. Dr. Krause was blinking rapidly, purposefully, and Heather had spent enough time watching him at the Parents' Association meetings to know that his incessant blinking was a prelude to bad news. *We're going to need to increase tuition by five percent.* Or *The construction of our new theater is six months behind schedule.* God, she wished that was what he was going to say. She would build that whole goddamn theater with her own two hands if it would make this entire fiasco disappear.

"Some concerned parents brought this distressing matter to my attention this morning," he continued.

"Concerned parents?" Heather sputtered, letting out an awkward, high-pitched laugh, but Dr. Krause's expression remained stone-faced. She rearranged her features. "Why would Violet's behavior off campus concern *other* parents?" She could hear the agitation creeping into her voice and struggled to tamp it down. This was a little bit much, wasn't it? It wasn't as if they were talking about *heroin,* for god's sake.

"The concern doesn't stem from what Violet did *away* from campus," he said, lifting a palm. "The concern is that Violet may be dealing drugs to her peers here at Crofton."

Heather shook her head, the words "dealing drugs" rattling back and forth in her ears. This was absurd. What kind of parent would read those nasty words written by an anonymous troll and, instead of feeling sympathy for Violet, decide to call the school, sharpened pitchfork in hand? What kind of a *person*?

The answer to her question unfolded, inch by infuriating inch, until it pressed against her skin with red-hot certainty: the *parents* of Caroline Ryan were behind this. They had their daughter smuggle in the phone and take the photo. They sent the photo to the anonymous Instagram account and planted the drug-dealing rumor. Then they called the school and clutched their pearls as if Violet had been spotted handing out vials of cocaine in the cafeteria.

Heather tilted her head, her eyes narrowing. "Which parents were concerned about this?"

"That I can't tell you, unfortunately." He adjusted his glasses on his nose. "School confidentiality. But I wanted to let you know the position we're in, so we can have an open line of communication here." He put his hands out, palms up in the "help me, help you" gesture. It filled Heather with a sudden, inexplicable, murderous rage. She resisted the urge to reach over and bat his stupid hands out of the air.

"Well, it doesn't seem as if anyone is concerned about Violet's right to confidentiality," she snapped.

"Dr. Krause," Oliver interjected in that measured tone of his. Heather noticed Dr. Krause's shoulders relax, seemingly relieved the likable one was finally speaking. "We appreciate you're in a tricky spot," Oliver continued. "But we can *assure* you, Violet is not dealing drugs. I'm sure we can agree that it's not hard to take a photo and throw it up on Instagram and label *anyone* a drug dealer."

Heather nodded, wishing she could grab her husband's face and give him a giant kiss on the mouth for pivoting the conversation. Because there was only one way they were going to fix this now.

Lift bus, throw Caroline Ryan under.

Heather crossed one leg over the other, leaned her body slightly forward, seizing her chance to cut in. "We didn't want to involve the school in this, but I think it's important to let you know that it was another Crofton student who orchestrated all of this." She was going off script and could see Oliver snap his gaze to her, his disapproving eyes burning a hole in the side of her face, but she plowed ahead. "A Crofton student took the unauthorized photo and arranged for it to be posted anonymously on the PSCON account." Heather made a point of saying each letter, rather than pronounce it the way Violet had, because it made the whole thing sound seedier. It was practically the dark web.

Dr. Krause tilted his head. Heather took this as a cue to carry on. "It's clear the motive was to disparage Violet's character and eliminate her as a threat in terms of boarding school applications." Heather made herself drop her shoulders, speak slowly, infuse her tone with faux compassion. "So, unfortunately, what we have on our hands is a clear-cut case of *cyberbullying*."

Cyberbullying. A trigger word for educators if ever there was one. All a parent had to do was utter the word and school administrators were crawling over themselves to weed out the perpetrator, lest the reputation of the school take a hit. Crofton had a zero-tolerance policy for cyberbullying—it was highlighted in the school handbook, which Heather had committed to memory when Violet was admitted. *Any student caught bullying another student online will be subject to immediate suspension,* it read in bold letters. Heather licked her lips, waiting for the inevitable question, already arranging her expression to ensure her response was tinged with an air of regret. *Which student? Well, I hate to name names, but I'll tell you what I saw . . .*

Heather hadn't fired the first shot in this war, but she was fully prepared to return fire.

Dr. Krause put his hands to his chin like he was praying. "Well, even if the photo was posted with nefarious intent, there is no way to know if the person who sent the photo was a student at Crofton."

"We *do* know she goes to Crofton because I know it was Caroline Ryan," Heather blurted, the accusation flying out of her mouth of its own accord.

Something like a wince slid over Dr. Krause's features.

"I know it was her because I was at the top of the stairs at Doubles and saw Caroline Ryan put her phone into her pocket and walk into the dance. Nobody else could have done it because nobody else had their phone with them." Her words were coming out fast, uncontrolled, one sentence blending into the next. "It's a club rule, but Caroline didn't follow the rule and *she* was the only one." Heather could hear that her tone was verging on manic, so she pressed her lips together to make herself stop talking.

Dr. Krause stared at them, his face inscrutable. The blood vessels in Heather's neck throbbed away the seconds.

One. Two. Three.

She was gripping the armrest so hard she noticed her fingers had made slight indentations in the leather.

Finally, he spoke. "Mr. and Mrs. Quinn."

Heather gritted her teeth. She was Mrs. Quinn now. They were back to formalities.

"Here at Crofton, we center our pedagogy around the five building blocks." He pointed a thumb at the framed print of the five words immortalized in bold—EXCELLENCE, CITIZENSHIP, KNOWLEDGE, COURAGE, RESPONSIBILITY. He paused, as if they needed a minute to familiarize themselves with them, as if they weren't written on every single fucking piece of school correspondence. "Children need to learn that while they are free to choose their behaviors, they must take *responsibility* for those choices."

"Choices?" Heather sputtered. "It wasn't my daughter's choice for someone to post a photo and a vicious lie about her. Caroline Ryan did that. And I would like to talk about *why* she did that.

Perhaps we should be calling *her* parents." Heather gestured to the sleek black phone on Dr. Krause's desk. She felt her eyes blinking in that way that Oliver always said was patronizing, but she couldn't help herself.

Dr. Krause's eyebrows gathered into a frown. "Ms. Ryan is an alumna and a current trustee of this school. It wouldn't be appropriate to pull her and her family into this office based on a random guess."

Heather felt a pressure in her head that she wanted to relieve by screaming. People had been sent to prison for *murder* with less evidence than she was presenting right now.

"It isn't a random guess. I *saw* her with the phone." To her embarrassment, her voice came out high and whiny. Oliver slid his hand over hers, gave it a squeeze. A warning sign that she was teetering on the edge of civility.

"Be that as it may," Dr. Krause said, "what you're suggesting is a fairly large leap to make. Caroline Ryan is not a known troublemaker."

"Violet has *never* been in trouble at school. Not even once," Heather said sharply. Her fingernails were digging angry, moon-shaped indents into the flesh of her palms.

"I recognize that," he said, his lips retreating into a flat line. "But students sign a code of conduct on the first day of school, which includes a prohibition on the use of illicit drugs and alcohol. On or off school grounds. If Violet is indeed ingesting drugs in this photo, that alone would be in direct violation of the code of conduct. And for that she would need to take . . ." He gestured with his thumb to the word "responsibility." "Which is why it's really important we don't jump to *any* conclusions here," he said, emphasizing the word "any."

His words pinned Heather to the cushion. She heard the barely concealed threat in them: *Back off of the Ryan family*. For a fleeting, rage-filled instant she envisioned snatching the scissors from his desk and holding the blade against his arrogant windpipe. She pushed the fantasy away, afraid it might come to fruition if she didn't.

"I'm sure you would agree that Crofton parents deserve and would *expect* a diligent investigation into any signs of drug dealing on our campus. Which is the principal reason for this meeting here today." He cleared his throat. "I wanted to let you know that, as part of our due diligence, we're going to need to have Violet's locker searched. Because there is a possibility the search could result in expulsion, our school policy is to notify parents beforehand."

Oliver's eyes flicked in Heather's direction, but Heather couldn't form her lips around a response. It was as if Dr. Krause's words had had some kind of immobilizing effect on her muscles. A verbal stun gun. Everything in her line of vision—the yellow sticky notes affixed to Dr. Krause's computer screen, the pile of papers lined up in the wooden inbox, the framed photo of him and his wife on their wedding day—was blurry, as if it were all submerged under five feet of water. "That's fine with us," she heard Oliver reply, his tone earnest. "We're confident there is nothing in there that shouldn't be."

Dr. Krause's shoulders relaxed. "Assuming we don't find anything, in light of Violet's sterling reputation, we'll be able to put this whole thing behind us." He gave his knees a satisfied smack with the palms of his hands before rising to his feet. Heather and Oliver were dismissed.

With Oliver's hand on her lower back, steadying her, they made their way down the hallway and pushed open the large, ornate front doors, back out into the painfully bright sunshine. Heather blinked rapidly, trying not to surrender to the tears that were threatening to spill forth with humiliating force. Threads of anger twisted in her stomach, pressing on her insides, evoking a familiar feeling: injustice. Crofton wasn't a meritocracy. If only that were *remotely* the case. Heather had made a gross miscalculation. Or, more accurately, she'd not run the numbers at all. The reality was that they, a family that had to stretch to write the hefty tuition check every year, would not have a fighting chance against the Ryans, whose name adorned the "builders' wall" on the STEM center.

It wasn't enough for people like that to have the advantage. They needed to stack the deck too.

Heather could feel it. Something inside of her, snapping.

"Deep breaths," Oliver whispered as her heels pounded against the sidewalk. "We'll figure this out." He reached for her hand, cupped it in his. She felt the righteousness of her anger pulsing through her skin like heat, the fury coalescing in the back of her throat. She already had one thing figured out, and her conviction was growing stronger with each step.

Over her dead body was the Ryan family going to get away with this.

Or someone's dead body.

To: Detective Joseph Danielli
FROM: Dr. Aaron Krause
<Tues, March 12 at 5:55pm>

Dear Detective Danielli,

My apologies for being so taken aback when you and your partner arrived on campus today. I'm sure you can understand that this is a very unusual circumstance for us at Crofton. We occasionally, but rarely, have had the police involved in a situation concerning one of our students, but never a member of our parent body. This is a first for us. I am truly shocked and dismayed by this tragic situation and am keeping everyone in my thoughts and prayers. As you requested, attached is a Crofton School parent directory, which includes the contact information of each parent, listed by grade. The name of our PA president is highlighted in yellow, and this may be a good place to start. I hope this is helpful in your ongoing investigation, and please feel free to reach out to me if there is anything else I can provide.

With gratitude,
Dr. Aaron Krause, PhD
Headmaster
The Crofton School

Chapter Seven

POPPY

THE SCENE OF the crime.

That was how Gretchen referred to The Doubles Club when she polled the eight women around the table. "So, who else's child was at 'the scene of the crime' last week?" she asked, raising one microbladed eyebrow. The expression on her face made her look like she was about to devour a particularly delicious piece of chocolate cake. Which was a move Poppy was certain Gretchen would never make. At least, not without sticking her fingers down her throat afterward.

Seven manicured hands went up around the table in response. If it was a vote, it would've been unanimous. Minus Poppy. She'd made the strategic decision to be absorbed in a message that required her full attention on her phone.

She knew better than to give anyone in this group a thread to pull.

The waiter appeared beside her, distributing artfully foamed lattes and herbal teas around the table, and setting down two baskets of shiny pastries in the middle. There wasn't a woman here who would let her hand come within six inches of the sugar-filled carbs, but they served the purpose of brightening up the table, like a floral centerpiece. And they were included in the forty-two-dollars-per-person continental breakfast menu at Gina La Fornarina, the go-to location for all Benefit Committee meetings.

Poppy wasn't a member of the Benefit Committee—she'd put in her time in previous years and considered herself officially retired—but Gretchen had asked her to attend the meeting as an authority on what had worked well in the past. As the school's largest donor, apparently Poppy was an expert on how to get wealthy parents to pry open their wallets and happily part with large sums of money.

It wasn't complicated. The answer was strong specialty cocktails. Yet here she sat.

Poppy set her phone on the table, screen-side up, and wrapped a manicured finger around the handle of her mug. There was a buzz of excitement in the air as each of the women tossed out a salacious detail to add to the pot.

"Apparently, that girl has been supplying the lacrosse team with steroids. A friend of my daughter confirmed it."

"I heard they found *heroin* in her locker!"

"She went to the dance to recruit more dealers. I'm friendly with the head of Doubles, and she said they're going to suspend the family's membership."

Poppy lifted the mug to her mouth, the mint tea burning her upper lip as she sipped. She could've predicted this conversation, as easily as predicting that the sun would rise. These meetings always had a tabloid quality to them. And a Crofton student being outed as a drug dealer was top news, not only among Crofton moms but moms at *all* private schools. In the past couple days, the photo had spread around the Upper East Side faster than a stomach virus. There had been no fewer than ten posts about it on UrbanMyth, ranging from the hyper-concerned (*My child was at this dance— should I mention it to her therapist?*) to the unaffected (*Call off the dogs, people, they're kids*) to the heads-on-spikes crowd (*Everyone involved should be held accountable—let's smoke them out of their holes!*).

Smoke them out of their holes. Poppy rolled her eyes thinking about that one. That was the main problem with technology these days. In her day, a teenager could experiment with cigarettes and drugs and the only risk of getting caught was the unmistakable odor that clung to your clothes. But nowadays one stealth iPhone and—*boom*—your reputation is tarnished forever. Look at Michael Phelps.

There were rumors that any child involved would face suspension. Poppy couldn't imagine what she'd do if Henry were facing that fate. She might as well set fire to his Andover application. Not even a sizable donation could counteract that level of damage. And it would be nothing short of a nightmare if Henry was the first in four generations of Ridleys not to attend Andover. Poppy would never hear the end of it.

Henry wasn't even *supposed* to be at the Doubles dance. Poppy had hired a tag team of private tutors in an effort to bring his dismal grades up to a respectable level, including a five-hundred-dollar-an-hour French tutor who came every Friday. But after seeing the posts on UrbanMyth about the Andover admissions director's plan to attend, Poppy couldn't pass up the opportunity to highlight Henry's top quality—his social side. Besides, it was just *French*. Surely a personal connection was more important than conjugating a few verbs.

But now . . .

"Wait, wasn't Henry at the dance too?" Gretchen's voice cut through her thoughts. Poppy looked up to see Gretchen's heart-shaped face staring at her expectantly, a single crease sharpening between her eyebrows. God, this woman was like a homing pigeon for potential scandal. Gretchen's daughter, Charlotte, was in the same grade as Henry and, if the number of times Poppy had seen her at the apartment lately was any indication, the two were an item. At the very least, good friends. It was so hard to tell these days with the way teenagers hung off of each other. Gretchen struck Poppy as the type of mother who would've pressed her daughter for a full roster of attendees. Maybe even their social security numbers to go along with it.

"He was." Poppy nodded, toying with the paper tab of her tea bag, measuring her answer. "But he told me he doesn't really know that girl, so . . ." She trailed off with a delicate shrug of one shoulder.

"Does he know who took the picture?" Gretchen probed.

Poppy stiffened. Gretchen wasn't going to be tossed off the scent that easily. The seven other women at the table cut their eyes her way, as if they could smell the brewing drama.

"No, but I assume it was one of the girl's friends," Poppy said, trying to sound breezy. "She and Henry don't exactly run in the same crowd."

"Okay, here's my question." A hawkish-looking woman with a sleek black bob interrupted, holding up her palm. Poppy flicked her gaze, relieved to be off the hook. She studied the woman's overly made-up face. What was her name again? Sienna? Savannah?

Sienna/Savannah paused, surveying the table to ensure she had everyone's attention. "Who *is* this girl in the photo? I mean, I know she goes to Crofton, but who *is* she?"

"Violet Quinn," Gretchen answered quickly. This was Gretchen's shtick—she collected information about people the way children collect Pokémon cards. And she doled it out with the pride of a cat dropping a dead bird at your feet. "She's a star student— service award, yada, yada, yada." She rolled her hand. "And now we know she's been selling *drugs* right underneath Dr. Krause's nose. A wolf in sheep's clothing."

Poppy mentally rolled her eyes.

"Wait . . . is that the author's daughter?" Sienna/Savannah's nose wrinkled slightly.

Gretchen bobbed her head.

The woman sitting beside Poppy let out a low whistle, shaking her head. "Wow. It's always the ones you least expect."

"Well, then let's be glad *our* children aren't the ones you'd least expect," Gretchen said, delighted with her own cleverness.

Polite laughter all around.

"Should we get down to business?" Poppy cut in, casting a pointed look at the time. These meetings had a way of stretching like one of those scarves a magician pulls from his mouth—on and on and on. The only way to bring them to a close was to refocus the group on the task at hand.

"Yes, okay. First up, does anyone know whether we can get that auctioneer from Sotheby's to run the live auction again? He was phenomenal last year."

"I think that's going to be tricky," a woman with pin-straight blond hair and a floral blouse said, scrunching up her nose as if she'd inhaled a whiff of body odor. She tossed a look over her shoulder before leaning in conspiratorially. "The woman who secured that for us last year—Susan, the CEO of Sotheby's—is going through a messy divorce now."

A few mouths dropped open.

"I'm only passing on what I've heard." She held her hands up as if to say *Don't shoot*. "You know I don't like to gossip, but let's just say it's not a good well to tap right now."

"Okay, noted." Gretchen made a big deal of scratching that off her list, the corners of her plump lips turned down, clearly perturbed the dirty details of the divorce were not going to be shared with the group. "We'll put a pin in that one for now."

Poppy's phone vibrated on the table. She picked it up and peered at the message, grateful for the excuse to remove herself from this conversation.

Headed to London. I've got a deal blowing up. Not sure if I'll be back in time for the party on Thursday.

She reread the message from Harris, feeling slightly unsettled but unable to pinpoint the source. Maybe it was the mention of the party she'd been strong-armed into hosting. Every year, the eighth-grade parents held a celebration on the evening the boarding school applications were due. "Lucky Cocktails," it had come to be called, thanks, in part, to the urban legend of parents who had skipped the party and later found their children shut out of their top-choice schools. Crofton parents had come to view Lucky Cocktails with the same reverence some Catholics reserve for Sunday mass. A Crofton student being shut out of their top-choice schools probably *was* akin to spending eternity in purgatory. It was an unspoken rule that the family with the largest apartment in the eighth-grade class hosted Lucky Cocktails, and Poppy could hardly conceal the fact that the title belonged to her.

You take the bad with the good, she supposed.

She pulled at her lower lip. It wasn't that Poppy was superstitious, but how was it going to look if Harris was a no-show at their own party? His presence, or lack thereof, wouldn't go unnoticed. "A big fish." That was how her mother had described Harris, and it was apt. Her mother had meant it in relation to his bank account, but it was fitting for both his personality and stature too. At six feet three inches tall and two hundred and forty pounds, he had the build of a retired linebacker, with his soft middle hanging over his belt, and a booming deep voice to match his size. His heft was what had first drawn Poppy to him. She'd just come off of dating a string of Napoleon-like men, men she'd towered over in stilettos. One of them had even insisted she wear flats when they went out. "Don't worry, I'm six feet tall when I stand on my wallet," he'd joked, and Poppy couldn't keep the wince off of her face, convinced "short man syndrome" was indeed a genuine disorder. "Poppy, I don't know why you're not taking advantage of these opportunities," her mother would moan after each breakup, as if these men were unexercised stock options rather than ex-boyfriends. So, when Poppy first laid eyes on Harris at the Harvard Club, she was struck by the way he claimed more space than any other man in the room. Not handsome, but imposing. No woman would need to make herself smaller around him. All of the single women in the room (and a few married ones) found themselves openly vying for an opportunity to be the future Mrs. Ridley, lured to that potent cocktail of power, money, and mass. For Poppy, the desperate, naked desire of the other women was its own aphrodisiac. When Harris had approached her, she'd relished the sweet feeling of being chosen. *Me. He chose me.* What Poppy hadn't realized at the time was how, years later, she'd feel like one of those Star Wars toys that collectors purchase and keep in a pristine, unopened box on a shelf, for display purposes only. Never played with. Never truly cherished. Harris Ridley liked to collect beautiful things. He had a Maserati he never drove, a Monet he hadn't hung, a vintage Rolex he never wore. And he had Poppy.

Poppy twisted the five-carat cushion-cut diamond engagement

ring on her finger now, watching the rainbows as it caught in the sunlight and danced across the untouched basket of pastries. "It's about time, Poppy," she could remember her mother saying the night they'd announced their engagement, exhaling the same sigh of relief she had when Poppy's brother had managed to dodge prison time for his DUI. Being unmarried at thirty probably was on par with doing hard time in her mother's eyes. Poppy wondered what her mother's reaction would be now if she knew what Poppy had been up to. *Don't risk your marriage for some pool boy,* she could imagine her mother saying. But he wasn't a pool boy, and she wasn't risking her marriage. They were having a little fun, that's all. And they hadn't even slept together, so technically it wasn't infidelity.

"Let's talk about the centerpieces," Gretchen said, turning the page in her Moleskine notebook.

"I've met with the florist on Madison and we're narrowing it down to three choices," Sienna/Savannah said with earnest dedication, as if it were her part in a war effort. "We're sticking with the color scheme, and he's promised us some unique little touches, so I think we're in good shape there."

"Great," Gretchen said, marking a check in her notebook. "Poppy, is it okay to use your apartment to store the silent-auction items until the big night?"

"Sure." She swallowed a sip of now-lukewarm tea and struggled to ignore the irritation creeping up her spine. Auction item storage—another penance for having a large apartment. Every year, she was compelled to agree to house the silent-auction items, which meant there would be endless deliveries of designer bags, vintage wine, rare artwork, and statement jewelry, all of which needed to be catalogued and safely stored in a spare bedroom with blackout shades (to protect the goods from the sun). Worst of all, opportunistic parents took it as an opening to peep inside her apartment under the guise of dropping off a donation.

Poppy's iPhone buzzed again, and her gaze zipped to the screen, irritation instantly morphing into pleasure. *We need to find a better spot to meet than the back seat of an Uber xxoo.* Tilting the screen away from the group, she reread the message, trying to suppress the giddy smile spreading across her face.

It had started as a harmless flirtation. She'd gone into Reflex, the new lacrosse training center on Third Avenue, where the old Modell's used to be, to sign Henry up for private instruction. "I hope you're not here looking for new sneakers, because you'd be the third person today," a deep, smooth voice called out, and Poppy raised her eyes from her phone to see a broad-shouldered man sporting a white button-down and an easy smile walking toward her. The tips of his sandy-blond curls were still slightly wet, and Poppy unintentionally pictured him in the shower, which, thanks to the strands of salt that peppered his hair, wasn't completely inappropriate. The sleeves of his shirt were partially rolled up and revealed muscled forearms as he extended his hand, introducing himself as the owner. Poppy was struck by his physicality—a rarity on the Upper East Side—and he flashed a boyish grin that let her know he'd caught her appreciating it. A few drop-ins later, and their flirting intensified—his hand on her shoulder as they spoke, some playful texts. Poppy had never stepped outside of her marriage before, but there was something about the way he looked at her—like he wanted to consume her, to swallow her whole—that unhooked a yearning inside her. One she'd kept firmly tamped down.

If that look were a drug Poppy would mainline it.

Two weeks ago, she'd made an excuse to stop by without Henry, and he'd offered her a tour of the back room. "It's where our athletes can review video of their performance, but I have to warn you it used to be dressing rooms, so there've been a lot of naked people in there," he'd joked. It was clear what was finally going to happen, and she was ready even before pivoting to follow him. The sound of the door chiming five minutes later interrupted them, just as she'd melted into his kiss and his hand was finding its way under her shirt, trailing up the side of her waist.

The opposite of being saved by the bell.

And then there was last week after she'd dropped Henry off at

Doubles. *I'm in an Uber around the corner . . . Join me?* his message had read. Despite having less than ten minutes to make her dinner reservation, an invisible force drew her to him like steel to a magnet. It was only after she'd reluctantly pried herself from his arms and out of the back seat that she noticed they'd inadvertently left the window down during their short tryst. Not her wisest move, she could admit. But contrary to what her mother would think, Poppy had no plans to sacrifice her marriage. She simply was *supplementing* it. Like popping a multivitamin to stave off a nutritional deficit.

"Poppy?" Gretchen's voice sliced through her reverie in a tone that made it clear this wasn't the first time she had called her name. Poppy flipped her phone facedown on the table so fast it nearly tumbled off the edge, and she turned her attention to Gretchen.

"Harris won't mind, will he?" she asked, touching her necklace as if checking it was still there.

Poppy stared at the sharp angles of Gretchen's nose and chin, marveling at how every question that came out of her mouth was like a trowel poised to excavate dirt. Had she always been like that? Or was Poppy being overly sensitive today, now that there was something to hide? "He won't even notice," Poppy replied with a flick of her delicate wrist, dismissing the idea.

"He won't even notice," Sienna/Savannah echoed, letting out a throaty laugh. But Poppy hadn't meant it to be one of those "Isn't my husband so clueless?" jokes that were often bantered around in this group. Harris used three rooms in their apartment—the master bedroom, the kitchen, and the home office. The Rockettes could be kicking their way through the other rooms and he would be none the wiser.

Poppy tapped a fingernail on the side of her mug, an idea unfurling in her mind.

"Okay, next item," Gretchen said, regaining her no-nonsense edge. Ignoring her, Poppy picked up her phone, angling it away from any curious eyes as she pecked out a response. A delicious shaky feeling pulsed in her legs, the kind she got when she was standing too close to the edge of a cliff.

Well . . . my husband is out of town and my apartment is empty . . .

Steeling herself, she hit send. Her fingers remained wrapped tightly around the phone as the waiter delivered a fresh pitcher of ice water to the table. The gray dots materialized below her message, then disappeared.

"Can I get you more hot water?" the waiter asked in what sounded like an Italian accent. Poppy shook her head without looking up from the screen. When the pulsating ellipsis appeared again, she realized she was holding her breath. She let it out slowly when the buzz of a new message vibrated against her skin.

Text me your address and I can be at your apartment in an hour.

She sprang to her feet, startling the freckled woman beside her. "Sorry, ladies. I hate to run, but I just got a text from my housekeeper and it sounds like there is some kind of issue with our . . . um . . ." Poppy hesitated before adding "pipes." She could feel the color darken on her cheeks as she fought to keep herself from cringing at the inadvertent sexual innuendo. But one look at the concerned expressions around the table and the murmurs of "Plumbing issues are the *worst*" and she knew it had flown over their well-coiffed heads.

She gathered her purse and stuffed her arms through the sleeves of her coat, assuring Gretchen this would not interfere with her ability to house the auction items (which, when she thought about it later, had been shortsighted of her. She could've used the same excuse both to get out of this meeting and to get out of the nuisance of using her apartment as a storage space, but the dopamine flooding her brain was impeding all rational thought).

"Let me know if you need the name of my plumber!" she heard a voice call out as she dashed out the door, barely avoiding a collision with the gray-haired couple who had stopped to peer at the menu posted in the window.

Poppy's body was tingling with anticipation by the time she swept into the lobby of her building. She did a quick appraisal of her reflection in the mirrored artwork on the wall, frantically ruffling her hair, trying to give it some volume.

"Good morning, Ms. Ridley," the fresh-faced doorman called

out from behind the desk. "Three packages came for you," he added as she flew past. She stopped mid-stride, irritation prickling her skin. She wasn't expecting any deliveries, which meant Gretchen had sent over some auction items before clearing it with her. "I'll have Fernando bring them up," he offered. "He's bringing up a FreshDirect delivery right now, but he should be back any minute."

Poppy flashed a look at her watch. "You know what, I'll take them now. I think that would be easier."

"One of them is pretty large." He held his hands about four feet apart, indicating the size.

"Then I'll call down and let you know when it's a good time. I have a guest coming over and I don't want to have the mess of all those boxes." She scrunched up her nose as if having the three parcels in her home now would be akin to an explosion of confetti raining down on her hardwood floors.

"Of course." He gave a brusque nod, pulling at the lapels of his forest-green uniform.

"Oh, and when my guest arrives, can you send him directly up?"

"Sure thing. Do you want me to add him to your list?"

"Yes. Please do." She turned on a heel and ducked into the closing elevator, silently congratulating herself for defusing that potential land mine. She'd always been good at the fine art of keeping a secret. You didn't grow up in a home like hers without learning how to keep skeletons locked firmly away in the closet.

The elevator doors dinged open on their private landing, and Poppy froze mid-step. In the top, far right-hand corner a flashing red light zeroed in on her with the brightness of E.T.'s finger.

"*Shit*," she hissed, as the voice of their real estate agent ran through her mind. "The safety of the residents is top priority here at 998 Fifth Avenue," the agent had opined, pointing a rolled-up Sotheby's International Realty flyer in the direction of the camera as if she were a flight attendant directing everyone's attention to the emergency exits. "There are security cameras on every floor that are fully monitored in a control room below. The recordings are available to you upon request, so some tenants use the system to keep tabs on their teenagers." She'd lifted the rolled-up flyer in front of her mouth before conspiratorially whispering to Poppy, "And their husbands."

Poppy took two steps and stood on her tiptoes now, stretching out her arm and wrapping her palm around the sphere. She gave it a wiggle. Another one, this time harder. The red light pitched.

It only took one more wrench—maybe two—before the lens was facing the wall.

UrbanMyth Message Board

I think there's some pay-to-play scheme going on at Crofton where the large donors get special treatment.

> OF COURSE THERE IS PAY TO PLAY. There are literally private cocktail parties with the headmaster if you donate above a certain threshold.

> In other news, water is wet.

> My son attends Crofton, and it is absolutely the most egalitarian private school on the UES. 15% of the student body is on financial aid.

> If you don't like it, send your kids to public.

I had a dream that my husband died last night, and honestly when I woke up I was a little disappointed he hadn't. I wouldn't say I'm going to kill him with my own two hands, but life would be easier without him.

> I wonder how long it will be until someone confesses to murder on this site . . .

> I swear the things people say here never cease to amaze me.

> Well, she didn't say SHE would kill him, only that she wishes someone else would do the job. This is the UES after all. We don't get our own hands messy. We have staff for that.

> Have you tried talking to someone? You sound depressed.

Chapter Eight

POPPY

Poppy rolled off of his body, her skin slick with sweat, raked her fingers through her damp hair, and let out a satisfied groan.

They were sprawled out on her California king bed, having made their way here after he'd pinned her up against a wall in the foyer, his urgent lips pressing against hers and then trailing kisses down her collarbone. The two of them weren't the only ones in the apartment, though—a thought that hadn't occurred to her until the unmistakable sound of the metal laundry cart being rolled down the hallway filled the air—so she'd swiftly extracted herself from his arms and shepherded him to the master bedroom, the only room in the apartment with a proper lock.

The last thing she wanted was Maya opening the door at an inopportune time.

Poppy arranged a pillow underneath her head, relishing the swell of endorphins coursing through her body. She tried to remember the last time she'd had sex in this room, or any room for that matter, but came up startlingly blank. Years. It had been years. Plural. She knew this was true but had a tough time admitting it to herself. Five years ago, she'd googled the words "sexless marriage" and learned that any marriage that involved sex fewer than ten times a year was considered "sexless." She could remember the sound "ha" exploding out of her mouth after reading that. Equating someone who was having sex nine times a year with what she was going through was like equating someone who'd skipped breakfast with someone who was struggling through a famine. A few months ago, after downing half a bottle of Moët and trawling UrbanMyth, she'd hastily posted *My husband doesn't want to have sex anymore. I'm not sure he ever did.* She needed to know there were other women out there who were married to men who wouldn't touch them, other women who'd allowed this part of them to atrophy. But the number of replies suggesting her husband see a doctor made her want to hurl her laptop against the wall. What kind of men were these people married to? If she so much as *hinted* to Harris that he should seek medical attention, he'd be at his lawyer's office before the sentence was out of her mouth. There was a tacit understanding in their relationship that she never mentioned sex, or lack thereof. And even if she *could* convince Harris to see a doctor, a small part of her feared what it would reveal. That everything was fine. That the problem was Poppy. A declining asset.

"That was *incredible,*" he panted, gripping the roots of his hair, releasing a familiar waft of sandalwood-scented shampoo.

Poppy turned her face away so he wouldn't notice the unexpected tears stinging the back of her eyes. He was right. It *was* incredible. The desire, the need, all of it unspooling inside her and around her. It was almost baptismal. For so long, she'd convinced herself it was fulfilling enough to be *envied,* but now she knew how big the chasm was between being envied and being *wanted*. It made her feel young, and alive, and light enough to levitate off this bed, and it all felt so fucking fantastic it was hard to believe she'd survived that many years without it. It was as if her head had been held underwater and she'd finally made it to the surface and inhaled a mouthful of oxygen. She was ready to fill her lungs with it.

Surreptitiously, she dabbed at each eye and slid her body closer to his, running a finger up and down the small patch of hair on his chest.

"I didn't know you had it in you, Bennett," she said coyly, marveling at how sweet his name tasted on her tongue.

The edge of his lips pulled up into a sexy half smile. "That's funny, because I knew you had it in you." His voice bordered on a growl, and she gave him a playful swat and settled her head into the crook of his arm. Her eyes ran the length of his toned body, watching the tendons in his hands flex as he adjusted the sheet around them. He reminded her of a sculpture that belonged in the Met. She wondered, not for the first time, how someone like Norah Ryan, a woman so dowdy she looked like the "before" photo in a *Today* show ambush makeover, ended up married to a man like Bennett. It went against the laws of nature, as far as Poppy was concerned. What could possibly be so spectacular about that plain Jane? Poppy felt an urgent itch under her skin to solve the mystery.

"Hey, are you coming to Lucky Cocktails?" she asked, lifting her eyes to meet his. He peered down at her with a questioning brow, so she continued. "You know, that Crofton parent cocktail party? I'm hosting it this Thursday night?"

He shook his head. "Nah, I'm almost positive that's not on Norah's radar. And if it were, she'd find an excuse not to go. She's not the class-party type." There was a note of pride in his voice, perhaps even a touch of judgment that Poppy couldn't help but feel was directed at her. What did it say about her if she *was* the class-party type? Agitation prickled her insides. Those kinds of women always bothered her, the ones who considered themselves intellectually above socializing. Because, really, this was a hundred-thousand-dollar cocktail party with the one percent of the one percent, not some tacky office party at the Olive Garden. She bit the inside of her cheek, doing her best to ignore the surprising and decidedly unwelcome knot of jealousy tightening across her chest. Bennett was *married* to this woman. What did Poppy expect? That he would disavow any feelings of love for her the minute they slept together?

Still. Poppy had never been good at playing second fiddle.

He ran the pad of his thumb across her shoulder. "It's probably a good thing for both of us that I won't be there." His throaty voice was teasing, playful. "Because the other parents might already be on to us."

"Nobody is *on* to us." She laughed, giving an exaggerated eye roll. "Is that why you don't want to come? Because I can assure you, I am *very* good at keeping a secret." Poppy didn't like the tone of her voice, which was verging on pleading. Was she testing him? Assessing whether she had the power to make him override his wife's stance on class parties? Maybe. But she couldn't help herself.

He tilted his head, and Poppy could see that glorious Adam's apple of his bob when he whispered, "But how can you be so sure your friends don't already know? Maybe they're good at keeping secrets too."

"Oh please, those people can't keep secrets. If they knew, it would be all *over* UrbanMyth. Trust me."

Now he was the one laughing, and Poppy loved the feeling of his chest shaking underneath her chin, the heat of his skin on hers. She could definitely get used to this.

"Sometimes I think you're speaking a different language," he said between chuckles.

She propped herself up on an elbow. "Bennett, you can't tell me you're the only person on the Upper East Side who doesn't know what UrbanMyth is?" With a mock reproachful shake of her head, she slid over and swiped up her phone from the rug where it had dropped from her back pocket mid-undress. She was feeling bold, empowered, sexy, as his eyes ran the length of her body. "Let me enlighten you. You can write anything you want on there and nobody knows it's you. Here." Her fingers flew across the screen like gnats. "See." She held up her screen.

He pulled his head back and squinted to read the post. *I just had the best sex of my life. It was not with my husband.*

He smiled wickedly. "Well, I love this site already," he growled. Then, in one swift motion, he'd maneuvered her so she was straddling him. His hands tightened around her waist. "Now I know how I can send you secret messages. Be on the lookout for a post that says, 'I have never seen a more beautiful woman than the one on top of me right now.'"

Poppy felt a bottle of champagne pop open in her stomach, the bubbles rising up and tickling the back of her throat. She was drunk with pleasure and could think of nothing other than how the word "beautiful" sounded coming out of his mouth, which is really the only explanation she could give for what she did next.

"Well, then I'd better download it for you right away," she said, her voice coy, and she lurched her body toward the bedside table, where she'd spotted his phone out of the corner of her eye. It was meant to be a flirtatious goad, but when she snatched the phone from the table everything in the room froze.

It took a moment for Poppy to process what she was looking at.

The screen of Bennett's phone wasn't dark, as it should've been. Instead, staring back at her was her own flushed, postcoital face, and above it a red rectangular timer counting the seconds.

Her throat closed up.

Bennett was recording a video.

Chapter Nine

POPPY

BENNETT WRENCHED THE phone out of Poppy's hands and was on his feet before the smile had dropped from her face. Without a word, he snatched his boxer shorts off of the floor where they'd been hastily discarded. The fingers of his right hand remained firmly clasped around his phone as if it were a detonator.

"Bennett." Poppy's voice was strangled.

The atmosphere in the room had changed so fast she could practically hear her ears pop.

He kept moving, pulling on his jeans, fastening the button, and scanning the room for his shirt as Poppy watched him, slack-jawed. Her emotions were cycling rapidly from confusion to irritation to fear.

"Bennett," she repeated, her sense of urgency rising as she swung her legs over the bed and planted her feet on the floor. Goosebumps rose on her clammy, naked skin, and she wrenched the sheet around her, pulling it up to her neck. "I want to see your phone." She stuck out her palm.

Ignoring her, he jammed the phone in the back pocket of his jeans and buttoned his shirt all the way to his throat. She could see the tight clench of his teeth in the line of his jaw, the shadow that had fallen over his features, and a certainty hit Poppy with a ferocious jolt. Bennett was not going to relinquish his phone. Because this hadn't been an accident. He'd purposely recorded them having sex.

He swiped a bead of sweat from his forehead with the back of his hand and met her stunned gaze. The affectionate glint behind his eyes had vanished. A tap that had been turned off.

A wave of dizziness engulfed her, and she planted a palm on the mattress to steady herself. *How?* How had he been able to do this right under her nose? Her mind whirled, reconstructing the last ninety minutes. When they'd swept into the master bedroom earlier they'd been kissing, their arms wild and unleashed—hungrily tugging off clothes, exploring each other's bodies. The small vase on the nightstand had tumbled over at one point, and Bennett had fumbled to right it. Every nerve ending in her body had been hyper-focused on the pleasure, so oblivious to everything around her, she realized now, that he could've bugged the entire bedroom with his free hand and Poppy wouldn't have noticed so long as he was still touching her with the other.

"Bennett, you *need* to delete that video." She lifted her chin, trying to emit an air of authority and composure she wasn't feeling.

His dark eyes latched on to hers. A small shake of his head. No.

"What the fuck is going on here?" she snapped, her eyes bouncing around the room, as if there were an entire team hiding behind the curtains waiting to jump out. *Surprise! We got you, Poppy!* It would not have blindsided her more than Bennett's behavior right now. Her heart pounded in her ears as she gathered her clothes from an inelegant heap on the floor, suddenly desperate to cover her naked body.

Bennett turned his head away and waited until she had fastened the top button of her pants before he opened his mouth to speak. As if on cue, the rumbling sound of the vacuum cleaner emanating from outside the door stopped.

Poppy could feel her heart stop along with it.

There was no distant honking from the traffic down below, no faint waft of street noise. It was as if the two of them were suspended together in a noiseless glass globe.

"I need something from you, Poppy," he said, breaking the silence. His tone had changed. He wasn't being flirty. Not flirty at all.

"What do you need?" Her voice sounded faraway, robotic.

He crossed his arms over his chest and rocked back on his heels. "Money."

"You need me to lend you *money*?"

He shook his head. His expression stayed stone still.

She let out an exasperated breath, locating her backbone. "I'm not really wanting to play charades. Explain to me what the hell you're talking about. You—"

"Not *lend*," he said, cutting her off. The two sharp lines in his forehead deepened. "*Give*."

It was completely involuntary, the sound that Poppy made in response. It was a cross between a cough and an expulsion of air. "*Give* you money? And why the hell would I do that?"

He slid the phone out of his pocket, gave it a jiggle. "Why do you think?"

Poppy's flinch was visible, as if he'd fired a gunshot into the air. The full understanding of what he was saying advanced cold and slow as a glacier and, with it, the terrifying agony of the position she'd put herself in. "I'm going to give you some advice," she remembered her family lawyer saying as she'd blissfully signed her name at the bottom of the ten-page prenup he'd billed her over a hundred thousand dollars to negotiate. "I hope you have a long and happy marriage, but because my job is to protect your assets, I need to say this. If you're going to engage in an extramarital affair"—he paused, holding up an index finger—"do not, under any circumstances, leave a paper trail. That means no texts, no emails. And second"—he held up another finger—"for the love of god, don't film yourselves having sex. I'm a good lawyer, but not even I can counteract that kind of damage."

Poppy had checked both boxes.

Her thoughts began careening down a slippery slope. A sex tape. Made in her husband's bed. Harris's shattered ego would be ruthless in the divorce proceedings. And he would use the infidelity clause in the prenup to slice Poppy's jugular. The clause was originally meant to protect Poppy. "In my experience, nothing soothes a jilted wife better than taking everything," her lawyer had proclaimed, crossing out the punitive figure Bennett's lawyer had proposed and doubling it. Poppy had agreed, of course. It had all seemed so logical, so wise at the time that she hadn't taken the time to consider one important fact.

The clause cut both ways.

She'd lose the apartment. Everything, gone.

An astronaut untethered from her vessel, careening through space.

Poppy licked her lips, the inside of her mouth bone-dry. "Are you saying what I think you're saying?" She narrowed her eyes, a drop of cold sweat trickling down her back. "Are you . . . is this . . . are you *blackmailing* me?"

He blew the hair from his forehead. "I guess you could call it that."

She could feel her jaw loosen, her mouth fall open. She was not an emotional person. Not prone to tears or outbursts, but she couldn't keep her lower lip from trembling as the truth spread over her, inch by excruciating inch. This was all a setup. Bennett had never actually wanted *her*. He'd wanted her *money*. The realization was like a blade sliding into her abdomen, hollowing out her insides. Heat traveled across her chest, all the way up to her neck. She remembered the first time she'd walked into Reflex, how charming he'd been—the compliments, the light touches on her arm, the overt flirting. It had all seemed natural, organic. But now she could see it for what it really was: a carefully calculated plan.

An avalanche of anger swept over her body, threatening to flatten her.

How savagely he'd humiliated her. How stupid she'd been.

With Bennett's gaze fixed upon her, she cast about for her poker face, wired it on. She forced herself to draw in a few even, slow breaths, which gave her time to collect herself and choose her next words carefully. "You're making a lot of assumptions here, Bennett. One of which is that Harris and I have a monogamous relationship." A shrill sound escaped from her lips. It was meant to be laughter, but it didn't hit the mark. "What makes you think I'd *care* if you showed him that video?"

Bennett cocked his head, studying her. She willed her expression to stay steady.

After a moment, Bennett laughed, a mirthless, condescending sound. "Come on, Poppy. I'm not stupid. Let's not make this harder than it needs to be."

She dug her fingernails into her palms, imagining digging them into his pretty face, clawing away his chiseled features. It was almost a relief, the way her anger was obliterating every other feeling in its path.

"Why are you doing this, Bennett?" she asked through gritted teeth. "You already *have* money."

"That's *other people's* money," he snapped, crossing his arms firmly over his chest. "And you and I both know that's different. People assume I have a shitload of money because my last name is Stillman, but you of all people should know the well eventually dries up."

"That's quite a sob story, but you and Norah don't exactly seem like you're begging for change." She could see him wince almost imperceptibly at the sound of his wife's name. Direct hit. Her spine straightened, regaining her steely edge. "You do realize you're putting your own marriage at risk, right?"

He snorted. "Oh, *now* you're concerned about my marriage?"

"Wait a second," she said slowly, threading her arms over her chest. "*This* is why you married someone like Norah. Because your trust fund was depleted and you needed her money."

His face darkened as her words landed. "What the hell do you mean 'someone like Norah'?"

"Well, it's obvious you didn't marry her for her looks." Poppy's voice was as sharp as a paring knife, and she relished his wounded expression.

"I didn't marry Norah for her money, and I've never used *any* of her money for myself. I'm only doing this because I've got a bit of a situation. Which has nothing to do with her."

"Screwing another woman for money has nothing to do with your wife?" She tilted her head condescendingly, raised a finger to her lips. "I wonder if she would agree with that."

He pushed his hands through his hair. "Well, you don't need to be concerned, because I have no doubt that I could convince Norah this was a one-time mistake if it came to it."

"Bullshit," she snapped.

He shrugged. "Then go ahead and call my bluff. But that's a pretty big risk to take. If you're wrong, then I guess we're *both* single."

Poppy glared at him as the weight of futility settled across her shoulders. Bennett was like an extremist with a bomb strapped to his torso, ready to blow up both of their lives.

"How much?" she spat. The words felt like fire in her throat, burning her esophagus.

He unbuttoned each sleeve, rolled them slowly up to his elbows. "Seven hundred and fifty thou."

She guffawed. She couldn't help it. This was absurd. "You think my husband won't notice a payment that size?"

"Tell him it's a charitable donation."

She released a high, strangled laugh. "You're insane if you think that's the size of my regular donations."

"I guess you're feeling extra generous then." He stuffed his hand in the front pocket of his jeans, extracted a folded Post-it note. "Here's the information you need for the transfer," he said, pressing it into her hands. "The name on the account is Feeding New York Inc., so Harris won't know the difference." He wiped a bead of sweat from his hairline and pushed his hands back into his pockets.

Poppy blinked away the moisture gathering in the back of her eyes.

"I'm not a monster, Poppy," he said, sounding almost practiced, as if he'd had to say it many times in the past.

Staring down at the yellow square in her palm, she connected the dots. "You've done this before, haven't you?" she said slowly. "You prey on married women and threaten to ruin their lives."

He scoffed, his breath hissing out of his mouth. "'Prey' is a really strong word, don't you think? Making someone face consequences for her choices doesn't turn her into a victim."

"You are a fucking asshole," she fumed, each word soaked with contempt.

He spread his arms in a "you got me" gesture. "You can call me whatever you want. The way I see it, I use my god-given gifts. You'd be surprised how many lonely married women are willing to cheat on their husbands. Enough that I could quit working for my dad and still maintain my lifestyle. But when I met Norah, I cashed out and started my own business." His expression was smug, and it sent a fresh surge of rage through her veins. "It's been years since I've had to tap this well, but this is only a one-time thing." He filled his cheeks with air, blew it out slowly. "I'm going to come back here at noon on Monday. If you've transferred the money, you can watch me delete the video, our messages, and any backups to the cloud, and we can both move on with our lives. If you haven't sent the money . . ." He left the implication hanging in the air.

"You're going to burn in hell," she heard herself say in a voice as hard as cement as she shouldered past him. She felt the threat of tears but clamped them down.

He took her words for what they were, a reluctant assent, and fell in line behind her as she stormed across the bedroom. With an unsteady hand, she wrenched open the bedroom door.

"Hello, Ms. Ridley," Maya called from the doorframe of a bathroom down the hall. She was on her knees, presumably wiping the porcelain with the rag in her hands. Poppy didn't miss the way her eyes widened when Bennett emerged behind her. Nor did she miss the way Bennett's appraising gaze swept over Maya, pausing briefly on her chest. Poppy recognized the look Bennett was giving Maya. It was the same one he used to give her. And now she could see it for what it was. It wasn't sexy. It wasn't sexy at all. It was lecherous.

Poppy forced herself to keep her chin up as she made her way past Maya, leading Bennett down the hallway. Somehow, her shaky legs continued to move forward.

"I'll see you Monday," Bennett said when they reached the foyer. She fixed him with a steely glare as he brought his fingertips to his forehead in salute.

She waited until the elevator had arrived and the doors had closed behind him before she released her hand from the knob and let the front door shut. As she put her palm against the wall, her eyelids closed, and she silently counted to five in an effort to slow her racing pulse. When she opened her eyes they locked on Maya, who had appeared at the far end of the hallway. The expression on her face made Poppy's blood run cold.

It wasn't her usual deference or uneasiness or awkwardness. It wasn't even curiosity.

Worse.

It was pity.

UrbanMyth Message Board

I want to fire my housekeeper, but I feel like she knows too much about my family. We don't have a nondisclosure agreement—can I force her to sign one now?

> Install a camera. Sooner or later she'll steal something. Use it as a bargaining chip to get a signature. Moral compass satisfied.

> You could kill her.

> You have to consider how long it will take to find another one, unless you want to be scrubbing your own toilets.

> With how much my housekeeper knows about me, I'm never letting her go. That woman knows where the bodies are buried.

I can't stop stealing things from stores—clothes, sunglasses—last week I stole an $8 jar of olives from Whole Foods. I just need the thrill, but if I ever got caught I would die of embarrassment. Anyone else do this? How do you stop?

> Don't blow up your whole life for an $8 jar of olives for fuck's sake.

> Is this Winona Ryder? Secretly living on the UES?

> I do this too. My therapist says it's because I'm depressed, but honestly, I think I just like free stuff. No harm, no foul.

> Wait . . . did you steal a red blouse from Intermix on Madison on Saturday? If so, I saw you and you're not exactly discreet. It's only a matter of time before you get caught.

Chapter Ten

HEATHER

AN EYE FOR an eye.

Heather could still picture her moral philosophy professor's earnest face as he stood at the front of the lecture hall, index finger pointed at the words written in bold letters on the illuminated white screen. *An eye for an eye.* "Can there be *justice* if the victim is not avenged?" he'd boomed, emphasizing the word "justice." "Can the moral order be restored in society if the offender does not suffer a punishment that fits the crime?"

An eye for an eye. The words ricocheted in Heather's mind now as she studied her reflection in the bathroom mirror, the impact of the past week unmistakably etched into dark circles under her tired eyes.

Five days. That was how long it had been since the infuriating meeting with Krause. Five days and Heather's certainty that Caroline Ryan was behind this mess had only solidified, her anger only festered, like a giant boil ready to burst. "We've completed our search and are happy to report there was no contraband found in Violet's locker," Dr. Krause had earnestly explained as Heather and Oliver huddled over her iPhone speaker. In Heather's experience, when someone said they were "happy" to do something, the opposite was true. Usually, they'd rather eat glass. And this was clearly the case with Dr. Krause. She knew what he really would've loved was to find a brick of cocaine atop the pile of textbooks stacked in Violet's locker, validating his outrageous, patently unjust overreaction. Heather had expected an apology, some sort of mea culpa, but instead Dr. Krause finished with "We'll consider this matter closed for now, but please convey to Violet that any infractions of the school's drug policy won't be tolerated." From the foreboding note in his tone, you would think it was a message for the ringleader of a drug cartel. He didn't address Caroline Ryan's obvious involvement, which made the message loud and clear: the Ryans were a vital part of the Crofton community, whereas Heather's family was a barnacle clinging to it. "Let's forget about Caroline Ryan," Oliver had said after they hung up the phone. "If she did this to Violet, karma will rectify things." Heather didn't know which part of that sentence annoyed her more: the way he'd emphasized "if," or his unwavering, ludicrous belief in karma, as if the universe were capable of restoring the moral order. The universe doesn't right wrongs. People do. If someone pushes you, you push them back twice as hard. You can't grow up in New Jersey and not believe that. It was practically the state motto.

"Are you sure you want to go tonight?" Oliver asked, shaking her out of her thoughts. "I really don't see how gathering a group of tense parents in one room is supposed to be good luck."

Heather lifted her head from the sink, turned off the tap, and patted her face and hands dry with a towel. Plucking a tube of concealer from her makeup bag, she eyed Oliver's reflection in the vanity mirror. He was in boxers and an undershirt, reluctantly tapping a razor against the side of the sink. This was his MO when he wasn't on board with her plans—taking an absurd amount of time to get ready in hopes that Heather would change her mind.

"We're not letting those people win," she said before turning her attention back to the mirror to dab concealer underneath each eye with her fingertip.

That's what Heather had developed in the past few days: a "them versus us" mentality. Perhaps because not a single one of "them" had reached out to her. Her life had been intertwined with these women's lives since their children were in kindergarten, volunteering alongside them at countless school fundraisers and fairs, singing "Happy Birthday" to their children at parties. Yet, none of them had bothered to check in with her. Instead, they were treating her as if she had some highly contagious flesh-eating disease and any contact with her would be deadly.

Yes, her daughter had been caught vaping weed, but she obviously wasn't the "resident Crofton drug dealer," for heaven's sake, despite the vicious rumors the Ryans were trying to spread.

Violet was the victim here.

"I'm worried about the pressure you're putting on yourself over this, Heath," Oliver said with another slow tap of his razor against the sink.

A familiar surge of resentment pushed against her spine. Lately, she couldn't shake the nagging thought that Oliver had pulled a bait and switch on her. When they'd met in college, he said he was *attracted* to her competitive side. And she to his. Together, they'd climbed the ladder with equal enthusiasm, always on the same page. But ever since Violet was born, it was as if he preferred her to tamp down that side of her personality, to wave the white flag and surrender whenever a challenge arose. The slightest inkling of pressure or stress and he would pull out the "Let's ease up" or the "Life's too short" crap. When, in fact, life is actually pretty long. And it would seem longer if Oliver insisted on dropping out of the game.

When she was feeling charitable, she put it down to a misguided sense of chivalry. He was trying to protect her from the agony of defeat. Lately, though, it was like nails on a chalkboard.

"I'm fine," she sighed, attempting to smother her irritation. "I looked at the RSVPs last night and Norah Ryan isn't coming," she added, swiping a mascara wand over her lashes. "So, you can stop worrying."

Heather had spent hours scouring Google, amassing scraps of knowledge about the Ryan family as if she could scrape them together into one giant mountain and push the Ryans off of it. A few clicks of her mouse and she discovered Bennett was the owner and head trainer at Reflex, the new lacrosse training center on the

Upper East Side, his smiling face adorning the company's home page, arms crossed and tucked under his biceps no doubt in an effort to make them appear larger. He was easy on the eyes, Heather supposed, in that "I've never spent a day in my life worrying about money" kind of way. Heather didn't know much more about Norah than what she'd gleaned online, which, given Norah's inactivity on social media, was limited to her employment and political-party donations. She could remember talking to Norah at a curriculum night or two, but Norah wasn't a regular at the monthly PA meetings or annual benefits. Apparently, not everyone felt the pressure to devote hundreds of hours of her life to the unending volunteer positions at Crofton the way Heather did.

Heather wanted her pound of flesh for what the Ryans had put her family through—yes—but more than that she wanted *vindication*. For Violet. For her. Proof that not only was the rumor patently false, but it was planted with malicious intent by Caroline Ryan. If only she could hack into Caroline's Instagram account and unearth the message she had sent to PSCON.

Is there someone I could hire to do that? Heather wondered as she dabbed a finger on her lashes, sliding off a rogue clump of mascara.

Oliver eyed her for a beat with that concerned face of his, which had become his default expression. He opened his mouth to speak before seemingly deciding against it. Dropping his razor into the ceramic cup, he headed back into the bedroom. Out of the corner of her eye, she could see him sliding on his dress pants, pulling the zipper up, and tightening the belt.

"I wasn't feeling that great today," he called out. "I think I might be coming down with something, so let's not stay too late."

"That's fine, we'll just make an appearance," she called back to him testily, as her phone vibrated against the marble vanity, the screen illuminating with an incoming text.

"It's about time," she muttered, relieved that at least one Crofton parent had the decency to reach out. She moved the mascara wand to her other eye as she considered her response. *I've heard there are pictures of some other Crofton students—would hate to see another child falsely accused!* That would sure motivate parents to find the culprit.

The Ryans weren't the only ones who knew how to plant false rumors.

She picked up her phone from the far end of the counter, where she'd set it down to keep it from getting wet, and checked the message. "Shit," she hissed, pressing the phone against her chest as if it were evidence of a crime.

"You okay?" Oliver's voice echoed from the walk-in closet.

She squeezed her eyes shut. "Yeah, I poked myself in the eye by mistake." She eased the door shut and leaned back against it, trying to settle her nerves. Her eyes skittered around the small space before she lowered herself onto the lid of the toilet, bracing herself as she reread the message.

Something came up on Saturday. Couldn't make it. But my fee has increased. The cost for the job will be $80,000.

She drew in a sharp breath. That was almost double what she thought it would cost. How the hell was she going to squirrel away that much money without Oliver noticing? Swiftly, she opened her Bank of America app, bringing up the account information. The dollar figure in their savings account was sizable, but not so much so that eighty thousand dollars wouldn't be missed.

Her lies were beginning to feel like a noose tightening around her neck.

She rested her thumbs on the screen, watching the cursor blink hypnotically as she considered her next move. She could refuse to part with another red cent and come clean to Oliver about everything. End the whole charade right now.

Or . . .

She pecked out a response.

Let's be reasonable. $65,000. I can have the money to you by the end of next month.

She dropped the phone in the pocket of her robe and pushed herself up off the toilet, gathering her resolve as if it were a pile of towels she could pick up off the floor. One of the very few useful things her mother had taught her, apart from how to survive on Pop-Tarts and Diet Coke, was how to put on a brave face. *You gotta tell yourself none of this crap ever happened,* she remembered her mom saying as she dabbed on lipstick in an attempt to conceal the purple tinge on the side of her swollen lip. *Just close your eyes and imagine an eraser wiping the whole memory clean.*

If there was anything her childhood had prepared her for, it was pretending everything was okay.

She dumped half of the dresses in her closet onto their California king bed before she selected a one-shoulder black cascade dress that came to her knee and silver drop earrings with diamonds on the ends that Oliver had given her for Christmas last year. Assessing herself in the full-length mirror, she noticed a small tremble in her fingers as she fastened the backs onto the earrings and smoothed her hands over the front of the dress.

"You can do this," she whispered, forcing her lips into a smile as if she were slipping on a mask. The Ryans would love it if they were no-shows at Lucky Cocktails, but Heather refused to give them the satisfaction. She could go to this party. She could blend in. Like beige paint.

Looping a finger through the backs of her peep-toe high heels, she padded down the hallway, dropping her shoes near the front door before heading into the kitchen. She extracted two highball glasses from the cupboard, twisted open a bottle of gin and tilted the bottle, watching the clear liquid cover the bottom of the glass, and topped it off with tonic water. Leaning against the counter, she swallowed a deep gulp, relishing the feeling of warmth traveling down her throat.

She swished her glass in a small circle, staring at the mosaic backsplash that ran the length of the kitchen until the pattern began to blur. How many times had she stood in this very spot, calling out reminders to Violet on her way out the front door? *Don't forget your homework . . . your clarinet . . . your science project . . . your bathing suit . . . your lacrosse stick!* God, there were so very many things to worry about when raising a child. Were they getting enough sleep, eating a well-balanced diet, consuming too much sugar, making friends at school, getting good grades, keeping up with their peers? Always, always something to worry about.

But she'd been asleep at the switch.

She'd left Violet unprotected, like a lioness who'd allowed a hungry hyena into her den.

I guess you're not so smart now, are ya Heath-ah? her father's voice mocked in her head. The man was long since dead, and she could still hear him berating her as clearly as if he were standing right beside her. Her father had relished it when she fucked up. It was the only time he paid her any attention at all.

Her fingers curled tighter around the glass. Seeing her daughter suffering at the hands of a bully like Caroline Ryan was like pressing on an old bruise.

She took a long, deep breath and then lifted her glass and took an even longer, deeper sip of her drink. Sliding her phone off the counter, she told herself not to look, but like an obsessive-compulsive at the mercy of a handwashing ritual, she couldn't help herself. UrbanMyth, once her respite, was now a digital land mine. One she reviewed with masochistic curiosity. *So, does Instagram girl only deal at Crofton or is it all UES private schools? / Let's just say I know this family, and I'm not surprised they're raising a drug dealer. / That photo is quintessential UES privilege. It's not like she needs the money. She should be kicked out of school.*

Heather gripped the side of the counter. Every post about Violet was like another quarter in an arcade pushing her closer and closer to the edge.

"Whoa, easy there, Tiger." Oliver appeared at the entrance to their galley kitchen, adjusting his patterned burgundy tie and smoothing down his shirt. "You do realize there will be cocktails *at* the party, right?" He gave an uneasy smile.

"Pregaming," she said, clearing her throat. She pointed at the empty glass she'd set out beside hers and raised her eyebrows in a question.

"Sure, one for the road. I wouldn't want to see you drinking alone."

She turned her head away as she poured, surreptitiously dabbing tears that had sprung up in the corners of her eyes, before passing him the glass. She raised hers in a toast, and they both took a long slug.

He rested a hand on her waist, gave her a gentle squeeze. "You sure you're going to be okay tonight?"

"Yes," she lied.

"Okay," he said, relenting. "Look, we'll get through this. Nobody is going to bring it up, but if they do we tell them what was written about Violet online wasn't true and we're dealing with it privately. People will get the picture. They don't want to talk about it any more than we do, and they're not going to want to make us uncomfortable."

She swished a sip of gin in her mouth. What was that like? she wondered. What was it like to have an unwavering faith in people, to believe that at the heart of it, they're good? What would Oliver say right now if she showed him what people were writing about their daughter on UrbanMyth, if she held up the screen of her phone and said, "This is how awful and mean-spirited people *actually* are"? She downed the rest of her drink and put the empty glass in the sink, not wanting to chew too long on the question.

"And if they do bring it up, the only thing I ask is that you keep your punches above the belt, and no hair-pulling," he tentatively teased.

"I can promise you violence is not on my agenda tonight, but I guess we'll see where the night takes us."

"You know I love to be kept in suspense." He cracked a grin and gave her backside a playful swat.

She slid on her heels and pushed her arms through her coat, stumbling slightly. Maybe she'd pregamed a little more than she thought.

"I'll need to keep an eye on you," he said, resting a steadying hand on her lower back and leading her out their front door. "Because I don't want to have to bail you out of jail if you decide to push someone off of Poppy's king-sized balcony."

Heather tilted her head back and laughed because the idea was ridiculous. Of course.

Chapter Eleven

NORAH

Norah stood in the lobby of her apartment building, her thumb hovering over the words "attending" and "regrets" on the screen of her phone. It felt like a tricky round of Would You Rather? *Would you rather spend the evening in uncomfortable heels making small talk with one hundred Upper East Side parents, or devastate your only child?* It was a dilemma she hadn't expected to face when she'd RSVP'd regrets to this party weeks ago. But, like a lot of situations involving Caroline these days, she'd managed to get it wrong.

In her defense, Caroline had always been blissfully indifferent to Norah's attendance at Crofton parent social events in the past. So much so that Norah had stopped mentioning the Rosé on the Roof or the Spring Garden Party invitations that peppered her inbox throughout the school year. Norah would fire off her regrets, delete the email, and consider herself lucky to be spending the evening home with her family instead.

But her luck had run out. Ironically, with an event called Lucky Cocktails.

The first text from Caroline had pinged on her phone over an hour ago. *Did you know there's a party for the parents tonight? Are you guys going?* Norah had been in the middle of a conference call and fired back a quick, *I have a date with Ted Lasso tonight. Care to join me?* missing the blatant hint Caroline was sending until she was hit over the head with it in the next message. *Can you go to the party instead?* Thinking Caroline had bought into the superstition, Norah had pecked out a gentle response to assure her that boarding school acceptances did not hinge on whether or not her mother attended a cocktail party. But when Caroline's reply flashed up on her screen, Norah's guilt-prone heart pinched. *I really want you guys to go. Can you, Mom? Please? I think it's already started.* Resigned, Norah had wrapped up her conference call, shot up from her desk, and grabbed the black A-line cocktail dress—the one she referred to as her "party uniform"—that she stored in her office for emergency work functions. Then she'd texted Bennett. *You're going to hate me, but can you put on a suit and meet me in the lobby in twenty minutes? Last-minute social function. I'll explain later (and make it up to you).*

The elevator doors pinged open now and Norah raised her attention from the screen, smiling at Bennett as he stepped off. "I don't know whether to be intrigued or alarmed by your text," he said wryly, slipping his wallet and phone into the breast pocket of his blazer. "But you always keep me on my toes." He leaned in for a quick kiss. "Let me guess. Important client?"

"Important, but not a client. Caroline."

He raised a questioning brow and stuck out his right arm for her to take.

"Looking good, Ms. Ryan and Mr. Stillman." The doorman grinned, readjusting the sleeves of his blazer.

Bennett clapped him on the back. "You know you can call me Bennett, Richy," he said. "Hey, did you see that overtime win last night? That puts the Rangers two points out of a playoff spot now." The two of them launched into conversation and Norah brushed the lint from her dress and cinched the belt of her coat, mentally calculating how long she could give them before she would need to pull him away. She was used to waiting for Bennett to wrap up a conversation—with an Uber driver, a barista, a salesperson. When people spoke, Bennett sat still and listened.

If it's true that you can tell a lot about a person by the way he treats service staff, then Norah had known everything she needed to know about her husband on the day she met him. She'd been sitting on a restaurant patio, having a rare solo Sunday morning brunch, an indulgence afforded to her due to the fact that Caroline was spending the day at a friend's house. She'd been digging into her eggs Benedict, perusing *The New York Times,* when a voice came from the table beside hers. "You won't believe how badly Eleven Madison Park got skewered by Pete Wells in the restaurant reviews." Norah had raised her eyes from the paper, unsure if the voice was meant for her. Bennett was smiling back at her. She instantly registered that he was attractive—with his wavy dark hair, athletic build, and resemblance to Bradley Cooper, it was difficult to miss—but it didn't occur to her that he might be flirting. Men who looked like him didn't tend to hit on women like her. Not that she bemoaned this fact. She'd always been both aware of and at peace with who she was. It was the men she dated who didn't seem to be. "Is it worse than the review he did of Peter Luger's?" she'd replied, setting down her fork and dabbing her mouth with a napkin. "Comparing the shrimp cocktail to cold latex made that one an instant classic." He threw his head back and laughed—a hearty guffaw that made Norah laugh too. "I think savage restaurant reviews are quickly becoming my favorite genre of writing," he'd said, flashing an appreciative grin. Twenty minutes later, he'd pulled up his chair to her table and they'd each ordered a second mimosa. As the peppy server delivered the brightly colored drinks to their table, she stumbled over a crack in the sidewalk, dumping the contents over Bennett's crisp white polo shirt. Red-faced and teary-eyed, she stuttered her apologies, but Bennett waved it off good-naturedly. "I wanted a reason to get rid of this shirt and now you've given me one," he'd said, bending down to help her collect the fallen glass. When Bennett and Norah left together an hour later Norah couldn't help but notice the generous tip he'd left on the table. And as they strolled down the sidewalk, Norah had felt intoxicated in a way that had nothing to do with the mimosas. When Bennett had asked her to marry him six months later, it was the first time in her life that she hadn't stopped to overanalyze her next move. She leapt. Bennett had a way of doing that. A way of making you leave your inhibitions at the door.

"I'd better head off, Rich," Bennett said, squeezing Norah's hand. "But let's hope they pick up another win tomorrow night and climb back into the playoff race."

Rich raised his crossed fingers and pulled open the brass-handled door with his other hand. Norah took hold of Bennett's elbow and gave a wave.

"Train or Uber?" Bennett asked, stepping out onto the sidewalk.

"Walk," she said distractedly, realizing she hadn't yet updated their RSVP. She pulled her phone out of her bag and tapped "attending." *No turning back now,* she thought, pulling the collar of her coat tighter, covering the patch of her collarbone not protected from the evening wind, as they made their way to the corner.

"Aren't you going to be uncomfortable walking in those?" He gestured at her rarely worn heels.

"It's only . . ." She checked the address on the invitation. "Four blocks away. It's a Crofton parent party."

His body visibly stiffened.

"I feel the same way," she said. "But apparently it's important to Caroline." She raised her eyebrows indicating she was as shocked as he was.

He slowed his steps. "Wait, *this* is why I had to drop everything and change? For some school thing?"

She pulled her head back, eyeing him. "What's up with you?"

"Nothing is *up* with me," he said, a decibel louder. "But when I got your text I assumed you needed me for a work function." A gray-haired couple walking a teacup dog in a plaid coat shuffled toward them, and Bennett softened his voice. "Norah, if Caroline asked you to go to a school thing, it's probably because she just wants the apartment to herself. Let's grab dinner and give her some space." He gestured to the Italian restaurant across the street.

"I know it doesn't sound like her, but trust me. She specifically asked me to go, and I promised her I would. I can't back out now. As much as I'd like to."

They paused on the corner of the sidewalk, and Bennett blew a long stream of air out of his cheeks. "Fine, but please tell me this isn't the event where some schmuck pays thirty thousand dollars so his kid can be the king of the school for the day," he said drolly.

She gave him a playful swat, relieved the tension had eased. A block of ice, melting. She should cut him some slack given that he'd spent what was likely an exhausting day at the small business conference at the Javits Center. Norah loved that Bennett had thrown himself into his new venture, creating something tangible of his own, rather than simply padding extra layers onto the wealth he'd been born into. She hoped the conference had been beneficial, but she knew better than to bring work up now. "No, that's the annual benefit," she said, smiling. "And I promise I won't drag you to that again." She shuddered, remembering the unsettling image of two of her male colleagues competitively bidding on the privilege of having Katy Perry sing "Happy Birthday" to one special child, each of them swinging the paddle in the air as if it were Wimbledon, driving the price well into six figures. Norah was no stranger to male pissing contests—they were practically a daily occurrence in her line of work—but she preferred not to have to put on a cocktail dress and pay six hundred dollars a ticket to witness one.

"This is called Lucky Cocktails," she explained. "And all I know is it's a silly tradition that has something to do with boarding school applications, which I think is why Caroline wanted us to go. I thought she'd let this whole boarding school thing go by now, but apparently not."

The light changed and they stepped off the curb into the crosswalk, navigating around a large puddle. She squinted to see the numbers on the awning up ahead. "Two more blocks," she said, pulling out a tube of tinted lip balm from her coat pocket and smearing some over her lips. "Oh, but you'll be happy to know that I leveraged our attendance to try and extract some information. I told Caroline I'd make her a deal. I'll go to the cocktail party if she'll tell me one thing about the dance other than that it was 'fine.'"

Bennett nodded distractedly, his mind clearly somewhere else.

Going to this party is the right thing, Norah told herself. *If only to smooth over things with Caroline.*

So, why was her stomach pooling with a sensation that resembled dread?

Norah had never been able to find her spot at these Crofton parent events. The Upper East Side ecosystem was a fragile one, and the truth was Norah messed it up. With her aversion to Botox and increasingly graying roots, she didn't look like the other moms. She didn't have the time or the inclination to volunteer on the endless school committees, and she did not stake her self-worth on whether her offspring attended an Ivy League school, despite having attended one herself. She didn't have a standing reservation at SoulCycle or Barry's Bootcamp, nor did she have any desire to vacation like a migratory bird—with Palm Beach in the winter and East Hampton in the summer. Add to the mix the fact that she was the main breadwinner of the family (gasp!) and she might as well have been showing up to this party in a Halloween costume, she was so out of place.

"I think this is it," Norah said, squinting at the green awning in front of the building with the limestone façade. She dropped his arm and pulled out her phone to double-check. "Yup, 998 Fifth Avenue." She registered the trepidation etched into Bennett's expression and felt a pinch of guilt. He hated these things as much as she did. *Twenty minutes,* she told herself. Twenty minutes of mingling and her mom duty would be fulfilled and they could leave.

"You know," he said, turning to her, doing that one eyebrow-raise that got her every time. "We technically have arrived at the party now. I don't think Caroline specifically said we had to go *inside,* so we could go grab dinner instead and still be able to check the box with Caroline." He kissed her temple. His lips were warm, and she closed her eyes, leaning into them.

"You're pulling out all the stops now, aren't you?" she teased, putting a palm against his chest. "Very tempting, but Caroline is too smart for that, and you know what a terrible liar I am." Peeling herself away, she hitched her purse up on her shoulder and led the way through the doors, across the sleek, marbled lobby. Norah noticed the uniformed doorman with the slicked-back black hair peering at them, an odd look on his face. She gave herself a quick once-over and smoothed down her hair with her hand. "We're here for the Ridley party," she said, approaching the desk.

He gestured to the model-esque woman stationed by the elevator, outfitted in a headset and tight black clothing, clutching an iPad. "She'll take care of you, ma'am."

As she approached the elevator, Norah took a deep breath and blew it out slowly through her lips. "Norah Ryan and Bennett Stillman," she announced. "We only recently RSVP'd so we might not be on the list." The bored-looking woman tapped the screen a few times before gesturing with a polished, cherry-red fingernail toward the elevator. Bennett took Norah's hand. His hesitant expression reminded her of Caroline on her first day of preschool.

"Come on," she whispered. "What's the worst that could happen?"

To: Detective Joseph Danielli
FROM: Gretchen Collins
<Wed, March 13 at 4:05pm>

Hi Detective Danielli,

As President of the Crofton Parents' Association, I want to thank you and your partner for your diligence in undertaking this important investigation. We are a tight-knit community here at Crofton, so this is all very unsettling. When you came to speak with me earlier today, you gave me your card and told me to email or call if I thought of any new information that might be helpful. I think it's important to let you know that I spoke to a number of other eighth-grade parents and can confirm I'm not the only one who was shocked by what occurred at Lucky Cocktails. It was a very disturbing scene, quite frankly. I don't want to tell you how to do your job, but I think delving into that incident would be the first place I would start. As I mentioned, please do keep me apprised as the investigation continues. I will keep my ear to the ground as well.

Warm regards,
Gretchen

Chapter Twelve

NORAH

THEY'D ONLY JUST arrived, but the champagne cocktail offered by smartly attired waiters at the threshold of the party was already improving Norah's mood.

"These are good," Bennett said, downing his in two deep gulps before placing it back on the tray and grabbing another one. Norah sipped hers, relishing the sweet taste on her tongue, and let her eyes roam around the room. The ceilings were twice as high as in a typical city apartment, with glittering windows that stretched all the way from the floor to the top, making the living room appear to be floating above the trees in Central Park. Vibrant flowers and abstract sculptures peppered the expansive, neutral décor, and the light from the chandelier ricocheted off the grand piano in the far corner, one that wouldn't have been out of place onstage with Billy Joel at Madison Square Garden.

Everything looked like a work of art and shockingly function-less. Which was very on brand for Harris.

She leaned her head closer to Bennett's. "You should go over there and start playing 'Chopsticks' on the piano," she whispered, trying to loosen his stiff demeanor. He forced a laugh, and they moved around a knot of guests, making their way deeper into the room. A string quartet was parked in front of the large marble fireplace, the soft sounds pairing well with the clink of champagne flutes and laughter, as catering staff circulated with trays of brightly colored drinks and elegant hors d'oeuvres. Norah eased her shoulders down, rearranged her features. This was a party, not an inquisition.

She reached for Bennett's arm as a trio of dads hailed him over.

"I'll catch up with you later," he said, giving her shoulder a squeeze before rubbing his hands together and disappearing into the crowd.

Norah sighed and did a perfunctory scan of the crowd, searching for a group to easily slip in and join, but came up dry. It was just as well, because she needed to get food into her system to soak up the champagne. She began weaving her way toward the artfully displayed sushi interspersed with fresh flowers at the far end of the room.

"Wagyu beef?" a waitress with a slicked-back bun offered, lowering her tray. "It's topped with truffle aioli, shaved pecorino, and mustard cress." Norah pinched the delicacy off the silver tray, reluctantly adhering to the party etiquette of taking only one, and accepted the proffered monogrammed cocktail napkin.

"OMG these are amaze!" a voice from over her shoulder exclaimed, and a manicured hand reached out, its long fingers pincering one from the tray. Norah shuffled out of the way, turning around and inadvertently inserting herself into the conversation of five well-coiffed women wearing jewel-toned cocktail dresses. She popped the hors d'oeuvre into her mouth, realizing too late that it was more of a two-bite endeavor. Raising the napkin to her lips, she chewed the ambitious bite, and swallowed a mass large enough that she could feel it slide down her esophagus, before smiling a greeting.

The one in the emerald-green number squinted at Norah, obviously rummaging for her name, and offered a thin smile before she continued talking. "So, I said, 'You're damn right we need the plans by next week, the co-op board won't give approval for the reno until we have them.'" Norah stole a glance at the other women. Judging from their expertly applied makeup, chiseled arms, and shiny hair blow-dried into submission, this circle of women took care of themselves like it was a full-time job. Norah peered down at her unpainted nails, wishing she'd at least had time for a manicure.

"Ugh." The woman with the sleek black hair frowned, but no creases appeared on her skin. "Dealing with architects is so infuriating." She sipped her drink with a quiet sigh as if imbibing something medicinal.

Norah nodded along to appear engaged and stifled a yawn. Upper East Siders talked about apartment renovations the way sports fans talked about football—passionately and incessantly. Norah, on the other hand, had purposely purchased an apartment her realtor had referred to as "turnkey" in order to avoid putting even an ounce of mental energy into considering grout colors. She hadn't so much as repainted before they moved in. She let her eyes roam the party in search of another tray of hors d'oeuvres. She spotted Harris near the piano, gesticulating wildly and exuding the air of gravitas that came with an eight-figure salary and standing a good four inches taller than the two men who were hanging on his every word.

Would Caroline ever fully appreciate the sacrifice Norah was making by being here tonight, rather than home on her couch? Probably not.

"And it's a landmark building so it's much more complicated . . ." the woman droned on, and Norah tried to tune back in. She shifted her weight to get some relief from the dull pain burning on the back of her left foot. One of her shoes had rubbed away the skin on her heel, leaving a throbbing blister. Somehow, though, it was still less painful than this conversation. She took a slug of her drink, calculating whether it would be rude to excuse herself midsentence. Given the intensity with which they were currently discussing building façades, it would probably go unnoticed.

"You're using my window guy, right?" a woman who bore a striking resemblance to Jessica Chastain piped in, arching her eyebrows as high as her botoxed forehead would allow.

Tipping her cocktail to her lips, Norah took another swallow, letting the alcohol work its magic, softening the jagged edges of her mood. Over the rim of the glass, she saw the familiar figure of Harris's wife insert herself into the circle, receiving air kisses from two of the women. Her eyes glinted across the room with the superiority of a queen. Norah's and Poppy's paths had crossed a number of times at various industry benefit dinners, even before their children had started kindergarten at Crofton, but their conversations never extended beyond perfunctory chitchat. Norah could still remember the bemusement on Poppy's face when Norah explained (twice) that she was not the *wife* of a managing director at Orca Asset Management, but rather she *was* a managing director, as if Norah had handed Poppy a banana and told her it was an orange.

"There is nothing worse than renovation issues," Poppy decreed now, and the other women nodded as if she'd delivered a prophecy. "I told Harris, 'You'd better like what we've done or we're moving.'" She gave a delicate laugh as the others laughed along.

"Poppy, your apartment is so lovely," Norah said, seizing the opportunity to join the conversation rather than stand mutely. "I love how you've decorated."

Poppy's heavily mascaraed eyes landed on Norah, and she reared back as if she'd been slapped. "Norah," she exclaimed, her voice a fraction louder than before. The five other women swiveled their heads in Norah's direction, detecting a shift in the air. With a manicured hand on her heart, Poppy rearranged her expression in a way that reminded Norah of an actress getting into character. "I . . . I didn't expect to see you here. When did you arrive?" Her tone made it sound like she couldn't imagine anything less appropriate.

"Oh, um, about twenty minutes ago," Norah replied, instantly regretting her decision to draw attention to herself. Considering her eleventh-hour change of plans, it probably would've been prudent to fly under the radar. She noticed red patches creeping up Poppy's pale neck, the tightening around her lips, and understood that Poppy must not take late RSVPs lightly. "Bennett and I had a last-minute change of plans and our evening freed up, so we changed our RSVP. So sorry about the late notice," she added, feeling slightly wilted.

Poppy's eyelashes fluttered, and she seemed to be looking not quite at Norah now, but at something behind her, which when Norah turned briefly, she could not identify. "Oh, that's no problem at all," she said after a moment, in a tone that indicated that it was, in fact, a colossal problem, her smile pulled so tightly across her lips it almost looked uncomfortable to hold the expression. "I didn't see you come in, but I guess I've been so wrapped up in making sure all of this is running smoothly." She waved her hand around the party indiscriminately.

"You've done a fabulous job, Poppy," a jewel-toned dress murmured, and the woman beside Norah bobbed her head like a trained seal.

"Shrimp tartlet?" a server in a starched white shirt offered, lowering the tray in front of Norah.

"She's allergic to shellfish," Poppy snipped, waving him away with an irritated hand.

"Just mollusks, actually," Norah quietly corrected her, watching the starched-shirt savior scuttle away. Norah had no memory of sharing this information with Poppy, although she must have.

Norah accepted another cocktail proffered by a passing waiter, placing her empty glass on the tray. This one was pale pink and served in a delicate, frosted martini glass with a lime wedge on the rim, and Norah wished she could swan-dive into it. She took a tentative sip and felt Poppy watching her with sharp eyes, seemingly taking measure of her, the tendons in her neck pulling through her skin as she gritted her teeth.

"I've been dying to hear what everyone thinks about this Doubles incident," the woman with the severely arched eyebrows said in a tone that was silky smooth, but not friendly.

"I didn't even realize teenagers today were still *using* Instagram," the sleek-haired one said with a touch of glee. "But apparently . . ." Her voice dropped to a hush.

"Norah Ryan, is that you?" Harris's voice boomed over the din of the room. He closed the gap between them in three long strides, slapping his meaty hand against her back. Norah tried to steady her drink, but a dribble of liquid sloshed over the rim of the glass onto the side of her hand. "I thought I saw you over here," Harris said, oblivious. "Are we actually letting our team out of the office these days?"

"From time to time," Norah replied with a tight-lipped smile, surreptitiously shaking the droplets off her hand. She shifted her body to invite him into the circle. She wouldn't have thought the addition of Harris would be a step up in the conversation, yet somehow it was. He had a glass of amber liquid in his right hand, and his gaudy cufflinks gleamed as he took a long sip.

"Don't worry, ladies, I didn't come over here to talk shop. Only to say hello." Norah noticed flecks of spit coming from his mouth as he said the word "hello," and Poppy's pained expression suggested she noticed it too.

"Are you going to play us a tune on the piano, Harris?" a jewel-toned dress teased, flashing her chemically whitened teeth.

Harris waved the notion away. "Nobody in our family plays an instrument, but we somehow wound up with a Steinway." He lifted one hand as if to say it was a mystery to him how a piano that costs six figures had wound up in the middle of his living room. "I'll let you all go back to your 'girl time.'" He carved out theatrical air quotes, and the women in the circle tittered as he backed away and moved on to the next group. Norah watched as he dropped a heavy arm around the shoulder of a woman whose brightly painted lips curled into an uncomfortable smile.

Harris was like a bumblebee, pollinating the clusters of guests with his overt chauvinism.

Norah craned her head slightly, plotting her own escape, and spotted the back of Bennett's head across the room. The men he'd been talking to had moved on, replaced by a woman in a one-shouldered black dress. Norah squinted. Based on the limited personal space between them, Bennett and the woman appeared to be having a very intense conversation.

"Cheers to that," one of the women said and Norah pulled her attention back to the group, raising her glass to clink theirs, unsure what they were toasting. The quartet in the corner launched into a new rhythm, and Norah's gaze fluttered back to Bennett. She tilted her head, studying them. Was it her imagination or did something seem off? Bennett rocked on his heels, grabbing the back of his neck, doing the aggressive one-handed massaging thing he did whenever he was angry. Norah's eyebrows knitted together. She was staring openly now and noticed Poppy was too, the edges of her lips turning down into a frown.

"Excuse me," Norah said to no one in particular and began threading her way through the knots of guests, her legs feeling wobbly on her heels. Even with her back to Poppy, she could feel her eyes on her like a spotlight tracking her every step. She picked up the pace, anxiety collecting in her stomach.

"Look, Heather, I don't know what you think you saw . . ." she heard Bennett say over the low murmur of conversation as she slid in beside him.

"Hi, guys," she said in a high-pitched voice that sounded nothing like her own. She rested a hand on Bennett's arm, gave it a gentle squeeze. His body was rigid. Norah recognized the woman he was talking to now. Heather Quinn. They'd had a few conversations over the years at school events, and she'd always seemed friendly, if a little intense.

"Oh, there you are." Heather turned to Norah, her lips pulling tight across her red-wine-stained teeth. Norah's expression froze. She'd always been a little uneasy around visibly drunk people. It was the unpredictability that bothered her. You never knew what was going to happen next. They could scream, weep, laugh, take a swing at you—it was anyone's guess. In her experience, the way to handle them was the same way you'd handle a bear in the wild. No sudden movements. Norah's eyes vaulted to Heather's husband, Oliver, whom Norah only now noticed was standing slightly off to her side. He had the expression of a hostage in captivity, practically blinking out the word "help" in Morse code.

"I haven't seen you guys in a while. How've you been?" Norah asked, in as friendly a tone as she could manage.

Heather dabbed her mouth with a bunched-up monogrammed cocktail napkin and tossed it onto a passing waiter's tray. The red wine in the glass in her other hand sloshed, coming dangerously close to spilling on her dress, but Heather didn't seem the least bit concerned.

"We've been good," Oliver answered, his voice tight. "Hey, it's great to see you two, but we were about to head out."

"We were having a very interesting conversation with your handsome husband here." Heather raised her voice over Oliver's, dropping an aggressive hand on Bennett's shoulder. "And it's a good thing you joined us because he seems to be implying that I'm a big fat liar."

Bennett closed his eyes for a fraction longer than a blink, shaking his head. "That isn't what I was saying at all, Heather. I said—"

Heather held a palm up to his face, cutting him off. "I would like to tell the facts to your wife now, if it pleases the court, your honor," she slurred.

Oliver put a hand on Heather's elbow, giving it a gentle pull, but she yanked her arm away. A cloud of defeat fell across his face. Heather was leaning so close now that Norah could see a sesame seed wedged between her teeth. She looked away, feeling embarrassed for her.

Witnessing Heather in this state felt like seeing her naked. Exposed.

"So, I'm sure you both know that your daughter has been trying to kneecap my daughter," Heather said, each word louder than the one before.

Norah's hackles shot up. She darted a look at Bennett and could see the muscles working in his jaw, as if he were chewing on a wad of tough meat that refused to be broken down. He rarely flushed, but spots of color were working their way up from his neck to the top of his cheeks. He reminded her of a steam engine ready to blow.

"Look, I have no idea what you're talking about, Heather," Norah said, dropping the joviality.

"Oh, I think you do know exactly what I'm talking about, *Norah*." She spat out her name like an expletive.

Norah could feel heat rising to her face, sensing the current of attention that had surged in their direction. Heather must have noticed the heads turning too because she lowered her voice a decibel. "I think you know your daughter went to the Doubles dance with the sole intention of ruining my daughter's reputation publicly and irrev . . . irrec." She paused to wipe saliva off the side of her mouth before enunciating each syllable. "Ir-re-vo-ca-bly."

Norah tightened her grip on the stem of her glass.

"Well, yes, Caroline *went* to the dance," she replied slowly, deliberately, keeping her voice as level as she could manage. "But she didn't mention any incident with Violet. Can you fill me in on what we're talking about here?"

Heather laughed in a sharp burst. "Oh, give me a break. Your Miss Innocent act doesn't work with me."

"That's enough," Bennett snapped. "I've been listening to this bullshit for the past ten minutes, and I'm done with it." He shifted his eyes to Oliver. "I think your wife needs to switch to water."

Heather kept her eyes trained on Norah. "So, you're telling me *you* weren't involved in planting the rumor on Instagram?" she slurred. "The one that the entire Upper East Side is talking about." She gestured dramatically at Poppy's floor-to-ceiling windows as if there were an entire crowd on the other side of the glass in deep discussion about the infamous Instagram post featuring her daughter.

Norah could feel sweat forming underneath her foundation. *Was this what the other women were talking about when they mentioned Instagram?*

"And I'm sure you'll also claim you didn't call Dr. Krause demanding my daughter's locker be searched. Christ, you're probably the one writing all the horrible things about Violet on UrbanMyth too."

"No," Norah drew out the word. "And that all sounds terrible, but I don't see what any of that has to do with Caroline." Bennett's hand found the small of her back, and she felt an overwhelming gratitude to have him beside her, mingled with guilt for subjecting him to this shit show.

"Oh, you don't?" Heather's voice slid up in pitch, and a few more heads turned in their direction. Norah willed her phone to ring, the smoke alarm to go off, a hole to open up in Poppy's solid oak floors. Anything to end this.

"Well, then, let me enlighten you. Your daughter took a photo of Violet and posted it on Instagram accusing her of being a drug dealer. And before you try and deny it, you should know that I have prooffff." Spittle flew from Heather's mouth. "Because I was at the top of the stairs that night, and do you know what Caroline had in her hands when she walked into the dance?" She paused.

Norah's heart did too.

"A cellphone." She spat out the word "cellphone" as if it were "high-powered rifle."

"Well, I can't imagine my daughter was the only one in a group of teenagers who had a cellphone." Norah chuckled nervously, tucking her hair behind her ears, and casting a glance at Bennett, whose eyes were closed as if it would make him disappear. *Take me with you,* she thought.

"Nobody is *allowed* a phone inside Doubles. You would think a *mother* would know the rules of the establishment where she dropped off her *child*. Apparently not."

Norah could feel herself reddening, equal parts embarrassment and anger. If she was being honest with herself, *this* was her underlying fear whenever she came to these things. Not of being loudly berated by a woman who's been overserved, but of being judged for being an absentee mother simply because she didn't micromanage every block of time in her daughter's calendar. For the most part, it was her belief that the mommy wars were largely overblown, the whole "working mom versus stay-at-home mom battle" a fabrication made up by the male media, hungry for contention in the female ranks.

And yet.

There was always one.

One rotten apple spoiling the whole damn bag.

"I don't know what happened to your daughter at the Doubles Dance or on Instagram, Heather, but my daughter didn't have any part in it." Norah straightened her spine, her voice firm. "Caroline doesn't even *have* an Instagram account."

Heather opened her mouth and a single, hostility-soaked syllable shot out. "Ha!"

An unpleasant feeling began to form in Norah's gut, one that had nothing to do with the cocktails or with Heather. It was achingly familiar. The last time she'd experienced it was when she'd brought Violet to the pediatrician for a routine checkup, only to discover she'd had a double ear infection. "I'm not sure how you've been able to ignore this for so long," the male doctor had said, peering into Violet's ears with an otoscope and shooting Norah a pointed look.

Did Caroline have an Instagram account? There seemed to be a lot she didn't know these days.

"How's everything going over here?" a high-pitched bordering on manic voice trilled from Norah's right side. She swiveled to see Poppy, smiling so hard it looked like her face might crack.

Norah opened her mouth to respond, but before she could force any words out there was a searing pain in her bicep. She gasped, and for a moment, time stopped. It was as if someone had turned a dial all the way up on her pulse, and everything outside her body— the soft sounds floating from the string quartet, the lithe brunette throwing her head back in laughter—slowed.

Whether it was intentional or whether the alcohol was to blame would become a matter of great debate among partygoers, but as Heather spun her attention to Poppy, her right fist had plowed directly into Norah's upper arm.

Norah wasn't even aware of the martini glass in her hand until it exploded at her feet.

Chapter Thirteen

NORAH

A LIVE GRENADE.

That's what you would've thought Norah had dropped in Poppy's living room with the way the seven uniformed staff had descended upon the fallen shards of glass, strong-arming the guests out of harm's way, as if they were in danger of being hit by flying shrapnel.

A live grenade was also what seemed to be sitting in the base of Norah's ribcage as the front door of her apartment closed behind her and she kicked off her uncomfortable heels. She noticed two small cuts on her calf, war wounds from her disastrous evening. Wrapping her arms around her abdomen, she followed Bennett into the kitchen.

"That woman is certifiably crazy," Bennett muttered, yanking open the refrigerator and glaring at the contents before slamming it shut. "And that's all there is to it."

Norah sighed, tilting her head to pull the backs off her uncomfortably heavy earrings and tossing them onto the kitchen counter, rubbing her earlobes in relief. "You know I hate it when you use that word."

"I'm making an exception for her." He grabbed the open bag of Tostitos on the counter and popped a chip into his mouth. "This is the *one* woman I'm allowed to call crazy. Batshit crazy."

Norah rolled her eyes. She had always considered "crazy" a harmful word, one used to either stigmatize or dismiss strong women. In her experience, whenever a woman got called crazy, her actions were, in fact, a perfectly *rational* response to the situation she was in. But she wasn't about to argue about it now. She picked up the bowl caked with dried salsa that was lying in the sink, rinsed it underneath the tap. So much for the pork stir-fry Norah had picked up from Whole Foods for Caroline's dinner. From the looks of it, chips and salsa had substituted. *Maybe Bennett hit the nail on the head from the beginning,* Norah considered as she ran a sponge along the crusted onion glued to the side of the dish. *Maybe all Caroline really wanted tonight was an evening without her parents hovering over her.*

"I'm going to check on Caroline," she said, crossing the kitchen as Bennett crunched another chip, ignoring the crumbs falling to the floor.

Norah found Caroline's bedroom door uncharacteristically closed, and she wondered when Caroline had stopped needing the crack of light from the hallway to fall asleep. One more thing that had changed. It was getting harder to keep track. She opened the door and whispered "We're home" into the darkness, and for a brief moment she had the overwhelming urge to wake Caroline up, to give her the play-by-play about her bizarre evening. Instead, she pulled the door shut and headed back into the living room, desperate to get off her blistered feet.

Bennett appeared, balancing two glasses of water in one hand and a bag of chips in the other. Norah accepted the proffered water and collapsed on the couch. Pulling her left foot onto her thigh, she inspected the blister on the back of her heel. The skin was angry and raw. Just like the rest of her.

"That's the last one of these parent things you're dragging me to," Bennett said, shifting a throw pillow before dropping down beside her on the couch. "If I want to be berated by a drunk middle-aged woman I'll visit my mother."

Norah laughed and settled into his chest, swinging her feet up on the cushion. He smelled like a mixture of laundry detergent, shaving gel, and wine, which was surprisingly comforting. She inhaled his sweet scent, feeling the ache that had lodged itself in her sternum subside.

"So, what did Poppy have to say about the whole scene?" she asked, massaging the soles of her feet. "Are we cut from all future guest lists now? Persona non grata?"

Bennett's chest muscles tensed underneath her cheek. "Poppy? Uh . . . well, I didn't talk to her all night, so I have no idea."

Norah lifted her head and peered at him. "Didn't I see you and Poppy talking when I came out of the bathroom?"

"Oh, yeah," Bennett said, raking a hand through his hair. "I forgot about that." He blew out a long breath and scrunched up his eyebrows as if he were trying to pull a memory from the recesses of his mind from decades—rather than an hour—ago.

Norah had shakily made a beeline for the bathroom after the incident with Heather, her calves coated in sticky liquid. Once the cocktail was sponged off of her skin, she'd put the lid down on the toilet and sat, waiting for her heart rate to return to normal. She wasn't sure how long she remained there, but the string quartet made it through at least four songs before she forced herself upright, splashed enough water on her face to put out the forest fire on her cheeks, and gripped the oversized vanity for a count of twenty, closing her eyes. When she'd opened them and looked in the mirror she'd realized, to her horror, she'd needed to dab away tears that had sprung up in her eyes. When she'd finally emerged from the bathroom, she spotted Bennett down the hall, his head mere inches from Poppy's in what was obviously the tail end of a hushed conversation.

"Uh." Bennett ran his palm down the stubble of his chin. "I can't remember exactly, but it was like 'Thanks for coming, don't worry about the spill, blah, blah, blah.'" He leaned forward and grabbed his glass from the coffee table and took a long chug, avoiding her eyes. She saw a flicker of something—a question, a worry—but it was gone before she could identify it.

"Well, it sounds like you got a better reception than I did," Norah said, running her eyes over Bennett's face and wondering why he looked so deeply uneasy. "I think she might have been pissed about the last-minute change in our RSVP."

He nodded. "Makes sense."

"Did she mention it?"

"No, but she seems like the type who would be uptight about that." He dropped his hand in the chip bag and popped two in his mouth. "I think the only reason she was even talking to me is her son had a private with me today at the studio, so she wanted to corner me to get an update on his progress."

Norah's brow furrowed. "But I thought you spent the day at the Javits Center at the small business conference?"

His knee began to bounce. "Right. I meant the lesson yesterday." He popped another chip in his mouth. Norah tried to read his energy but was having trouble deciphering it. He was jittery. Off. But after the way things had gone tonight, who could blame him? She rested her head back on his chest and could hear his heart pounding at a rapid speed.

He stroked her hair. "Hey, here's what I still don't understand. Who the fuck cares if Caroline had a phone on her at the dance? I'm sure they all did. Isn't that what teenagers do?"

Norah fiddled with a loose thread on the hem of her dress. The silence swelled between them.

"Did she?"

"Did she what?"

"Did Caroline have her phone on her when she went inside? When she wasn't supposed to?"

"How the hell should I know? I dropped her at the door and said goodbye." He shifted his weight, and she sat up. He was staring at her incredulously.

"But how was she when you picked her up?" Norah probed. "I mean, how did she seem?"

His expression darkened. "You aren't seriously buying what that woman said, are you? Nor, she's nuts. She's one of those tiger moms who thinks all the other kids are out to get her kid."

Norah pinched the bridge of her nose. "You're right. No, I know you're right."

Bennett pushed the hair off of her face and kissed the top of her head. "She's a good kid, Nor. Teenagers are weird and unpredictable, but at the heart of it she's a good kid. That woman was drunk and completely off her rocker." He tugged his vibrating phone out of his pocket, frowned at the screen, and then dropped it back in his pocket, before returning his attention to her. "Let's go to bed," he said, tapping her knee. "It's been a long night."

"I wish I could, but I should get a few things done before I turn in."

"Okay, but you work too hard." He dropped another kiss on top of her head and pushed himself off the couch. Her eyes trailed him down the hallway before he disappeared into the master bedroom.

Outside the window, an ambulance siren wailed, matching pitch with the hum of worry reverberating in her head. She couldn't escape the restless feeling crawling up her skin like ants—the one that told her she was overlooking something important. Without thinking about what she was doing, she grabbed her phone off the table and swiped through her apps until she found Instagram. The last time she had perused any social media was months ago, and even then, it was only because Caroline was featured in a photo on Crofton's account. Sliding her thumb up the screen, she scrolled past photos of sunsets, targeted ads from Bloomingdale's, and children posing with birthday balloons. She let out a frustrated sigh. Trying to find a particular photo on Instagram felt like searching for a particular blade of grass in Central Park.

She lay her thumbs on the tiny keypad, changing course.

When UrbanMyth had launched, Norah had found it fascinating to peep into the secrets of strangers, and had even posted a few of her own, finding the simple act of confession therapeutic. But the novelty of the whole thing wore off quickly, and it had been ages since she'd used the app. Staring at the home page, she considered her game plan. The site wasn't searchable, and posts weren't archived, so the only way to find anything was to sift through everything. It was far from user-friendly, but she supposed that was the point. She began scanning.

My husband thinks I'm an alcoholic. Can that be true if I only drink wine?

*My daughter had a take-home math quiz today
and I spent the afternoon filling out the answers
for her. Everyone cheats on those, right?*

*I'm not in love with my husband. I don't think I
ever was.*

Norah could feel a headache gathering at the back of her skull and was ready to turn in when she saw it. *So, when is the Crofton Instagram girl going to be kicked out of school? Anyone taking bets? Children have been disappeared from private schools for less.* Norah held her breath as she scrolled through the comments.

Crofton has always been known for druggies. The teachers are probably her suppliers.

Where is the parent supervision? Terrible!

That girl looks deranged.

The words snapped against Norah's heart like a rubber band. Despite everything that had happened tonight, she felt a wash of compassion for Heather. What would Norah do if Caroline were the subject of these nasty comments? She'd probably want to burn everything to the ground too. She tilted her head back and stared at the ceiling. She wished Caroline had never attended that stupid dance. Choosing to wear a dress and hang out at a private club was as out of character for Caroline as pitching a tent in the middle of Park Avenue, so why the hell did she decide to go?

Norah could see the writing on the wall. She just couldn't read what it said.

She pushed herself off the couch and padded down the darkened hallway, past the bedroom she shared with Bennett, to Caroline's door. Twisting the knob, she tiptoed into the room and sat on the foot of the bed. Her eyes ran over Caroline's pink-tipped hair splayed across the pillow, the curves of her face lit by the glow from the moonlight creeping in through the shades. Her mouth was slightly open, and her body was tucked in the fetal position, with her arms wrapped tightly around one of her pillows. It was the same way she used to hug her teddy bear. Caroline was such a contented baby that whenever Norah would look in on her she would find her smiling in her sleep. Smiling! It used to placate Norah's worries about her long hours. Whatever she was doing, her daughter was happy, right? But tonight, Caroline's lips were pressed into a thin line.

Norah ran a finger over her face, a featherlight touch on her soft cheek. During those younger years, there were many nights when Norah would get home late from work, long after her sister had already put Caroline to bed for the night. Norah could remember sneaking into Caroline's room to go through the laundry after her sister had gone home, wanting to see the clothes Caroline had worn that day, eager to paint a mental picture. *Oh, she wore her favorite shirt, the one with the smiley-faced watermelon. There's a pasta-sauce stain down the front—she must have enjoyed her spaghetti.* Collecting puzzle pieces to put together all the things she'd missed.

Here she was again. Playing detective.

She felt a sudden and intense pang of nostalgia. Those baby years were hard, yes, but they were also uncomplicated. *Small children, small problems; big children, big problems,* her sister would tell her whenever Norah lamented a sleep regression or an embarrassingly public tantrum. Now she understood. She would much rather be trying to decipher which treat Caroline had selected from the ice-cream truck than worrying about whether she'd been involved in cyberbullying.

Norah's eyes ran over the surface of the bedside tables. There was a charging pad with a lone case for earbuds on top. She crouched down, eased open the drawer on the nightstand, pushed aside some crumpled-up papers. Nothing. She let out a sigh. The headache that had formed earlier had metastasized to her entire skull, pushing on her frontal lobe. She should go to bed. She readjusted the polka-dot duvet over Caroline's middle and leaned down to drop another kiss on her head. As Norah turned to leave, a teal object peeking out from underneath the pillow snagged her attention: Caroline's phone.

Norah rested an index finger on the corner of the case, easing the phone toward her. She felt like a voyeur, but worse, she felt like a stranger. She knew Caroline. She knew the way her right eye crinkled a little more than her left when she smiled, the way a single patch of red appeared on her neck when she ate spicy food. She knew that until Caroline was six she thought strawberries were called "straw babies" and Norah didn't have the heart to correct her. She knew that she couldn't for the life of her keep the clothes in her closet organized but had single-handedly organized a coat drive for the homeless last winter.

She knew Caroline the way she knew the rhythms of her own breath.

Except.

She didn't know why she'd had a last-minute change of heart about the dance.

What else didn't she know?

With her hand gripped around the phone, she plopped onto the swivel chair in the corner of the room. Steeling herself, she typed in the password, and began swiping through Caroline's photos. There was a selfie of Caroline standing in front of her bedroom mirror, hair in a messy bun, wearing a shirt that said NO VALIDATION NEEDED. There was one of her with a friend, filtered to give the girls cat eyes and whiskers, with hearts in the corners of the frame. Another one of four brightly colored scoops of gelato. Norah kept sliding her finger across the screen, her narrowed gaze locked on the date at the top of each photo. Finally, she reached a picture in Caroline's photo roll that matched the date of the Doubles dance.

It took a moment for her mind to catch up with what her eyes were looking at. Then all of her organs seemed to cave in on themselves.

"Oh, Caroline," she whispered, squeezing her eyes shut and bringing a palm to her mouth, poised between tears and rage.

How.

How had this happened?

UrbanMyth Message Board

Spotted: the mother of the Crofton dealer getting wasted at a school-sanctioned party. Like mother, like daughter.

> I've said it before, and I'll say it again, Crofton is full of pill poppers and pill pushers.

> Private school parents need to drink to avoid thinking about those fifty-thousand-dollar checks they're writing for kindergarten.

> This has to be a Crofton parent who wrote this, which goes to show you the backstabbing that happens at that school. This would never happen at Dalton.

> Guys, this is a child we're talking about FFS. Let's go back to talking about screwing your doorman or whatever else you consenting adults are doing with your free time.

Should I leave my wife? She's gained twenty pounds since we were married and our sex life has been reduced to once every few months.

> Well, don't you sound like a peach.

> No, she's the one who should leave you.

> Ignore the posters above. You should absolutely leave her.

> Wait . . . there are men using this site??

Chapter Fourteen

HEATHER

When Heather stepped out from under the shade of the awning, the rays of sun assaulted her eyes, penetrating through her sunglasses and into the back of her skull. Groaning, she hitched Violet's lacrosse stick farther up on her shoulder and twisted off the cap on the bottle of juice labeled "Dirty Detox." Juice Press was cutting a little close to the bone with the names of their pressed juices these days. She took a slug of the charcoal-colored liquid and hustled across the street to get to the shady side. *Sunshine is either a gift from God or a punishment from God, depending on how you're living*, her Catholic mother used to say. Usually it was muttered under her breath as she dropped another one of Dad's empty beer bottles into the recycling bin, watching from the kitchen window as he stumbled out the door for work, shielding his eyes from the sun's rays as if they were laser beams melting his retinas. One morning, when the pile of discarded colored bottles was particularly high, her mother had raised the venetian blinds, filling the room with such an intense brightness that it ricocheted off of the dust floating in the air. "*That,* Heather, is what I call a message from God," she'd said.

Heather didn't want to consider the message being sent to her today.

To say the morning had been rough would be an understatement.

"Where am I?" she'd croaked in response to the sound of Oliver's voice penetrating her sleep, his hand on her shoulder giving her a gentle shake. Based on the pain radiating through her body, her first guess would've been the emergency room after being struck by a large bus.

"You're in bed, Heather. At home," he'd answered flatly.

Peeling open one eye, it took a few seconds for his face to come into focus. "What time is it?"

"Ten in the morning." He placed a large mug of coffee on her bedside table beside the untouched glass of water. "You didn't wake up with the alarm, so I turned it off and let you rest."

Heather sat up quickly, a move she instantly regretted.

"Vi's already at school," he assured her. "I did the morning routine and told her you weren't feeling well."

Heather let her head fall back down, grabbed a pillow from Oliver's side of the bed, and pressed it to her face, letting out a groan. Violet wasn't an idiot. She would put two and two together and realize her mom was hungover. Kids can sense these things. Heather had enough experience on that front to know that was true.

Oliver plucked the pillow away from her head. "I feel like you're going to be really dehydrated if you don't get some liquid in you soon."

She peeled her head heavily off the pillow, pushed up on an elbow, and accepted the coffee in the "World's Best Mom" mug. Her husband could be the King of Passive-Aggressive when he wanted to be. As the hot liquid slid down her throat, details emerged in her mind from the alcohol-soaked evening: seeing Bennett from across the room in conversation with three other men, drink in hand and throwing his head back, laughing as if he were some kind of mad fucking scientist. The frantic shake of Oliver's head as he tightened his grip on her hand. Yanking it free from his sweaty palm. Stumbling, catching herself. A big ball of rage careening down a mountain, gaining traction as it plowed forward. The zigzag of worry lines etched in Bennett's pompous forehead when she announced she knew what he'd done. His denial. Norah's frozen, fake expression. Their satisfied smiles like a raised middle finger. Had Heather thrown something at Bennett? She could distinctly recall a balled-up cocktail napkin in her fist at some point, but the rest of her memories from the evening were blurred around the edges.

Except the end of the night—that she remembered clearly. For better or for worse.

"If you're wondering if it was as bad as you're thinking, the answer is probably 'Yes,'" Oliver informed her, and the coffee suddenly tasted bitter on her tongue. He eyed her as if she were made of delicate crystal that might break, before he dropped onto the foot of the bed and put a palm over the mound of her feet. "I'm as upset as you are about what unfolded, but last night . . ." He blew out a long breath and rubbed his eyes behind his glasses. "Heather, you really need to let this Caroline Ryan thing go. For *all* of our sakes."

A large truck blared its horn, startling Heather and shaking her back to the present. She gripped Caroline's lacrosse stick tighter and paused on the corner, staring at the blinking red hand as Oliver's parting words reverberated in her brain. *Take a step back and put it into perspective.* But she was the only one who *had* it in perspective. A bully had spread a vicious rumor about Violet. Did Oliver really think the right course of action was to let that go? Show Violet that the bully wins? Heather knew firsthand what happened to girls who let themselves be pushed around by bullies.

Heather was determined to regain a sense of power.

She took a final gulp of her Dirty Detox juice before tossing the bottle into an overflowing trash can, crossing the street and hanging a left on Ninety-sixth Street, toward the elaborate prewar exterior adorned with tiny gargoyles. As she ascended the wide staircase to the entrance of The Crofton School, she swallowed down the nausea creeping up her throat and pulled open the heavy glass door.

"Good afternoon, Ms. Quinn," the round-faced security guard called out. "Hey, my wife bought your book yesterday."

Heather forced her lips into what she hoped was a friendly

smile. "Oh, that's so nice of her, Wally. Tell her I'd be happy to sign it if she'd like."

His smile widened. "Wow. She'd love that."

Heather waggled the lacrosse stick. "Guess what Violet forgot."

"Ah, it happens." He extended his hand. "I'll make sure she gets it."

Heather curled her fingers around the stick, struck by a sudden need to deliver it herself, if only to refute the presumption that she was too hungover to function this morning. "Do you mind if I pop into the gym and drop it off for her?"

"By all means." He swept his arm in the direction of the gymnasium. "But make sure you tell her she's lucky to have a dedicated mom like you." He winked.

Heather gave a small wave of thanks, ignoring the needles of guilt puncturing her insides, and started down the corridor. Being inside the Crofton School building usually filled her with the type of pride one felt walking into a newly purchased home. Today, though, it felt like she was trespassing. Even the brass-winged creatures dotting the ornate spiral staircase seemed to be eyeing her judgmentally.

She pinched her cheeks in an effort to bring some color into her gray complexion, hoping she didn't look as bad as she felt when she passed a group of pony-tailed kindergartners walking two-by-two. "Hands to yourselves," she heard the perky teacher call out over a few high-pitched squeals. A dull ache encircled Heather's head like a halo as she wove her way down the carpeted hallway, past the meticulously arranged trophy case, to the door marked HAWTHORNE GYMNASIUM.

She lifted an eyebrow, wondering, not for the first time, how significant the donation had to be to have the gymnasium named after your family. And whether the school would rename the gym now that the patriarch of the Hawthorne family had been indicted for embezzlement.

Not likely.

So much for Krause's precious building block of "responsibility,"

Heather thought, rolling her eyes as she rested a hand on the silver bar and pushed open the substantial metal door.

Her rubber-soled ballet flats squeaked against the polished floor, echoing off the walls of the empty gymnasium. She checked the time on her watch. Quarter to three. Practice should've started by now. Frowning, she scanned the cavernous room, as if perhaps she'd simply overlooked the presence of twenty teenage girls. Her eyes landed on a line of backpacks on the far wall, each with a lacrosse stick stationed beside it. The coach must've started with a warm-up run around the reservoir.

Ignoring the sound of her shoes squeaking, Heather made her way to the other side of the gym, scanning the overhead banners that advertised three straight years of NYSAIS girls' lacrosse championship wins. If all went well, Crofton would win their fourth straight championship at the end of the season, which would mean Violet played on two different sports teams that brought home titles for Crofton this year. Would that be enough to tip her scale over to the "yes" category at Andover?

Not a chance in hell if the admissions director caught wind of the PSCON story.

A sudden wave of vertigo swept over Heather, and she had to stop and close her eyes, count to five, breathing through it. When she opened them, she scanned the line of multicolored backpacks and spotted Violet's at the end of the row. Carefully, she rested the lacrosse stick beside it. She briefly considered tucking a note into the side pocket of her backpack (*Have a great practice!*) before nixing the idea. Violet would see through that transparently guilty move. As Heather pivoted to leave, a familiar teal object caught her eye, poking out from the backpack next to Violet's.

A phone case.

Exactly like the one she saw Caroline tuck into her pocket on the night of the dance.

Heather's breath hitched. It was as if she'd stumbled upon the smoking gun. She shot a look at the entrance before easing her arm down and gingerly pinching the phone case between her thumb and index finger as if it were a bomb at risk of detonating. She turned it over in her hands. Even through the leather, she could feel the warmth. It must've been used only minutes earlier. She slid a finger along the edge of the case and flipped it open.

Her eyes widened.

The screen was illuminated.

A smile spread across her face. Her mother had been wrong. Sunshine wasn't a message from God. An unlocked phone sitting within arm's reach without a single soul to witness her sneak a peek? Now *that* was a message from God.

She slid a shaky finger along the screen searching through the brightly colored icons. When she located Instagram, she hesitated, her conscience in a game of tug-of-war with her drive for vindication. It was easy to imagine gleefully seizing this opportunity when it was hypothetical, but now that it was reality, she found herself struggling to pull the trigger. She lowered her hand, ready to deposit the phone beside the backpack. But her fingers wouldn't uncurl.

It would be ludicrous to throw away this gift from the universe, wouldn't it? It would be moral peacocking. If the roles were reversed, Norah would've dropped an exorbitant amount of money on a private investigator to break into Violet's phone, Heather assured herself, finding her way back to the moral high ground.

Heather was simply protecting her child. Every mammal protected its own young. It was hardwired into our biology. It was basic animal instinct.

You can't fight nature.

She shot another look at the door. Then she lifted the phone closer to her face and tapped open Instagram. She went straight to the DMs, squinting at the names beside the circled photos, bending and extending her thumb, searching for any correspondence with the PSCON account, but she went as far back as four weeks and came up empty. Swiftly, she swiped Instagram away and tapped the rainbow-colored Photos icon. A mosaic of tiny square images filled the screen and Heather only hesitated for a second before she began searching through, eyes glued to the date in the top left-hand corner, moving closer and closer toward the night of the Doubles dance. What was she going to do with the photo once she found it? For once, she didn't have a plan. But the deep, desperate need for irrefutable proof was so great it felt like a hurricane-force wind pushing her forward.

She scrolled past selfies and sunsets and snaps of neon-colored Starbucks drinks. Caroline took dozens of photos a day, but when Heather reached the day of the dance there was only a single square. She pinched the screen, narrowing her eyes, trying to make out the subject of the dimly lit image. It took her mind a moment to process what she was seeing.

She sucked in a sharp breath.

It wasn't Violet.

If she hadn't seen her that evening, she probably wouldn't be able to recognize her from the photo. She was only visible from behind, her buttercream-blond hair cascading down the top of the flawless, blush-colored cashmere coat. Heather could make out a sliver of the profile, but she didn't need to see her face to identify the woman. It was Poppy. She was in the back seat of a car, visible through a rolled-down window, and her back was to the camera. But that wasn't why every muscle in Heather's body was instantly immobilized. The reason for that was the person in the back seat with Poppy. His face was mashed up against her neck, his hand curled around the back of her head in a way that, even with the blur of the photo, Heather could tell was passion. She used her thumb and index finger to zoom in. Squinting, she could make out a mess of curly, coffee-colored hair.

"Holy shit," she whispered.

The loud screech of the metal doors ricocheted off the corners of the gym, and Heather flinched, dropping the phone as if it were radioactive, flinching again as it clanked on the polished floor. A gaggle of crimson-faced teenage girls in white-and-navy uniforms spilled through the doors, their high-pitched voices filling the cavernous space. Heather's pulse jackhammered as she scooted over to where the phone had landed and used the tip of her shoe to nudge it back to the spot where she'd found it. Out of the corner of her eye, she could see the photo was still illuminated on the screen, but there was no way to rectify that now. She lifted a shaky hand and waved to a sheepish-looking Violet in the crowd.

"Mom, you look all pale and sweaty," Violet whisper-hissed when she got closer, crinkling her nose, unable to conceal her mortification caused by her mother's mere existence. "What's *wrong*?"

Heather wrenched her lips into what she hoped was a convincing smile. "Nothing," she said, a tad too manically, shaking her head, trying to ignore the dizzy feeling sweeping through it.

Everything, she thought.

Everything was wrong.

Including, to her great shock, Heather.

UrbanMyth Message Board

If a parent of a child is cheating on his spouse, could that have any effect on a boarding school application? A divorce would look bad, right?

> Yes, the only reason I'm staying in my marriage is to present a nuclear family during admission season. After my son gets into Deerfield it'll be splitsville.

> Is this a serious question? Why would any school CARE?

> Give me a break, if this were true the hedge-fund warriors who are on their third wives would be screwed.

> Confession: I think parents who willingly send their young teens away should be reported to social services.

Chapter Fifteen

NORAH

How DID THE saying go? *When people show you who they are, believe them.* It was her mother's favorite piece of advice. She'd written it on a yellow Post-it and stuck it on the wall of Norah's dorm room after Norah had mentioned reconciling with an old boyfriend who'd been unfaithful. *When people show you who they are, believe them.* The words drifted back to Norah now as she pushed open her bedroom door, pulling her black roller bag in behind her. Lemon-yellow sunlight spilled through the blinds, casting linear shadows across the unmade sheets. She hoisted the suitcase onto the king-sized bed and pulled the zipper along the side, flipping it open to reveal the neatly packed contents: two freshly pressed, un-worn pencil skirts and neatly folded blouses to match, a pair of sensible one-inch heels, and the undergarments to keep everything in place. She'd packed her things on Friday, and now, on Monday morning, she methodically put them away again.

"You need to fly to Chicago *tonight*?" Bennett had asked when he'd returned home from work on Friday and found her arranging her shoes in the suitcase. She'd punctuated her motions with huffs, ensuring she looked suitably irritated by a compulsory meeting being sprung on her at the last minute. "What kind of person schedules an early morning meeting on a *Saturday*?" His tone was irate on her behalf, and for a second, his support almost softened the edges of her red-hot anger.

Almost.

"Unfortunately, the kind of person who signs my paychecks," she'd answered, blowing out a resigned sigh for good measure, as she'd slipped a burgundy silk blouse off of a padded hanger and carefully folded it into her suitcase. All to throw Bennett off the scent. "I'm going to bring Caroline with me, so you won't be on stepdad duty while I'm away this time."

Bennett had cocked his head at this, knitted his eyebrows together, and Norah wondered if the jig was up. They both knew Caroline never accompanied her on work trips.

"I'm going to try to spin it as a girls' weekend," Norah lobbed, avoiding his eyes as she drifted into the bathroom, collecting her toiletry bag.

"You really think Caroline is going to buy that?" he'd teased, sliding his feet into running shoes and popping his earbuds in.

Norah had stretched her mouth into a shaky smile, gave a light eye roll as if they were both in on the same joke. Then she'd kissed him goodbye on his way out for a run around the reservoir. "I'll be back Monday," she'd said with a wave. It had required a herculean effort to make her voice sound chipper.

Apparently, Bennett wasn't the only one with the ability to lie directly to someone's face.

She'd waited until she heard the front door slam behind him, and then she collected the file marked "transcripts" from her home office—the one that didn't contain a single transcript, but instead a collection of her financial documents—and slid it into the side pocket of the suitcase. Then she threw some of Caroline's clothes into an old Land's End tote bag, picked her up from debate club, and headed straight to the Pierre hotel in Midtown, taking a taxi rather than an Uber in case Bennett could track her Uber account. "It's important that your husband doesn't catch wind of any of this," her lawyer had warned when she'd called him first thing that morning. "Or he could start strategically withdrawing money from your joint accounts and socking it away where we can't find it."

This was how Norah handled grief: power through a list of tasks, enough to form an impervious levee against the emotion threatening to flood in. When her beloved grandmother died, Norah had filled the weeks that followed with selecting the casket, organizing the service, and boxing up the knickknacks left behind, while her sisters had bathed in their sadness.

A well-thought-out plan was Norah's suit of armor, the scaffolding holding her up. Without it, she'd collapse.

"Mom, tell me again why we're here," Caroline had huffed as Norah swiped the key card and pushed open the door to the twentieth-floor suite at The Pierre. "Because I'm not really in the mood for a staycation if that's what you had in mind." Norah was silent as she watched Caroline toss her backpack onto the couch, pull aside the curtain, and assess the view of Central Park before flopping onto the king-sized bed. Now that she had Caroline alone, she was struggling to arrange the words she needed to say in a digestible order. Tentatively, she perched on the corner of the bed and rested a hand on Caroline's slender ankle.

"You look like somebody died," Caroline said drolly. "Wait." She sat bolt upright, a look of horror sweeping across her face. "*Did* somebody die? Is that why you brought me here?"

"Nobody died, honey," Norah said in a gentle voice, turning her face to the window. Was it wrong to fantasize that Bennett *had* died? Probably. And not the example she wanted to set. Turning her gaze back to Caroline, she gave her ankle a little squeeze. Caroline's breath quickened, the way it did when they would watch scary movies together, so Norah forced herself to expel the words that were sitting like a rock in her throat. "Honey, I know about the photo on your phone. The one of Bennett." Caroline's leg tensed underneath Norah's palm, and Norah girded herself for indignant shrieks about an invasion of her privacy, but to her surprise, Caroline's face crumpled.

"I'm sorry, Mom. I wanted to tell you. I really did."

Norah scooted closer, pulling her into her arms, and Caroline buried her face in her chest. Norah ran a hand down the back of her head. "It's not your fault," she murmured. "Please don't think any of this is your fault."

The words poured out of Caroline, as if a pressure valve had finally been released. "I think it's been going on for a long time, Mom, because every time you travel he always disappears for, like, hours at a time, and he has these whispered conversations in your bedroom. So, I started to think that something wasn't right. It was the strangest feeling, but I just knew it." Caroline lifted her head from Norah's chest, wiping her nose with the back of her hand. "And then the day before that stupid Doubles dance, he left his phone on the counter. He *never* leaves it in plain view, but this time he did, and I saw a text come in. It said, 'Can we push Henry's Saturday morning lacrosse session an hour later? Big Friday night plans—Doubles dance.' And it had two kissing emojis."

Norah rubbed her back as she took a shuddery breath.

"I wanted to see for myself if that text meant anything or if I was imagining the weirdness. So, after he dropped me off, I started to go down the stairs. But then I went back up to see if he was talking to anyone. I actually thought he'd left, but then I saw a car parked on the corner and I walked toward it and . . ."

Norah closed her eyes. It felt like someone was wringing out her heart like a wet dishrag. "You saw Bennett in the back seat with someone else," she filled in, so Caroline didn't have to, doing her best to keep her voice even. She didn't want Caroline to think for one second that even a drop of that anger was directed at her.

"At first, I didn't really know who it was because I took the photo quickly and ran right back into the dance after, but then I looked at the picture later and could tell it was Henry Ridley's mom."

Norah's muscles clenched. She hadn't ID'd Poppy from the blurry photo—just registered that there had been another woman's face attached to her husband's face, all captured on Caroline's mobile device. The identity of the woman was meaningless.

It only occurred to Norah later, after she and Caroline had ordered room service, changed into pajamas, and Caroline had begun to snore softly beside her, that her instincts had been correct the evening of that ironically named Lucky Cocktails. Bennett was, in fact, being cagey about his conversation with Poppy. And she'd ignored her gut.

From her calm, sunlit bedroom now, Norah heard the front door open and close with a bang, the sound moving through the apartment like a gunshot, startling her back to the present. She swung a hard look over her shoulder. It was nine o'clock on a Monday morning and Bennett was supposed to be at work. Her plan had been to text him in an hour and ask him to meet her at home, say that it was an emergency. That way they could have this conversation before Caroline returned home from school. Clearly, she'd lost track of what her husband did during working hours. She tossed the pair of socks she'd been clutching back into the suitcase and gave herself a mental pep talk. Then she headed out into the hallway, her skin pulsing with adrenaline.

He was sitting on the couch in the living room, hunched over his laptop, pecking at the keys so intensely he didn't notice her presence, not even when she was close enough to see the two bright squares of the computer screen reflected in his forest-green-rimmed glasses.

She studied him, blinking back unexpected tears. How could this have happened right under her nose? But she knew how. When Bennett had come into her life, she'd been a frayed wire in an overloaded breaker box, and Bennett closed the circuit. He was by her side as she navigated her mom's ever-changing medical needs and willingly took over parental duty anytime she was absent. With him, Norah finally had a solid handrail with which to steady herself after years of teetering on her own, and she'd let that security obscure her vision. She disregarded the way his eyes would trail attractive women on the beach, overlooked how he'd tilt his phone away from her when it pinged with a message, made excuses for the times when his schedule didn't match up with where he said he'd been, told herself she was being paranoid when she'd catch him in a blatant lie. She accepted every line of his story. Plot holes and all.

"Bennett," she snapped.

He jerked his head up, shock registering on his face. "Shit, you scared me, Nor," he said, his expression morphing into a slick smile as he pulled out an earbud. "I didn't know you were home. How was . . ."

"I want a divorce," she said, her voice firm and sharp as a tack.

He pulled back as if she'd slapped him. His wounded expression pulled at her heart, so she trained her eyes on the painting that hung behind the couch, the painting his mother had given them for a wedding present and which Bennett had insisted be displayed prominently, despite the fact that the colors were too dark and dreary.

One more compromise she'd made for him.

"Norah," he said, his eyes searching for hers. "You're not serious."

"Deadly."

He rose to his feet slowly, as if she were a wild animal he was trying to prevent from pouncing. "What is this about, Nor?"

"I know about Poppy," she retorted, cutting to the chase.

The lines on his forehead deepened. "Poppy? You mean Poppy Ridley? I coach her son." He raised his palms. "That's it."

"Oh, fuck off, Bennett," she spat, the force of her words surprising them both. "Don't insult my intelligence. I know what happened after you dropped off Caroline at the dance." There was a hitch in her voice at the sound of her daughter's name. It ripped apart her insides to think about how difficult it must have been for Caroline to carry that knowledge around, her teenage mind ill-equipped to handle it. Thinking about it sent a fresh shot of rage through her bloodstream.

"Norah, we were just talking." He raked his fingers through his hair. "I might have given her a friendly hug, but nothing beyond that. I swear on my life."

She studied his face. He was the picture of innocence wronged, his beseeching expression so convincing, so utterly blindsided, that for a moment there was a flicker of doubt in her mind. The photo *was* a little blurry. Maybe she really did have this all wrong.

She changed course.

"You do realize that you're not the only one who has access to the security cameras at Reflex, right?" she said, crossing her arms over her chest. It was a shot in the dark, but judging from the way the color drained from his face, it had hit the target.

His expression collapsed, and he dropped back onto the couch, covering his face with his hands, like a child trying to hide. When he spoke again, his voice was muffled. "I'm so, so sorry. I don't know what's wrong with me," he moaned. "When things are finally going good in my life, I go and fuck it all up. I got myself into a little financial trouble, so I—" He pushed his fingertips into his eye sockets so hard it looked like he was trying to drive the rest of the sentence out of his skull. "Norah, Poppy didn't *mean* anything to me. I would never do anything to hurt our family. You know I—"

"We're not your family, Bennett," she guillotined the rest of his sentence. "Not anymore." Any lingering doubts she had coalesced into fury. "You have fifteen minutes to get anything you need out of the apartment."

His shoulders were shaking. He'd started to weep.

"Nor." He reached for her hand, but she took a step back. "You need to have faith in me. I can change."

"Faith?" She choked on the word. "I've had *blind* faith in you for way too long. Not anymore. My lawyer has prepared the divorce papers, Bennett. They're being filed today."

His face slowly hardened, from a puddle into a glacier.

She'd never seen this expression on his features before. It was as if he'd peeled off a mask and revealed someone unrecognizable.

In an instant, he was on his feet towering over her, muscled arms crossed firmly over his chest. "I don't think you're going to want to do that," he said flatly. "Not unless you want me to take half of all this with me." He gestured around the living room. *Her* living room.

"You think so? You might want to talk to your mother about that. Because she was *very* concerned about *me* stealing the family fortune, remember? I think that's why she insisted that we waive all community property in the prenup. Which means we can only walk away with what we each brought into this marriage."

His eyes blazed, and a vein in the furrow of his forehead began to pulse.

Surprisingly, it hadn't been Norah who had insisted on a prenuptial agreement. Waverley had been the one to suggest it, minutes after they'd announced their engagement at a Sunday dinner at the Stillman estate in South Hampton. "It makes good sense for each of you to protect yourselves, dear," she'd whispered in Norah's ear, as they'd raised a glass of Dom Pérignon in a toast to the upcoming nuptials. "It would make us more comfortable about your *intentions*." She'd emphasized the last word as if she were auditioning for the part of an overly protective father preserving a teenage girl's reputation. Waverley clearly had a misconception of how much money her son personally brought into the marriage. That was the funny thing about old money: those who had it lived under the assumption that as long as the bloodline existed, so did the wealth, as if it were wrapped up in their DNA. Norah had acquiesced, choosing to focus instead on the wedding planning and yielding her powers of refusal to prevent Waverley from turning the big day into an event that would be splashed on the pages of the Hampton social diary. But even Norah's seasoned lawyer was surprised when Waverley had insisted on a rider waiving all community property, meaning no joint assets. Norah had executed the document sitting in her bridal suite while her hair was being swept up into a sleek bun. "It can be your something blue," her sister had joked as she handed Norah the blue-ink Bic pen, rolling her eyes at the absurdity of Norah's future mother-in-law.

The red tide creeping up Bennett's neck now confirmed what she already knew: he hadn't bothered to read the document he'd signed. It was very on-brand for Bennett to blindly trust his family.

"You're bluffing," Bennett snarled, the rise and fall of his chest quickening.

Norah shook her head. "You're entitled to nothing but the assets you brought into this marriage, Bennett. Not even alimony."

He stared at her for an unbearable amount of time without saying a word.

With his nostrils flaring and cords bulging in his neck, he reminded her of a fighter sizing up his opponent. Norah returned the full-force eye contact. A surge of fight-or-flight adrenaline pulsed under her skin, and she found herself calculating her path to the front door. He'd never raised a hand to her in the past, but she didn't trust the man standing in front of her now.

Without warning, he closed the gap between them in two angry steps. Norah recoiled, catching a shelf with the back of her head, and a ceramic plate with an impression of Violet's kindergarten hand, decorated to look like a flower, tumbled to the floor and fractured into three pieces.

Bennett drew in a sharp breath and froze.

Norah swept a hand to the back of her head, pressing the tender spot that was already swelling.

"I—" he started, his voice shaky, but Norah waved a firm hand, silencing him.

"Leave, Bennett," she said through clenched teeth. "And don't come back."

He swung around, snapped his laptop closed, and yanked the power cord out of the outlet so hard it bent the two prongs sideways. "Crazy bitch," he muttered, tucking the laptop and mangled charger under his arm. She threaded her arms across her chest, not taking her eyes off of him as he thudded past her and into their bedroom. She could hear him sliding out a suitcase from the closet, the zipping and unzipping, the sound of him tossing in clothes and god knows what else. She stayed rooted to her spot, listening to him riffle through papers, slam drawers shut. Finally, he emerged, his hand gripped around the handle of his roller suitcase, a small duffel bag slung across his chest.

His feet pounded on the floor, across the apartment, only pausing when he reached the foyer. Norah drew a sharp inhale. "It doesn't have to be this way, Norah," he called out, his voice thick. "But if I walk out this door, you'll regret it. I can promise you that. And the next time you hear from me it will be through my lawyer."

She closed her eyes, felt the throbbing on the back of her head. "Make sure your mom hires you a good one this time."

Norah didn't exhale until the door slammed shut.

Chapter Sixteen

POPPY

WHEN THE CALL from the doorman's desk cut through the morning silence of her apartment, the initial feeling that flooded Poppy's bloodstream was relief.

Bennett was early.

Her nerves had been on a razor's edge since the night of the cocktail party, when Norah had appeared beside her in the living room like a Dickensian hallucination. Norah's presence at the party had caught Poppy so off guard that for a moment she'd wondered if Norah was in on Bennett's scheme, like some screwed-up Upper East Side Bonnie and Clyde. But it was quickly evident that Norah was too oblivious to be one half of a calculated blackmailing plot. Poppy had never been so grateful for a drunken invitee creating a scene as she had been for Heather. Sure, Poppy would have preferred the evening not be remembered for a physical altercation between the guests, but the incident had accelerated the swift departure of Bennett, so ultimately it was worth it. The cause of the confrontation was still a mystery to Poppy, but she wasn't going to expel any energy tracking down the answer. Sooner or later Bennett was going to try his scam with the wrong woman, and Poppy did not want to be part of the narrative when he did.

Despite her best efforts, Bennett had managed to corner her in the hallway on his way out of the party. "D-Day is Monday. I'll be back here at noon, and I hope for your sake you do the right thing, so I can delete this," he'd whispered in her ear, waggling his phone inches from her face. But when he darted his eyes apprehensively in the direction of the bathroom door, he'd inadvertently played his hand. Bennett wasn't going to reveal the existence of the video to Harris, because Bennett stood to lose as much as Poppy did. Not dollar for dollar, of course, but enough to make him want to keep his mouth closed and his iCloud to himself. Norah might've turned a blind eye to his indiscretions in the past, but she wouldn't in this case. Because here was the thing with turning a blind eye—it was impossible to do once somebody flicked on the neon lights and forced your lids open. Poppy would know—her mother had practiced turning a blind eye as if it were a religion. She could still hear her say, in a voice as steely as the concrete holding up this building, "It had *better* not be one of my friends," when her father stumbled through the front door in the wee hours of the morning, smelling like wine and perfume. To Poppy's knowledge, her father had heeded the warning. Because even partners who accepted regular infidelity as a part of their marriage, like her mother had, weren't going to accept being made a fool of. Every celebrity divorce proved that.

Today, Poppy intended to call Bennett's bluff. The conversation obviously couldn't happen via text or email, lest she pad her already sizable and incriminating paper trail, and frankly she was glad it would be in person, if only to see that fucker's face crumble when he realized he wasn't going to receive one red cent from her.

But Poppy's relief that Bennett was early was short-lived when the doorman revealed the name of the visitor.

It was not Bennett.

Poppy took a minute to collect herself before she pulled open the front door, organizing her features in a way she hoped concealed her palpable anxiety. "Hi, Gretch," she said smoothly, eyeing the two large shopping bags swinging from Gretchen's grip.

"Auction items!" Gretchen singsonged, holding up the bags, her overly glossed lips spreading into a smile.

"You didn't need to come all the way up. My doorman could've delivered these." Poppy extended her hand to relieve Gretchen of the bags while using her body language to convey the message that she would not be inviting her in.

"Well, there's a Himalaya Birkin in this one." Gretchen held up her right hand. "Crocodile. So, I figured I shouldn't risk it." She scrunched up her nose and maneuvered around Poppy with the agility of a football player avoiding a tackle. "The Benefit Committee would have my *head* if it ever went astray."

Poppy had to close her eyes for a second to keep them from rolling. Gretchen always spoke about the Benefit Committee as if it was a de facto government agency, wielding just as much power. Poppy didn't have the stomach for this inane conversation on the best of days.

And today was *not* the best of days.

"Thanks, Gretch. I'll take it from here," she said stiffly, her hand glued to the doorknob. But Gretchen had already set the bags down in the foyer and slipped off her coat, draping it over her forearm. Poppy's body was so tense that when the shopping bags hit the floor, she flinched.

"That was such a fun party Thursday night," Gretchen said, oblivious, craning her neck to peep down the hallway, as if she might spot a leftover guest or two sprawled out on the chaise.

"Yes, it was," Poppy said, not bothering to conceal her impatience. If Bennett stuck with his plan, he would be here in two hours, and she did not want there to be any possibility of these two crossing paths in the lobby. News like that in the hands of Gretchen would travel like a lit fuse.

Gretchen spun to face her, a wicked gleam in her eye. "Hey, so I didn't really see what happened with Heather Quinn, but I heard she slapped Norah Ryan. Is that true?" she asked with the type of unbridled pleasure usually reserved for an orgasm.

The mere mention of Norah's name threw Poppy off-balance. She took a careful breath, leveling her thoughts. "What an odd thing for someone to tell you," she answered icily, her equilibrium restored the instant Gretchen's cheeks turned pink. "All that happened was they bumped into each other accidently and one of them dropped a glass." She lifted one shoulder, as if it were all so benign. She didn't dare utter Norah's name. Gretchen would home in on her obvious discomfort faster than a heat-seeking missile. "Actually, now that I think about it, I should ensure the cleaners didn't overlook any shards of glass. I'm sure you can imagine how busy I am after hosting a party that size . . ." Poppy trailed off, letting the dismissal hang in the air.

"Of course," Gretchen said, tucking a strand of hair behind her ear. "I should let you get to that. Let me do one final check to see that everything is in order." She made a show of crouching over the shopping bags, moving aside what appeared to be a red Cartier box, peering in. With her back to Poppy now, she said, "You know, Heather Quinn is the drug dealer's mother. It wouldn't surprise me if she was *high* at your party."

Poppy didn't take the bait. There was only one way to make someone like Gretchen vaporize. Silence. It was their kryptonite.

Seemingly realizing that one could only prolong the process of looking inside two bags so long, Gretchen slid them closer to the wall, on the left side of the handcrafted console table, lingering to arrange them just so, and stood up. "You know my Charlotte said that girl approached her at school to try to get *her* to start dealing too," she said, sliding her hand through the sleeve of her coat at a painstakingly slow pace. "It sounds like she's trying to recruit some of the other eighth-graders too."

"Mm," Poppy answered noncommittally.

Gretchen looked squarely at Poppy, her sparse eyebrows pulled together. "As a trustee, you must worry about what that could do to the *reputation* of the school."

Poppy's grip tightened around the doorknob; she was a tad unnerved by the way Gretchen had emphasized the word "reputation." Tilting her head, she scrutinized Gretchen. *Is there a possibility she's caught wind of what is happening with Bennett?* No, if Gretchen was privy to that kind of gossip her whole head would explode. She must have sensed Poppy was keeping a piece of information close to the vest and this was her pathetic attempt to tease it out—an appeal to Poppy's sense of duty. People like Gretchen always assumed that because Poppy was a trustee, it was akin to being a frontline worker in the endless pursuit of greatness for The Crofton School. In truth, an unnamed bookkeeper had assessed Poppy's net worth and—*poof*—she was a trustee. The students of Crofton could be cooking meth in the cafeteria as far as Poppy was concerned, just as long as the school managed to springboard Henry into Andover despite his terrible transcript littered with C's.

"I think Crofton's reputation is safe," Poppy said, pointedly looking at her watch. Her voice sounded tight and strained, so she made an effort to lighten it. "Anyway, I should—"

"Now, *who* do we have here?" Gretchen interrupted with a cunning smile, gesturing with her thumb down the hallway, in the direction of the master bedroom.

Poppy's knees went weak beneath her. Flashes of what had occurred in that room—Bennett's firm body on top of hers, her fingernails digging into his muscled back—flooded her vision and sent a fresh surge of panic through her.

Gretchen leaned closer to Poppy, holding her hand flat to the side of her mouth, stage whispering, "I don't think I'd want my husband seeing a woman who looked like *that* floating around *my* apartment." Poppy exhaled a sigh of relief when she realized Gretchen was referring to Maya, who could now be heard humming softly. Gretchen opened her eyes wide and lifted her palms in a "don't shoot" gesture before she added, "Not that you have anything to worry about with Harris, I'm sure. But you know what they say about too much temptation."

Poppy forced herself to laugh along, her unease deepening. She couldn't help but worry that Gretchen was deliberately steering this conversation in a calculated direction.

Gretchen shot another look down the hallway at Maya before pivoting back to Poppy. "So, I wasn't going to mention anything, but speaking of *temptation,* have you heard which Crofton dad has been caught stepping out on his spouse?" She raised a single, pred-atory eyebrow.

Every muscle in Poppy's body tensed. Gretchen had the satis-fied expression of a gangster poised to fire the kill shot. It was all Poppy could do to not throw herself at Gretchen's mercy, beg for discretion, offer to buy every item at this goddamn benefit at a premium. But she could only get a single word to emerge from her mouth.

"Who?"

It was only a second before Gretchen answered, but to Poppy it was a decade.

"Bennett Stillman."

Bang.

The blood drained from Poppy's face. Her eyes locked on Gretchen's, narrowed a fraction. Gretchen blinked expectantly, waiting for Poppy's response.

Poppy lifted her hand from the knob and let the front door slam shut, mentally shifting around her chess pieces. Humiliation min-gled with fury as she gathered her resolve. "Gretchen." She licked her lips. "This needs to—" The end of the sentence was intended to be "stay between us," but the words died on her lips when Gretchen interrupted her, holding up the infuriating "don't shoot" hands again, eyes saucer-wide.

"No, not me! *I'm* not the one sleeping with him," Gretchen squealed, misinterpreting Poppy's desperation for an accusation. A sly smile unfolded across Gretchen's face. "But let's just say it's not going to be a secret for long because . . . okay, I almost *never* read this site, but there was a not-so-subtle post about it on Urban-Myth . . ."

Gretchen was still talking, but Poppy couldn't make out what she was saying over the sound of Bennett's baritone voice in her ear. *Now I know how I can send you secret messages.*

Holy. Shit.

"Gretchen," Poppy interrupted, her volume louder than she'd intended. Gretchen reared back, looking wounded. "I really need to get a start on my day now. I'll take care of the auction items, but I have a ton of things to get done, so I really need to cut this conversation short now."

Poppy waved her out the door and shut and locked it behind her. She was at her laptop before Gretchen's prim ballet flats hit the tiled lobby. A few taps on the cold trackpad, and the implication was clear.

Bennett had flipped over his trump card.

And he wasn't bluffing.

To: Detective Joseph Danielli
From: Savannah Cowley
<Thurs, March 14 at 2:55pm>

Dear Detective Danielli,

My name is Savannah Cowley, and I'm a parent at The Crofton
School. Gretchen Collins mentioned you'd spoken to her in
regard to your investigation to gather some information on
the family, and I wanted to drop you a note. I don't know if
this is something that is already on your radar, but have you
ever heard of an app called UrbanMyth? Off the record,
I would like to bring it to your attention, as I saw a few
disturbing posts on there that might be of interest to you.
(I am not a frequent user, by any means, but I happened to
come across the posts while I was seeking local restaurant
recommendations.) I don't want to repeat what was written
because I can't recall the exact quote and would not want to
be accused of giving false information to the police. (That
happened to someone on a Law & Order episode I watched
recently.) I will let you uncover it yourself and do with it what
you will. UrbanMyth isn't searchable, so it will require time to
sift through and find what I am referring to, but I'm sure you
have people to do that for you.

Best,
Savannah

Chapter Seventeen

POPPY

"It's so wonderful to see you, Ms. Ridley," the pencil-skirted twentysomething with a messy bun cooed as she led Poppy down the carpeted corridor, past ringing phones and the click-clacking of fingernails on keys. The offices of the private banking division of Lochwood Trust were located at Fifth Avenue and Fifty-ninth Street, in a reflective glass behemoth overlooking the flagship Apple Store in the heart of Midtown. It was a strategic location for an institution that catered to high-net-worth clients, but today Poppy wished the offices were a little more off the beaten track. Perhaps in an abandoned warehouse, three states over.

"I didn't realize you were coming in today," the secretary added, stretching her crimson-red lipsticked mouth into a smile.

You and me both, Poppy thought as they rounded the corner. Outside the floor-to-ceiling windows, the skyscraper that housed Harris's office came into view and it did not escape her that Harris was, quite literally, looming over her right now. She forced the thought out of her mind. There was already enough stress pressing down on her chest to snap her entire body in half. She didn't need to throw a possible run-in with Harris into the mix.

They stopped at the doorway of a corner office with a brass nameplate that read NICK PENNER, SENIOR VICE PRESIDENT, PRIVATE WEALTH MANAGEMENT, and the twentysomething held out her hands in a "ta-da" gesture that made Poppy wonder exactly how much caffeine this woman had consumed that morning.

"Poppy Ridley," the pasty-faced man with the receding hair-line exclaimed as he rose from his high-backed chair, greeting her with a hearty handshake. He gestured for her to sit, and Poppy lowered herself into the chrome-and-leather chair opposite his desk, gripping the armrests to conceal the tremble in her hands. "Always a pleasure to see you," he said, and Poppy smiled in a way that indicated that the pleasure was all hers.

But the pleasure was *not* all hers.

Being here ranked below cleaning toilets at Grand Central Ter-minal in things she wanted to be doing right now, but what choice did she have? After the warning shot Bennett had fired, the answer was clear.

None.

It hadn't been a challenge to find the post after Gretchen left, not when it sat atop the "most popular" column. *Confession time: I'm sleeping with my child's lacrosse coach—the one from Reflex on the UES. I think he's willing to end his marriage. Should I end mine?* It had racked up seventy-seven responses, mostly chastising the stupidity of giving the specifics. *It doesn't take Sherlock Holmes to figure this one out, honey. The Upper East Side is a small town. I'd delete this ASAP.* But it wasn't deleted. Not even when someone lifted the veil of anonymity and asked the question, *Bennett Stillman? Does this mean my son's lacrosse lessons will increase in price if he needs to pay alimony?*

The post was a direct communication from Bennett, as if he was a mobster sending a severed, bloodied ear in the mail to remind Poppy what was at stake. He was making it clear to her that he didn't have anything to lose.

And no one is more dangerous than a man with nothing to lose.

"Can I get you something to drink?" Nick asked, bringing her back to the present. He rubbed his palms together. "Juice, Coke, water, something stronger? My secretary can bring us in a glass of prosecco if you'd like." He gestured with his thumb to the door.

"I'd love a water," she said, her tongue suddenly feeling like sandpaper.

He yanked open the small refrigerator in the corner, peering in.

"It's not as cold as it should be," he said, resting a thick hand against the side of a bottle of Poland Spring before passing it across the desk and dropping himself back into his chair. "That's the problem with these mini fridges: these overloaded outlets can never give them enough juice."

Poppy bobbed her head as if she, too, had this issue with mini fridges and understood completely, hoping he didn't notice the tremble in her fingers as she accepted the proffered bottle.

"I'll buzz my secretary and get you some ice." He tapped the red button on his speaker phone, but Poppy waved him off.

"This is fine, Nick. Really."

"Never mind, Jess," he bellowed into the speaker before hitting the button again and returning his attention to Poppy.

"Now, how can I be of assistance to you today?" he asked, gripping his hands together and planting his forearms on the desk, his head slightly bowed in deference. The unabashed eagerness in his posture reminded Poppy of her personal shopper, the one who routinely invited her to come in after hours because he knew Poppy couldn't stand the Midwestern tourists shouting things like "Mom, this dress is over *five thousand* dollars!" while she was trying to shop. It wasn't lost on Poppy that most people in her orbit were willing to go above and beyond what was expected in order to please her. As they should. Because here was the thing about this level of wealth—she made those around her wealthier too. Not by donating money to them (although she was a generous philanthropist), but simply by being a client. That personal shopper kept the store open for her because he earned thousands of dollars in commission every time Poppy entered. And there was no doubt that the Ridley account was the reason Nick had four "Private Wealth Manager of the Year" awards lined up; nor was there any doubt that it had paid for the house Nick and his wife were posing in front of in the framed photo displayed prominently on his desk. Poppy had never been one to abuse her power per se. Not like her friend who'd forced her real estate broker to miss his brother's wedding because she didn't want him leaving the city while their townhouse was on the market. "It's not like I asked him to *murder* his brother," she'd said, cackling as the waiter had topped off her wine. "Although he probably would've done that too if we'd asked him, given how we've lined his pockets over the years." No, Poppy wasn't *that* bad. But she was well aware that very little was off the table when the price was right.

A wild thought flew through her mind. *What would Nick say?* Her eyes drifted to the edge of the folded yellow sticky note peeking out of the side pocket of her purse, the one with Bennett's account number on it. What would he say if she leaned forward and, in a voice as clear as the faux crystal of his "Private Wealth Manager of the Year" awards, said, *Well, Nick. I'll tell you exactly how you can be of assistance to me. I said earlier that I'd love a water, but what I'd really love is if you would disappear someone for me.* With Nick's soft frame and round cheeks, he wasn't the likeliest candidate to be a hitman, but given that most of his clients probably earned their money in ways that fell into gray areas of the law, chances were high he knew someone. It wasn't the most outrageous of possibilities. She could pay someone to take Bennett to the roof of a building. A push. A shove. It would be so easy. And cheaper than paying Bennett's blood money.

Not to mention, permanent.

The piercing ring of the phone on Nick's desk severed her thoughts, and Nick jabbed a finger at the keypad, silencing the ringer. She twisted off the cap of her bottle of Poland Spring and took a long swallow, hoping to lubricate her desert-dry mouth.

"I'd like to move some money around," she said, infusing her voice with a coolness she wasn't feeling. She proceeded to give him instructions for three different money transfers in order to avoid suspicion. Nick didn't appear to be the type to question his client's spending habits, but Poppy wasn't taking chances. Not anymore.

Nick peered down at the account numbers on the paper she'd slid across the desk and rested a hand on his mouse. "Now, which account will we be doing the transfer from?" he asked, adjusting the frameless glasses on his nose, squinting at the screen, and hammering a thick index finger on the mouse.

Click. Click. Click.

The sound was menacing, like the relentless tick of a time bomb.

Poppy cleared her throat. "My personal account, please." It was an account Harris wasn't aware she had. She'd set it up at the advice of her mother. *You should always have a bank account that your husband has no knowledge of. You don't need him peeking over your shoulder when you're feeling in the mood for spending.* Poppy had socked away around three million dollars in her private account years ago, but the truth was she hadn't felt the need to make a single withdrawal. Harris couldn't have cared less what she spent money on so long as she didn't bother him with the details. As long as the houses were properly maintained, the strategic dinner parties and events were planned, and the aesthetics of their lives exceeded that of his peers, he didn't ask questions.

Harris wasn't perfect. God knows. But there were women who would kill to be married to him. Poppy could be replaced faster than a click of that mouse.

"The last four digits of the account are 4987," she said, twisting the diamond engagement ring on her finger.

Nick nodded, not taking his eyes off the screen. The wrinkles in his forehead deepened and two small red patches bloomed on the apples of his cheeks.

Poppy examined his face, noting beads of sweat springing up on his top lip. Did he suspect something was amiss? Maybe Harris had given him strict orders to flag any large transaction Poppy made. It would explain why Harris had never questioned her about her spending before.

No. Harris had far too little time to get involved in the day-to-day minutiae of Poppy's life. And she always had the charitable donation alibi to fall back on. Sure, a $750,000 donation would be unusual, but it wouldn't even be close to their largest charitable donation. That was reserved for Harvard, Harris's alma mater. Ten million dollars, paid in five installments, across five years. "We'll call it insurance money," Harris had joked. "Because I get the feeling Henry's brain isn't going to open any doors for him."

Poppy slid her phone from her purse and checked the time. Eleven-fifteen. Bennett would be at her apartment in forty-five minutes. Her knee started to bounce. "Is this going to take much longer?"

Nick ran a hand across the shiny bald spot on the back of his head, unruffled. "I should have you out of here in a few minutes, but it could take up to an hour for the wires to hit."

"That's fine as long as I have confirmation it was sent." She slid her purse onto her lap, readying herself to leave, as her phone vibrated against her thigh. She scrambled to read the message.

I realized I have one more auction item to drop off today—oops! I'll swing by in an hour.

"Shit," Poppy hissed under her breath.

I'm at a lunch in Midtown and won't be home until late afternoon. Poppy typed, then paused. Reevaluating, she added *Come by at 1pm tomorrow instead and we can combine it with a boozy lunch. Have some time to chat!* Poppy knew the offer would be catnip for Gretchen and would throw her off the scent. She slid the phone back into her purse, suppressing a bubble of unease. The timing of the message was almost *too* fortuitous. Maybe Gretchen had caught a flash of panic on Poppy's face, however brief, in response to Bennett's name. It was surprising, given Gretchen's talent for collecting secrets, that Poppy hadn't heard about Bennett's grift years ago. Maybe Gretchen was losing her touch.

Either that or Bennett really was true to his word. Pay the money, keep the secret.

"Okay, let me grab a couple signatures from you," Nick said, clapping his hands together, as Poppy's phone began to vibrate with an incoming call. She narrowed her eyes, reading the name of the caller on the screen.

Her chest tightened. *For fuck's sake, what now?*

Holding up an index finger, she flashed a tight smile. "I need to take this."

Chapter Eighteen

HEATHER

HEATHER PAUSED ON the corner of Seventy-ninth Street and Fifth Avenue, set down the shopping bag, and massaged the angry red indentations on the palm of her right hand. She hadn't expected this stupid quilt to be so heavy. Maybe she should've hopped into an Uber twenty blocks ago, but once she'd made the decision to walk up from Midtown to get her exercise for the day, she was committed.

And unlike *some* people, Heather *honored* her commitments.

She peeked inside the bag, ensuring every corner of the quilt was safely ensconced. Being on the Crofton Quilt Committee had to be her most undesirable volunteer position to date. Every year, the committee arranged for each of the eighth-grade students to decorate a square of fabric to be sewn into a custom quilt, hand-stitched in the Garment District. The quilt was always the most sought-after auction item at the benefit, fetching well into six figures, because every private school parent knew that there is no better way to establish yourself atop the financial hierarchy than to outbid your peers for an item that is essentially worthless. "Priceless" the auction catalog asserted without satire. Heather, of course, wouldn't be in the running to win the quilt, but she damn well hoped that all the grunt work she'd put into creating the priceless item would count for something.

She tented a hand over her eyes, squinting at the numbers on the awning down the block, gathering her nerve. Even before Lucky Cocktails, she was familiar with the location of Poppy's palazzo-style apartment building, having detoured there a number of times to lustfully sneak a peek into the gleaming, white-glove-manned lobby. Today, though, she wouldn't be on the outside looking in. Hand-delivering an important auction item gave her a legitimate reason not only to enter the building, but also to go up to Poppy's palatial penthouse. And after what Heather had seen on Caroline's phone in the gym, she found herself in an unfamiliar position: a position of power. Not that Poppy would recognize it. Still, Heather relished it. It was like being gifted a set of antique china. She wasn't sure she would ever have an opportunity to *use* it, but it was reassuring to have in the cupboard should she ever need to pull it out.

Heather hoisted the bag, changing hands, and made her way down the sidewalk, doing her best not to think about what had transpired the last time she was inside Poppy's opulent living space. She was positive her behavior was not as bad as Oliver had made it out to be. "Mortifying" was the word he'd used to describe it. Honestly, her husband could be a tad out of touch with reality sometimes. If only she could say to Oliver that while he might have been a little embarrassed, it wasn't as if Heather had been caught canoodling in the back seat with another Crofton parent. *That* would certainly fall under the "put it in perspective" advice Oliver loved to dish out.

"Good morning," a doorman with jet-black hair and a green tailored uniform called out as Heather pivoted toward the entrance. "Almost afternoon!" he corrected himself, looking at his watch, smiling a toothy grin.

"I'm here to see Poppy Ridley," Heather said, throwing her shoulders back, hoping to make it clear she was a peer rather than a delivery person—despite her sweaty forehead and overstuffed shopping bag.

"Fernando at the desk can assist you," he replied, pulling open the glass door and gesturing her inside.

As Heather entered the lobby, her senses were hit with the pleasant smell of freshly washed linens, and she wondered if the scent was pumped into the expansive space via the vents. Even the air was better in these buildings, she marveled, as her phone vibrated in her purse. She stepped to the side, avoiding the curious stare of the man with the chiseled features she assumed was Fernando, and paused to read the text.

I'll take $70,000, but I need the money by next week.

Heather's nostrils flared with a sudden intake of breath, and she shot a look over her shoulder, ensuring no one was close enough to see her screen. There hadn't been any contact since the text Heather had sent while getting ready for Lucky Cocktails, and she'd been under the assumption that the silence was akin to acceptance. Apparently not.

I need more time than that, she fired back with a shaky thumb.

The response was almost instantaneous. *Well, I need $70,000 by next week.*

Heather's fingers stiffened around the phone. How the hell was she supposed to come up with that amount of money by next week without rousing Oliver's attention?

She shook her head, resigned. She would find a way. She had to.

Fine, she pecked back bitterly and dropped the phone into her purse. Pinching the bridge of her nose, she fought a sudden wave of dizziness that threatened to overwhelm her.

"Can I help you, ma'am?" Fernando inquired from behind the desk, watching her with measuring eyes.

Heather cleared her throat and strode to the desk. "Yes, thank you. Um. I'm here to see Poppy Ridley. She's not expecting me. . . . Well, no, she *is* expecting me, actually." Heather wiped a bead of sweat from her forehead and continued babbling. "I have an important delivery to give her that she *is* expecting, but she might not be expecting it right at this moment." Heather tucked a strand of hair behind her ear, trying to regain her composure.

So much for her power position.

That text had completely thrown her off her game.

"Ms. Ridley isn't home right now, ma'am," he replied coolly. "But you're welcome to leave it with me, and I'll see that she gets it." He stepped out from behind the desk to relieve her of her wares, extending a muscled arm.

Heather yanked the bag closer to her body. "I'd really rather deliver it myself," she snapped, surprising herself. Ordinarily, she would have reluctantly handed over the bag, disappointed not to be getting the credit for the delivery. Today, though, it felt critical to show her face, if only to prove she wasn't in hiding after what had happened at Lucky Cocktails.

If there was anyone who *should* be in hiding, it was Poppy and Bennett. Not Heather.

Heather straightened her spine, ignoring Fernando's barely concealed eye roll.

"No problem at all," he said with a brusque nod. "Maybe you can arrange with Ms. Ridley a good time to come back then?"

Heather nodded, readjusting the bag on her sore hand. But she knew what Poppy's response would be if Heather tried to coordinate a face-to-face drop-off. She'd casually insist Heather leave it with the doorman. That is, if Poppy deemed Heather worthy of any response at all.

Heather bit her lip, checking her watch: 11:30 A.M. She didn't need to be anywhere for another hour. Her eyes drifted to the pristine sitting area in the corner of the lobby.

"I have some time," she said. "I think I'll wait."

Chapter Nineteen

POPPY

Poppy shifted her weight on the leather loveseat and checked her watch. Half past twelve. She was officially thirty minutes late to meet Bennett. She drummed her fingers on the armrest. *Where the hell is this man?*

"Dr. Krause will be with you in a minute," the thin-lipped assistant had assured her in a no-nonsense tone as she'd escorted Poppy into the headmaster's office. Her expression was tight, bordering on grim, and Poppy wondered if it reflected her knowledge of the reason for this meeting or if it was simply the woman's default countenance.

It'd better be the latter.

"No problem at all," Poppy had replied, forcing her lips into an acquiescent smile.

But it *was* a problem. It was a big fucking problem. And Poppy could do nothing about it. It was a foreign feeling for her, this feeling of utter powerlessness. It was as if she'd been taken hostage. First by Bennett and now by Dr. Krause, who'd insisted she come to the school ASAP to discuss what he'd termed "an unfortunate incident." "It really is a matter that needs to be discussed in person," he'd explained in an ominous tone after she'd made the rational suggestion to discuss it over the phone. "I'd like at least one parent to come. If you're not available, perhaps Mr. Ridley can come in." It took everything Poppy had to keep herself from smashing her iPhone against the brass nameplate outside Nick's office door. But Krause held Henry's future in his sweaty little palm, so like a captured enemy soldier, she fell into line. She bid Nick goodbye (with confirmation of the wire transfer in hand), ducked into the waiting Escalade, and fired off one quick text to ensure Bennett wasn't left hanging.

God forbid he thought he was stood up and started Paul Revereing their affair all over the Upper East Side.

Poppy clasped her hands on her lap now and twiddled her thumbs. She'd been sitting in this stifling office for twenty minutes. Her stomach felt like a pressure cooker poised to explode. She couldn't remember the last time she'd been kept waiting this long for anything. Who else in this city but the headmaster of an elite private school could elicit the type of deference usually reserved for a head of state or a drug lord?

No one.

Fishing her phone out of the side pocket of her purse, she checked the screen for the third time in the last forty-five seconds. No new messages.

"Poppy Ridley," Dr. Krause said, breezing into the office, a red-faced Henry trailing behind him. Poppy dropped the phone back into her purse and leaned forward, readying herself to stand, but he waved her off. "Please. No need to get up."

The sides of Poppy's lips felt like they had weights pulling them down, but she lifted them into a smile and extended a hand to shake his. Her eyes shifted to Henry, trying to catch his, but his focus remained firmly fixed on his feet, as he shuffled to the love-seat and plopped down beside her with such force that her body bounced. Dropping a hand to brace herself, her pinky grazed the side of Henry's palm. He snapped it away, raking his fingers through his thick blond hair.

Dr. Krause took his place in the upholstered chair across from them, resting his palms on his knees. He had a practiced sympathetic look on his face, like a funeral director who had passed over a brochure with color options for a loved one's casket. "I never like to ask parents to come to my office in the middle of the school day," he started. "I'm sure the timing wasn't great."

Poppy gritted her teeth. *You have no fucking idea.*

"Unfortunately, Henry's actions have backed us into a corner."

Keeping her lips compressed, she fought the urge to remind him that the Ridley family's annual donation helped pay for that penthouse he and his family currently occupied, and *that* should help him find his way out of whatever corner he *thought* he'd been backed into.

Thankfully, there was a small drop of self-control remaining in her reservoir.

Dr. Krause touched the tips of his fingers together, flexed them a few times. The room fell silent, save for the ticks from the grandfather clock in the corner of his office. *Tick. Tick. Tick.* A constant reminder that, somewhere, Bennett was a time bomb ready to blow.

Hurry the hell up! she wanted to scream.

Finally, he spoke. "Henry was in Latin class with Mr. Garza, and from what I understand, he was reaching into his blazer pocket when this fell out and rolled across the floor." Dr. Krause held up an object, waved it around, as if he were a prosecutor introducing a particularly damning piece of evidence.

Poppy narrowed her eyes. Dr. Krause's fingers were wrapped around a shiny cobalt-blue vape. Irritation surged on her skin.

This? This is what he defines as an "unfortunate incident"?

She struggled to hold her face still.

He lowered his hand, tucking the vape into the inside pocket of his blazer. "We have certain expectations for our students," Dr. Krause continued earnestly, but a vibration coming from her purse interrupted Poppy's focus. The buzz of a new text. She tucked her hands in between her crossed legs to keep from clawing the phone out of her bag. Dr. Krause was still speaking—something about the five building blocks—but Poppy couldn't make out the words over the alarm bells sounding in her head. *Is Bennett texting? Is he demanding an immediate response? Has Gretchen wormed her way into this? Oh god, is she at the apartment?*

The sound of a door slamming outside the office shook Poppy's focus back to Dr. Krause.

"You've probably heard there was a somewhat public incident, where another student was accused of dealing drugs at Crofton. It rattled some of the parents." Krause's voice trailed up at the end, and Poppy gave a nod of acknowledgment. "So, student drug use has become a bit of a"—he paused, tapped his prayer hands against his chin—"hot-button topic lately. One I had to assure the Parents' Association we were taking aggressive steps to address. And one of those steps was a commitment to enforcing our rules here on campus."

Poppy nodded, trying to keep her eyes firmly locked on Dr. Krause, but she could feel them skittering to the clock on the wall. She felt her lack of control at the edges of her fingernails.

"So, Henry being caught with drug paraphernalia on campus has put us in a tricky spot."

Poppy seized her opportunity to move the conversation along. "I completely understand, and am so disappointed Henry did this," she said in as stern a tone as her impatience would allow. She swung her gaze to Henry, who, to his credit, looked like a remorseful puppy who had chewed a pair of her favorite shoes. "That certainly isn't anything we tolerate at home, and I really appreciate you bringing this to my attention."

Dr. Krause took a deep breath through his nose, blew it out slowly. Poppy was beginning to think every move this man made was in slow motion. "As the rule stands, anyone caught with drug paraphernalia *on campus* is subject to an immediate suspension."

Her blinking sped up.

"Now, because you and your husband have been such generous patrons of the school, I thought it would be best if we took a different approach. Especially since Henry will be applying to boarding school this year . . ."

"I appreciate you taking that into consideration," Poppy said, filling the charged silence. She snuck another peek at the clock on the wall to the left of Dr. Krause's head. This conversation had already eaten up thirty whole minutes. She rested a hand on her knee to keep it from bouncing. If she could've written a six-figure check right then and called it a day she would've. But discretion was key here.

"If Henry tells me that he never intended to *use* the vape, and he had it in his pocket because . . ." He waved his fingers as though pulling an idea from the air. "Maybe he found it on the sidewalk on the way to school and picked it up, not aware of what it was. If that were the case, we of course wouldn't need to resort to suspension." He raised his eyebrows, indicating that Poppy and Henry were now both in on the plan. "Which is why I needed to have you come in today. It's school policy that, when it involves matters that could involve suspension, we don't question students without a parent present."

The side of Poppy's purse vibrated again. Was it her imagination or did the buzz seem more agitated this time?

Krause slid his hand into his pocket, pulled out the vape, and pointed it at Henry. "Henry, did you intend to use this?"

Poppy held her breath.

Henry gave a slow shake of his head. "I . . . I found it on the way to school," he said, his voice wobbling. "And I . . . I didn't want any of the younger kids to pick it up. I was going to throw it out."

Dr. Krause smiled like a proud parent and tossed the vape into a trash can beside his desk. The clank it made against the metal at the bottom made Henry's shoulders jump. "I don't see the need for any further action, given the circumstances," he said. Then he clapped his hands together, letting them all know that the meeting was adjourned. Poppy and Henry were out of the office before Krause sat back down at his desk.

"I can explain, Mom," Henry mumbled, hustling to keep up with her long, angry strides.

"Goddammit, Henry, not a word," she fumed. A gray-haired woman clutching a pile of manila folders eyed them pointedly from behind her glasses as she passed. Poppy snuck a glance over her shoulder, as the nosy woman disappeared behind a door.

"Henry," she whisper-hissed, shooting another look behind her to ensure no one was within earshot before pulling him into a small hallway that—based on the marked doorway a few feet from them—led to the men's bathroom. "I told you to distance yourself from that Doubles drama, and then you go and bring the exact vape pen from the Instagram photo to *school*? What the hell were you thinking?"

From the moment Poppy laid eyes on the now infamous photo, she'd known Henry was the person sitting beside Violet. The only part of him visible was the underside of his left forearm, outstretched to receive the vape, but one look at Henry's arm dangled over his bed that morning, tattooed in purple ink with the telltale loopy handwriting of a girl named Skylar, and Poppy knew it was a match. She'd forced Henry to scrub off every identifying mark, rubbing until his skin turned pink, ensuring he couldn't be identified. Maybe it was overkill, but with boarding school applications on the line, it was important to keep Henry's hands clean. Literally.

"It's bad enough you were vaping when the admissions director was somewhere in the club, but to go and risk—"

"Mom," Henry groaned, cutting her off. "The admissions director wasn't even *there*. So, you can stop freaking out about that."

Poppy closed her eyes, shook her head. "You might not have seen her, but she was—"

"Mom," he cut her off again, more forcefully this time. "I know she wasn't there because *I'm* the only reason you thought she would be."

Poppy blinked at him, not computing.

He let out a long sigh, pushed a frustrated hand through his mop of hair. "I wrote that post on UrbanMyth about the admissions director coming to the Doubles dance so you would let me go to the dance instead of the tutor."

She shook her head, refusing to process what he was saying. It was as if he were insisting the world was flat when she knew it was round.

"It was Charlotte's idea. She knew all the parents would fall for it because she said you guys all read that stupid site, like, obsessively."

Poppy's mouth dropped open.

"But what I'm *trying* to tell you is I didn't have anything to do with taking that photo or putting it on Instagram or spreading the rumors about Violet Quinn. I mean, I know Charlotte had her phone because she made me hide it in the inside pocket of my blazer to sneak it in because she wanted to make a TikTok inside Doubles. And then we were playing around, and she dared me to get Violet to take a puff from my vape. But I had no idea she was going to take a picture and post it. I swear." He held up his hand, palm up.

This was why Gretchen kept digging, Poppy realized. She was trying to take Poppy's temperature, to feel out if Poppy had caught wind of anything from Henry. Likely, she wanted to ensure they were on the same page. Whatever page that was.

"Why would Charlotte set you up like that?"

Before Henry could answer, a toilet flushed, and they both turned their attention to the bathroom door. A goateed man in a janitor's shirt emerged, nodded a greeting in their direction, and disappeared around the corner.

"Aren't you listening, Mom?" Henry said after the man was out of earshot. "She wasn't setting *me* up. She was setting Violet up. I asked her why, and she said I wouldn't understand because her family can't *buy* her way in like we can."

Poppy raised her eyes to the ceiling. "Jesus Christ," she muttered. Leave it to the daughter of Gretchen to do something so diabolical. She had more questions, but now was not the time to ruminate on them. "I need to go, Henry." She gripped the strap of her purse. "Go back to class and stay out of trouble." As if on cue, her phone vibrated from the side pocket, an ominous reminder of what was waiting for her back home.

Striding toward the exit, Poppy slid the phone out and checked the screen. Three new text messages were waiting for her. The first one was from Gretchen. *Tomorrow sounds perfect! See you at one!* The second one was from Harris. *Why the hell do I have a voicemail from Henry's school?*

Her fingers tensed around the edges of her case as she read the third one. It was from Bennett. She blinked anxiously at the screen, reading it once, twice, three times as her brain scrabbled to process the words. The message was written in all caps, which made it feel like he was shouting it at her.

I WAS WAITING OUTSIDE OF YOUR BUILDING AT THE AGREED TIME AND I DO NOT WAIT FOR ANYONE!

Chapter Twenty

NORAH

"Say something, Mom." Norah hugged the throw pillow in her lap closer, studying her mother's wrinkled features, trying to gauge her reaction.

Lunch with her mother was a weekly tradition and one Norah usually looked forward to. When both of her parents lost their ability to drive, Norah had hired a driver to come three times a week, allowing them to retain the independence to do their own grocery shopping, see a movie, or attend doctors' appointments without the challenges that came with public transportation or taxis. On Sundays, the driver would bring her mother into the city for a mother-daughter lunch at Norah's apartment. Caroline would join them most days, but this afternoon Norah had strategically sent her and a friend to an exhibit at the Guggenheim for an art history project they were working on at school. Norah needed time alone with her mother to break the news about Bennett. This, she realized, was the hardest part about her impending divorce: the potential that it would upset her parents. If she could've put off telling her, she would've, but it had been almost a week since she'd kicked Bennett out, almost a week with him out of her life, and the odds of getting through this lunch without her mother catching on that something was wrong were slim. Her mother had always had polygraph-like capabilities when it came to discerning whether Norah was being honest.

Norah had kept the conversation to the weather ("Yes, the rain today is terrible") as she'd helped her mother out of the black sedan and guided her up to the apartment and into the living room, arranging her mother's sun-spotted hands on Norah's shoulder to bear her weight as she eased her onto the couch. Then she'd sat gingerly beside her and, without any preamble because her mother was the queen of "cut to the chase," she said, "I hope this isn't too hard on you, Mom, but Bennett and I are getting a divorce."

After what felt like five hours, but was probably only five seconds, her mom finally spoke. "Divorce?" Her wrinkled lips were pursed.

Norah nodded. Her mother's eyes moistened, and her shaky hand reached over, took Norah's hand, and clutched it fervently. Norah braced herself.

"Norah, honey, this was one time in my life that I did *not* want to be right, but I *knew* that man would never be faithful. From the first time we all had dinner together. Do you remember?" Her soft, watery blue eyes searched Norah's.

"I remember the dinner, Mom," Norah said slowly, unsure where this was going. Norah hadn't mentioned Bennett's infidelity, which only served to prove that her mother was capable of reading Norah like a picture book.

"Well, when the dessert menu came, he couldn't make up his mind, so he ordered both the cheesecake and the crème brûlée. That was the proof." She lifted a slender index finger, nodded as if agreeing with herself. "If a grown man can't commit to a dessert, how can he be trusted to fully commit to a marriage?"

Norah laughed and tossed the throw pillow off her lap, scooching close enough to her mom to put her arm around her. The smell of her mother—a mix of floral-scented lotion and burnt coffee—was better than therapy. Now that she thought about it, she could remember her mother being out of sorts during the dinner when she'd introduced Bennett. She should've been paying more attention to Bennett's dessert choices. She should've been paying more attention to a lot of things.

"It was a gut feeling, but I pushed it away. I'm so angry at myself for not telling you what I thought." The side of her thin lips quivered.

"No, Mom." Norah shook her head vehemently. "This is nobody's fault but Bennett's."

Her mother let out a resigned huff. "Well, I know someone who could break both of his arms for you."

"Mom!"

"I'm serious," she said, sounding it.

Norah's phone vibrated on the coffee table, and she leaned forward to see who was calling.

"Let me grab this," she said, reluctantly, swiping the phone off the table and standing up. "Hold that thought."

"Oh, I will."

"No, I mean, *don't* hold that thought," Norah said with a chuckle, waving a scolding finger. "Never mind, I'll be right back."

Norah headed into her bedroom, pulled her earbud case out of the pocket of her jeans, and popped one in each ear, steeling herself.

The first call had come in at nine this morning, as she and Caroline were digging into their blueberry pancakes. Her phone was on the far side of the counter, and Norah was going to let it go to voicemail, but she got up to check in case it was her mother. The name Waverley Stillman flashed and managed to appear aggressive even on a tiny screen. Norah could imagine accepting the call and hearing Waverley spout off gems like "My son has always been too good for you" or "He's better off without you." So, she'd sent it to voicemail and gone back to her breakfast. She'd ignored the next call too. And the next. But Waverley wasn't the type to be stymied by an unanswered call (or five), and Norah didn't want her time with her mom to be repeatedly interrupted by a ringing phone, so it was time to take her lumps.

She pressed her finger to the green circle on the screen, answering the call.

Waverley didn't bother waiting for Norah to say hello before firing questions. "Where's Bennett? What's happened?" Waverley demanded in the tone of someone summoned to the ER after the accident of a loved one.

Norah, accustomed to her mother-in-law's hysterics, leaned against the kitchen counter, raising her eyes to the ceiling. With Waverley, it was impossible to determine the severity of the affront du jour based on her tone: it could be that someone had the audacity to add croutons to her salad or that a masked gunman had pistol-whipped her and made off with her purse. Both scenarios would give rise to equal levels of indignation.

"Bennett isn't here, Waverley," she answered flatly, hoping to neutralize her. "I don't know where he is."

"Well, I know he's not *there*. Because he's supposed to be *here*. It's my birthday for heaven's sake. And he is officially late."

Norah bowed her head and squeezed the bridge of her nose. Waverley's birthday was a national holiday in the Stillman home. Every year she invited a hundred of her closest friends for an "intimate" birthday party at their home in Tuxedo, waving her hand in faux embarrassment and uttering lines like "You didn't need to do all this." The fact that it had fallen off her radar was a testament to just how distracted Norah was. She wouldn't have attended, of course, but she would've taken a moment to feel gratitude that she was no longer obligated to attend.

"Waverley, I'm sorry about Bennett missing your birthday, but there's been a lot going on. Bennett and I . . ." She paused, unsure of how she wanted to fill in the rest of the sentence. Had Bennett really not informed his parents of what had happened? She'd assumed it would be Bennett's first call. And Norah would've bet her bank account that Waverley had a divorce lawyer on speed dial to ensure her family fortune was safe from Norah's grubby hands.

"Bennett hasn't been home all week, Waverley." She expelled a sigh of frustration. "Not since Monday." Leave it to Bennett to make her do all the heavy lifting, even in the end. "I don't know where he is, but I'm sure you can reach him on his phone."

The sharp edge of silence on the other end of the line was enough to slice your jugular.

"Bennett hasn't been home all week? And you're not *worried* that you haven't seen your husband, *my son,* all week?"

"No, I'm not, but this is really something the two of you need to talk about. Why don't you—"

"I've called him!" she cried. "I've *been* calling him. I must've left twenty voicemails. And now he isn't at my party." She gave an indignant sniff. "Something must be terribly wrong. Bennett would *never* stand me up. Not on my birthday. Never."

In Waverley's defense, it was out of character. Bennett had always followed the decrees of his mother with the type of blind faith usually reserved for the Pope. In the past, Norah had considered his commitment to his family admirable, but now she saw this type of behavior for what it was: shockingly pathetic.

It was amazing, the clarity that came with removing the rose-colored glasses.

But Waverley was a wizard when it came to convincing other people to do her dirty work, her sleights of hand so quick that before Norah knew what was happening, she'd agreed to leave her dry, warm apartment and venture into the soggy afternoon to track down Bennett at Reflex and pass along the message that he needed to call his worried mother ASAP.

After finishing lunch with her mom and helping her into the back seat of the car, Norah waved goodbye and ventured down the sidewalk. Cinching the belt of her raincoat tight, she cursed the fact that she'd forgotten her umbrella. The drizzle that had started as a fine mist was thickening into rain now. She picked up the pace, dashing across Park Avenue, keeping her eyes on the crosswalk sign with the large orange numbers decreasing from seven to zero, avoiding a murky-looking puddle as she stepped up onto the curb. A gray-suited man on the corner struggled with his umbrella before the wind caught it, ripping the fabric from the spokes. Norah took shelter under a green awning as the man jammed the skeleton of his umbrella into the trash. *Why the hell did I agree to this?* she wondered sourly as her phone vibrated deep in her coat pocket. She fished it out with a wet hand. Beads of water dripped from her hood onto the screen. She wiped them away and played the message, holding on to the slim hope that Waverley had located Bennett. Instead, it was Waverley reminding Norah exactly how many people she had at her house right now, eager to see Bennett. Seventy-seven apparently.

Norah shoved her phone and her hands in her coat pockets and jogged down the damp sidewalk, ignoring the swells of water splattering her ankles. By the time she pulled open the door of Reflex, her jeans were soaked through up to her knees and her well of patience was dry. She mentally groaned when she saw who was manning the reception desk. It was Brinley, the employee who greeted anyone who walked through the door with the annoyed expression of a woman who'd been interrupted while taking a shower. "Brinley has the customer service skills of a damp dish-cloth," she remembered warning Bennett. But Brinley had been blessed with pin-straight blond hair and cheekbones sharp enough to double as weapons which, apparently, was enough to qualify her to greet customers, in Bennett's eyes.

Another red flag. She'd ignored them before. Now she couldn't unsee them.

"Hi, Brinley." Norah infused her voice with as much friendliness as she could muster. "Is Bennett here?"

"Nah, Bennett hasn't been in all week," Brinley answered without lifting her eyes from her phone. "He's missed a ton of appointments too. Like, a ton. I've got a million messages from angry parents."

"Did he . . . Did he give a reason?" Norah asked, ignoring the awkwardness that came with looking for answers a wife should already have. "I mean, did he tell you why he's missed so much work?"

Brinley shrugged her pointy shoulders. "Maybe he lost his phone and doesn't have his schedule. He hasn't been answering any messages, so that would make sense."

"I'm just going to take a quick look in his office," Norah said, but Brinley was already bored with her and had returned her attention to her phone. Norah dug her fingernails into her palms, arms swinging, as she headed to the back. Bennett could be stationed behind his desk, and Brinley wouldn't have a clue. But when she turned the knob and swung the door open, Bennett was nowhere to be found. Norah's forehead wrinkled as she inspected the half-empty Starbucks cup on the desk, the remnants of coffee crystalized on the spout of the lid. A wave of unease gathered in her stomach as her eyes swept the unoccupied space, but quickly it ebbed. Bennett had specifically told Norah he would make her regret kicking him out, and now it was glaringly obvious what he was doing. He was intentionally running the business—the business they were fifty-fifty partners in—into the ground out of spite. And, as a bonus, forcing her to be the one to deal with his insufferable mother.

Norah stomped back to the front, low-frequency anger pulsing with every heartbeat.

"When you see Bennett, can you tell him to call his mother?" she called out, trying to suppress her resentment. Brinley lifted her gaze, and Norah swore she saw what looked like a glint of gratification, but just as quickly her expression reverted to barely concealed impatience. Brinley lifted an obnoxious thumbs-up in response as Norah yanked open the glass door. Hiking the damp hood over her head, she scurried down Third Avenue to a canopy for shelter. Bracing herself, she dialed Waverley's number.

"Are you serious?" Waverley screeched after Norah relayed what Brinley had said. "He hasn't been to work all *week,* and he hasn't been home?"

"Waverley." She let out a beleaguered sigh. "When Bennett left the apartment on Monday we both agreed he wouldn't be coming back, so he's probably left the city. We didn't end on good terms, so I'm not expecting to hear from him anytime soon."

There was a freshly sharpened edge to her mother-in-law's voice when she spoke. "Something is *wrong,* Norah. I can feel it in my bones. A mother knows these things." Norah heard rustling on the other end of the line. "Francis!" Waverley called loud enough that Norah had to pull the phone away from her ear. "We need to call the police." Norah heard more muffled noises in the background before Waverley came on again. "Francis is on the phone with our local police. We're reporting Bennett missing. Something *you* should've done a week ago."

And then the line went dead.

Norah stared down at her phone. A prickle of worry traveled up her spine, but she shrugged it away. Bennett was a master manipulator. That was obvious now. She stuffed her phone back into her pocket and pulled her hood up over her head. Looking both ways, she headed back in the direction of her apartment.

Later, after Norah had explained to the professionally patient police officer on the other end of the line that yes, her mother-in-law was in her right mind and wasn't in need of a long-term care facility, but no, Norah was not concerned about her husband's whereabouts, one part of their conversation kept playing on a loop in her head. "I have to be honest," the police officer's deep voice had said from the other end of the line. "This sounds to me like a man who's decided to take a little time away from his overbearing mother. It's not a crime for an adult to walk away from their life for a little while. You'd be surprised how often it happens. But Ms. Stillman has indicated that he might be in danger, so we're going to need to consider this a missing person case." Norah hadn't argued. Why would she? If Waverley wanted to turn this into a dramatic, embarrassing waste of police resources then that was her prerogative.

But no matter how many times she tossed and turned in her bed that night and employed the 4-7-8 breathing technique, she couldn't silence the voice in the back of her head—the one that told her she hadn't been one hundred percent honest when she'd answered the police officer's final question.

"There isn't anybody out there who might want to hurt your husband, is there?"

Chapter Twenty-one

POPPY

POPPY RAN THE tip of her index finger down the cold trackpad, scrutinizing each post on UrbanMyth as if she were a code breaker in World War II. She was seated in the kitchen with her laptop stationed on the table in front of her, debating whether she should pour herself something stronger than green tea. But it wasn't even ten in the morning.

One week. That was how long it had been since she'd wired the money to Bennett. True to his text, he had not been waiting for her when she'd returned home from her ill-timed meeting with Krause. She'd held on to a kernel of hope that he'd left behind some sort of proof the video had been deleted. A printout of a screenshot perhaps. She'd entered the lobby, asked the doorman in as breezy a tone as her wobbly voice would allow whether any packages had arrived for her. He'd double-checked. Nothing.

No packages. No texts. No phone calls. No drop-ins. No word from Bennett.

The video could still be sitting in Bennett's iCloud. Like a grenade with the pin yanked out.

Any moment. *Boom*.

It was a terrible feeling knowing your life could implode without warning. It was enough to make a person unravel. A few days ago, she'd gone to Reflex in an attempt to catch Bennett at work. It was a risk, speaking to him in public, but what choice did she have? He wasn't answering his phone, and she couldn't add another text to the mountain of evidence he already had against her. "I think he's sick," the standoffish receptionist had informed her, but Poppy could have sworn she saw a glimmer of judgment when her eyes ran the length of Poppy's body. Bennett had probably spread lies about her to his entire staff, painted her as unhinged. Maybe he had even posted a photo of her in the back room, warning, "If you see this mom, do not engage." Worse, Poppy *felt* deranged. She'd even purchased a prepaid phone so that he wouldn't be able to screen her number, called him a few times. Sent texts. Nothing. That all-caps text from him was their last communication. Searching UrbanMyth now was her last-ditch effort.

Maybe it was grasping at straws, but straws were all she had left.

She chewed at a loose piece of skin on her lip and scrolled down the post she'd entered a half hour ago. *I need to contact the person blackmailing me. Any suggestions?* It was a desperate smoke signal, one that had been largely ignored. There were three useless responses, all questioning her sobriety. She let out a defeated sigh and took a sip of tea, which was now room temperature. *Screw it,* she thought, slamming her mug down on the table. Her fingers hammered on the keyboard. *You win, Bennett. You have your money. Now hold up your end of the deal.*

With her hand on the laptop, ready to snap it closed, a new post pinged on the screen. *Has anyone seen the article in the Post about the missing UES man? Scary stuff.* Poppy's eyes widened, reading the words twice before her mind processed them. Her fingers dropped on the keyboard and in under five seconds she'd navigated to nypost.com and found the article titled UES MAN DISAPPEARS WITHOUT A TRACE.

Bennett Stillman, son of socialite Waverley Stillman, and owner of Reflex lacrosse studio on the Upper East Side, was reported missing yesterday. A source close to the investigation said the police do not suspect foul play at this time. A spokesperson for the NYPD declined to comment.

Poppy's hand flew up to her throat.

No. No. No.

She gasped for a breath but couldn't pull in any air. It was as if a vise were tightening around her windpipe. Fumbling for the mouse, Poppy clicked back to UrbanMyth, and with wild eyes, searched for a way to delete her last post.

What had she done? What the *hell* had she done?

A loud, rumbling noise pierced the silence and Poppy jumped in her seat. Her muscles unclenched when she realized it was only the refrigerator dropping ice cubes into the tray. She had to get ahold of herself. Her posts on UrbanMyth were anonymous. That was the whole *point*. Nobody knew it was her. And nobody would *ever* know.

What was the tagline again? "Your secrets are safe with us." They goddamn better be.

She pivoted back to her laptop and reread the *Post* article, drumming her fingernails on the side of the keyboard. Was that why Bennett needed money? Had Poppy inadvertently funded him skipping town? Bennett had mentioned being in a jam. But if that was the case, how long would it be before he came back to her with his hand out for more? Leaning closer to the screen, she examined the photo embedded in the article, the one of Bennett grinning in a tuxedo. She recognized it as an old photo lifted from the website of Patrick McMullan, the omnipresent Manhattan-social-scene photographer. The text underneath the photo read *Anyone with information on the whereabouts of Bennett Stillman is advised to call Crime Stoppers*.

She lifted both fists to her mouth and pushed back her chair with such force it toppled over behind her.

"Are you okay, Ms. Ridley? Can I help you with that?"

Poppy jerked her head to the left, where Maya stood in the entryway to the kitchen, her eyes the size of quarters.

Goddammit, this woman was everywhere Poppy didn't want her to be.

Poppy shuffled back two small steps, rested a hand against the counter, steadying herself. Panic buzzed in her hands and feet.

"Help me with what?" she snapped, her chest rising and falling at a rate so rapid she briefly thought she might be in cardiac arrest.

Maya pointed a tentative finger to the chair resting on its side on the tiled floor.

"Oh." Poppy waved it away with a dismissive hand. "That happens all the time." She swept her laptop off the table and tucked it under her arm, storming out of the kitchen and down the hallway toward her bedroom. The questions in her head were scattering in a million different directions, like a jarful of marbles that had fallen to the floor. Would someone report her UrbanMyth post to Crime Stoppers? Would the police find out about the money she wired to Bennett's account? Would they bring her in for questioning? What the hell would she tell Harris?

Harris.

He was still somewhere in the apartment, she realized. He'd slept in, disappeared into his office about thirty minutes ago, muttering something about taking a call, and had yet to emerge. He hadn't worked from home in a while, so it had slipped her mind.

She couldn't let him see her like this, teetering on the edge.

When she reached the master bedroom, she jammed her trembling hands into the pockets of her robe and began pacing an angry lap around her bedroom, strategizing. As long as the police didn't have access to Bennett's phone, she was fine. Her paranoia was getting the better of her. She would move through the daily rhythms of her life as if everything were perfectly normal. Because it *was* normal. Poppy hadn't done anything wrong. All she'd done is wire money. That wasn't a crime. It wasn't like she was standing there with his blood on her hands for god's sake.

Oh god.

His DNA.

Her eyes flicked around the room. His DNA was all over this apartment. All it took was a single strand of hair somewhere in this bedroom and they'd know he'd been in here. She pressed her fingertips against her temples. She was unwinding faster than a yo-yo.

Air.

She needed some air.

She strode to her walk-in closet, peeled off her pajamas, and pulled a pair of Sweaty Betty leggings out of the drawer. She'd go to Pilates, she decided, sliding a leg through the stretchy fabric and pulling a loose top over her head. Being seen in public would send the message that Bennett was as tangential to Poppy's life as her mailman. She pulled the phone from the pocket of the robe discarded on the floor and slung her gym bag over her shoulder. She'd check UrbanMyth on the way, see if there were any responses to her post. Maybe someone had reported it for violating the rules of anonymity and it'd been removed. Striding out of the walk-in closet, she tapped the phone awake.

"Poppy?" Harris's voice boomed.

She jerked her head up to see Harris looming under the doorframe, staring with an intensity that bolted her feet to the floor. The tight clench of his teeth in the line of his jaw caused every hair on her body to snap to attention. Tilting her head, she forced her lips into an innocent smile.

That was when she saw it. The object pinched between his fingers.

Bennett's glasses.

His dark eyes seared into hers as he lifted his hand. "Who the hell do these belong to?"

Looking back, there were so many plausible answers she could've given. They could've belonged to any one of the ninety-five Crofton parents who'd been in their apartment for the cocktail party. Or the caterers, party planner, or myriad others. Harris had no clue who came in and out of their front door on a daily basis. But Poppy knew who they belonged to, and the vein pulsing in Harris's forehead warned her he might too. The possibility filled her with an electric shock of terror, paralyzing all rational thought.

So, she did what she hadn't ever done in her forty-two years on this earth.

She panicked.

Chapter Twenty-two

POPPY

POPPY TRAILED HARRIS as he thundered down the hallway, arms swinging.

"Harris, what is going on with you today?" she called, terror bumping the edges of her voice. She broke into a jog to keep up with his long strides. "Slow down! Let me talk to you."

Harris spun around, eyes wild. His skin was covered with angry red splotches, and with a manic smile spreading across his face, he looked dangerously unhinged. The last time Poppy had seen him like this was when a childhood rival had successfully outbid him on a waterfront home in East Hampton, with a figure that had come in (according to Harris) well after the auction deadline. Poppy had implored Harris to let the whole thing go, especially after they found a much more suitable property six months later. Instead, Harris had used his connections with the East Hampton Building Department to torpedo all permits for the planned gut renovation, leaving the house essentially uninhabitable. "Nobody cheats a Ridley," Harris had proclaimed, with an unsettling intensity, when the property was back on the market a year later. If Harris found out about what happened with Bennett, she'd be the one in the crosshairs of his vengeance. It would be swift, and it would be apocalyptic.

It would implode life as she knew it.

"Why are you so worked up right now?" she asked, trying and failing to keep her tone even. "You're worrying me."

Harris was panting, his chest rising and falling as if the distance between the master bedroom and foyer were the length of a marathon, and Poppy briefly wondered if he might have a heart attack.

Which, truth be told, would not have been the worst of possibilities.

"What's there to be worried about?" He leveled a cold stare. "Unless you're worried your story won't hold up?"

"It's not a *story,* Harris." She forced a laugh, hoping it didn't come across as laughing *at* him, a regrettable action that had once triggered the biggest fight of their marriage, confirming the theory that a man's biggest fear is that a woman will laugh at him. Of course, the second half of that theory is that a woman's biggest fear is that a man will kill her, an outcome that seemed entirely possible now based on the rage splattered across Harris's face.

Poppy needed to *think,* to steer this ship away from the iceberg.

"You're getting yourself all worked up over nothing, and I know you're *much* too busy to be dealing with this right now." It was a trick she employed whenever she wanted to keep his nose out of what she was doing—whether it was his predictably garish decorating opinions or his overly aggressive approach to parenting. Tell Harris he was too *important* to deal with a trivial matter and it was impossible for him to disagree.

Harris gave a righteous sniff, considering this.

In the weighted silence, there was a faint sound of a sink turning on, turning off again, the scuff of a foot against a tiled floor. Harris's ears perked up, detecting the movement in the kitchen. Poppy's stomach clenched, watching his features morph.

"I'm not too busy to find out who's been in my apartment when I'm not here. And if you're telling the truth, this won't take any time at all." He spun around and stomped toward the kitchen. Poppy hustled after him, her pulse throbbing in her neck so hard it felt like she might choke.

"Maya!" Harris roared, and Poppy saw Maya's shoulders jump.

Maya whirled around, wet dishrag in hand. She looked like a deer that had been lined up in the crosshairs of a hunter. Right before he shot her between the eyes.

"Maya, stop what you're doing," Harris commanded.

"Is . . . is everything okay?" she sputtered, taking a step back and bumping into the counter. Maya's eyes pinballed between the two of them. Poppy wrung her hands, trying desperately to transmit a silent message. She knew how Harris was coming across—deranged, dangerous—and frankly, she wasn't sure how this would play out if this girl did not give him the answer Poppy *needed* her to give.

"Of course, everything is okay," Poppy trilled. "Harris, let's leave Maya to do her work and go talk about this in the privacy of our bedroom." She rested her hand on his forearm, but he wrenched it away. He took another step toward Maya.

"How's your eyesight?" he asked without a drip of humor in his tone.

Poppy's chest rose almost imperceptibly. She was holding her breath.

"Um . . . it's okay, I guess," Maya stammered.

He took another step closer. Maya held herself possum-still.

Harris narrowed his eyes, inspecting Maya's face. "But I see you're not wearing glasses today. Do you *ever* wear glasses?"

Maya's gaze flicked to Poppy, beseeching her for the correct answer. Poppy gave a minuscule nod of her head, praying Harris didn't take that nanosecond to shift his angry glare in her direction.

Maya cleared her throat. "Sometimes," she hedged.

"Sometimes," Harris echoed, his veined nostrils flaring.

Maya fidgeted with the rag in her hands, twisting it so hard it looked like it could snap.

There was a feverish blaze in Harris's eye when he lifted his arm and dangled the pair of forest-green-rimmed glasses away from his body as if they were a dirty pair of underwear. "Are these yours?"

Maya's eyes slid back to Poppy. Poppy stared at her with the intensity of someone performing mind control, mentally pleading with her to say yes.

Harris's question hung in the air, swinging like a pendulum.

"Yes," Maya finally said, bobbing her head. "They're mine."

Poppy's jaw released. A slight exhale lowered her shoulder blades.

"They're yours," Harris repeated, his voice flat. His words agreed, but his tone did not.

Maya nodded, this time with more force, like a bobble-head toy. "I need them when I drive to read the signs. And sometimes I put them on to read the small lettering on the back of cleaning products." She swept the bottle of organic all-purpose cleaner off the counter and held it up as if it were indisputable proof.

Harris's expression hardened. His fists clenched and unclenched in the icy silence.

"Well, I'm paying you to *clean* this apartment, not to leave your crap everywhere." He tossed the glasses onto the counter and turned around, muttering a "Jesus Christ" as he shouldered past Poppy on his way out of the kitchen. "Get the staff in order, for fuck's sake."

Poppy and Maya stood perfectly still as his footsteps disappeared down the hallway toward the foyer. They flinched in unison when the front door slammed shut.

Poppy opened her mouth to speak and then closed it. Opened it. Closed. After a few seconds, she threw her shoulders back, re-establishing her place in the hierarchy. "That will be all for now, Maya. Please see me before you leave today," she said curtly, before pivoting to leave.

The next time Poppy sought out Maya was at the end of her shift. She found her in the laundry room, changing out of her cleaning slippers and back into her sneakers. Poppy threaded her arms across her chest, taking in the tiled space, wondering how she'd managed to overlook this room in the renovation. Had she ever stepped foot in here before? Probably not. Maya's head was down. She was focusing on tying her laces, oblivious to Poppy's presence. Poppy clicked her pen with her right hand and Maya leapt to her feet.

"Oh, sorry, Ms. Ridley, I didn't see you there." She stood up straighter like a soldier awaiting inspection.

Poppy cleared her throat. "I should've done this when you started with us, but now is as good a time as any." She placed a stapled document featuring the words "nondisclosure agreement," which were underlined and set in bold, on the washing machine, the product of a frantic phone call to her lawyer after Harris had departed for work. She clicked the pen again and rested it on top, staring at Maya expectantly.

Maya eyed the document, then Poppy.

"They're all standard terms," Poppy said quickly. "The long and the short of it is that you don't disclose any information that you've gathered during your employment with us. I'm sure you've signed one of these before at your previous positions."

Maya shook her head.

"Well, as I said, they're quite standard, and there's obviously no detriment to you to sign, but there'll be an additional thousand dollars in your next paycheck." She picked up the pen and held it out to Maya before adding, "As a gesture of goodwill."

"I'm . . . I'm sorry, but we're not supposed to sign anything without it going through the agency first. I . . . I would get in trouble."

Poppy pursed her lips. Was that true? She didn't remember anything in the fine print that indicated she couldn't ask a staff member to sign a separate contract once employment had commenced. But despite Poppy's not-so-gentle coaxing, assuring Maya that there would be no repercussions from the staffing agency, Maya wouldn't relent. She departed for the day with the promise to read over the contract and clear it with someone at the agency.

Poppy didn't say it outright, but she hoped the implication was clear: Maya would be fired if she failed to sign the agreement. It was as simple as that.

Except it wasn't.

UrbanMyth Message Board

***What is with the weird posts on this site today? Who is Bennett
and why does he win?***

> Surely, that's not the weirdest thing you've read on here.

> Because people with Waspy names like Bennett always win.
  Tell us something we don't know.

> I think using someone's actual name is against the rules and
  should be reported.

> Wait, isn't that the name of the missing lacrosse coach???

Chapter Twenty-three

CROFTON PARENTS

They were at an online safety seminar, of all places, when the news broke.

One parent from each family was required to attend, in light of what Dr. Krause had vaguely referred to as "recent cyber incidents affecting our students." *It's important that parents are given the tools they need to keep their children safe,* the email read. *And for that reason, the seminar will be mandatory.* The word "mandatory" was in bold, and within minutes of the email pinging into eighth-grade Crofton parent inboxes, the WhatsApp group blew up. *A mandatory seminar with one week's notice?! Does anyone else think that's a bit much?!?!* one of the mothers wrote, taking the time to alternate the exclamation points and question marks. Multiple raised-hand emojis followed, along with one all-caps *PREACH.* A meme with a power-hungry Elmo raising his hands in front of a background of flames prompted a handful of crying-laughing emojis. *I think some reading material would be sufficient,* one humorless mother chimed in. Multiple responders concurred. But despite the calls to take up arms, nobody was willing to risk noncompliance. All bark and no bite. They had boarding school applications to consider.

If Dr. Krause said "Jump," the resounding response was going to be "How high?"

As they funneled into the theater for the mandatory morning seminar, the atmosphere was heavy, as if a storm were coming. It had already been a trying few days for the Crofton parent body. Having one of their own reported missing was not a common occurrence. There was an undercurrent of unease, perhaps even a whiff of schadenfreude, when the news made the rounds in hushed conversations.

Have you noticed his eyes are always bloodshot?

I wouldn't be surprised if he's off on a bender.

Doesn't his family have mafia connections? I bet that has something to do with it.

I heard he drained the bank account before he took off.

As the parents made their way to their seats, travel cups of coffee in hand, there were even whispers that the police were talking to a few Crofton families. "Not as potential suspects," Gretchen assured the four moms hanging on her every word. "They're just gathering information about the family." Gretchen's face glowed with unbridled joy when she delivered this tidbit.

There was nothing juicier than a police investigation involving a Crofton parent.

Dr. Krause approached the podium with the air of an evangelical preacher poised to deliver a televised sermon, and the conversations stopped. Attention was redirected toward the stage. He adjusted the microphone and opened with a run-through of the five building blocks, with practiced hand gestures for emphasis on the word "knowledge." "If we have the *knowledge* of how to keep our children safe online, we can *achieve* it," he said before introducing the guest speaker, an earnest-looking woman with a blond pixie cut.

She was thirty minutes into her presentation, rattling off alarming statistics and moving through her PowerPoint slide titled "Preserving Cyber Identities," when the buzzing started. A cacophony of vibrations from devices stowed away in expensive leather purses. One hundred silenced iPhones being anything but silent.

What Heather would remember was the illuminated screens, glowing in unison.

What Poppy would remember was the sound of the muffled gasps.

What Norah would remember was her phone remaining curiously silent. Proving she was, in fact, the only mother who had turned off notifications for WhatsApp.

Not one of them would recall which member of Crofton Eighth Grade Mamas sent the infamous message to the WhatsApp group. That was how human memory worked in response to a traumatic event—critical details are burned into your consciousness, at the expense of the peripheral ones. When a person is staring down the barrel of a gun, the brain is focused on the weapon, not the person with his finger on the trigger.

The message was only three words, but it was the link pasted below those words that reverberated through the room and beyond the four walls of the now-ironically named online safety seminar.

Three words.

Is this real?

New York Post
Major Data Breach for Popular Anonymous Forum

Is nothing on the internet sacred? In a scene reminiscent of the 2015 Ashley Madison data breach, the hacktivists have struck again. Employees at TallTale Media Corp., the parent company behind the popular app UrbanMyth, were met with loud blares and the following message when they logged on this morning.

Access Denied Mother F******. All user information compromised. To view, visit tattletales.com.

A hacktivist group identifying itself by the name "Eat the Rich" has taken credit for the information leak, a leak that will affect the nearly one million users who frequent the site. The popular anonymous forum, which *Entertainment Weekly* once likened to "group therapy for those too paranoid for group therapy," touted full anonymity for its users, collecting no personal information other than an email address. An email address that, thanks to Eat the Rich, can now be used to look up the entirety of a user's history in an easy-to-use database.

So much for anonymity.

Unlike the Ashley Madison data dump, these hackers have cut out the middleman and gone right to a searchable database. To use it, simply plug in an email address and the site will provide a list of every post attributed to that address. If you know your neighbor's email address, you'll soon learn how much trust they put in cybersecurity.

Executives from TallTale Media Corp. could not be reached for comment.

Chapter Twenty-four

HEATHER

HEATHER LOOKED UP from her phone and gazed around the theater, a small smile twitching at the corners of her lips. *This* was certainly going to ruffle some feathers. It reminded her of one of those old Scared Straight programs, the ones designed to show the realities of prison to motivate troubled teens to turn their lives around, but for screen-addicted Upper East Side parents. *See! This is what could happen if you put too much trust in Big Tech and don't heed my warning today. It could happen not only to your children, but to YOU.* It was pretty impressive that Digital Media Coalition could pull this off. Of course, calling the hacker group "Eat the Rich" was cutting close to the bone. Krause surely hadn't vetted that part.

She stifled a snort as she watched the thumbs anxiously swipe across the glowing screens, the horrified eyes widening, from her spot in the back row. She'd strategically selected a seat isolated from the rest of the parents and was now happy with her vantage point. It would be entertaining to watch this all unfold. She imagined the woman onstage pointing her finger at the crowd calling out *Gotcha!* with a satisfied smile. *This is why you should never put anything on the internet that you wouldn't want on the front page of* The New York Times, she would say, pleased with herself.

Except.

The minutes ticked by.

"That concludes today's presentation," the blond pixie cut said, a smile pulled across her thin lips. Heather examined her, waiting for her expression to morph. When not a single hand went up for the Q and A and Dr. Krause gave a perfunctory word of thanks, reminding everyone to ensure they'd signed in to receive credit for their attendance, Heather had to resist the urge to leap up and shout *You've forgotten the punch line!* It wasn't until she saw the presenter slip her laptop in her purse and push her arms through the sleeves of her coat that Heather realized she'd been catastrophically mistaken.

This wasn't part of the show.

The overhead lights in the theater came on. All around her, faces marbled red, heads lowered to avoid eye contact, hands trembled as they collected purses, briefcases, discarded coffee cups. The air was thick with nervous sweat and regret.

It was as if someone had flicked the lights on at an orgy.

"Holy shit," the woman to the left of Heather hissed, pressing her shaky fingers into her temples. Was she crying? Heather didn't wait for the answer. She swung her purse over her shoulder and joined the other parents fleeing the theater with the speed of escaping convicts. Bypassing the crowd by the elevator, Heather pushed open the heavy door to the stairwell, taking the six flights down two at a time. When she was safely outside of the school building, she broke into a run, not bothering to stop when the red hand blinked manically on the corner of Ninetieth Street.

"Watch it, lady," a man in an orange construction vest hollered as she wove between him and a pony-tailed woman pushing a double stroller, but Heather didn't slow her pace. Like a shark, she had to keep moving in order to breathe. By the time she reached the door to her apartment, the back of her cardigan was soaked through with sweat and her heart was beating so hard it felt like it might break one of her ribs. She didn't even know how she managed to get the key into the lock given how hard her hands were shaking.

"Oliver!" she shrieked into the apartment, relieved when she was met with silence. He would be at work by now. Thankfully. She leaned her back against the weight of the door, sliding down to the floor until she was crouched in the foyer. She ground the heels of her palms into her eye sockets. UrbanMyth posts began to move through her mind the way credits roll at the end of a movie.

Has anyone ever received a loan from a bank without their spouse's knowledge? I'm curious how this would work.

Where is the best place to go if you need to sell jewelry? Husband thinks it's been stolen so can't be a local place.

"*No, no, no, no,*" she repeated in between panted breaths as if she could wipe the slate clean if she pleaded hard enough, but the posts kept marching through her mind, a relentless army of her own typed words blitzing through her brain. But it was the last post she'd written that was burning in her gut, eating away at her stomach lining. It was buried on UrbanMyth like a land mine, waiting to explode the second someone stumbled upon it.

Her entire life blown up in an instant.

She couldn't let that happen. She gathered her limbs, climbed to her feet, and hurried down the hallway to her office. Flicking on the desk lamp, she shot a look over her shoulder—as if Oliver might've arrived home in the past two seconds and was silently trailing her—before dropping onto the chair and swiping the mouse. The screen lit up, displaying the four open tabs on her browser, UrbanMyth in the first gray rectangle. With frantic energy, she navigated to tattletales.com, where she was greeted with a paragraph in bold at the top of the screen.

Mission Statement—Destroy Big Tech

Our mission, which we choose to accept, is to blow up the One Percent, who've earned their place in this world standing on the tired backs of the Ninety-nine. Step one: Destroy Big Tech. UrbanMyth is a wholly owned subsidiary of TallTale Media Corp., whose CEO was paid a seventeen-

million-dollar bonus last year but denied workers the forty
hours a week that would have entitled them to benefits. He
wouldn't let go of the brass ring, so it's time to pry his
greedy fingers off of it. Let this data dump be a warning to
Big Tech everywhere—pay your workers a living wage or
you're next. Happy reading.

The cursor pulsed rhythmically, almost hypnotically, in the white rectangular box next to the words "insert email." Heather stared at it, hating herself for having been lulled into a false sense of security by this fucking thing.

Anonymous. How easily she'd bought into the promise.

She pulled back the sleeves of her shirt and keyed in her email address, the one she'd used to create an UrbanMyth account. It was the same one included with her contact information in the Crofton parent directory, she realized with a start, accessible to anyone with a sliver of interest in tracking it down. Heather dropped her face into her palms. She wasn't sure she could face what she was about to see. She was even less sure she could take one more second of not knowing.

Holding her breath, she hit enter.

What appeared on the screen resembled a multipage Word document. No images, no targeted ads, no eye-catching font. Only text. Lines and lines and lines of text. It only took a cursory glance for Heather to be certain. Every single word on this screen was a word she'd typed.

All of her posts, all of her secrets, instantly declassified.

With wild eyes, she started at the top. *New to this site but looks like fun!*

She'd created her UrbanMyth account over a year ago on a whim, mostly lurking, as if sitting in the back row of an A.A. meeting, judging others for their sordid confessions. Within weeks, her defenses were lowered, and she was tossing in comments like "I've done this too" on posts about shoplifting or writing your child's essay for them. It felt like opening a safety release valve, relieving some pent-up pressure, and it was much more effective than the confessional booth she'd been forced to sit in when she was ten years old, that one year her parents had attempted regular church attendance.

But Heather hadn't stopped at unburdening her conscience.

Why the hell hadn't she stopped there?

Heather's leg bounced as she bulldozed through over a year's worth of posts, her sense of privacy unraveling as if someone had grabbed a fraying hem and yanked.

Every new post she read, another pull.

An hour passed. She rubbed her eyes and kept reading. She felt peeled. Exposed. Naked in front of an auditorium of people. Finally, blessedly, she reached the bottom of the long list. The last post. Her chest tightened as she scanned her words. And even though she was expecting it, even though she'd braced for what she knew she'd find, it still felt like a punch to the throat. She read it over once, twice, the implications detonating in her mind. Anyone could now see that she had written this. Oliver could see it. They'd put two and two together.

They'd know what she'd done.

How the hell was she going to cover this up?

A buzz from the intercom sliced through her thoughts like a machete.

She threw a look over her shoulder to the door of the office. She wasn't expecting any deliveries. Hastily, she closed the tab, cleared her browser history, and shut down her computer. Rising to her feet, she eyeballed the monitor with the intensity of a person standing over the dead body of a thwarted attacker. If she could've taken a sledgehammer to her computer without arousing suspicion from Oliver, she would've. Giving her office a final once-over, ensuring there wasn't any damning evidence, she headed toward the foyer, as the intercom buzzed again.

Uneasiness thrummed in her chest.

Bracing herself with a hand on the wall, she closed her eyes and counted to three. Tentatively, she lifted the receiver to her ear.

"Ms. Quinn," the doorman said, his voice shaky. "There are two detectives in the lobby here to see you."

The earth stopped spinning on its axis. Somehow her voice found its way outside her head, and it sounded only slightly strangled.

"You can send them up."

Chapter Twenty-five

HEATHER

HEATHER WAS STANDING in the foyer waiting, but the fist still startled her when it rattled against the other side of the door. A quick, staccato knock. She pressed an eye against the peephole. Two tight-lipped, distorted faces filled her vision. She'd briefly debated telling the doorman no, he couldn't send them up, but she knew if she made an excuse now, they would only come back later. Maybe when Oliver and Violet were home. It was in her best interests to get this over with.

Rip off the Band-Aid.

So why wouldn't her body cooperate and open the damn door?

Heather put a palm against her chest, commanding her heartbeat to slow its thunderous pace. It didn't *mean* anything that they were here to talk to her. They were simply checking a box, making their way down a long list of Crofton parents. "Gathering information" she'd heard Gretchen say. She wiped a bead of sweat from her forehead with the sleeve of her cashmere cardigan, rested her hand on the knob, took a breath, and pulled open the door.

Neither of the broad-shouldered men in the hallway were in uniform and for a brief, glorious moment Heather wondered if they were impostors posing as police, here to rob her of her worldly possessions. She would've gladly handed over anything of value to make them go away. But one of them—the clean-cut, dark-haired man with the threadlike scar woven through his eyebrow—was holding out a shiny detective shield. He was speaking in a low baritone, but she couldn't make out all of the words over the blood roaring in her ears. She tightened her grip on the doorknob and forced herself to focus.

"Missing person . . . part of our investigation . . . ask you a few questions."

The room needed to stop spinning so she could get her footing.

"Can we come in?"

Heather wasn't even sure she'd opened her mouth to respond, but she must have, because the two men were sliding past her into her foyer, their eyes flicking around the entryway, running over the contents of her console table and over her shoulder into the apartment.

"Can I get you some coffee?" Heather heard herself ask, hoping it sounded breezy. "Or some water?" She swallowed, suddenly aware of the tightness in her throat.

The two men shook their heads in unison.

"No, we don't want to take up too much of your time," the shorter, mustached one said. His round face was friendly, almost benevolent, like he was going to roll up his sleeves and offer to fix her garbage disposal while he was here. His partner, on the other hand, had heavy eyelids and gray-speckled stubble running down his jawline, giving him the air of a bad-tempered bounty hunter, ready to drag her away and collect his sizable reward.

Good cop, bad cop. If she hadn't been so terrified, she might have cracked a joke.

"Is there someplace we can sit?" Good Cop asked, craning his neck to peer farther into her apartment.

"Of course." Heather clutched her hands together to hide the tremor as she led them to the living room. She noticed Bad Cop's eyes swinging around her apartment like searchlights on a helicopter, and she instantly regretted her choice of sitting areas. It would've been more strategic to guide them into the kitchen. Those rigid, uncomfortable chairs that her decorator had selected for the breakfast table had a maximum sitting time of fifteen minutes, whereas the plush furniture in the living room invited guests to sit and stay awhile.

Unfortunately, her default setting was to be hospitable.

Each detective lowered himself into an upholstered wingback chair. Heather perched on the end of the plush sofa across from them, knitting her fingers together in her lap. Her head was already beginning to throb. She focused her eyes on a polished silver frame on the side table to steady herself.

"Thanks for agreeing to speak with us," Good Cop said, pulling a small green spiral notepad and pen out of the breast pocket of his blazer. "We've been talking to a number of people, trying to track down any information that might help us with our investigation."

Heather tucked a strand of hair behind her ear and nodded in a way that she hoped conveyed a willingness to help.

"You have a child at The Crofton School, correct?"

"Yes, that's right," Heather replied stiffly. "That's how I know . . ." She paused a beat before adding "them." She gave a little cough. "The family I mean."

He scribbled in his notepad. "How well do you know the family?"

"Not very well. We have children in the same school, but I wouldn't call us close friends. More like acquaintances." She was careful not to add details that would steer her too far away from the truth.

The truth. What a slippery concept.

"Have you ever socialized with them?" He raised one eyebrow.

Was there a hint of judgment in his tone?

Heather cleared a rasp from her throat. "Um, a bit." She shrugged one shoulder, as if it were all too dull to mention. "But just school events. Parent cocktail parties, curriculum nights, that kind of thing."

Another nod, another scribble.

"Did anything unusual happen at any of these school events?"

Heather knitted her brow. "Unusual?" Her heart rate picked up speed. "Not unless you count middle-aged parents drinking a little too much as unusual." She attempted a smile, a light eye roll, looking for a connection. But his expression remained expertly neutral.

His head cocked to one side. "Did you ever see anything that would lead you to believe anyone would want to harm the family?"

"*Harm* them?" Heather swallowed hard. "Do you think that's what happened?"

"We haven't ruled out foul play."

Her knee started to bounce. She forced herself to stop by crossing her legs.

He launched into more questions. "Did you ever see anyone hanging around the school?" "Are you aware of any domestic disputes within the family?"

Heather shook her head no, not trusting her voice. The less she said, the better. She turned the silver bracelet on her wrist, around and around and around, as he continued. This was taking longer than she'd expected, the questions becoming startling in their specificity. Why on earth did she agree to this? She should speak up now, tell them she wouldn't answer another question without legal counsel present.

No. That would look suspicious now.

Guilty.

Besides, it wasn't like she was being accused of anything. Was she?

An ambulance siren wailed from down below, jolting Heather out of her head. Had she answered all of his questions? She must have, because Good Cop was flipping over a marked-up page, reviewing his notes.

He tapped a thick thumb against his knee, his brow furrowed.

Heather shifted her weight on the couch. Her back was aching, and she realized she'd been rigid with tension since they'd arrived. "Is this going to take much longer?" she asked. "I have someplace I need to be in fifteen minutes." She made a show of looking at her watch.

It wasn't a crime to have things she needed to do.

Bad Cop kept his gaze leveled on her, his elbows planted on the arms of the chair. Heather could see his sidearm peeking out from the holster.

Good Cop raised his eyes from his notepad. "Is there *any* other information you can think of that might be useful for us as we investigate this disappearance?" he asked, his voice gentle, like a parent trying to coax information from a frightened child.

"Um." Heather wiped her damp palms on her lap. There was a moment, just a breath, where silence fell between them, and she considered telling them everything. The words rested right behind her lips, ready to break free. *Let me start at the beginning,* she would say. She imagined it all coming out in a tumble. An avalanche of truth. Maybe if she laid every sordid detail on the table she could convince them to see things from her point of view. She wasn't a monster, for god's sake. She only did what she had to do. Anyone in her position would've done the same thing.

Confession—it was good for the soul, right? She'd heard that somewhere.

"No." Heather ignored the hitch in her voice as she expelled the word. "Sorry, I wish I could be more helpful."

She wasn't under oath. She didn't have to be honest. Not even to herself.

Good Cop's forehead creased into a frown. Another nod. She could see the muscle flex in his jaw as he clenched his teeth.

One second. Two seconds.

The air in the room seemed to tighten. Why weren't they getting up to leave?

Bad Cop let out a long sigh and leaned forward in his chair. "Well, let's start over then," he said, burrowing his eyes into hers.

He clicked his pen a few times, as if he were cocking a gun.

The hairs on her arms stood up.

"How long has the affair been going on?"

Chapter Twenty-six

HEATHER

HEATHER SQUINTED, THE sunlight ricocheting off the window and shining directly into her retinas like a hundred-watt lightbulb. Bad Cop licked his lips, his pen suspended over his small green spiral notepad, the satisfied blaze in his eye one of a prosecutor who had tripped up the witness on the stand. Heather's head felt detached from her body, a helium balloon released into the atmosphere, floating overhead watching it all unfold. She imagined the three of them in an interrogation room, one of those windowless ones with concrete cinder-block walls, a coffee cup on top of a puckered metal table, the chill in the air intended to cause maximum discomfort. She'd always thought those kinds of transparent interrogation tactics were only effective on weak people.

Yet here she was in her own living room, mentally unwinding.

"Ms. Quinn?" a voice cut through her haze.

Heather lifted her eyes from the vase of flowers on the coffee table and met Bad Cop's gaze. He raised his eyebrows expectantly.

She brought a fist to her mouth, coughed a few times, biding time.

"I'm sorry?" she said, her intonation turning the two words into a question. She arranged her features to convey innocent confusion. Forehead slightly furrowed. Head tilted just so.

There was no way they could know. Was there?

It had been a reckless thing to do, she knew that now, but *some-*

thing needed to be done after what had happened at the cocktail party. Norah and Bennett hadn't shown an ounce of concern about Violet's reputation being shredded by a vengeful, anonymous rumor, so it was obviously up to Heather to give them a heaping tablespoon of their medicine. With her bloodstream full of alcohol and rage-fueled adrenaline and Oliver snoring beside her, she'd typed *Confession time: I'm sleeping with my child's lacrosse coach—the one from Reflex on the UES. I think he's willing to end his marriage. Should I end mine?* It had been mollifying to plant an online rumor of her own. A shot across the bows. She imagined Norah's growing awareness of the whispers when she passed, or perhaps reading the words herself on UrbanMyth, cut by the razor-sharp irony that an anonymous digital grapevine was now being used to hang *her*. If ever there were an example of the punishment fitting the crime, the perfect tit for tat, this was it. Of course, Heather knew now that Norah's daughter *wasn't* the one who took the photo. But that was beside the point. Heather never would've written that post if Norah had shown her a baseline courtesy and agreed to check Caroline's phone for the photo. It was such a simple, logical request. Heather could've eliminated Caroline as a suspect and moved on. Really, all of this was Norah's fault.

"How long has the affair been going on?" Bad Cop repeated, louder this time.

Heather's thumb tapped against the armrest of the couch. A Morse code of distress. She cleared the tremor in her throat and opened her mouth to speak. "What affair are you referring to?" she heard herself ask, mentally cringing. As if the affair with Bennett was one of a hundred affairs in her memory bank.

For someone with so much practice stretching the truth, she was not performing well.

Good Cop gripped the back of his neck with a meaty hand, massaged it a few times, as if the mere act of watching Heather lie to his face had caused him unbearable discomfort.

"Ms. Quinn," Bad Cop said, crossing his left knee over his right and leaning back in the chair, appraising her. "Let me take this back a few steps for you. Did you attend a cocktail party at the residence of Poppy Ridley on . . ." He lowered his eyes to his small spiral notepad, flipped back a few pages to one Heather could see was marked with blue ink. "February twenty-eighth?"

Heather cleared her throat. "Yes, I attended the cocktail party, but I didn't stay very long."

"But we can agree that you were there?"

She nodded.

"Well, we've spoken to another attendee who witnessed you in a very heated exchange with Bennett Stillman and Norah Ryan at the party."

"Well, I don't know if I would call it *heated* . . ." She faltered, her face flushing.

Bad Cop held up a hand, cutting her off. "All the same, Ms. Quinn. We can agree that, at a recent party, you had some form of a conversation with Bennett that was noteworthy enough for someone else at the party to recall it." He clicked his pen a few times.

Heather's head spun as she tried to land on which Crofton parent would have had the audacity to point the finger at her because of one slightly animated conversation at one lousy cocktail party. It could've been any one of them, she realized with a jolt of anger. Heather had no allies. Which was exactly why it was up to her to look out for *herself*.

Bad Cop stopped clicking the pen, let his thumb hover over the top. "On our way over here, we were informed about a cyberattack on an anonymous app that's popular in this neighborhood." He paused to make sure she was with him. But she *wasn't* with him. She was untethered, hurtling around the room. "So, on a whim," he continued, "we flipped through that parent directory we were given and plugged in your email address." He leaned forward, planted his forearms on his knees. The light from the chandelier glinted off of his sidearm. His expression hardened. "Now that we're clear, let me ask you again. How long has the affair with Bennett Stillman been going on?"

Heather felt as if he'd drawn his weapon and was holding it against her temple.

"I'm not sleeping with Bennett Stillman," she sputtered, wrapping her arms around her abdomen, pulling her gray cashmere cardigan closer, like a life jacket. "I've never even been alone in the same room with that man."

Bad Cop sighed, low and long. A slight eye roll. He was used to this.

She swung her gaze to Good Cop. The softness in his eyes had given way to irritation. She was losing him too.

"Ms. Quinn, would you like to revisit the statement you made earlier about the nature of your relationship with Bennett Stillman?" Good Cop offered.

The temperature in the room rose sharply.

Her statement? The nature of her relationship? What the hell was happening here?

Reading her reticence as confusion, Good Cop filled in: "You told us earlier that you and Bennett Stillman were acquaintances and you didn't know each other well. But that conflicts with what you posted on this"—he rolled his hand—"Urban something."

"I did *post* that," Heather conceded, speaking quickly now. "But it wasn't actually true. I just wanted his wife to *think* he was sleeping with someone." Her tone sounded shrill, and she could feel the corners of her eyes burning. She blinked rapidly to keep the tears at bay.

"You wanted Norah Ryan to think *you* were sleeping with her husband," Bad Cop said, his expression even more skeptical than his tone.

"Well, no, not sleeping with *me*. Just sleeping with someone who wasn't *her*. Cheating on her. I'll admit it was a stupid and childish thing to do, but I was . . . angry."

Good Cop grimaced, ran a palm along his dark mustache.

"Angry?" Bad Cop cocked his head.

Heather wanted to claw back the word, but it hung in the air like a noose.

"What were you angry about, Ms. Quinn?" Good Cop probed.

She turned her face, watched specks of dust floating in a ray of sunshine. The apartment was uncharacteristically quiet, not a single horn from the street down below or footstep from the apartment up above, as if someone had hit pause on everything around them as they waited for her to answer the question. She felt a sudden urge to pierce the silence with a wild scream, to demand that they tell her what lengths *they* would go to if it was *their* child's name being dragged through the mud. Yes, maybe she'd made a mistake and pointed the finger at the wrong family, but entire wars have been fought over less evidence than she'd possessed. *Weapons of mass destruction, for god's sake, doesn't anyone remember that?*

She squeezed her fingers into fists.

What am I angry about?

She took three slow, deep breaths. Then the words tumbled out of her mouth. She told him about the Doubles Dance, watching Caroline sneak a phone in, the Instagram post accusing Violet of being a drug dealer, Violet's tears, the school searching her locker as if she were a common criminal, the competitive boarding school process, her certainty that Caroline Ryan's motive was to sabotage Violet, likely with her mom's blessing. It wasn't completely unheard of for parents to be involved in that type of sinister behavior, she pointed out—look at the college admissions scandal. That woman from *Full House* would've done the same thing in a heartbeat. "And with all the evidence in my corner, Bennett still accused *me* of being a liar," Heather said with a puff of indignation. "And he wouldn't even *entertain* my request to check Caroline's phone for the photo. Which proves he was trying to cover it up." She ended the story there. The truth about the photo didn't fit her narrative and it threatened to blow up the foundation of her moral high ground, a position Heather still firmly believed she occupied. Despite being wrong about the contents of Caroline's phone, it was still *her* daughter who was the victim here.

Heather sat up straighter, swiping at the moisture on her lip. She thought it would feel good, maybe even righteous to finally tell someone *her* side of things, but she couldn't help wondering now if it all sounded slightly unhinged.

Guilty.

Was she guilty? Of lying she supposed. But lying wasn't a crime. It was an anonymous forum they were talking about, for heaven's sake, not a witness stand. Although, if the disapproval clouding Bad Cop's features was any indication, he did not recognize the distinction.

"So, you *claimed* to be having an affair with Bennett Stillman to get back at this family?" he asked drolly.

"I wrote that post on UrbanMyth after I got home from the party. And I'll admit it: I had a little too much to drink that night and did something silly. Juvenile. But there's absolutely no truth to what I posted." She unclenched her hands, shifted her weight on the couch. Her fingernails had pressed tiny moons onto her skin.

Bad Cop tapped his pen against his knee, studying Heather. His expression was inscrutable.

"I'm sure I'm not the first person in the world who's posted something online that wasn't true," she said, letting out an awkward little laugh.

Their skeptical eyes torpedoed her attempt to lighten the mood.

"Look, I really don't have any information regarding Bennett's whereabouts now. The night of the party was the last time I saw them. *Either* of them." She forced herself to stop talking. Even *she* could hear the defensiveness that was creeping into her voice now. Biting the inside of her cheek, she considered the advantages of telling them about Bennett and Poppy. It would certainly end this line of questioning. But bringing that up would require explaining how she'd broken into Caroline's phone—which didn't exactly scream "innocent." And with the kind of power a member of the Ridley family could wield, it was vital for Heather to tread carefully.

Bad Cop stuck a meaty hand into his breast pocket, pulled out his phone, and frowned at the screen before dropping his phone back in. The scratch of Good Cop's pen against paper was the only sound in the room. In the quiet, Heather swore she could hear the creak of the wooden floorboards in the foyer, of Oliver coming home. But her mind was playing tricks on her. Oliver would still be at his office, blissfully unaware of the scene unfolding in his living room. Tears pricked the backs of her eyes as a gut-wrenching certainty hit her. She wasn't going to be able to hide this conversation from Oliver.

There was a lot she was not going to be able to hide now.

She swiped a hand underneath each eye. Was she crying? Her cheeks felt wet. She wasn't even sure if she was breathing at this point. She felt a sudden, urgent need to remove herself from the sweltering spotlight before she fully unraveled.

There was only one way to do that.

"You know." Her voice grew thoughtful, as if the idea was just occurring to her. "I've heard Poppy Ridley is *quite* friendly with Bennett. She would probably be a good person for you to talk to."

Their expressions suggested this was not within the range of things they expected to come out of her mouth.

"Is there a reason you think that?" Good Cop asked, the wrinkle between his eyes deepening.

Heather paused, weighing her answer. It was a risk, bringing the Ridley name into the conversation, but it was only a breadcrumb, and if she kept her information vague it wouldn't be traced back to her. "I can't remember who I heard it from, but somebody told me she'd seen the two of them together without their spouses." She raised a pointed eyebrow.

Bad Cop shot Good Cop a look.

Outside the window, Heather could hear the faint chimes of church bells. Twelve o'clock. Fifteen minutes past the time she'd claimed she needed to leave.

"I'm sorry, but I really do need to run." She made a point of tilting her wrist and eyeing her watch. "Dentist appointment." She rose to her feet. The detectives reluctantly followed suit, trailing her out of the living room and back down the hallway.

Before they reached the front door, Bad Cop slowed his step. "Your husband isn't home, is he?"

Heather shook her head. "He's at work. Why?"

"I wanted to ask him a few questions."

"Oliver won't have anything to add," she said quickly, regretting providing Oliver's name. She didn't want to give these two another morsel of information. And the last thing she wanted was to have Oliver dragged into this.

"I've been doing this long enough to know that *everyone* has something to add." Bad Cop reached inside his jacket and flicked out a card between two fingers. "Number's on the bottom. Tell your husband to give us a call."

Heather accepted the proffered card, slid it into the back pocket of her jeans.

It felt like thumbtacks were sliding up her throat as she pushed out the words, "Of course."

Chapter Twenty-seven

POPPY

POPPY HAD JUST returned from her lawyer's office and was making a hasty trail from the back seat of the Escalade to the elevator bank of her building when she noticed the two large men approaching the doorman's desk.

Still incensed from the meeting, she was mentally picking over what her lawyer had explained in that unaffected tone of his, the one that had always sounded professionally detached but today had come across as downright inhumane. "I'm going to be honest with you," he'd said after he'd ushered Poppy into his corner office, smelling like the steakhouse she'd demanded his assistant pull him away from. "I've already had three calls from other clients about this UrbanMyth hack. And I'm eager to help, to the extent that I can, but the truth is the world of cybersecurity is like the Wild West. As your lawyer, I can pursue a civil action on your behalf for any emotional distress you suffer as a result of this hack, but there's no cease-and-desist letter in the world that could make this information disappear from the internet."

"Useless!" Poppy fumed, replaying the conversation as her heels pounded across the sidewalk and into the tiled lobby of her building. Pandora's box had been wrenched open, and that man had the nerve to tell her that despite her thirty-thousand-dollar-a-month retainer, there wasn't a goddamn thing he was going to do about it.

It was unfathomable to have a problem that could not be solved if enough money was thrown at it.

She'd spent the twenty-minute car ride back to her apartment reviewing her UrbanMyth posts, as if assessing the amount of blood coming from a stab wound before registering the full depth of the pain. Her posts about Bennett, her proclivity for taking things from stores without paying for them, the lack of sex in her marriage, her fantasies of her husband dying—there was enough dirt on that site to bury her. It was imperative to ensure it could never be exhumed. Thankfully, she'd used her "shopping email" to create her UrbanMyth account, the one she used solely for on-line purchases to avoid the inevitable deluge of spam clogging up her main inbox. It was created using her maiden name, wouldn't be listed in the Crofton directory, and didn't contain a single message in the sent folder. Without access to her personal profile on the websites she routinely patronized, no one would ever know it existed. To be safe, though, she needed to delete all online accounts connected to that email. Wipe it out of virtual existence.

A catacomb sealed shut.

She was mentally compiling a list of accounts to delete and had accumulated at least five in her mind by the time she passed the sleek cherrywood desk, unaware of the doorman lifting his hand and pointing in her direction.

"That's Ms. Ridley over there," she heard the doorman say, and Poppy's first thought was *If this is one more fucking auction item, I'm going to burn it.*

But then the two men were walking toward her and one of them, the doughy-faced, mustached one, called out her name. "Poppy Ridley?"

"Yes, that's me," she said shortly, shooting an annoyed look at the doorman. Fernando, was that his name? Why the hell was he allowing deliverymen to accost her like this? Fernando had the ashen, clammy complexion of someone who was minutes away from throwing up, presumably now cognizant of his egregious error. Through the fog of her irritation, she returned her attention to the two men.

The man who hadn't yet spoken—the one with the receding, close-cropped, salt-and-pepper hair and stubble on his neck—was holding up a shiny badge, giving a name Poppy failed to catch, saying something about asking her questions, and gesturing to the seating area on the far side of the lobby.

Her head swiveled to the glass coffee table flanked by two starkly contemporary couches, as if the furniture could explain what the hell was happening, and then back to the two men. One was tucking his leather bifold badge back into his breast pocket, running a hand along his stubble. The mustached one had a hand on his hip, and Poppy could see the glint of a firearm in a holster. A wave of dizzying panic swept over her as her mind played catch-up. These men weren't delivering a package for the auction. They were cops.

"Have the police talked to you guys about Bennett yet?" Gretchen had inquired in a hushed voice this morning as they'd funneled into the theater for the mandatory parent seminar. "I'm sure they'll get to everyone, but as president of the Parents' Association, they wanted to talk to me first." There was an achingly pathetic amount of glee in her voice, as if it was a visit from the queen, rather than two city workers with badges. Poppy had kept her face impassive at the time, despite her elevating anxiety, tucking the news away to deal with later. But the UrbanMyth hack had knocked it off the top of Poppy's pyramid of worries, and she hadn't thought about it since.

Nor had she prepared for it.

"Should we sit down over here?" she heard one of the men ask.

Poppy blinked numbly. She'd never seen anyone sit in the meticulously arranged sitting area. She could recall the agent mentioning bespoke furniture in the lobby, but those couches could have been made out of cardboard for all she knew. And she was acutely aware that, however this conversation might go, it needed to be private. Seeing three people utilizing the sitting area would be remarkable enough for any resident of this building to take notice. Seeing Poppy Ridley sitting there talking to two detectives when a prominent Upper East Side man was missing? Now that would be unforgettable.

"Why don't we go upstairs?" Poppy offered grudgingly. She pivoted in the direction of the elevator bank and the men fell in step behind her. Her own personal police escort. She snuck a surreptitious glance at Fernando. His expression had morphed from nauseated to horrified. He clearly thought she'd made the wrong choice.

A well-put-together gray-haired woman with a leather Dior bag the size of her torso regarded the men with an appalled glare as the three of them stepped onto the elevator with her. Poppy recognized the woman as the mother of the Eastern European couple who occupied the fifth floor with their tennis-racket-toting brood of blond children. Could she tell that these men were cops? Or was the source of her wrath simply that she assumed they belonged in the service elevator instead?

"Are they with you?" the woman asked, giving a small, disapproving shake of her head.

Poppy replied with a curt nod, without further explanation, adhering to the game plan she engaged for any sticky situation: answer only the question asked. And she stuck to that game plan once the three of them were safely ensconced in the north sitting area of her oversized living room, the two men on the sofa across from her, pens hovering over their spiral notepads poised to record her responses.

Answer only the question asked. Did she know Bennett Stillman? Yes, he was her son's lacrosse coach. Had her son had any sessions with him in the past ten days? No. Did she know Norah Ryan? Yes, Norah worked with her husband. Poppy's answers were so benign she was almost starting to believe that Bennett was little more than an acquaintance.

If only.

Poppy crossed her legs and leaned forward on the velvet accent chair, sneaking a peek at her watch. They'd been at this for ten minutes now. How many different ways could she say the same thing? It was taking monk-like self-control for Poppy to prevent herself from screaming at them to get the hell out of her apartment. She was not accustomed to relinquishing power to someone who made less than her housekeeper.

She eyed the one with the mustache as he rearranged himself on the sofa, which was too low for his six-foot-one frame. Cross legs. Uncross. Brush lint. Cross at ankles. The beefier one, the one she now knew was named Joe Danielli, put a fist to his mouth, cleared the phlegm from his throat, a disgusting, guttural sound. Poppy's nose wrinkled.

"So, let me make sure I understand this." He tapped a pen on his spiral notepad. "Bennett Stillman is your son's occasional lacrosse coach, your children attend the same school, and your husband works with Norah Ryan, but other than that you've had little to no contact with either him or his wife, correct?"

"That's correct," Poppy replied, the lie slipping seamlessly between her teeth. Out of the corner of her eye, she noticed Maya in the reflection of the window, dusting a console table in the hallway. Poppy's lips retreated into a thin line. It wasn't like Maya to hover when Poppy had guests. It was an unwritten rule. Guests arrive, you disappear. *Poof.* Like magic.

"And you don't have any information that might be helpful in tracking down the whereabouts of Bennett."

"I wish I did," she said coolly. This wasn't a lie. She *did* want to know where that asshole was. But not for the same reasons as these two.

Joe flipped back a few pages in his notepad, narrowing his eyes to read what was written. "Was the last time you saw Bennett Stillman at the cocktail party at your apartment on February twenty-eighth?"

She tilted her head. Had she told them the date of the party?

Poppy was aware of the tension in her back now and made herself pause a second before she answered. "Yes, I believe so."

"Did you speak to Bennett at the party?"

She considered this, uneasiness threading down her throat into her stomach. "No, not that I recall."

He nodded slowly, frowning. "Why not?"

"No reason other than that I was focused on hosting a party for over one hundred people in my home, so I didn't get a chance to speak with every guest who attended," she replied, sounding appropriately nonchalant, with a hint of irritation.

He scribbled down a note. "Another parent said Heather and Oliver Quinn were in a heated conversation with Bennett and Norah during the party." He lifted his eyes to meet hers, and his voice trailed up at the end of the sentence like a question, which hung in the air.

A fishing line cast.

Poppy didn't bite.

Joe cocked his head to one side. "Have any idea what that was about?" he probed.

"I'm not sure, to be honest," she said, as if she was being anything *close* to honest. Poppy's gaze drifted back to the reflection in the window. She could see Maya had stopped dusting, was holding herself perfectly still now, staring into the living room with unconcealed interest. Poppy studied her out of the corner of her eye. She still didn't have Maya's signature on that nondisclosure agreement. That needed to be rectified. ASAP.

"Ms. Ridley." Joe's voice interrupted her thoughts.

Poppy shifted her attention back to his stubbly face. He was studying her, as if he were trying to figure out from across the poker table what cards she was holding. Poppy tugged on her earlobe, a nervous tic she had never even noticed before.

"Have you spent any time with Bennett Stillman outside of Reflex when he's not in the company of his wife?"

Poppy's expression shifted almost imperceptibly, like an animal scenting danger.

"No," she said, regretting her answer as soon as it slipped out. It would've been smarter to hedge. But they had no reason not to believe her, no reason to dig through countless days of security footage of her lobby. And she was smart enough to know that getting access would require a warrant.

"Did your husband have any contact with Bennett at the party?"

Poppy drummed a fingernail on the armrest, her eyes flitting back to the reflection in the window. Maya had disappeared. "I can't recall seeing them talk, but as I said I was focused on other things. I'm sure you can imagine there's a lot to manage with the caterers and the staff." She emphasized the word "staff," trying to summon any authority she could access.

A not-so-subtle reminder of her place in the social hierarchy. And theirs.

"Can you think of anyone who would have any reason to be angry with Bennett Stillman?"

"Angry?" There was something about the way he'd phrased the question that made the hairs stand up on the back of her neck. As if there could be a long line of people with personal vendettas against Bennett. Which there probably were, when Poppy considered it. All of the women he'd masterfully duped. For the first time, it struck Poppy that Bennett might not be on the lam, having absconded with her money. Someone else might've followed through with the type of violence against him that Poppy reserved for her fantasies. A woman driven by shame. A man possessed with jealousy. Off-kilter now, she opened her mouth, prepared to give a long-winded answer to keep the police from exploring the revenge theory any further. As far as she knew, Bennett was a respected member of the Crofton community and any interaction she'd had with him had always been positive. . . . *Answer only the question asked,* a frantic voice in her head cautioned.

"No." She cleared the tremor in her throat. "I wish I had relevant information to share, but I really don't know the couple very well." She shot a pointed look at her watch. "Looking at the time now, I unfortunately need to run."

They exchanged a brief look.

"Well, thanks for agreeing to speak with us," the mustached one said, his knees cracking as he rose to his feet. He reached into his breast pocket and withdrew a creased business card, handing it to her. "If you can think of anything, call anytime."

"Of course." She picked up her phone from the side table, and ushered them out of the living room, back down the hallway.

"You have a very nice apartment," Joe said, craning his neck to get a peek at the hand-painted embossed leather walls in the dining room.

Poppy nodded, impervious to his calculated attempt at small talk.

Ten steps from the front door, Joe slowed his pace, the soles of his shoes scuffing along the herringbone floor. "Oh, we should've done this at the beginning, but we need to get your contact information. In case we have any follow-up questions." He slid his hand into his breast pocket, dug around.

Poppy bit back her frustration at being held up inches from the finish line. Was this man purposely moving in slow motion now? She suddenly had the patience of a three-year-old and wanted nothing other than these two out of her home.

"Why don't I airdrop my contact card to you?" she offered, a touch of pique in her tone.

He stuck out his lower lip, nodding. "That works."

With a few quick taps, she accelerated their departure.

"All set," she said, sliding her phone into her back pocket.

When the front door closed behind them and the sound of the elevator departing for the lobby had faded, her heart rate returned to normal. She was pleased with her performance.

Sometimes, her ability to deceive people impressed even her.

Chapter Twenty-eight

HEATHER

HEATHER WAS ON a stool at the breakfast bar in her kitchen, tapping the stiff edge of Bad Cop's card against her palm when she heard the key in the lock of the front door. She slid the card into her back pocket and topped up her wine, pouring the last dregs from the bottle into her glass.

"Here you are," Oliver said, appearing at the other end of the galley kitchen, his brow furrowing as he took in her splotchy skin and the empty bottle of wine.

Heather never drank before five, but today she'd opened the bottle of pinot noir soon after the detectives left. How else could she be expected to get through an afternoon researching criminal lawyers while simultaneously bracing herself for the dismantling of her life? By two o'clock, news of the hack was up on Gothamist and CNN, and her "one glass" promise to herself had long since been broken.

"Where's Violet?" Oliver asked, the line between his eyebrows deepening.

"She won't be home for a few hours," Heather said, her voice sounding very far away. "Lacrosse practice."

Oliver blew a stream of air out of his cheeks, unbuttoned his coat, and plopped down on the stool next to hers, running a hand down his face. "What's going on, Heath?" His tone was taut. "You can't send me a message saying you need me to come home ASAP and then turn your phone off. If this is about—"

"Have you ever heard of a website called UrbanMyth?" Heather interrupted.

"Yeah," he drew out the word as if it had twice as many letters, eyeing her. "I heard that their stock tanked today because of some cyberattack. Wait . . ." He slapped his palms onto the counter. "Did you move any of our money into their stock? Is that what this is about?"

She shook her head. If only. If only that's what this was about.

Her hand wobbled as she twisted the stem of her glass between her fingers. The wine circled the sides of the glass, and she kept her gaze fixed on the ripples. "Oliver, UrbanMyth is where people reveal secrets and ask questions they don't want to ask other people face-to-face and it's all supposed to be confidential. That was the whole point." She forced herself to take a breath. "And I posted a lot of things on there, some of them true, some of them not. But now, thanks to this hack, everyone can see what I posted." She picked up her wineglass by the stem, took a slug.

"Like what kind of things?"

She found herself looking at the floor, the refrigerator, the box of Cheerios sitting on the counter, anywhere but his face, at anything but his eyes. The words were wedged below her lungs, and she struggled to push them out. "I wrote that I'm having an affair with Bennett Stillman."

The color drained from his face.

"I'm not really having an affair with him," she said quickly. "I was pretending to be someone else to get back at him. I wrote that because . . ."

"Jesus Christ," he muttered, lowering his head and rubbing his brow. "You did it because of that damn Instagram post about Violet." He rested his forehead on his knuckles. Heather didn't even have to look at him. The electric charge radiating from his body was enough to let her know how angry he was.

"Well, I couldn't let him get away with it, Oliver," she said, her guilt splintering and giving way to righteous anger. "You weren't doing anything about it, and *someone* had to pay for what happened to her." She didn't mention that the person whom she'd made pay for it was not, in fact, the person who'd done anything to Violet. That was beside the point now.

Oliver stood with a sudden backward scrape of his stool and started pacing. "So now what? Is this the end of it, Heath? You accosted them at a school party, you posted lies about him on some random website, you got whatever payback you needed. Tell me this is the end of it. This has to be the end."

Heather let out a shaky breath, tapping a fingernail against the side of her wineglass. The pain that had been pulsing in her head all day had parked itself behind her eyebrows. A reservoir of secrets overflowing in her skull.

"Oliver, the police came by today," she said flatly.

He froze mid-step and stared at her, mouth agape.

"The police? What do you mean they came by? Came by *here*?" He pointed to the floor.

She nodded. "You know how Bennett Stillman was reported missing? The police are talking to all of the Crofton parents as part of their investigation, so I guess today was my turn," she said, stretching the truth. A "select few" was probably more accurate. She realized now she'd never thought to ask.

Oliver's normally soothing hazel eyes darted over her face. "What kind of questions did they ask you?"

"Just general ones," she said, infusing her tone with as much nonchalance as possible, trying to neutralize the panic rolling off of Oliver in waves. "It sounded like they were covering their bases by asking everyone the same questions, hoping someone has seen him recently or has some other type of information on where he could be."

Oliver grabbed the back of his neck, gave it a squeeze.

"It's really not that big of a deal, Oli," she said, without a trace of conviction in her voice to back it up. It was, Heather knew, a big fucking deal.

"They must think he's dead somewhere or at the very least in danger if they're talking to that many people. Wait. What if the police find out you're the one who wrote that post?" Oliver's voice was verging on hysterical, and Heather trained her eyes on a water mark on the counter to steady herself. "Don't you think it's going to look really weird that not only were you shouting at this guy at a party in front of a ton of witnesses, but you also claimed to be sleeping with him?"

Yes, I do.

She raised her eyes, ready to tell him that the police already knew about her post, but the look of concern on his face was so strong her voice melted.

Oliver collapsed back onto the stool, his face ashen. "Do you think someone told them what happened at the party and that's why they came? They think you have some vendetta against him?"

"No, of course not. I think I was just next on their list," she said unconvincingly.

The silence unspooled between them, and in the stillness Heather considered coming clean. Laying all the cards on the table. What she'd told the police, what she'd seen on Caroline's phone. Everything. *The girl's phone was right there on the floor of the gym, Oli, who wouldn't take a look?*

But the truth stayed lodged inside her chest, a stubborn, stabbing pain.

She rested her forehead on her fingertips, feeling the wine pushing up the back of her throat. "Oli, the police want to talk to you too."

His eyebrows shot up. "Are you kidding me?"

She shook her head gravely.

"And you're telling me you think this is not that big of a deal?" His voice rose. "Jesus Christ, what if they come to my office, Heather? I can't lie to the police and say 'Oh, Bennett Stillman? No sir, my wife has never mentioned the name to me before.'" He ran a hand down his clammy face. "We're really going to need to get our story straight now."

She bit her bottom lip, staring down into the burgundy-colored sediment sticking to the bottom of her glass. He was right. It was critical that their stories matched. They had to be on the same page now. With *everything*. If the police took the time to read the rest of her posts, her loose relationship with the truth would become glaringly obvious. These lies—not lies exactly, but omissions—expanded in the back of her throat like a sponge, threatening to cut off her air.

"Why do I get the feeling there's something you're not telling me?" he said slowly, studying her.

The only way out was through.

She filled her lungs with air and wrenched the words out of her mouth. "Oliver, I'm not really a writer. I paid someone to write my first book for me, and I recently took out a loan from the bank to pay her to write another one."

Oliver's eyes were wide and wild, gawking at her as if she'd confessed she was part chimp.

"What the hell are you talking about?" he sputtered. "You . . . Why the hell would you do that?"

Her eyes fell shut. She'd done it for the same reason she did everything. For Violet. But it was never supposed to go this far. If she hadn't been on that stupid Benefit Committee years ago it never would have. But Heather had learned early on that there were two ways to ingratiate yourself (and, in turn, your child) to Crofton's development office: make a large donation or volunteer with gusto. They couldn't afford option A, which left option B as the only viable choice. When Violet was in kindergarten, Heather joined the Library Committee, the Teacher Appreciation Committee, and the Community Service Club, volunteering alongside stay-at-home moms with full-time nannies and no idea of limits. Three months into the school year, it was clear she would need an after-school babysitter for Violet to keep up with her rigorous committee-meeting schedule. She found the woman Oliver referred to as "Mary Poppins" using City Sitters, a website that vetted childcare providers, promising college-educated helpers looking to make extra money. Heather couldn't believe her luck when Lori, a fresh-faced ball of energy with an MFA from UCLA arrived at her door. Lori was supplementing her writing income, she explained, and was happy to help out as much as Heather needed. With Lori at her beck and call, Heather was free to work her way up the volunteer hierarchy, and by the time Violet was in the fourth grade she'd made it to the top of the food chain: the Benefit Committee. That was where she met Sunny Brown, a mother of four whose three eldest children attended Andover. When the conversation at their biweekly committee meetings inevitably meandered into talk about boarding school applications, Heather hung on Sunny's words as if she were a prophet. "I'll tell you what boarding schools want now," Sunny had said, lifting an authoritative finger. "They want diversity among the professions of the parent body, so if you're a banker or a lawyer you're completely screwed. You need to be an artist or a writer or, I don't know . . . sing on Broadway." Sunny had rolled her eyes as if it was all too insufferable to bear, but Heather had taken it all in, chewed on it, rolled it around in her mind like a hard candy, trying to figure out how this new information could be used to her advantage. Then fate stepped in. What else would you call it when, the very next day, in casual conversation, Lori mentioned she was doing some ghostwriting. "You wouldn't believe the amount of money some people are willing to pay to have their name on the cover of a book in Barnes & Noble," she'd marveled. Until then, it had never occurred to Heather that someone could *pay* to become an author. How could she pass up the opportunity that had fallen out of the sky and landed in her lap? It was the ultimate shortcut. Of course, she hadn't dared tell Oliver the details—only that she wanted to try her hand at writing—and engaged the help of her ghostwriting Mary Poppins to the tune of sixty thousand dollars. It had been easier to siphon off money back then. They were doing a gut renovation of their apartment at the time and paying cash to take advantage of the ten percent discount. With how much money was flying out of their savings account, Oliver hadn't questioned it when there were three unexplained withdrawals totaling sixty thousand dollars. He still thought the flooring went fifteen thousand dollars over budget and grumbled about it whenever Violet pushed her dining room chair out too swiftly across the walnut floors.

When Heather had received a two-book offer from a big publisher, she and Oliver had celebrated with dinner at Nobu. "I can't believe you've had this talent all along and I never knew," Oliver had gushed, pointing his chopstick at her. Heather hadn't been able to wipe the grin from her face, her happiness eradicating any prickles of guilt. She had done it. Heather Quinn: published writer—an interesting, diverse career. The boarding schools would eat it up, and it had all come together so perfectly, so seamlessly she'd never once stopped to consider the plan for the *second* book in the contract. It wasn't as if she could *write* it.

"My wife is an author," Oliver would tell people, beaming, when in truth she was no more qualified to be an author than Oliver was to play second base for the Yankees.

Heather slid her wineglass out of reach now to keep from fidgeting with it. "Someone told me creative careers are a big draw for boarding schools and it gives applicants a leg up, so . . ." she said, losing the words in her mouth.

So, I lied to you.

So, I invented an entire career.

So, I handed over a huge chunk of our money you knew nothing about.

Nothing was said for a few painfully long minutes. The only sound in the room was the low hum of a vacuum cleaner coming from the apartment directly above theirs. Oliver was looking down at the two fists clenched in his lap, but Heather could see the flush of anger creeping up his neck. She used to joke that his face was like a thermometer, the red mercury rising as he got angrier. She'd never seen it get past his cheeks before, but when he finally lifted his head, the crimson color had reached his hairline.

"I can't believe you took it this far." His voice was low, controlled. And simmering. "When the whole college admissions scandal broke, we both agreed it was completely screwed up. That we'd never *pay* to get our child into a school."

"But this isn't like that. Violet *deserves* to go to that school." Her voice came out high and strangled, shame mingling with indignation. "What I did is the same thing as someone getting their child an internship in order to pad their résumé. *Everyone* does that."

"Will you listen to yourself?" The words exploded out of his mouth, echoing off of their designer cabinets. "For god's *sake*, Heather. You don't even realize how far gone you are." His eyes burned into her. Normally so calm and earnest, now so full of fire.

She shrank into the stool. Tears had sprung to her eyes, blurring her vision, but she heard the slap of Oliver's palm against the granite counter.

"What you've done has crossed so many lines." He held up his hand, counting the transgressions, spittle sparking on his lips. "You lied to your daughter, you lied to me, you created a career that was a lie." The vein on his neck bulged and throbbed. In their seventeen years of marriage, she had never seen the fury that was simmering under his expression now. "You risked our marriage over this. Over a fucking boarding school that—newsflash—I'm not even sure Violet really *wants* to attend. I want the best for Violet too. But you . . . this . . ." He waved his hands indiscriminately. "Isn't it." He pushed his stool back. "You're a liar, and you made Violet and me liars too. You had our daughter posing with your book in the window of The Corner Bookstore, and you *knew* it was all a big fucking lie. And the worst part is your plan was to *keep* lying and let me go around like an idiot telling everyone my wife was working on her second book. I was actually *proud* of you." He scoffed and gave a disgusted shake of his head. "And now I'm ashamed."

His words were like shards of glass in her stomach. "Oli, I'm sorry," she cried. "I was going to—" She searched for the right words, but the rest of the sentence melted away when she lifted her eyes to meet his. He was staring at her so hatefully that for a moment she wondered if she was going to be slapped.

After a second, he blinked. Hastily, he leapt to his feet, the legs of the stool screeching against the floor as he pushed it back. "You were *never* going to tell me if you didn't get caught. *That's* what you were going to do. Be honest with me for *once*." He spun and stormed out of the kitchen.

Heather listened to the sound of his feet hammering down the hallway, followed by the slam of the front door behind him. She remained frozen for a minute, wondering if she should go after him. But she couldn't. A wave of nausea surged from her gut and her fist flew to her mouth. She scrambled to the sink before the bottle of wine came up, splattering deep red liquid across her white ceramic tile, the bitter bile burning her throat. Sweat and tears and snot streamed out too. Eyes closed, chest heaving, she twisted the tap on and cupped her palm under the stream, bringing it to her lips, swishing out her mouth and spitting. She ripped a paper towel from the roll by the sink and dabbed at her mouth and damp face. Tossing the crumpled-up paper towel into the trash, she swiped an index finger under each watery eye and surveyed the scene. Her kitchen looked like someone had butchered a small animal on her countertops.

A metaphor for the mess she'd made of her life.

Now it was up to Heather to figure out how to clean it up.

Chapter Twenty-nine

NORAH

NORAH WAS SITTING on the end of their bed—no, *her* bed—when the familiar number blinked on her screen.

"What now?" she sighed, swiping the phone off the duvet. Her insides felt like a wrung-out dish rag, and she wasn't eager to subject herself to another twist. In the past week, Caroline had been vacillating between relief at no longer harboring the secret of her stepfather's trysts, to guilt over being, in her eyes, the reason for the dissolution of her mother's marriage. Norah had ridden the waves with her, reassuring her sensitive daughter that nobody was responsible for a marriage other than the two people in it. But it was a tough sell. Tougher still, was the hypercritical voice in Norah's head, wrestling its way into her consciousness, the one telling her she could've prevented this from happening to Caroline. Because, in truth, she could've.

She *should've.*

Norah had forgotten—no, she'd blocked—the suspicions she'd had about her husband. But the internet doesn't forget. After Norah heard about the UrbanMyth hack, she'd inputted her email into the search, curious to see if these hackers really had managed to dump the amount of information claimed in the article. And they had. All twelve posts Norah had written on that silly app fanned out on her laptop screen, including the last one. Reading it, Norah was hit with an excruciating realization: she knew Bennett was a cheater long before the proof was in her hands.

My husband is hiding something, but I don't know what.

She couldn't remember typing those words, although she must have. Probably in some faraway hotel room, jet-lagged and over-worked, mentally stripped to the bone and searching for a reason-able explanation for his inconsistent behavior. Her gut had articulated what her voice would not. It'd probably been a relief to put the words out into the universe, a backhoe excavating the un-comfortable thought from her brain and depositing it somewhere else. But the fact that she'd ignored her gut, which was so plainly telling her something was off, made her dizzy with regret. It need not have happened. Or, more accurately, it need not have hap-pened as it had, with Caroline put in a position where she bore the unnecessary weight on her still child-sized shoulders.

Norah readjusted herself on the bed now, flipped over the phone, and stared at the name on the glowing screen. *Joseph Dani-elli.* She'd hadn't spoken to Detective Danielli since their initial call when she'd provided him a list of places Bennett liked to frequent, speculated where Bennett might retreat to if he wanted some time to himself. Detective Danielli had thanked her, told her he would be in touch, and asked Norah to call him when she heard from Bennett. Norah could remember he'd used the word "when," reit-erating her belief that Bennett contacting her was inevitable.

Taking a deep breath, Norah tapped the green circle and tilted her head to free her hair from her ear.

"Hi, Ms. Ryan, it's Joe Danielli. Sorry to bother you. Is now a good time to run through a few things?"

"Sure," she said, pushing herself off the bed and pacing a small circle around her bedroom.

"My partner went to talk to some of Bennett's employees at his place of business today and the receptionist, Brinley, showed us Bennett's back office. I know you mentioned you'd already taken a look at his office and didn't see anything unusual, but Brinley opened a few of the cupboards and my partner noticed a bur-gundy suitcase tucked away. She thought it'd always been in there, but I wanted to run it past you since you previously told us he'd left the apartment with a suitcase. Do you remember what color it was?"

"It was burgundy." Norah chewed the side of her thumbnail. "I don't know if he kept another one at his office, though. I think there might have been a lot of things I didn't know."

There was a long pause and for a second she thought the line had gone dead.

"There is no easy way to say this, but in our preliminary questioning of some of the other people who knew your husband, it appears as though there is a possibility of some infidelity in your marriage."

Norah stared at the opposite wall, slack-jawed. Who'd told them? Poppy didn't strike Norah as the type to confess. Was Norah really so out of touch in her own life that it was common knowledge among the other mothers? The thought lodged in her throat, making it hard to pull breath into her lungs.

"Ms. Ryan? Are you still there?"

"Yes," she answered, expelling a small cough. Her thoughts were growing muddier despite her efforts to sift through them. "I'm sorry, but this isn't what I expected to hear."

"I understand," he said with forced sympathy. Norah could hear the sound of his fingers typing on a keyboard as he spoke. *Click. Click. Click.* Norah imagined he delivered all kinds of bad news. Car accidents, arrests, deaths. A grown man cheating on his wife wouldn't even register on his Richter scale. "These sorts of things often come as a bit of a shock. Did you *suspect* any infidelity in your marriage?"

She gripped the phone tighter, as if it were a stress ball.

"Yes," she answered, heat rising up her throat. Norah had explained to Detective Danielli during the course of their initial conversation that she and Bennett had fought over her filing for divorce, that Bennett had packed up and left the apartment, told her she wouldn't see him again. However, when Detective Danielli had probed for Norah's reasons for filing, she'd answered "irreconcilable differences," being purposely vague. Given the prominence of Bennett's family, Norah hadn't wanted to risk the information getting out and the media digging into their marriage. Now it seemed someone else had taken it upon themselves to provide the police with some clarity.

"I did suspect Bennett had been unfaithful, which is what led to the irreconcilable differences," she said finally.

Another pause.

"And do you have any idea *who* he might have become involved with, Ms. Ryan?" There was a new edge in his tone that Norah hadn't heard before. This time he wasn't posing the question simply to placate Norah's overbearing mother-in-law.

Something had changed.

She felt her tongue start to form the word "yes," but a small voice in the back of her head cautioned her. If she revealed she knew it was Poppy, one question would lead to another, and Norah would inevitably need to reveal the existence of the photo, which would drag Caroline into the conversation.

Her daughter had been through enough.

"No," she said. "But from his actions it was clear to me he'd been unfaithful. Call it women's intuition."

"Right." Norah could hear the skepticism in his tone. She resumed pacing, avoiding her reflection in the mirror above the vanity.

She could hear rustling on the other end of the line. After a moment, he expelled a long breath. "Have you heard of an app called UrbanMyth?"

She froze mid-stride.

Without waiting for an answer, he continued, "A Crofton parent by the name of Heather Quinn posted on the site, and I quote: 'Confession time: I'm sleeping with my child's lacrosse coach—the one from Reflex on the UES. I think he's willing to end his marriage. Should I end mine?'"

Norah dropped down onto the bed. "That . . . that surprises me," she managed.

"So, Heather Quinn wasn't one of the women you suspected of having a relationship with your husband?"

"No," she answered, utterly confused. *Was this why Heather had accosted them at the party?*

More typing on his keyboard. "Well, Ms. Quinn has denied the relationship. She seemed to have some nonrelated issue that prompted her to write the post. Has Ms. Quinn ever threatened you or your family?"

"Threatened? No." Norah's brow furrowed. "Are you . . ." She gripped her forehead, fighting against the sharp pain in her temples. "Are you saying that you think something has *happened* to Bennett? In our last conversation, you said you thought he was blowing off steam somewhere."

"We're exploring all the avenues, Ms. Ryan. With Bennett's prominence in the neighborhood and the fact that the press has run with the story now, we need to make sure we're doing our legwork." He moved the phone away from his mouth to clear the phlegm from his throat before resuming. "If we have any new information about your husband's whereabouts, you'll be the first to know. For now, let us know if you hear from him."

If.

Norah didn't miss the way he'd said "if" this time.

The call ended and Norah stared at the phone so long the screen went dark. It slipped out of her fingers and onto her lap. She'd been nursing the idea that Bennett was punishing her with his absence. *If I walk out this door, you'll regret it. I can promise you that.* In the silence of her bedroom, her thoughts began hurtling off a steep cliff.

An accident. A self-inflicted wound. A heart attack. Lying in a ditch.

She shook her head, shaking the scenarios away. This was exactly what Bennett wanted. For Norah to worry about him. To turn her into an emotional hostage. And she refused to give this man another drop of her emotional energy.

"Where the hell are you, Bennett?" she whispered, the question mounting like an itch beneath her fingernails. She pushed herself off the bed, and in five long strides she was at the door of his walk-in closet, yanking it open. *His and hers walk-in closets,* Norah remembered the agent pointing out as Norah walked through the apartment with her hand on her pregnant belly. *Not his and hers, mine and mine,* Norah had silently corrected her. When she and Bennett had gotten engaged, emptying her things out of one of the closets to make room for his possessions had felt like more of a commitment than the ring on her finger.

Another sacrifice made for him.

With a steadying breath, she stood in the middle of the closet trying to decide her plan of attack. She scanned the hangered rows of hoodies, dress shirts coated in plastic from the dry-cleaning delivery, and polos. Spotting the blazer he'd worn to Poppy's cocktail party, she shoved her hands deep into each pocket, finding only a crumpled monogrammed cocktail napkin and two toothpicks. She picked up a pile of indigo jeans from one of the shelves, wondering exactly when her husband had managed to collect seven pairs of the same jean, and rifled through the pockets. Crumpled CVS receipts and a folded twenty-dollar bill. Nothing earth-shattering. She flipped open lids of shoeboxes, emptying the contents onto the floor of the closet. Another one. Another one. Another one. By the time she stopped to take a breath, it looked like the closet had been ransacked by armed intruders. Norah was ready to throw in the towel when her attention snagged on an old messenger bag hanging on the back of the door. It appeared to be empty, but she unzipped the side pocket and jammed her hand inside, pricking her pinky on something sharp. Flinching, she brought her finger to her mouth, before using her other hand to extract the source of her pain from the bag: a small spiral notebook.

Stepping over the mess, Norah headed back into her bedroom and dropped onto the edge of the bed. She flipped open the notebook, her heart rate quickening. Narrowing her eyes, she tried to make sense of the notations, which were written in faded pencil—as if when Bennett wrote them he'd hoped they'd disappear. Numbers were scattered along the white, lined page, peppered with the words "odds," "bet," and "loss." Turning the pages, she saw what looked like some kind of running tally. She kept flipping. A phone number she didn't recognize. The name Justin. More numbers. Norah squinted. Were those dates? She flipped the page. More numbers. These ones had a *k* beside them. Mostly negative ones now. She kept flipping until she reached the last note he took.

A date.

It was the same day that Norah had confronted him. The day he stormed out of the apartment. But it wasn't the date that caused her stomach to climb up into her throat.

It was the name circled below it.

Chapter Thirty

HEATHER

HEATHER IGNORED THE peppy-looking blonde trying to shove a flyer into her hand, gesturing to the earbuds that were planted firmly in her ears—an indication that she was on a call. She wasn't, but it was a good cover story. She had been standing on the corner of Eighty-eighth and Park for the past twenty minutes. Her head throbbed. Oliver hadn't come home last night, and after spending the evening with her retinas glued to the blue light of her computer screen, Heather felt as though every cell in her body had been wrung out. She needed fluids. She squinted at her watch, wondering if there was time to pop down to the deli two blocks away and pick up a bottle of water. But she couldn't risk missing her opportunity.

The brownstone-lined sidewalks were eerily quiet for a Saturday morning. No parents jogging behind overzealous preschoolers on scooters, no yoga-pant-clad women with manicured hands wrapped around a fresh green juice. As if in defiance of Heather's mood, the sun shone brightly, illuminating the pale pink buds dotting the branches on the trees that lined the street. It was a gorgeous morning, despite the fact that the majority of the residents of the Upper East Side wouldn't emerge from their homes during daylight hours to experience it.

News of the UrbanMyth hack had erupted like a dirty bomb, defiling everything in a ten-block radius of Crofton. It was as if they'd all walked in on each other in the bathroom and were now incapable of making eye contact. Those who could fled to their country houses to hunker down. Others were holed up in their apartments, cauterizing the damage to their reputations, their marriages, their friendships, their careers, their lives.

Unlike her peers, Heather was well schooled in facing adversity. And she was going to tackle it the way she always had: by taking matters into her own hands.

A dark-haired woman with a Yankees baseball cap pulled low over her face emerged from the glass doors of the prewar building. She looked like a celebrity trying to avoid the paparazzi. An electrical charge pulsed through Heather as she watched the woman cross her arms impatiently over her chest, peering up and down the street. Heather adjusted her aviator sunglasses on her face and stepped toward her, until she was close enough to confirm her identity.

Heather had plugged in email after email from the Crofton parent directory, trying to track down the person who'd spearheaded Violet's character assassination. She was on her eighth email address when the words appeared on her screen.

Let's just say I know this family and I'm not surprised they're raising a drug dealer.

When is the Crofton drug dealer going to be expelled?

The Crofton drug dealer is recruiting at other private schools.

There were thirty-two posts in all about Violet from the one user. The user had engaged in a calculated, systematic attack on Violet, igniting a fuse of fear underneath other Crofton parents and leading the rallying cry for Violet's expulsion.

And now that user was standing in front of her.

"Gretchen!" Heather called out, her voice like a knife. Sharp and cold.

Gretchen tilted her head to peek from under her baseball cap. Heather was close enough now to see her eyes, which were so red and swollen it looked like she'd washed her face with pollen. Heather wondered which UrbanMyth confession had triggered the most tears, the one where she'd revealed she'd found the Viagra in her husband's coat pocket with two missing pills or the one where she talked about wishing her husband were dead. A toss-up. Heather would bet her life savings that the vitriol Gretchen had spewed about Violet didn't even register on her scale of regrets.

"Hi, Heather." Gretchen's tone was impatient. "I can't talk now. I'm meeting someone." She pulled her hoodie tighter around her chest, averting her eyes as if Heather were a panhandler whose gaze she wished to avoid.

Heather shook her head. "No, you're not."

It took until the wee hours of the morning to work her way through every word Gretchen had written on UrbanMyth and develop an action plan in response. But the toughest part had been figuring out how to get Gretchen to leave the safe cocoon of her apartment. Heather wasn't going to put anything in writing—fool her once—but she also couldn't afford to play it safe and wait for the opportune time to strike. It wasn't clear how things would play out with the police, and if she left this loose end untied, she'd never be able to forgive herself.

She'd always had a strong sense of justice.

Gretchen cocked her head, forcing a puff of laughter out of her nose. "What do you mean, 'No, you're not'?"

"I know you're the one who wrote all that crap about Violet."

Gretchen's blinking sped up as she connected the dots. "Did you . . ." She swiveled her head, realizing there wasn't a FedEx truck anywhere on the block. "Did you make up a story to get me out here?"

It was easy once Heather had remembered Gretchen's Achilles' heel. Gretchen might want to take up residence under a rock right now, but she was still beholden to one of the most powerful entities at Crofton: the Benefit Committee. Heather had approached a FedEx delivery driver making his rounds, offered him one hundred dollars to call Gretchen and tell her he had a delivery, one that the sender had said should not be left with the doorman under any circumstances. "In the list of contents, it says it's an auction item," the deliveryman had said, flawlessly adhering to Heather's requested script. "Unfortunately, we're short-staffed and I can't come inside the building."

Hook, line, sinker.

"Why did you do it, Gretchen? What the hell has my daughter ever done to you?"

Gretchen held up a palm. "Oh, grow up, Heather. Nobody gives a crap about your precious Violet right now."

"I do," Heather snapped. She could feel the breath in her flared nostrils. She wanted to push Gretchen's face against the dirty sidewalk.

"Okay, this is ridiculous." Gretchen choked out a mocking laugh. "I always knew you were a psychopath." She pivoted back toward the entrance of her building.

"I know about the SSAT," Heather blurted, and Gretchen froze.

The SSAT. The three-hour entrance exam every eighth-grader in New York City applying to a private high school was subjected to, the score of which made up a significant portion of each student's application package. SSAT tutors pimped their experience to the tune of seven hundred dollars an hour, a fee that New York City parents would gladly pay if it meant increasing an eighty-five percent to ninety-five. Parents who couldn't foot the bill, or who had been asleep at the switch and failed to line up one of the top tutors, were left scrambling with workbooks, SSAT practice apps, and a prayer.

But, like everything in the Upper East Side, there was always a loophole to be exploited.

Gretchen turned back around, drilled Heather with a look.

"You had an awful lot of questions about which doctors are loose with their requirements for a disability report," Heather continued, taking pleasure in watching the terror spread across Gretchen's face. "And I couldn't help but wonder if you were seeking a falsified accommodation for Charlotte."

The first time Heather had heard a disability report referred to as a "golden ticket" was at a client dinner with Oliver, when one of the other wives had imbibed one too many glasses of wine and waxed poetic about getting her son into Exeter. "You get a specialist to say your child has test anxiety or has a fear of number-two pencils or whatever, and *poof.*" She'd drunkenly snapped her fingers. "An extra hour to take the test. And the best part is the schools never know because it's all confidential which students have accommodations." Her husband had quickly ushered his wife out of the dinner party, and Heather had taken out her cellphone and typed in the words "disability report—golden ticket." But Violet had gone ahead and rocked the first SSAT she took, so there was no need to go any further down the rabbit hole.

Apparently, the same could not be said for Charlotte.

"You don't have any proof of anything," Gretchen said without an ounce of conviction.

"It's funny you should use the word 'proof' because that is exactly the word you used in your posts. You remember: when you asked which specialists were known *not* to require 'proof'?" Heather enforced her point with air quotes. "And then there are five more posts where you ask if someone can tell you the questions posed in a clinical exam for test anxiety and whether the test could be successfully gamed." Heather cocked her head. "That's a lot of curiosity about a path you didn't intend to pursue."

A doorman in a black-blazered uniform emerged from the glass doors, gripping the brass handle as a white-haired woman slowly shuffled through. Both women watched, halting their conversation.

"What do you want from me, Heather?" Gretchen spat when the woman was out of earshot. "An apology? Fine, sorry. Happy now?" She threw up her hands. "But in case you've missed the thread here, nobody is going to care what someone wrote about a silly SSAT test when it's buried under literally thousands of other posts."

"Well, the schools that Charlotte has applied to might care."

Heather dipped her hand into her purse, extracted a manila envelope, and held it up. "And they won't need to sift through any posts because I'm going to send them the highlight reel. Anonymously, of course. I've got my own personal FedEx driver willing to make the drops." Heather gestured with a thumb over her shoulder.

Gretchen's red-rimmed eyes blazed. "What the hell do you *want*, Heather?"

Heather tapped the sharp corner of the envelope against her palm. She imagined Gretchen with her keyboard courage, hiding behind the cloak of anonymity as she typed in *If that girl isn't expelled there is going to be a mass exodus from Crofton*. Gretchen knew Violet wasn't peddling drugs to her fellow eighth-graders out of her locker. Yet, she'd tried to set fire to everything Violet had worked so hard for.

If Heather didn't make her *pay* for that, what kind of parent would she be?

"I want you to withdraw Charlotte's high school applications."

"Wh . . . where would she go to high school then?" Gretchen sputtered.

"Where ninety-five percent of the kids in this country go—public school."

Gretchen's mouth dropped open. She looked at Heather as if she'd just suggested her daughter join ISIS. "You . . . you can't be serious."

"Those are your choices, Gretchen. And if you want my opinion, I think Charlotte has a slightly better chance of getting into a decent college if her transcript isn't flagged for academic fraud. The schools are very touchy about that subject now, you know." Heather tucked the envelope back in her purse, hitched it up farther on her shoulder. "Think of it this way. At least at a new school you can use a different email for the parent directory." She turned on a heel and left Gretchen standing on the sidewalk, mouth agape, her eyes burning a hole in Heather's back.

Heather silently congratulated herself for taking care of the first action item of her plan. But it was the second action item that was sitting like a brick in her gut. When she was one block from her building, she checked her phone. No messages from the police. No messages from Oliver.

She took a deep breath and dialed Poppy's number.

Chapter Thirty-one

POPPY

"We appreciate you agreeing to speak with us again, Ms. Ridley," the detective said, flipping open his spiral notepad and leaning forward on the couch.

Poppy set her iPhone down beside her on the armrest of the accent chair and flashed a tight smile, fighting the impulse to add a curt *Well, did I have a choice?* Poppy was aware she could've demanded her lawyer be present, but she was also aware that there is no brighter neon sign blinking I HAVE SOMETHING TO HIDE than a person who refuses to answer a few simple questions about a missing person without lawyering-up first.

And Poppy didn't *need* to lawyer up.

In the eyes of these two detectives, Poppy was a minor character in this story, her only touchpoint being that she was the one to host a large social event with other Crofton parents. And Poppy intended to stay a minor character. She'd been slightly alarmed to see the two detectives waiting for her in the lobby twenty-four short hours after their first appearance, but they must've heard more about the scuffle between Norah and Heather from other Crofton parents and wanted to nail down some details from the hostess. The whole scene was so low brow it would've been seared into the memory of her well-heeled guests, who likely recounted it to the police as if recounting it to a therapist. Poppy had downplayed the argument to the detectives in their previous conversation, in an effort to remove herself from the narrative entirely, but today she was revising her strategy. Keeping the focus squarely on Heather, she realized, meant keeping it off of her.

A gazelle doesn't need to outrun a lion. It simply needs to outrun one other gazelle in the herd.

"We wanted to circle back on a few things we talked about before," the mustached one said as the sound of Poppy's phone ringing filled the large room, lighting up the name of the caller on the screen.

Poppy's eyes narrowed. *Maybe: Heather Quinn*. Why the hell would that woman be calling her? Irritably, Poppy tapped "decline," laced her fingers together, and rested her hands in her lap, doing the best to convey *Get on with it* with her body language.

"Do you need to get that?" The detective motioned with his pen to her phone.

Poppy shook her head and slid a finger along the side of the phone to set it to silent mode. A second later, it vibrated against her leg and an incoming text flashed on the screen, snagging the attention of both men. Poppy tilted the screen toward her, quickly reading the message before swiping it away. *I need to talk to you. Can you call me when you have a chance? This is Heather Quinn.*

"Somebody must really need to talk to you," Detective Danielli said, raising an eyebrow. "We can wait if you need us to."

"It's nobody important," Poppy said, meaning it. She flipped the phone screen-side down, realizing this was probably Heather's desperate attempt to rewrite the history of her tantrum at the party. Fat chance.

He licked his teeth. "You told us yesterday that the last time you had contact with Bennett Stillman was at the cocktail party held at your home. Is that correct?"

She fiddled with the bezel of her Cartier watch. "Well, I wouldn't say I had any real contact with him that evening, but that was the last time I saw him, yes." She lifted a finger to her lips, as if a thought was only now occurring to her. "You know, when I think about it, I do remember seeing him that evening with Norah.

I didn't get a chance to speak with him, but he did appear to be distressed over the altercation they were having with Heather. At one point, it got a little violent. A punch was thrown. I think a glass was too." She paused to arrange her expression to ensure it appeared appropriately concerned. "I hope this doesn't have anything to do with Bennett's disappearance."

They exchanged a look. Why weren't either of them writing any of that down?

"Did you make any attempt to contact Bennett *after* the evening of the party? In any way?"

Goosebumps rose along Poppy's arm. That was an odd follow-up question. "I think I did call him to try to arrange a training session for Henry," she said, hedging. "But I never heard back."

"Did you call his work number or his mobile number? Or email? Perhaps another method . . ."

Tugging her ear, Poppy snuck a glance at Joe, whose eyes remained glued to her. There was something different about him this time. It was in his body language, which was a degree stiffer than it had been. He was squeezing his lower lip between his thumb and index finger, a glint she couldn't quite identify shining in his eye.

She felt an instinctive tightening in her chest.

"Mobile, I think. He's impossible to get ahold of on the work number, and I prefer not to leave messages that go unanswered." She attempted a light eye roll, but it fell flat.

He nodded. This time, he wrote in his notepad.

Poppy bit the inside of her cheek, and it occurred to her that it had been a mistake to hedge. It was likely a standard question they were posing to everyone, and now she'd opened herself up to more scrutiny. She was off her game.

His pen stopped. "It sounds like Mr. Stillman was a hard person to get in contact with . . ." He let the silence hang and Poppy chose not to fill it. Outside the window, the sunny day had clouded over and sporadic raindrops began pelting against the floor-to-ceiling windows, briefly pulling Detective Danielli's gaze away from Poppy.

"Nice view," he said, the words sounding more like an accusation than a compliment. He turned his attention back to her and tapped a thick thumb against his knee, assessing her. Her jaw ached, and she realized she was gritting her teeth.

"Ms. Ridley, it's clear to anyone who comes in here that you have . . ." He paused, seemingly searching for the right word. With a little sigh he continued, "An abundance of resources."

She narrowed her eyes. He had the smug look of a magician about to let you in on the secret to the trick.

"Have you ever been the victim of blackmail?"

"What the hell kind of question is that?" she snapped, instantly regretting the outburst. It was possible they'd caught wind of Bennett's grift and were asking every Crofton mother the same question. Probing for a reaction. A reaction she'd now given them. She crossed one leg over the other, her foot jiggling as she mentally scrambled for control. But her regret was morphing into a much more comfortable feeling: indignation. How dare they? How dare they assume she was the kind of weak person Bennett could victimize?

A ring pierced the suddenly charged silence, and the left side of Joe's blazer illuminated. Jamming a hand in his pocket and retrieving his phone, Joe frowned down at the screen. "I should take this," he grumbled, shooting his partner a grave look before rising to his feet and stomping toward the hallway. "Joe Danielli," Poppy heard him say.

"While he's taking that, mind if I use your bathroom?" the other one asked.

"First door on your left." Poppy gestured with an irritated hand.

As Poppy watched him disappear from the room, a terrifying thought clawed its way into her consciousness. She'd posted on UrbanMyth about a person blackmailing her, asking for suggestions on how to contact him. But there was no way they could find it and trace it back to Poppy. Could they? Panic ricocheted through her chest as her fingers scrabbled for the phone next to her. It would be impossible, she told herself. Impossible. Her heart pounded against her ribs as she brought up her list of contacts. She blinked into the screen.

No.

No. No. No.

Poppy had two contact cards with her name in her contact list. One was under Poppy Ridley, which Poppy had populated with her contact information herself, and the other was under her maiden name, automatically created by iOS when she set up an Apple ID. The contact card with her maiden name contained the email address she had used to create her Apple ID. Her shopping email address.

Poppy couldn't be sure which one, in her haste, had been air-dropped to Joe.

The horizon line seemed to tilt the trees outside the window on their sides. Poppy shot a frantic look over her shoulder, as if one of the detectives might have snuck up behind her. Her mind was going in seven different directions, scrambling for a game plan. She needed to remember the exact words she'd posted, while also try-ing to figure out a way she could spin them so they could not be related to Bennett. It was critical for her to stay one step ahead.

"Can a post I wrote on UrbanMyth be used against me in any way?" Poppy had asked her lawyer yesterday, declining to provide any identifying details. "I can't give you a full answer without knowing the specifics," he'd answered, in that annoyingly useless way of his. "But if you're asking if posts on social media or other types of electronic data can be used as evidence against you, the answer is yes. I've seen social media used to persuade a jury that a person is capable of the crimes he's accused of."

Poppy dragged her fingertips down her cheeks. Crime. Jury. Accused. The words collected in her throat like magnets, making her choke.

Joe came back into the living room with his partner trailing him, and Poppy snapped to attention, unpeeling her fingers from her phone and returning it to the side table. Her heart was beating so hard in her chest she worried they could hear it.

"Where were we?" Joe yanked at the thighs of his dress pants before dropping back onto the couch. There were small red patches on his neck that hadn't been there before.

She dabbed at a bead of sweat on her forehead and tried to mask her efforts to take a deep breath, mentally reassemble herself. It was a game of chess, and she had to think three moves ahead. "I was startled by the word 'blackmail,'" she said smoothly. "But to answer your question, I did have a former housekeeper who demanded I pay her a large amount of money for the return of some personal, sentimental items she took from our apartment during her employment here. It was very distressing. I'm not sure if that's relevant here, though." She blinked her eyes. The picture of innocence.

Joe was pressing his lips together, and she could see the edges turning white.

Your move, she thought, her gaze drifting to the spot in her living room where she'd spotted Bennett the night of the cocktail party. Her skin burned with white-hot rage as she pictured him now in her mind's eye, standing in her home in his perfectly tailored charcoal suit, the obnoxious grin on his face that might as well have been a giant "fuck you" to her.

Except.

Her heart rate ticked up.

Bennett wasn't wearing glasses that night. Poppy remembered that now. With crystal clarity. She'd commented on it when he'd accosted her on his way out. "Are the glasses fake too?" she'd hissed, unable to conceal her anger. It had been reckless of her to show that kind of emotion, and she'd darted her eyes around to ensure no one had heard.

Had they?

She didn't think so at the time, but now she couldn't help but second-guess herself.

"When would you say that was?" a voice asked.

"I'm sorry?" She blinked several times, trying to regain her footing while her thoughts careened.

"Was your former housekeeper blackmailing you before or after the cocktail party?" Joe barked impatiently.

Her mind was whirling now. Other than at the party, Bennett had only been in her apartment one other time. The day they'd slept together. And he had not set foot in the office. Poppy was as sure of that as she was of her own name. So how could Harris have found them there?

She straightened her spine. "I don't see how any of that would be relevant."

Joe leaned back, pulled at his lip again. "Well, then let me enlighten you." He flipped over a page in his notepad. "Last night, we were doing a little digging around the data leaked from the app UrbanMyth. We'd already tried your email from the parent directory and came up dry. But then I looked at the contact information you provided us and, lo and behold, there was a different email address." The sides of his mouth twitched. He was enjoying this. "There were two posts that caught our eye." He peered down at this notepad. "One," he planted his elbow on the armrest, lifting an index finger. "And I quote: 'I need to contact the person blackmailing me. Any suggestions?' And two." He lifted another finger. "'You win, Bennett. You have your money. Now hold up your end of the deal.'"

Checkmate.

He tilted his head. "So, Ms. Ridley, what exactly was Mr. Stillman's end of the deal?"

Poppy could feel the room shrinking as if it might collapse on her. Her body was surging with something different now. It wasn't impatience or exasperation. It was foreboding.

She looked up from her hands sharply. "I think we're done here." The words shot out of her mouth, surprising her with their force. Judging from the way Joe's eyebrows shot up, it surprised him too.

Her animal instincts were kicking in. When cornered, attack.

Joe's eyes burrowed into her, and she held his icy glare, the unsettling silence unspooling between them. She sat very still, a warning signal blaring in her brain, filling her with a near-blinding urgency to get these two men out of her apartment.

Now.

Joe leaned forward and planted his forearms on his knees. "I have to be honest, Ms. Ridley. I'm getting the feeling that there's something you're not telling us."

"And I have the feeling there's something you're not telling me," she shot back, her nostrils flaring. "Like why you think it's appropriate to treat an acquaintance of Bennett Stillman like some kind of *suspect*."

Joe cocked his head, stared at her for a beat.

"Now, why would we be talking about suspects when we're simply trying to track down a man's whereabouts? Unless there's something else you know . . ." He let his sentence dangle dangerously close to an accusation.

The heat in Poppy's body spiked. One more second under the scrutiny of these two and she felt she might spontaneously combust. She leapt to her feet. Her vision tipped and blurred. She shouldn't have gotten up so fast.

"We're done here," she repeated.

"Sure, that can be all for now," Joe said smugly, rising to his feet. "We'll show ourselves out."

Fewer than five minutes after they'd left, Poppy's phone rang again.

This time, she answered it.

Chapter Thirty-two

HEATHER

Heather was leaning against her kitchen counter, readying herself to tap the red circle on the screen to avoid listening to Poppy's voicemail greeting again, when Poppy picked up on the fifth ring.

"What do you want, Heather?" Poppy's voice filled Heather's earbuds, her tone razor-sharp, and Heather flinched. This wasn't the poised, aloof greeting she'd expected, and it instantly threw her off-balance. *Maybe this is a bad idea,* she fretted, balling her hands into fists. She should call back later when Poppy was in a better mood.

"Hello?" Poppy barked impatiently.

Heather gripped the side of the counter and leveled her gaze on a photo of Oliver and Violet stuck to the whiteboard on the far wall of her kitchen, gathering her nerve.

It was a Sophie's choice, like an inmate being asked to choose the method of his own execution. Lethal injection or electric chair? Did Heather want the police to harass Oliver, who was already mentally perched on a cliff's edge, ready to divorce her? Or did she want to shift the police focus off of her family so she could heal her relationship with Oliver—knowing she would be atop the Ridley shit list? Heather was reluctantly picking option number two, but hoping that by contacting Poppy first, she might be shown some mercy.

"Poppy, it's Heather Quinn. Violet's mother?" Her voice trailed up, as if she wasn't sure. She squeezed her eyes shut, pinching her nose. This was not going the way she'd rehearsed it. She could hear Poppy's breath heaving on the other end of the line, as if she'd recently returned from the gym, and a fresh surge of resentment coursed through Heather's bloodstream. Poppy was the one who'd done something wrong, yet she was going about her daily life, probably finishing up a session with a private trainer in her palatial apartment, while Heather was dealing with the aftermath of the UrbanMyth hack, a police investigation, and a husband who was so angry with her he refused to come home.

There really was no justice in this world.

"I know who you are, Heather," Poppy spat. "But why do you keep calling me?"

Heather felt her face flush. Poppy could never be accused of being friendly, but this was ridiculous. Realizing she must be annoyed with her about what had happened at Lucky Cocktails, Heather wanted the opportunity to plead her case, but now was not the time. She readjusted the earbud in her ear, wishing she could readjust the beginning of this conversation along with it. "Poppy, you may already know this, but I'm chair of the Quilt Committee this year," she began.

The sound of Poppy's heels clacking against what Heather presumed were Poppy's wood floors came to a halt. "This is about the *quilt*? Jesus Christ," Poppy muttered. "I'm busy, Heather. Leave it with my door—"

"No," Heather interrupted louder than she'd intended, trying to stop Poppy from hanging up. "I'm . . . I'm not down in your lobby now. But I *was* down in your lobby the Monday after your cocktail party."

The line went pin-drop silent. Heather couldn't even hear Poppy breathing.

Heather had waited in Poppy's lobby that day, as she'd told the doorman she would, for nearly forty minutes before throwing in the towel and leaving, quilt in hand. She'd been positioned on the couch in the corner, wondering how much Poppy paid in monthly fees to occupy a full floor in the stunningly appointed building, when a familiar, triggering voice had snagged her attention like a sharp fingernail.

"I'm on the list. Bennett Stillman," he'd said smoothly, breezing past the doorman's desk and disappearing into the elevator. Heather's jaw had dropped, so stunned by the brazen move that she'd convinced herself Poppy and Bennett's relationship must not be a secret, not when Bennett was on the list of people cleared to go straight up to the Ridley apartment without being announced and given permission first. Open marriages were more common these days, she supposed, and with the wealth Poppy and Harris came from, their union was probably similar to an arranged one. Two prosperous families forming an alliance, keeping their bloodline blue.

"Are you there?" Heather asked into the dead air now.

"I'm here."

Another long pause. A deep breath.

"Well, I don't know why you were in my lobby waiting for me like some kind of stalker," Poppy said, the ice returning to her voice. "But you should've given the quilt to my doorman."

"This isn't about the quilt, Poppy," Heather snapped, finding her backbone. "When I was waiting to give you the quilt, I saw Bennett come into the lobby of your building and go up to your apartment. And I don't care what you were doing. Really." She held up a palm as if swearing an oath in court. "But the police came by my apartment yesterday to ask some questions about Bennett, and they were really pressing me about when I last saw him. I didn't tell them about seeing him in your lobby, because . . ." Heather considered how to articulate that her fear of the social annihilation Poppy could trigger was on par with her fear of being sent to a federal prison.

"Because we're friends," Poppy filled in, her tone suddenly as smooth as silk. "And friends don't drag friends into these kinds of messes unnecessarily, right?" she continued without waiting for an answer. "I'm sorry I was so curt earlier. I've been under so much stress, as I'm sure you have, because you *think* you saw Bennett when you didn't. Why don't you come over to my place and have a glass of wine and we can connect?"

Heather blinked, dizzy from the sharp turn this conversation had taken.

"I'll see you in twenty minutes," Poppy said without waiting for a reply, ending the call.

HEATHER LOWERED HERSELF onto the butter-soft couch, accepting the glass of chilled Sancerre from Poppy's outstretched hand. "Thanks." She forced her lips into a smile, surreptitiously dabbing a bead of sweat from her brow as she pulled the sunglasses off the top of her head and set them on the coffee table. She wished she'd had time to change into something a little nicer or at least put some earrings on before coming over. Being in Poppy's living room holding stemware that likely cost more than her entire outfit made Heather feel like she'd shown up for a state dinner at the White House dressed in jeans. More pressingly, though, Heather wished she were here for any other reason than the one at hand. But this wasn't a social call, she reminded herself. She couldn't allow herself to be pushed off course from her plan to tell the police the truth.

Well, *most* of the truth.

"I'm so glad you could come over," Poppy said with a sigh, settling down next to Heather on the couch, wine in hand, crossing one slim leg over the other. "It sounded like you were really frazzled on the phone earlier, which you have every right to be after having a conversation with the police. The whole Bennett thing is *really* distressing."

Heather nodded, averting her eyes, and took a gulp of her wine, holding it in her mouth a second before swallowing. She couldn't say if it was good because she couldn't taste it. The metallic tang on her tongue, the one she got when her adrenaline was pumping, wouldn't dissipate.

Poppy swirled the stem of her glass in tiny circles, keeping her gaze locked on Heather, appraising her. "I'm really grateful you called me, though, so I can talk you through the mix-up. I know you think you saw Bennett in my lobby, but we have a few neighbors in our building who resemble Bennett. Like, the hair, the eyes." She waved a hand in front of her face, giving a deliberate laugh. "Everything. I've even caught myself doing a double-take sometimes. So, I can see why you got confused." She dialed up her smile by another fifty watts.

Heather bit her lip. Under the mesmerizing warmth of Poppy's attention, a pocket of doubt was beginning to open up in her mind. It had happened so quickly that she supposed it could've been someone who resembled Bennett. A good portion of the residents of this building probably did have the same Waspy look. Except . . . the man Heather saw *said* his name was Bennett. Because it *was* Bennett. She took another shaky slug of wine, forcing it down with a hard swallow, collecting her thoughts, letting the weight of her certainty wrap around her.

"Poppy, I'm sure you're right that you have neighbors who look like Bennett, but it was Bennett who I saw going up to your apartment. He told your doorman his name and said he was on your list." Heather paused, unnerved by what looked like anger falling over Poppy's features as she spoke. "I'm not trying to poke into your business. I'm only telling you this because I need to let the police know that I saw him that day."

"No, you don't," Poppy said coolly, brushing her hair away from her face with an irritated flick. "Just as I don't need to tell the police how you *assaulted* Bennett at my party. Which was *awful*. Some would even call it *violent*." She raised an eyebrow and tilted her glass, taking a pointed sip.

Heather curled her toes in an attempt to suppress her irritation. For someone who was screwing a man who wasn't her husband, Poppy sure had strong opinions about Heather's moral code when it came to cocktail party etiquette. "The police already know about what happened at your party," Heather replied firmly. "Look, I'm really sorry if this causes you or your family any trouble, but I have to tell the police the truth. I should've done it in the first place, but as you said we're friends, so I wanted to let you know first. I didn't want you to be caught off guard by anything."

The cords in Poppy's neck tightened as she leaned forward and set her wineglass on a sterling-silver coaster on the coffee table. Heather could practically see Poppy's mind running through a list of the ammunition at her disposal. Foot soldiers fell into line for women like Poppy. She wasn't conditioned to accept anything less.

The fingers of Heather's free hand spread out wide on the soft cushion, as she braced herself for an onslaught of threats. In truth, this was why Heather had made the call to Poppy, why she'd dashed over the moment she was beckoned. She needed to find out what the Ridley family intended to do to her if she revealed Bennett's appearance at their apartment to the police. She imagined the Ridleys were the type of family who would do anything to avoid having their name associated with a man who was now missing. And families who have *everything* really can do *anything*.

Heather had always been the type of person who preferred to determine what type of music it would be before she had to face it.

Poppy was looking straight ahead, rather than at Heather, when she spoke. "Where did you go to college, Heather?"

Heather's forehead furrowed, examining Poppy's profile. Poppy's breathing was even, but her eyes were glassy, like stones. "Um. Rutgers," she answered, her voice thin, unsure where this was going, certain it was nowhere good.

Poppy replied with a quiet "Hm," seemingly deliberating.

Heather set her wineglass down on the coaster, worried it might slip from her sweaty hands. "I . . . I went to business school there too," she added to fill the unsettling silence.

Poppy licked her lips. "Well, I don't know if you know this, but there is a building at Harvard named for my husband's family." She turned her head and locked eyes with Heather. "Needless to say, the Ridley name carries a lot of weight."

Heather's whole body tensed, as if she were in the passenger seat of a car headed straight for a brick wall. On her way over here, she'd mentally run through a list of things Poppy could do to her—ensure she was barred from every private club in New York City, excommunicate her from the influential committees, direct important clients away from Oliver's firm—but this was worse than she'd feared.

Poppy was going right for Heather's jugular. Violet's college admissions.

"If you are willing to forget about what you saw," Poppy continued, her tone startlingly calm now, "I can ensure that you are appointed a trustee of Harvard endowment fund next year. My husband has the power to fill those seats, and since you've spent time working on Wall Street, he can make it happen like that." She snapped her fingers.

Heather's mouth dropped open. Poppy took her silence to be a negotiation tactic and kept talking.

"I'm sure you recognize the importance of this position in terms of admission to Harvard. There has never been a child of a trustee who hasn't been accepted. Early decision. Henry will be attending after he graduates from Andover. That's the route Harris and Harris's father took, and it's important to Harris that Henry continue his family's legacy at both institutions. But it sounds like you don't have Violet's path laid out in the same way." Poppy tilted her head, raising her eyebrows in a question, but Heather remained frozen. "Well, I don't know what your high school plans were, but your college plans could be set."

Heather turned her face away, blinking rapidly, trying to orient her thoughts. Poppy wasn't threatening to destroy her, as she'd feared. Poppy was offering her a key to her kingdom. The corner of Heather's lips twitched up into a smile. The first genuine one that had formed on her face since the whole Instagram fiasco happened. If Heather was a trustee of the Harvard endowment fund, Violet wouldn't need to be accepted into Andover. She could go to the high school of Oliver's choosing and still have a direct line to an Ivy. Every obstacle in her way would be removed. Heather's eyes roved Poppy's lavish living room, evidence of what a life without obstacles could look like. Heather had seen firsthand how easy it was to win a hundred-yard dash when you start on the ninety-yard line.

"Do we have a deal?" Poppy asked.

Heather bit her lip, deliberating. A voice in her head was imploring her to consider what was best for her fractured marriage. That was priority number one. But this was like being offered a winning lottery ticket. It would be ludicrous not to take it. She didn't know why Poppy was so adamant about making this blood pact, and frankly, she had no intention of finding out. All she needed to do was endure the police suspicion, their incessant questions, and give Oliver the support and assurance he needed while he endured the same. She could do that.

Conviction began to pulse with every beat of Heather's heart.

She could convince Oliver that she'd never lie to him again.

He would forgive her. He always did.

For Violet's future, Heather could do anything.

Heather nodded, inhaling the sweet smell of success. "Deal."

Chapter Thirty-three

POPPY

Poppy eased the front door closed behind Heather, wrestling her breathing under control, and made her way down the hallway to the office. Tapping her phone against her palm, she surveyed the room. The floor-to-ceiling built-in shelving that housed her custom-jacketed books was spotless, the surface of the antique executive desk at the far end of the room was clear save for a small horse sculpture, the bespoke sofa and club chairs didn't have a cushion out of place. There was not a single thing in here that she could imagine Bennett being after. But this is where Harris had found Bennett's glasses, and Poppy now knew Bennett *had* been inside her apartment when she wasn't home, apparently having been sent right up after giving his name to the doorman. But what the hell would he have been looking for in this room?

Poppy dragged her fingers through her hair and walked the perimeter, uneasiness clawing at the back of her neck. She couldn't shake the feeling that she was one wrong step away from detonating a land mine. Dropping onto the couch, she unlocked her phone, and brought up the contact list, scrolling to her lawyer's name, mentally parsing through the details she needed to divulge in order for him to properly advise her about next steps with the police. She would need to mention Bennett's being on the list with the doormen, she realized now, a fact that could be dug up if someone was digging in the right place. *Auction item drop-off,*

Poppy could claim. Bennett had offered to donate a gift card to Reflex.

An easy fix.

She nodded, agreeing with herself. If there was one thing Poppy knew about the truth, it was that it should be doled out sparingly. And only when your hand was to the flame.

Poppy's knee started to bounce; she was still unsettled. It had completely slipped her mind that—the day they had slept together—she'd added him to the list in an effort to minimize his time in the lobby. What a colossal mistake.

Among many.

She couldn't afford to make any more. Toggling to her exchange with Bennett, she studied the last message he'd sent her as if it were a puzzle she could solve. I WAS WAITING OUTSIDE OF YOUR BUILDING AT THE AGREED TIME AND I DO NOT WAIT FOR ANYONE!

A loud crash rang out from the kitchen, and Poppy's entire body flinched, sending the phone to the floor. "Jesus Christ," she muttered, bending over and fumbling for the phone. With Bennett's words on the screen screaming at her, a realization flew through her mind with the force of a hurricane. *She hadn't remembered Bennett was on the list until Heather had told her. That fact hadn't even been on Poppy's radar.*

The room started to spin.

She jabbed a frantic finger on the screen, rereading the last message she'd sent to Bennett. *You're so bad,* accompanied by a winking and kissing emoji. A stark contrast to the gray oval with the all-caps message that followed it.

"Holy shit," she whispered, staring at the space between the messages.

She couldn't believe she'd overlooked this particular link in the chain of events. Yet she had.

MAYA WAS ON all fours when Poppy found her in the kitchen, glistening shards of glass scattered around her like confetti. She scrambled to her feet, running her hands across the front of her pants. "I don't know how it happened, Ms. Ridley, but I was running a cloth across the counter, and your glass fruit bowl, it—" She gave a frantic wave of her hand.

"Crystal," Poppy interrupted.

Maya's busy hands paused. "I'm sorry?"

"The bowl. It's crystal," Poppy said dully. "Not glass."

"Oh," Maya said slowly, brushing her palms together, the lines in her forehead deepening. "I . . . I will clean up this . . . um . . . crystal, and I'm sorry about this. I've never broken anything before while working." Her lower lip looked unsteady.

Poppy tilted her head, appraising her as if seeing her for the first time. It was intimate, Maya's job. She picked up Poppy's trash, stacked her papers, hovered in the background when she had guests. But how well did Poppy know this woman who had access to every corner of her life?

"Maya, did you get the text I sent you about two weeks ago? The one where I said my friend would be stopping by?"

Maya's busy hands froze.

Poppy hadn't wanted Bennett to linger outside of her building too long or, god forbid, in her lobby, and her frenzied mind hadn't realized he was still on the list with her doorman from the afternoon they'd slept together, so from the back seat of the Escalade, riding uptown for her meeting with Krause, she'd pecked out a message to Maya. *A friend of mine is stopping by the apartment. Can you have the doorman send him up as soon as the call comes in and have him wait in the living room. I'm running thirty minutes late.*

"Yes, I got your message," Maya replied, her voice thin.

Poppy took a small step closer. "But my friend never came?"

Maya regarded Poppy dully, as if on a time delay, before shaking her head.

Poppy bit the inside of her cheek, her frustration mounting. She hated being lied to. And this woman was an awful liar. But Poppy sensed the only way to get what she was after was to approach Maya the way one would approach a frightened puppy. Tentatively.

"There's blood," Poppy whispered, pointing a slender finger.

The color drained from Maya's face.

"On your thumb. You're bleeding, Maya." Poppy wrapped her fingers around Maya's forearm and ushered her over to the sink, turning the tap on and directing her palm underneath the stream. The water from the faucet cascaded over Maya's hand, sending rust-tinted pools spinning down the drain. Poppy yanked open a drawer with neatly folded tea towels, pulled one out, and passed it over. Maya's gaze remained lowered, directed at the sink, as she wrapped it around her hand, pulling it tight.

Poppy leaned back against the counter, crossing her arms over her chest. "Maya, did you see the two policemen who came here?"

The muscles in Maya's back tensed. She lifted her uninjured hand from the towel, rested it on the tap, turning off the stream. Her movements were slow. Deliberate. "I saw you had guests, Ms. Ridley, but I didn't know they were policemen. I hope everything is okay."

Poppy tiptoed between the shards of glass to the other side of the island and pivoted to face her. Maya squeezed the tea towel harder around her wounded thumb, wincing.

"The police are looking for that man who was supposed to come over here. And I don't know if you're aware of this—if you've seen them when you've been cleaning—but we have cameras throughout the apartment." Poppy raised one eyebrow, let the sentence hang heavy in the air. Her breathing slowed. Oddly, she was at her most relaxed when she was lying. Maya, on the other hand, was not. Her eyes were now darting like mice trapped in a cage.

"I'll ask you again. Did a man named Bennett come inside this apartment the day that I texted you? I need to know where he is, Maya. I know he's not a good man, so if he threatened you in any way, I can help you."

Maya shook her head back and forth a bit too emphatically and brought her towel-wrapped hand to her mouth. Poppy stepped forward, rested a palm on her quaking shoulder. "Whatever you tell me stays between us. All I care about is knowing Bennett's game plan."

Maya sank her head into her hands. She was speaking, but the words were unintelligible against the towel.

"I can't hear you." Poppy sighed, her impatience simmering.

Maya lifted her chin and looked at Poppy through lashes clumped with moisture. "He doesn't have a game plan."

Poppy's throat thickened. "Why . . . why do you say that?"

Maya tipped her face downward and a drop of moisture hovered on the end of her nose. Her breath was coming in shaky gasps. "Because he's dead," she whispered.

Poppy took a step back, slack-jawed. The slow shake of her head wasn't a denial; it was a plea. But one look at Maya's petrified expression was all it took for Poppy to know her plea would go unanswered. Maya wrapped her arms across her chest, gripping her elbows, her body swaying. Poppy felt like she was watching a glass teeter at the edge of a table. Right before it fell to the floor and shattered.

"I killed him," Maya managed to say.

Poppy's legs went loose in the joints. She clasped Maya's elbow, steadying herself, steering them both to the kitchen table. They dropped heavily onto opposite chairs. Maya seemed to be staring at something behind Poppy that wasn't there, her focus scattered and undefined.

"I didn't hear the man come in," she whispered, her eyes anguished. "I had already finished my work in the living room and had moved into the office. I like to get the office clean when you and Mr. Ridley aren't in the apartment, because Mr. Ridley doesn't like to see me in that room." The speed of the words coming out of her mouth increased until they were pouring out, fast and uncontrolled, tumbling over each other. "But I know you expect it to be cleaned, so I'm always careful about when I clean it. I was on a step stool dusting the shelf, and all of a sudden, someone was behind me, grabbing me, putting his hand between my legs and I—" She squeezed her eyes shut with a force that contorted her whole face.

Poppy had stopped breathing. She was absolutely frozen.

"I pushed him." Her voice was gravelly, tears pooling in the corners of her closed eyes. "I didn't mean to *kill* him. I was afraid, so I jerked my elbow back like this." She lifted her elbow and threw it back with one swift motion. "But he was unsteady, and it hit him here, I think." She pointed to the bridge of her nose. "He went off-balance and fell against the side of your desk. There was a loud crack and . . ." She faltered, her eyes going somewhere else momentarily.

"No." Poppy's brow was furrowed, and her head was shaking back and forth quickly. "Bennett texted me. He said he wasn't going to wait for me, and he left." Her eyes flew wildly around the kitchen for her phone, as if it were indisputable proof of life.

"He didn't send that message," Maya whispered. "Fernando did. He was working that day. He was the one who sent your friend up here because he was on your list of approved people. But he thought something was off because he knew you weren't home, so he texted me to make sure everything was okay. But I didn't see the message. Fernando was the one I called when—"

Poppy held up a palm, cutting her off. Alarm bells were blaring in her head. She'd already heard too much. No more details. Plausible deniability. The clink of her rings against the table was the only sound in the room as Poppy struggled to dig her way out of the avalanche that had fallen on top of her.

"No one needs to know." A disembodied voice reverberated from the entrance to the kitchen, slicing through the silence like a machete.

Poppy's head jerked toward the source.

"Heather?" she choked, uncertain whether the figure staring back at her was a hallucination.

For a moment, everyone in the room was immobilized.

"I . . . I left my purse behind by mistake," Heather stuttered, tapping the leather strap hanging from her shoulder. "I was in the lobby when I realized, so I came back up. Nobody was answering the door when I knocked, but it wasn't closed all the way, so I let myself in. I didn't mean to eavesdrop, but I . . . I could hear you two talking from the hallway."

Panic rose in Poppy like a bird trapped in a room. She shut her eyes and tried to breathe steadily, but she was choking on the air. When she opened them, Heather was looming over her, her characteristic anxious energy crystallizing into something entirely different: fierce determination.

"No one needs to know," Heather repeated, her tone resolute. "We just need to come up with a plan."

Poppy stuck her thumbnail between her teeth, her heart racing at the chaos a murder investigation could cause in her life. There would be questions about why Bennett had been in her home that day. Her relationship with Bennett would be examined. Maya would surely divulge that Bennett had been in here before, had emerged from Poppy's bedroom. Financial forensics could uncover the money transfer. It wouldn't implicate Poppy in Bennett's death, but her marriage would be over. The infidelity clause triggered. Worse, because of her social status, it would likely play out in the media.

Poppy's life would be just like the crystal bowl: shattered.

Okay, she thought, then realized it was aloud. "Okay, okay, okay," she repeated, barely above a whisper. She extended her hand across the table and grabbed ahold of Maya's. "Let's not panic," she said, her own voice rising in panic. "Did Fernando say whether there were other people in the lobby when Bennett arrived?"

"There was one woman who was waiting for you when Bennett came into the lobby, but Fernando said she left a few minutes after Bennett went up to your apartment."

Poppy and Heather exchanged a look. Heather pulled out a chair, joining them at the table. "That was me, and I saw nothing," she said, and from her steadfast expression, Poppy almost believed it was true.

Poppy's attention shifted back to Maya. "But there must have been other doormen on duty," she fretted.

"Fernando was the only one when the man arrived." Maya wrung her hands. "The other two doormen were making deliveries at the time. They were back at the desk when I called Fernando for help, so he went on break and used the stairs to come up so they wouldn't see where he was going. And he was able to get the lobby surveillance footage erased afterward."

"Okay. Good. Let's think this through."

The three of them were so deep into the details that when the sound of the buzzer echoed through the apartment, they all flinched.

Chapter Thirty-four

NORAH

When the front door opened, Norah recoiled. She didn't know what she'd been expecting, but what was standing in front of her wasn't it. Poppy's eyes were bloodshot and hooded with bruises, her skin was pink and raw, stripped down to its core, and her forehead glistened with sweat. She looked like she'd been jumped by muggers on her way to the door. Most unsettling was the haunted look on her face, as if whoever had jumped her was standing behind Norah, ready to pounce again.

Instinctively, Norah took a step back.

Poppy ran a palm along the halo of frizz surrounding her blond hair, and Norah realized, to her relief, that she'd misjudged the situation. The marks on Poppy's face weren't bruises. They were smudged mascara. Not the streaky mess that streams down your cheeks after a bout of crying, but the lemur-like rings that result from grinding the heels of your palms into your eye sockets. Norah would know. It was what had greeted her in the mirror the night she found the photo on Caroline's phone.

"Norah, hi," Poppy cooed, wrenching her face into a smile with such a colossal amount of effort it almost looked uncomfortable to hold the expression. "Um, if this is about dropping off an auction item, you're welcome to leave it with the doorman downstairs. He makes deliveries up to the apartment in one big load, which makes it easier for me to receive." Her smile stretched farther across her teeth, which seemed like an impossible task.

"I think you know why I'm here, Poppy," she said, steel in her voice.

Poppy's smile cracked down the middle. She blinked a few times, the way people do after they've woken up from an afternoon nap and need to get their bearings. Her brow knitted momentarily, deliberating, before she stepped out of the way, making room for Norah to step inside. Poppy peered into the elevator landing, ensuring no one was behind Norah, before closing and locking the door.

All five of Norah's senses were on high alert as she followed Poppy down the hallway. A strange zip of worry traveled down her spine, but she chalked it up to the disconcerting artwork on the walls. Norah could never understand why expensive artwork had to be so . . . grim. What was wrong with a pleasant-looking beach scene? She averted her eyes and gripped the handle of her purse harder.

"Make yourself at home," Poppy said with a hardness to her voice as she gestured to one of three sitting areas in the living room. "I'll be with you in a minute."

Before Norah could respond, Poppy had spun around, click-clacking down the hallway, and disappeared behind one of the doors. Norah crossed her arms over her chest and drifted slowly around the living room, letting her eyes run over the contents as if she were wandering through a gallery. The room looked larger without a hundred people standing in it, and Norah's gaze was pulled to the spot near the fireplace where she'd been standing with Bennett the night of the party. A surprising pang of longing pricked her heart. Bennett had been her ally that night, and she could remember the overwhelming gratitude she felt having him at her side. Now it reminded her of something her mother used to say. *A fistful of Monopoly money doesn't make a person rich.*

There was a muffled sound coming from another room, and Norah's ears perked up. Someone else was in the apartment. She briefly wondered if Harris was home, before remembering he'd gone to Toronto for the afternoon for a shareholder meeting.

Thankfully. His presence here would complicate things. She fiddled with her pendant, reminding herself that Poppy was the type to have an army of staff stationed around the apartment. But as the distant wail of an ambulance siren echoed from down below, a creeping sensation made its way across her scalp. Something didn't feel right. She dragged her hands through her hair and gathered it at the neck, her clammy palms coating the strands.

She should go.

"I'm back," Poppy announced, floating into the living room looking decidedly more refreshed. The makeup had been cleaned off her face, her hair was pulled back into a sleek ponytail, and she'd changed her shirt. She was a walking "before and after" photo. She gestured for Norah to sit on the long, sleek sofa, and Norah briefly considered saying she'd stand. It was an old trick her mentor had taught her. *When you're negotiating, always be the tallest one in the room,* he'd advised. *Even if it means you spend an hour on your feet.* But Norah wasn't here to negotiate. She was here for answers. And after seeing Poppy's name penciled into Bennett's notebook, she had no doubt that Poppy was the one who could provide them.

Norah perched on the edge of the pristine cream-colored sofa, keeping her spine straight in hopes her posture would convey that she was not to be fucked with. Poppy sat down heavily in a chair across from her. She straightened with a deep inhale, the puff sleeves of the fresh blouse she'd put on standing at attention—the picture of civility, save for the tiny tremble on the right side of her cheek. Poppy pursed her lips in what Norah assumed was an attempt to conceal it. As she watched Poppy set her phone down beside her, screen-side up, it struck her why Poppy might be rattled. The cyberattack. Norah had checked her own email, but it hadn't occurred to her that everyone else's was fair game now too. But she had no interest in digging into other people's secrets. There was only one piece of information she was after.

"I want to know where Bennett is, Poppy," she said without preamble. "And I think you have some information that would be helpful to me."

Poppy's pink lips fell into a deep frown. "I'm not sure I understand what you're referring to. I heard your husband was missing, and I'm so sorry about that." She pressed an insincere palm to her chest. "But I already told the police everything I know, which unfortunately isn't much."

"Cut the bullshit. I know you're in some kind of relationship with my husband." Her voice hitched on the word "husband." "Soon to be *ex*-husband," she corrected herself, emphasizing the "ex." "And I think you gave him a large sum of money and might be helping him wherever he is now. I don't understand why, and I don't want to. But a police investigation? It's just taking it too far, so tell Bennett to come clean and let his parents know where he is so all of this can be done."

"I'm not sleeping with your husband," Poppy replied flatly.

"Really? Because I have a photo of the two of you together that maybe Harris would like to see."

Poppy choked out a humorless laugh. "Good god, you sound exactly like him." She turned her head to the wall of windows, her features pinched with annoyance. Norah could see the muscle in the side of her neck twitching.

"What the hell does that mean?"

Poppy snapped her attention back to Norah, her eyelashes fluttering with irritation. "Your husband issued the same threat. Yes, I slept with Bennett once, and yes, I understand that knocks me off the moral high ground, but this is what your husband does."

Norah scoffed. "Sleeps with other women? Yeah, I—"

Poppy held her hand up like an angry schoolteacher quieting an unruly class, and despite herself, Norah hushed.

"He seduces married women, Norah, and then blackmails them. I paid him seven hundred and fifty thousand dollars, and god knows how many other women have done the same. He's got a whole racket going."

Norah stopped breathing, caught between inhaling and exhaling.

She felt like a tiny boat in the middle of a storm surge, and she needed an anchor for her mind to latch on to. She'd already deduced Bennett had a very expensive gambling habit, based on the figures in his notebook. Odds, baseball teams, dollar figures. What Norah hadn't been able to figure out was how Bennett had bankrolled it. Norah's accounts didn't have any unexplained withdrawals, and she knew Bennett had cut into a substantial portion of his savings to open up Reflex, which was currently operating in the red. She'd come over here thinking Poppy was somehow funding his habit, but she'd assumed Poppy had given the money willingly. Not like this.

"Your husband was not a good guy, Norah," Poppy said, but Norah had trouble hearing her over the dull ringing in her ears. There was too much happening, too many blows for her to process. She was trying to focus on Bennett's betrayal when her thoughts snagged on one word that had come out of Poppy's mouth.

"Wait." Norah's already elevated heart rate picked up speed, a rock tumbling down a hill. "Why did you say 'was'?"

Poppy's forehead furrowed.

"You said Bennett *was* not a good guy."

Poppy's posture slackened, devolving into a less prim version of herself. She opened her mouth as if to speak, then briefly closed her eyes, deciding against it. She pressed her lips together, seemingly weighing her options.

A cold sensation spread over Norah's body as the silence stretched. She kept her eyes on Poppy, watching as her expression slowly morphed from resigned to calculated, as if grudgingly moved from plan A to plan B. But Norah still hadn't figured out plan A.

"You seem like the kind of person who wants to do the right thing," Poppy finally said, her voice robotically calm. "But I think we both have enough life experience to know that sometimes the right thing isn't always clear. I'm going to tell you something, but you need to promise me that you will think through what you do with this information before going to the police with it."

Norah searched her face, waiting for it to collapse into the saccharine smile. But Poppy's hard expression didn't falter. It didn't even flicker.

"What are you . . . Did you . . . ?" Norah choked, the rest of the question lodged in her throat.

She could hear someone approaching from the hallway. Instinctively, Norah leapt to her feet. Poppy followed suit. Norah's eyes grew wide as the figure entered the living room. The woman had puffy, red-rimmed eyes and the dazed appearance of a person who'd emerged from a horrific car accident, as if someone needed to drape her in a foil blanket, put an arm around her shoulders, and guide her to the nearest ambulance. Norah could see splatters of stains on her shirt that she assumed were paint. But upon closer inspection she realized she was wrong. The splatters were the unmistakable rust color of blood.

"What the hell is going on here?" Panic bumped the edge of Norah's voice.

"I tried to get her to stay in the kitchen," a frantic voice called, trailing her into the room. "She wouldn't listen to me."

Norah's eyes bounced between the frightened young woman and, inexplicably, Heather Quinn, as she tried to process what was unfolding in front of her. She suddenly wasn't sure if her body could remain upright, if her knees would continue to hold her weight. She took a step back and dropped herself back down onto the couch.

The young woman's chest heaved. "It was an accident. A horrible, terrible accident," she cried, her voice quivering, weighed down by a desperate intensity. Norah found herself too stunned to move, to speak, to break the spell. Heather was waving her hands wildly, trying to stop the woman, but she continued. "I was cleaning, and I didn't hear him come in, but he forced his hand between my legs and I . . . was so scared and reacted without thinking. It was like something took over my body. He hit his head, and I . . . I didn't mean to kill him." Her voice shriveled to a whisper, the gravity of her confession settling over the room like a fog. It was a heavy, unnatural silence, save for the sound of the woman's soft sobs.

Norah sat paralyzed, struggling to rearrange the woman's words into digestible sentences. The full impact spread over her one inch at a time until she had the whole picture. Bennett hadn't purposely run away from his life. He wasn't making good on his threat to make her regret kicking him out. Bennett was dead. This woman standing in front of Norah had killed him after he'd tried to assault her.

"I think we should all consider the best course of action here." Poppy's voice filled the room as if from another frequency.

"I agree," Heather piped up.

"Where is he?" Norah choked out. "His body."

"It won't be found," Heather answered definitively, exchanging a look with Poppy.

"We . . ." Norah swallowed hard against the acid rising in her throat. "We have to go to the police."

Heather shook her head. "I don't think that's a good idea."

Poppy laced her fingers around her knee. "Norah, Bennett is dead no matter what happens in this room right now," she said, an icy calm enveloping her voice. "The question is, how many more lives is he going to ruin on his way out?"

Norah's eyes met Poppy's and they looked at each other with a cool, deep understanding of what Poppy was asking. Norah's bones began to feel heavy and hot. The young woman's body was quaking, her face drooping toward the floor like melted wax. Threads of empathy wove through Norah's insides. What had Bennett done to her? What had he been capable of? She didn't know anymore, but there was one thing that was certain. Whatever he did, he would've gotten away with it. Because men like Bennett always did. Norah pictured the shattered woman in front of her put in handcuffs, lowered into a police cruiser, the tawdry trial that would ensue. HIRED HELP MURDERS MILLIONAIRE. The media would eat it up. What would that do to Caroline, whose mental health was as fragile as a Fabergé egg right now? Norah knew the answer, and it felt like a fishhook snagging at her heart.

Norah drew a ragged breath.

She'd made her decision.

Clearing her throat, Norah told the three women what she intended to do. Then, like a sleepwalker, she took a step forward. Then another and another, out of the living room, down the hallway, until she reached the front door. She rested her hand on the knob, only hesitating for a moment, before she pulled it open and let it slam behind her.

Two hours later, she sat in the police station waiting to talk to Detective Danielli.

Chapter Thirty-five

NORAH

NORAH HAD ONLY spoken with Detective Danielli once in person, so she hadn't accumulated the type of familiarity required to interpret his body language, but one look at his sober expression as he walked toward her and she knew. This conversation was not going to go the way she'd planned.

"Ms. Ryan, I didn't realize you were coming in today," he said, his voice cracking. "But I'm . . . I'm glad you're here." He clapped his hands together, and the sound echoed off the four corners of the dreary, institutional lobby of the 23rd Precinct station house. "Let's find a place we can talk."

Norah's shoes squeaked loudly on the vinyl floor as she followed him down the hallway, past glass-walled offices and cubicles with potted ferns and messy stacks of manila folders. Phones rang, printers whirred, and the dull throbbing in Norah's head intensified with each step. He slowed his pace when they arrived at the door with a metal nameplate reading JOSEPH DANIELLI, DETECTIVE, peering through the glass before seemingly deciding against it and continuing down the hall. "I moved offices last week, and it's a mess in there," he said by way of explanation.

She forced a closed-mouth smile, adjusting her purse on her shoulder, mentally adjusting her plan along with it. "As far as I'm concerned, we never had this conversation," Norah had told the three women. "I was never here." She took solace in the way

Maya's expression had changed, like a deer realizing that the car behind the headlights was not going to run her over. Her plan had been to come to the police station to deliver Bennett's notebook and, in doing so, what she hoped would be a valid theory for Bennett's sudden disappearance. Judging from what he wrote, Bennett had accumulated sizable gambling debts, which could motivate a person to walk away from his life, lay low, off the radar of debt collectors. Possibly forever. Before she'd tucked the notebook into her purse, she'd made sure to rip out the page with Poppy's name and the two behind it, in case the pencil had left any impressions. She imagined it would make her look helpful to bring it down here in person. *All the information I have, I've given you.* But there was one thing she hadn't factored in. And judging from Danielli's gait as he led her into the small room at the end of the hallway—shoulders hunched with the weight of a grand piano resting on them—it was time to start factoring.

There was a large metal filing cabinet in the corner of the room and a round table with three cushioned chairs haphazardly arranged around it, as if the last people who'd been sitting in them had left with the haste of someone responding to a 911 call, and when Norah thought about it, maybe they had. Detective Danielli picked up a rogue napkin off the table, crumpling it up and tossing it into the small plastic garbage bin by the door before gesturing for her to sit.

Norah sat stiffly, her forearms resting on the armrests, as if she were strapped into an electric chair. There was a strong odor of old Chinese food and mildew permeating the air, and she couldn't decide if it was the smell making her eyes water or if it was a preemptive reaction to the news she was certain she was about to hear.

Detective Danielli's chair creaked as he shifted his weight and interlaced his meaty fingers. "We received a call a short time ago, and I was waiting on a little more information before I came by your home today to talk to you about it. I'm so sorry to be the one to tell you this." He stared down at his clenched hands resting on the table. "But the body of an adult male has been found that matches the description of your husband."

Norah's mind turned to static, a television that had lost its signal. Words kept streaming out of his mouth—the East River, decomposed, a logoed Reflex shirt—bending and overlapping in the air between them, but her consciousness couldn't make sense of them. She tried to force herself to focus, relying on the advice of a yoga instructor from the wellness spa her well-intentioned sister had dragged her to. *Locking your gaze on one focal point in the room will cultivate a deep state of concentration.* Norah focused her eyes on the dents in the metal filing cabinet behind Detective Danielli as she tried to get her footing.

A body. Decomposed.

She swallowed hard, suddenly self-conscious about her reaction. Bennett being deceased *should* have been new information to her. She attempted to arrange her features accordingly.

"I understand this is a lot to take in," she heard him say, and she forced her head to nod. "And I know you came down here hoping for a better update. I wish I could've given you one. I'm so sorry."

Silence filled the small room, and she realized he was waiting for her to speak.

"Yes," she said, her throat tightening around a hard lump. "This isn't what I expected." Her voice sounded foreign to her ears, faraway and robotic.

He pushed himself out of the chair, yanked open the top drawer of the filing cabinet, pulled out a flower-patterned box of tissues and held it out to her. She lifted her fingertips to her cheek. Was she crying? Her fingertips came back wet. She pulled out two tissues, dabbed at the watery mixture of guilt and grief that had pooled in the corners of her eyes, trying not to picture Bennett's bloated body being pulled from the water, his mess of hair tangled with seagrass, his lips a bluish white. The image made it feel like someone was standing on her chest.

"Ms. Ryan," Detective Danielli said, his voice gentle.

She wadded the tissue into a ball in her hand, an unexpected stab of pain drilling through her shock.

"This may sound like an odd question, but have you heard of an app called UrbanMyth?"

A splinter of apprehension lodged in Norah's throat.

"Yes," she choked out. She stared at the muscle twitching in his jawline, gripping the tissue tighter as the realization crept across her skin, and with it the terrifying understanding of why he was bringing this up. Joe Danielli suspected *she* was responsible for Bennett's death. And the post Norah had written on UrbanMyth had cemented his suspicions.

Instinctively, her eyes darted toward the exit, her thoughts scattering. Was she allowed to leave? Were they going to search her home? Could she call her mother? She couldn't risk being accused of the murder. What would that do to Caroline? Swiftly, the ocean that was roaring in her ears ebbed, leaving behind a brutal truth: she had to tell him what had happened over at Poppy's apartment. It was the only way to clear herself as a suspect.

Tears stabbed the back of her eyes as she opened her mouth to speak.

"And were you aware that your husband was a frequent poster on UrbanMyth?" Detective Danielli asked before she could get the words out.

Norah shook her head numbly.

"Your mother-in-law, Waverley Stillman, gave us Bennett's personal email address back when she first reported him missing. She wanted us to access his inbox for clues, but we aren't authorized to do something like that. When we heard about this cyberattack, my partner began running a few email addresses from the Crofton parent directory through the database in hopes of turning up some useful information." He licked his lips, reached into the breast pocket of his blazer, and extracted a small spiral notepad. "We tried Bennett's email, but nothing turned up. When we returned to the station and reviewed our notes, we realized we'd tried Bennett's work email, but not the one his mother gave us." His brow knitted as he flipped the pages, landing on one. "Your husband made sixty-two posts where he talked about killing himself. He wrote, 'If my spouse was cheating on me, I'd kill myself.' 'If my wife was shoplifting, I'd kill myself.' That kind of thing. It was a frequent response, no matter the subject he was responding to." He looked up from his notepad, his eyes filled with such sincere sympathy it nearly broke Norah. "Has your husband talked about taking his own life before?"

She shook her head. Her voice was inaccessible.

"There were other posts that lead us to believe he had a gambling problem?" He lifted the end of the sentence like a question.

Norah answered with a small nod.

He blew out a long breath, tucked the notepad back into the pocket of his blazer. "The details of these types of deaths can be difficult to establish once it's been over a week with the body submerged, but given the circumstances, we think your husband may have jumped from the bridge."

"Jumped," she whispered, the backs of her eyes stinging.

"Had he been depressed lately?" The wrinkles in Danielli's forehead deepened.

She forced herself to swallow. Up until now, she hadn't committed a crime. She was under no obligation to tell the police that Poppy's housekeeper had confessed to killing Bennett. Norah had paid close enough attention in school to be aware that merely *knowing* a crime had occurred did not make a person an accessory to the crime. But overtly lying to the police about her husband's mental state in order to buttress a false conclusion, diverting attention from the guilty party, would surely push her over the tipping point into a felony.

At heart, Norah was a rule follower, the type of person who paused at stop signs for a full three seconds even when no one was around and always put her phone in airplane mode on a flight. She liked rules. They created order. But following rules didn't always result in doing what was right. Bennett dying by suicide meant the terrified woman in Poppy's apartment wouldn't go to prison. The press wouldn't write salacious headlines, camp outside their apartment harassing Caroline on the way to school. They could all put this behind them. Was Norah really going to sacrifice that woman's freedom and her daughter's mental health at the altar of rule following?

She could see her mother's face in her mind now, feel the weight of her mother's warm hand on her shoulder, hear the words she would utter every time Norah was faced with a difficult choice in life. *Always trust your gut. Your gut knows what your head hasn't yet figured out.* Norah had ignored her mother's advice only one time in her life—on her wedding day, when she married Bennett. And look how that had turned out.

Norah met his gaze and could feel the weight of the moment's irreversibility.

"Now that I think about it"—she cleared a tremor in her throat—"he had been depressed lately."

Detective Danielli closed his eyes, gave a somber nod. "I'm sorry, Ms. Ryan. I think all signs point to the fact that your husband died by suicide. Let's see what the coroner has to say."

Chapter Thirty-six

MAYA

I RAN AN index finger along the edge of the check, eyeing the line of zeros. It reminded me of the junk mail that arrived in my family's mailbox addressed to my mom, claiming she was the recipient of one million dollars, except the fine print on the oversized check in the envelope read *This could be yours if you're a sweepstakes winner!* For all I knew, this check could be equally worthless.

"Next please, step down," the impatient-sounding teller called out. A white-haired woman at the front of the line adjusted her purse in the front basket of her walker and rolled toward the vacated window.

"Jesus Christ," the twentysomething man in front of me muttered, lifting his eyes from his phone momentarily as he moved forward.

I heard an impatient sigh behind me, coupled with a "Why are there only two tellers working?"

I shuffled along with the line, folding the check in half to conceal the rust-colored splotch in the right-hand corner. It was a fossilized memory I didn't want to unearth.

I chewed at a loose piece of skin on my lower lip, wondering if the long line was an indicator the tellers were being especially diligent with their deposits today. A sign that they were asking a lot of questions. As I tossed a look over my shoulder at the ATMs by the entrance, my thoughts swung like a pendulum. *Should I?*

Shouldn't I? I'd bypassed them on the way in, unsure if a check this size could be deposited that way (surely ID was required once it hit six figures?), but maybe it was a safer bet. An ATM couldn't interrogate you the way a human could. *Before we deposit this check, can you let us know the circumstances around this money being obtained?* I pictured them asking. On the other hand, trusting a deposit this size to an ATM might raise red flags too. They could freeze my account.

I was overthinking this.

Overthinking. It was something I was doing a lot of lately. *Was there any possible evidence I hadn't factored in? Was it wrong of me to get Fernando involved in all this? What would've happened if I hadn't been able to fend that man off?*

But I knew what would've happened.

Of course I did.

Because it wasn't the first time a man had forced himself on me. The first time, I was fourteen, holding a sweating can of Bud Light, perched on a scratchy couch that had been relegated to the back deck, alone with the boy I'd snuck out of my house to meet. We'd just popped open our drinks when he'd flashed a crooked smile and suggested we play The Nervous Game. I didn't know which one of my classmates had invented the stupid game—or if it was a game played in every high school—but I knew the gist. Someone put his hand on your knee and slowly moved it up the length of your thigh, asking "Are you nervous?" and stopping when the answer was yes. I thought he was being flirty, but instead he'd ignored my answer when he'd reached mid-thigh, thrusting his hand roughly between my legs, overpowering me with his strength.

My teenage self hadn't known what to do.

But my twenty-eight-year-old self had.

I credit my self-defense class for the elbow I directed toward the bridge of Bennett's nose. But the way his head hit the side of the solid desk was a freak accident. Up, down, to the side and he would've been fine. As it was, the man's neck was bent in such a grotesque way that there was little doubt he was dead. "I'm glad you called me," Fernando had assured me when he'd found me ashen-faced and frozen beside the crumpled body. My older sister had once broken down the rules for dating: ten dates before sex, twenty dates before saying "I love you," thirty dates before bringing him home to meet the parents. Fernando hadn't yet met my parents, but we'd exchanged "I love you"s. Did that mean our relationship was ready for the frantic call I'd made from the floor of the Ridleys' apartment? Fernando seemed to think it was. His features had remained stone still as he rested a finger against the man's left wrist, but it was already a foregone conclusion. Only then did the terrifying realization wash over me: I recognized the dead man's face. He was the one who had emerged from Ms. Ridley's bedroom, eyeing me as if I were part of the buffet.

Fernando and I hadn't verbalized what we were about to do, but our bodies moved with a self-preserving instinct. I'd mopped the sticky, amoeba-shaped pool of blood while Fernando retrieved industrial-sized plastic bags and the garbage cart from the basement. "I know where the cameras are in the building and how we can get him down to the garage and into the trunk of my car," he'd promised, his adrenaline-fueled voice wobbly. And we'd set to work as if crime scene cleanup was part of our job description. Fernando meticulously deleting the footage from the entryway cameras. Me retrieving the phone from the dead man's back pocket and holding it in front of his lifeless face to unlock it, pecking out a message to Ms. Ridley to put off questions I hadn't yet worked out how to answer. "Let me take a quick look at what you wrote," Fernando had said, revising the text to make it all caps before hitting send. "We want him to sound angry." There had been something about focusing on the task at hand for those thirty radioactive minutes that had allowed me to disassociate from everything around me. But there hadn't been an hour since then that I hadn't thought about the reverberating crack that filled the room when his head hit the desk, about his eyes open and vacant below the dent in his skull, about the unnatural way his body folded into itself.

My phone vibrated in the back pocket of my jeans, shaking me out of my intrusive thoughts, and I slid it out, the muscles in my neck tightening as I read the message. *Saw the news. Call me when you can.* As I shuffled forward in line, my eyes flitted to the TV mounted on the far wall, the news ticker at the bottom of the screen snagging my attention.

DEATH OF UES MAN RULED SUICIDE.

Holding my breath, I watched—trancelike—as the man with the close-cropped blond helmet hair solemnly delivered the alleged details from behind the news desk, just as he had two hours ago when I'd watched the twenty-four-hour local news station from home. He was the same newscaster who had been on my TV screen all week, the one who resembled a fifty-year-old Ken doll. I could recite the schedule, the top stories, and I saw his face in my sleep. I'd already spent countless hours imagining how he'd report my fall from grace. *Twenty-eight-year-old former housekeeper has been arrested for the murder of a prominent Upper East Side man.* "Prominent." That's the word they'd use to describe him. Not "sexual assailant." They would post a photo of him clean-shaven and donning a suit and tie, while managing to dig up a photo of me looking like I'd come off of a shift at a strip club. Conclusive proof of culpability. Guilty before even stepping into a courtroom. I'd been dreading the inevitable knock on my door (Would they knock? Or would they break down the door, guns drawn?) ever since his body had been located. "The body of the missing Upper East Side man has been found," the Ken doll had reported last week in his most somber tone. I'd leapt from my couch and moved closer to the television as if being called up to the front of the room by a teacher. "Foul play isn't suspected," he'd noted before pivoting to a feel-good story about donated teacher supplies.

"Do you think that means they're not investigating anymore? That it's done?" Fernando had asked in a hushed tone during a walk around the neighborhood. We never risked talking about anything to do with that day over the phone or at home, thanks in part to Fernando's earnest belief that our phones could be bugged: *Rich people have their ways of tracking us.*

"I don't know if we're out of the woods yet, but if any of those women are going to talk, now is when they'd do it," I'd whispered. But deep down, I knew they wouldn't.

Our pact was like nuclear war. If any of us pushed the button, we'd all be screwed.

I shifted my weight now, shooting glances behind me, as if one of the bank patrons would piece together that the benign-looking woman standing in line with the red patches sprouting on her cheeks was responsible for the crime they were reading about on the screen. *Unconfirmed sources have told NY1 News that an email address used by Bennett Stillman was linked to numerous posts on the website UrbanMyth, which viewers will remember suffered a cyberattack recently, crippling the site. No word on whether the cyberattack was a contributing factor to the man's death,* the captions read.

I took a deep breath, attempting to uncoil my insides, fearing this was my new normal: unexpected bouts of paralyzing paranoia.

Maybe.

It would be my penance. A small price to pay.

The Ken doll was still talking, reporting now on what appeared to be a political scandal with a female staffer, but my mind was somewhere else. If I closed my eyes I was there, in Ms. Ridley's kitchen, a tiny shard of glass wedged into my thumb, the blood springing from the fresh wound. I'd been carrying around the unbearable weight of what I'd done, and the intensity of my guilt was acute, tangible, noxious. It made the rhythms of daily life— brushing my teeth, riding on the subway—feel like swimming against the tide with my legs tied together. Unsustainable. When I'd listened to the policeman talking to Ms. Ridley about the dead man's family, I didn't think I could keep myself afloat any longer, and couldn't stop myself from being washed away in a tsunami of remorse.

Ms. Ridley had lied to me. There were no cameras in the Ridley apartment. I knew that. She thought she'd cornered me into telling the truth, but it wasn't the threat of being caught that compelled me to confess. The moment I saw the blood springing from my skin, all I wanted to do was squeeze every last drop out of my body, as if the secret I was keeping was a demon that needed to be exorcised. When I'd opened my mouth to answer Ms. Ridley's question, the confession had tumbled out of me like vomit. I'd expected Ms. Ridley to scream, scramble for her phone, and call the police. But that wasn't what she did.

And then. Then. That other woman.

And the wife.

Not even she cared that the man was gone.

And I could feel it. The virus that had infected my body being purged. Right there in the apartment where it had first entered my bloodstream.

Free.

Behind me someone cleared their throat, bringing me back to the present. My eyelids blinked rapidly as I tried to get my bearings. A cold palm rested on my shoulder, and I jumped.

"She's calling you." A woman with purple spiky hair and a large nose ring gestured to the teller.

"Thanks," I mumbled, forcing my legs to move forward.

"How can I help you today?" the bespectacled woman behind the bulletproof glass asked in a wearied tone that implied she'd really like to be doing anything but. Her mousy brown hair was knotted neatly at the nape of her neck, her plum-colored lips tugged slightly down, and she reminded me of an authoritarian teacher, the kind who would gladly put the entire class in detention if she caught a single person passing a note.

It did not bode well.

"I want to deposit this check," I said, sliding it into the dip underneath the glass. Beneath her watchful gaze, I ran a hand through my hair and felt dampness against my scalp.

"Go ahead and swipe your card," the teller said flatly, gesturing with a fire-engine-red fingernail to the keypad bolted to the counter. "And I need to see your ID."

I extracted my wallet from my purse, pulled out my driver's license, and deposited it in the dip. The teller clasped the check and unfolded it, adjusting her glasses before bringing it closer to her face. I saw a slight hiccup of her eyebrows when she read the amount, but nothing else registered in her expression. She was all business.

It shocked the hell out of me too, I wished I could say. It would be a relief to talk to someone about it.

"I'd like to give you this," Ms. Ridley had said, her tone as sharp as the corners of the check she was pressing into my wounded hand. She kept her volume low, despite the fact that the other two women had left and we were the only two people in the apartment. "We'll consider it a severance payment." I'd accepted the check, tucking it into my wallet without telling another soul about it. I didn't need her to tell me it would be my last day. I knew I'd never come back there. When Bennett's body surfaced in the East River, I prepared myself for a knock, a phone call, a team of police with sirens wailing, and considered tearing up the check, at one point holding it over the garbage can readying my hands to shred it. If I were going to be indicted for murder, I didn't want my parents to think I'd been a hired hitman. And taking one hundred thousand dollars from your employer would surely not sit well with a jury when you're supposed to be a sympathetic defendant. But this morning, as I watched the Ken doll earnestly report that Bennett Stillman had taken his own life, it was as if I'd been given a Get Out of Jail Free card.

"Excuse me a minute," the teller said, the corners of her mouth tugging down farther. Her tweed skirt rustled as she turned around and thudded on her sensible heels toward a woman with a navy blazer and a severe haircut.

Heat burned on my cheeks as I watched the teller lean in, say something to the other woman. My stomach wrenched, realizing Ms. Ridley had probably reconsidered and canceled the check. Could I be arrested for attempting to deposit a canceled check? Was that fraud? I shot a look over my shoulder at the exit, calculating. I could make it there in three seconds flat if I had to.

There was a smile on the other woman's face now as she reached into a drawer and produced a small cloth. I kept my eyes locked on the teller as she removed her frameless glasses and held them up to the light, wiped her lenses, and put them back on before returning the cloth to the drawer.

"Okay, where were we?" she said, returning to her station. She peered over her nose at the monitor without waiting for an answer, her long fingernails clicking against her keyboard.

The tips of my fingers tingled with relief as the blood rushed back across my body. My breath slowed as the teller stamped the check and slid my driver's license back, along with a receipt showing my new bank balance.

"Would you like to make any withdrawals today?"

I wiped my damp palms on my jeans before gathering my ID and receipt. My throat thickened as I looked down at the figure written in light gray figures. Balance—$102,546.88. It was nearly three times my annual salary.

"Ma'am, would you like to make any withdrawals today?" the teller repeated, impatience seeping into her tone again.

I shook my head, not trusting my own voice.

"Well, is there anything else I can help you with then?"

I stared down at my bank balance, absorbing the possibilities ahead of me. This money wouldn't erase what had happened to me. Nor would it expunge what I'd done. But I could choose to see it for what it was: a safety net. I would finally be one of those people who moved through the world with a safety net.

"No," I replied, folding the receipt and slipping it into my back pocket. "I'm all set."

Acknowledgments

WHEN I OUTLINED this book, I had no idea that I'd be writing it during a global pandemic, in between virtual schooling and endless quarantines. To say the writing conditions weren't ideal would be a gross understatement, and the book never would've made it past the outline stage if not for my endlessly patient editor, Anne Speyer. Anne, I don't know how you managed not to despair after reading my initial draft, but for that I am truly grateful! Working with you has been a masterclass in the difference that a good editor can make. Huge thanks to the many others on the talented team at Bantam, which includes Alexis Capitini, Kara Cesare, Denise Cronin, Jennifer Garza, Jennifer Hershey, Kim Hovey, Brianna Kusilek, Jennifer Rodriguez, Quinne Rogers, Allison Schuster, Jesse Shuman, Rachel Walker, Derek Walls, and Kara Welsh. I will never stop being amazed that so many people devoted their time and energy into bringing *No One Needs to Know* to life!

My brilliant agent, Alexa Stark, thank you for your expertise and guidance and for always being gentle when you asked, "How's the book coming along?" Having you in my corner makes every step of the publishing process smoother.

I wouldn't be where I am today without the boundless love and encouragement of my parents, for which I am eternally grateful. Mom, you always told me I was a writer even when I didn't know it myself. Dad, this is my first book without you here, but you will remain in my acknowledgments forever. You are deeply loved and wholeheartedly missed. If there is any lesson to be taken from Covid times, it is how much I cherish the time I spend with my family and extended family. My heartfelt thanks to the Lamprechts, Magrakens, Akerlys, Bohakers, Camerons, Royales, Brandts, Brookses, Ellen Montizambert, and all of the Reef Road alums. We're a motley crew and I love you for it.

I'm fortunate to have the kind of friends who would bury a body for me, and while I promise to never take them up on that, it's a good thing to have in my back pocket if needed. Although they haven't had to pick up a shovel (yet), they give me life every day. A billion thank-yous to Gosia Bawolska, Sara and Doug DiPasquale, Kimberley Hall, Marie-Claude Jones, Jennifer Mermel, Hyewon Miller, Michele Murphy, Serena Palumbo, and Ceylan Yazar.

I have a huge soft spot for Bookstagrammers and reviewers, whose never-ending passion for reading and enthusiastic support of authors blows me away. I was thrilled when you embraced my work and shouted about it from the rooftops. One thousand hearts and prayer-hands emojis to the following fabulous accounts: @firepitandbooks, @graceatwood, @booksandbasta, @blondethrillerbooklover, @beautyandthebook, @jordys.book .club, and so many others. You make this social-media-averse author happy to be on Instagram.

A special shout-out to my fellow Upper East Siders! To answer the inevitable question—no, the people in this book are not based on anyone I know (unless you see yourself in one of the characters, in which case it is absolutely you).

Last but not least, thank you to the loves of my life. Gord, thank you for always responding with an enthusiastic, "Let's celebrate!" when I tell you I finished my book today even though you know I will make the same announcement at least ten more times. More than the others, this book was a team effort, and I couldn't ask for a better teammate in life than you. Ethan and Elise, thank you for allowing me to remain hunched over my laptop while you scavenged for snacks. Being your mother is my greatest gift, and our pride in you both is immeasurable. Keep shining your light. The world needs it.

NO ONE
NEEDS TO
KNOW

LINDSAY
CAMERON

Random
House
Book Club

Because
Stories Are
Better Shared ™

A BOOK CLUB GUIDE

Dear Reader,

Thank you for reading *No One Needs to Know*! The initial spark for this story was ignited when I attended a Meetup for new mothers after having my first child. One of the women in the group told me about an anonymous discussion board for local parents, whispering, "Let's just say that it goes far beyond questions like how to find a good nanny." I wasn't sure what she meant, but the storyteller in me was dying to find out! I created an account and was soon spending time during late-night feedings scrolling through other people's confessions: infidelity, white-collar crime, private family issues—nothing was off-limits. The veil of anonymity was like truth serum, and I found myself wondering about the identities of the people behind the posts. Was the woman standing next to me in the elevator, holding the hand of a curly-haired boy in a shiny soccer jersey, the same person who posted about a weekend tryst with her son's soccer coach? Maybe! The Real Housewives had nothing on what was unfolding in that forum.

Years later, the infamous hack of the extramarital affair website Ashley Madison exposed its user records and hit the news, shattering the illusion of online anonymity. It also fanned the spark of the story idea in my mind. I thought back to all of the sordid secrets people divulged on that seemingly anonymous neighborhood forum. The identities of the users behind those posts were only one data breach away from being revealed. And because I love a good thriller, I began to imagine what would happen if some of those secrets were worth killing for.

I had so much fun creating these characters and seeing which way the story would take me. I hope you love the book as much as I loved writing it. And I hope you think twice before trusting that your digital footprint will remain strictly confidential!

I'm on Instagram (@lindsaycameronauthor) and would love to connect.

Happy reading!

Lindsay

Questions and Topics for Discussion

1. Parenthood is a significant theme throughout the book. Discuss each mother's relationship with her children. How are they different from one another? How are they similar? Why do you think Lindsay Cameron chose mothers as her main characters?

2. All three of the main women, Heather, Norah, and Poppy, come from different class and educational backgrounds. How do their pasts influence the decisions they make in the present? Did your perceptions of these characters change at all as you read, and if so, how? Which character did you relate to, or empathize with, the most?

3. Getting accepted into Andover is seen as a crucial step toward future success. How do money, class, privilege, and education factor into this story?

4. When does being involved in your child's life cross over into being overbearing? Are any parents able to find the perfect balance?

5.   Does true anonymity exist? How does the veil of anonymity free some people and hinder others from sharing their unfiltered thoughts?

6.   How would this novel be different if its story was told from the perspective of the children?

7.   Why do the parents in the book trust UrbanMyth with all of their secrets? Would you trust such a website?

8.   The author specifically chose to set the story in New York City's Upper East Side. How did you feel the location affected the plot? If you were to write a novel about where you live, which characteristics of your neighborhood would you give your setting?

9.   What would you do in the scenarios these various women find themselves in? How far would you go to protect your own secrets, and your own family?

10. Discuss the ending of the novel. Were you surprised to learn the truth? Do you agree with the decision the women made at the end? Was their behavior justified?

LINDSAY CAMERON worked as a corporate lawyer in Vancouver and New York before becoming a novelist. She is the author of *Just One Look* and *Biglaw*.

lindsayjcameron.com
Twitter: @LindsayJCameron
Instagram: @lindsaycameronauthor
Find Lindsay Cameron on Facebook

About the Type

This book was set in Bembo, a typeface based on an old-style Roman face that was used for Cardinal Pietro Bembo's tract *De Aetna* in 1495. Bembo was cut by Francesco Griffo (1450–1518) in the early sixteenth century for Italian Renaissance printer and publisher Aldus Manutius (1449–1515). The Lanston Monotype Company of Philadelphia brought the well-proportioned letterforms of Bembo to the United States in the 1930s.